JAN 18

LAST
STAR
BURNING

LAST
ST★R
BURNING

CAITLIN SANGSTER

SIMON PULSE
New York   London   Toronto   Sydney   New Delhi

To Allen

SIMON PULSE

An imprint of Simon & Schuster Children's Publishing Division

1230 Avenue of the Americas, New York, New York 10020

First Simon Pulse hardcover edition October 2017

Text copyright © 2017 by Caitlin Sangster

Jacket illustration copyright © 2017 by Aaron Limonick and David Field

All rights reserved, including the right of reproduction in whole or in part in any form.

SIMON PULSE and colophon are registered trademarks of Simon & Schuster, Inc.

For information about special discounts for bulk purchases, please contact Simon & Schuster

Special Sales at 1-866-506-1949 or business@simonandschuster.com.

The Simon & Schuster Speakers Bureau can bring authors to your live event.

For more information or to book an event contact the Simon & Schuster Speakers Bureau

at 1-866-248-3049 or visit our website at www.simonspeakers.com.

Jacket designed by Jessica Handelman

Interior designed by Mike Rosamilia

The text of this book was set in Venetian 301 BT Std.

Manufactured in the United States of America

2 4 6 8 10 9 7 5 3 1

Library of Congress Cataloging-in-Publication Data

Names: Sangster, Caitlin, author.

Title: Last star burning / by Caitlin Sangster.

Description: First Simon Pulse hardcover edition. | New York : Simon Pulse, 2017. |

Summary: "To escape execution for a crime she didn't commit, seventeen-year-old Sev is forced

to run away from her city into the wilderness. With nowhere to turn, Sev has to figure out who she

can trust in a world where trusting the wrong person could mean not only her life

but the lives of everyone she loves"— Provided by publisher. |

Description based on print version record and CIP data provided by publisher; resource not viewed.

Identifiers: LCCN 2016046285 (print) | LCCN 2017021830 (eBook) |

ISBN 9781481486156 (eBook) | ISBN 9781481486132 (hardcover)

Subjects: | CYAC: Epidemics—Fiction. | Fugitives from justice—Fiction. |

Survival—Fiction. | Fantasy.

Classification: LCC PZ7.1.S263 (eBook) | LCC PZ7.1.S263 Las 2017 (print) |

DDC [Fic]—dc23

LC record available at https://lccn.loc.gov/2016046285

PART I

CHAPTER 1

THEY SAY WAR IS NO DINNER PARTY. NOT REFINED, graceful, courteous, or magnanimous. It's complete devastation. Every foul human impulse distilled into quick bursts of chaos. And yet here I sit at a table, stones to mark my soldiers in front of me in pretty lines on a grid, the conversation perfectly quiet and polite. All I need is a snack.

"Yuan's ax, Sevvy." Tai-ge laughs as he flicks the edge of the weiqi board. "Is there a strategy buried under here somewhere? You don't have anywhere else to play."

"My game is too advanced for you to comprehend." My stones are pitiful and lonely spots of white in a sea of Tai-ge's black, a besieged army with no hope. Picking up one of the smooth pieces, I weigh each of the open spaces, attempting to keep dismay from leaking through my cheerful mask. "In one or two moves, I'll have you right where I want you." But Tai-ge is right. Most of my stones are dead.

Tai-ge twirls the gold ring on his middle finger, light catching the City seal stamped into the soft metal, then rubs the two raised white lines scarring the skin between his thumb and forefinger. "You've got as much chance to win as if you were fighting a gore with a broken bottle."

"I don't believe in gores. If gores were real, there wouldn't be so many soldiers alive and well to spin stories about them."

Tai-ge taps the board one last time. "You concede?"

I take a theatrical breath and let it out, bowing low over the table.

A little smile softens the angular lines of Tai-ge's face as he shakes his head. Reserved gloating, as though smiling too widely would break something inside of him. "One more game? We probably don't have time, but maybe if I walk you home . . . ?"

I nod and sit back in my chair as he resets the pieces, looking to the bay window behind him. The last streams of orange and pink fade into black over the smokestack skyline around us as I consider the view. The City makes a wheel shape cut into the side of our mountain, ringed entirely by a high outer wall. The three spokes of the wheel divide the City into thirds to keep the different parts to themselves, with a central market hub the only common point connecting them. Below Tai-ge's house, I can just glimpse the chimney tops and factory lights above the wall that separates the industrial Third Quarter from the martial Second Quarter. On this side of the wall, peaked roofs as clean and orderly as the Seconds themselves rise up the side of the mountain. I can't see the First Quarter from my vantage point here. Firsts reside higher up the mountain, towering above the other two quarters where they can keep an eye on the rest of us—that is, if they bother to take a break from their experiments and research to spare us a thought.

At least the Seconds and Thirds have their own quarters. I touch my collar, where my four metal stars are pinned. There isn't a place for Fourths here.

The horizon beyond the outer wall seems unreal somehow, as if the mountaintops poking up through the clouds are just a painting, a backdrop the Firsts invented for us.

I shiver. I'll take the fairy-tale painting. If Outside is distant and out of focus, I won't have to watch the desperate survivors out there trying to kill each other.

Under the table, I continue digging a cluster of Tai-ge's pencils point-first into the red candle I stole from the Hong family shrine downstairs. I hate seeing Tai-ge so smug from beating me, but it's not like I can tell him I've been sabotaging his writing supplies, not to mention desecrating his ancestors' shrine. But the next time he sits down with his Watch reports, he'll know exactly why I was so distracted during our game of weiqi. He'll swear over his red-smeared reports, but then I know he'll laugh. And my friend needs more reasons to laugh.

Dark wood paneling makes the room seem small and dim in the waning light. Nothing has changed much in Tai-ge's room since we were kids. Everything is so red. Down to his striped bedcover, the accents in the hardwood bookcase, and the portrait of our City's founder, Yuan Zhiwei, matted in red on the wall. I suppose it's typical in the Second Quarter to deck out everything in City colors. They're proud to protect the City. Though I do wonder sometimes if sleeping in this room coats Tai-ge's dreams in red paint.

Before the board is clear of stones, Tai-ge's door pops open.

"Tai-ge, Fenghua just brought in . . ." Comrade Hong trails off as she notices me across the table from her son. "What are you doing up here?"

I jump to my feet, subtly dropping the pencils and pocketing the stolen candle so she won't see it, keeping my eyes on my boots. The peeling leather toes are half-hidden by the City's star-and-beaker seal cut into the deep red fibers of the carpet. I smile a little to make up for the humble bow, refusing to give in completely to the tight disapproval in Comrade Hong's voice. "We were playing weiqi, Comrade."

Tai-ge gestures to the empty board from his seat at the table. "Well, I was playing. I'm not quite sure what Sevvy was doing."

Comrade Hong does not look amused.

General Hong and his wife may have graciously volunteered to reeducate me after my parents' blunders—it was an honor for their family to be trusted with a subject as corrupted as I, and there are few families so true to Yuan Zhiwei's vision that they'd even be allowed near me—but Comrade Hong's eyes don't seem to register that any improvement has taken place over the last eight years. Her hair is cropped short in the new City fashion, the utilitarian line only accentuating how beautiful she is. Tai-ge's mother is shorter than I am, her heavy Watch uniform making her look as though she's a child playing war. Her perfectly shaped eyebrows are raised in dismay, as though the neighbors might have glimpsed me sitting across from her perfect Second son with something other than reeducation materials in front of us. Not many of the high-ranking Seconds would permit a Fourth within a block of their homes up here on the Steppe, much less inside, playing an unsanctioned game of weiqi with their children.

"You were supposed to be back down in the Third Quarter over an hour ago, Jiang Sev. Just because the General is too busy for reeducation tonight does not mean you can sit up here wasting time." Her eyes freeze on the pin hanging cockeyed at my collar, as if she can't see me past those four red stars. "Sister Lei will be hearing about this. Now get out of my house."

Tai-ge pulls himself up from the table, the lamplight glossing over his thick hair, trimmed so close to his scalp. He glances out the window where the lamps are starting to glow in the falling darkness. "Come on, Sevvy. I'll walk you down."

The little glow of warmth I feel at hearing my nickname on Tai-ge's lips winks out when Comrade Hong snaps back, "No, Tai-ge, you stay here. And don't call her that. It's too informal."

Tai-ge smiles at his mother as he guides me past her and out into the hallway. "That's her name." But when Comrade Hong's expression blackens, he drops the smile and gives a respectful nod. "Sorry. Jiang Sev. I'm the one who told her to stay, so I'll walk her back. The Watchman on the bridge at night is always crabby."

"She knows the rules." Comrade Hong follows us down the stairs and past the family shrine. Hongs long gone, somber-eyed in their portraits, watch us through the screen of smoke issuing from a garden of newly lit incense. The missing red candle makes the table look off balance, but Tai-ge's mother is too busy arguing to notice. "Your father is never going to be able to teach Jiang Sev correct social theory or her place in it if she can't even adhere to basic policy. . . ."

Tai-ge grabs both our jackets from the hooks in the entryway, and before his mother can protest any further, he throws open the front door and drags me down the steps.

"Be quick!" Comrade Hong yells after us. "If you aren't back in the next ten minutes . . . !" But the rest of whatever she wanted to say is lost as we run through the circular gate that connects the Hong compound to the street, our breath misting out in front of us in the frozen air.

Tai-ge tows me around a corner, but slips on the icy paving stones when I don't move fast enough, sending me sliding into a patch of early snow. The fall knocks the wind out of me, but I manage to kick his feet out from under him before he's done laughing. We both lie on the ground for a few minutes, looking up at the stars. It's a miracle we can even see the first few in the twilight. Smoke from the Third Quarter factories usually keeps the whole City under a cover of smog.

It almost seems impossible that it has been eight years since I stood sullenly outside the Hong's house, hand still scabbed over from the brand newly burned into my skin. It sort of looks like a star. A melted, ruined star, seared into the flesh between my thumb and forefinger.

The man who gave it to me didn't say anything. Just unpinned the star from his collar. I sat there watching as he stuck the pin in the fire until the metal glowed red, only a rag protecting his hand from the brutal heat. I closed my eyes before he pressed the pin to the single line that marked me as a First, charring away any evidence that I ever had a place in the City. I don't remember if it hurt, how it smelled, or whether I said thank you afterward. I only remember the vertigo of my entire world shifting from First to Fourth.

Tai-ge was out on the front steps that day to usher me in before his parents could shoo him away, as if he didn't care how far my family had fallen. He was the army personified, honored to take part in my reintegration into the politically correct proletariat. But the moment his parents looked away, Tai-ge's military straight posture relaxed and he shoved a red cellophane–wrapped candy into my sore hands, the same shifty look in his eye as Mother had when she used to make a game of slipping my sister, Aya, and me sweets, seeing how many we could hide before Father noticed.

I close my eyes and shake the thought away before it can burn like molten lead at the back of my mind. No thoughts of Aya tonight.

When I open my eyes, Tai-ge is pointing up at a blinking light as it slowly pulses across the sky. "Satellite or Kamari heli-plane?" he asks me, the lamps hanging over the nearest compound gates casting a golden sheen over his skin.

"Better hope it's a satellite. A Kamari bombing spree would definitely keep you out here longer than ten minutes, and I don't think your mother would consider an enemy attack a good enough excuse for your being late."

"It's probably just a City patroller." Tai-ge squints at the sky as if trying to decide.

When Tai-ge stands, he pulls me up with him, brushing at the snow clinging to the dark wool of my coat. My face pinkens as his hand catches on one of my buttons.

"I don't think you have to worry." I pretend to look up the street to hide my blush, the mountain pricked yellow and white above us, lights from the First and Second Quarters too dim to wash out our view of the stars. "Even Kamar seems to know that bombs so close to the First Quarter are unacceptable. They keep it to the Thirds and the factories."

"Where they can destroy our munitions and food. It makes sense."

"Well, if I were in charge, I'd go straight to the top." I point up the mountain to the highest lights twinkling in the darkness. "The First Circle all live right in the same neighborhood, don't they? If you cut the head off, the chicken might flap around for a little bit trying to pretend it's still alive, but it'll still lie down dead in the end."

"Lucky I'm not a First, I guess. Don't let my parents hear you talking like that, or they'll be checking your room for knives."

I close my mouth, wishing it would just cement shut. "You might as well be First, Hong Tai-ge. Or don't you see the way we all jump when your father barks? Perhaps Reds will move up to the First Quarter, and a new era will begin where Second comes before First."

Reds. Tai-ge shakes his head at the nickname, looking down at the two lines scored into the skin on the back of his hand that mark him a Second. I'm not the only one who calls Seconds "Reds." It's hard not to, with their City-red coats, City-red carpet, and City-red souls.

Tai-ge reaches across to flick some snow from my cheek, snapping my attention away from my thoughts. I can't help but look at him now, his hand warm against my cold skin. His eyes are so dark the irises look black. He doesn't move, as if the cold has frozen the two of us together.

But then he blinks, pulling his hand away from me to stick it deep in his jacket pocket. "My father knows his place. He knows mine, too, and often reminds me that it isn't playing with you in the snow." He starts down the street without me, but then waits for me to draw even with him, leaving a few feet of space between us.

I run my fingers through my long hair to brush out the last bits of damp clinging to me, trying to shake the hollow feeling that growls deep in my chest as he keeps the appropriate distance between us on our walk. Tai-ge is right to keep his distance. And I should be more careful about keeping mine. I won't ruin his future. Not on purpose, at least.

We silently turn down the road toward the Aihu River bridge that marks the edge of the Second Quarter, both of us trying to ignore the awkwardness between us. Somewhere up the mountain is a lake that feeds the river, above the First Quarter and the blunt cliffs that edge the whole east side of the City. On the other side of the bridge lies the dividing wall that will forever separate my life from Tai-ge's. A Third climbs a ladder propped up against the closest bridge support as we walk by, only allowed on this side of the barrier to blow the red paper lanterns strung across the bridge back to life. The lights sparkle in the dark waves of the river and across the sheen of frost coating the bridge.

We stand together, companionably watching puffs of smoke creep toward us from the Third Quarter below. A sigh streams out of me as the last bit of light drains out of the sky. Time to go back or they'll send out the Watch to find me.

Before I can suggest we move, Tai-ge breaks the silence, pointing to the dedication painted in red and black across the huge wooden supports just in front of the barrier that blocks the Third Quarter off from the river. He points to the characters as he reads, each syllable sharp and clear. "'Aihu Bridge, erected Year Four by the Liberation Army. United to stop Sleeping Sickness,'" he recites, shaking his head. "That was Yuan Zhiwei's dream, but look at us now, almost a century later. We sit up here with nowhere to hide. Bombs fall on us at least once a month. How much longer before they send their armies up here, do you think? Just cut us all down."

"Kamar couldn't walk a whole army up this high on the mountain; that was the point—"

"They were never supposed to find us at all." Tai-ge stares up at the sky again, as if he's searching for the blinking light we saw earlier. "Everyone thought we'd be safe, and we *were* up until . . ." He breaks off when he looks down, and I realize my hands are twined together as if I can hide the brand. "I'm sorry, Sevvy. I didn't mean to say it like that."

I nod, but turn from him before he can see the cracks in my expression, thoughts I can't let crystallize hovering too close to the surface.

A figure thick with layers of clothing steps out from behind the pillar beneath the sign, making for a good distraction. Winter is coming, leaving this man with his coat buttoned up to his throat and fur hat pulled down around his eyebrows with the flaps tied tightly under his chin. He looks a little like one of the grainy old photographs from the Great Wars, needing only a bolt-action rifle and mustache to complete the picture. Lantern light glints off the two stars pinned to his red coat. A member of the Watch.

My smile is back by the time he gets to us, ready to face whatever he might say, trying very hard not to notice Tai-ge's arm nudging mine in apology. There's no reason for him to apologize. I am not my stars, whatever most people believe.

The Watchman eyes me and then looks pointedly at his wristwatch. "Do you know what time it is, Fourth?"

I wish hiding my stars weren't a punishable offense, but I suppose keeping them out of sight wouldn't help anyway. The Watch knows my face, the birthmark curling out from under my ear and onto my cheek. They know the burn that mars the skin between my thumb and forefinger. It's their job to know. I pull my ID card from my coat pocket and hold it out to him. "Yes, I know I don't have much time before the walls close, Comrade."

He takes it, scowling. Looking at the bright silver likeness of Yuan Zhiwei printed next to my picture, he spits on the ground at my feet. "Trash like you shouldn't even be allowed to disgrace his image."

Tai-ge steps forward. "She's not late yet. Let her go past."

The Watchman takes a careful look at Tai-ge. "You should watch where you go with her kind of garbage. Even if you are the General's son." He spits again on the ground and walks back to the Watch station policing the door between my quarter and Tai-ge's.

I shrug off Tai-ge's interjection and wave good-bye, the bridge's lights framing my friend in a warm glow.

As soon as I cross the barrier, my eyes take a moment to adjust to the darkness, as if even the light on this side of the wall is gray. It's hard to make out the peaked roofs down the hill, where most families don't have the electricity rations to use their cheap incandescents at night. I wait until the empty stalls from the afternoon market hide me before I start to run, not wanting Tai-ge to know just how late I actually am. I'll have to explain missing dinner, but I don't care. A smile steals across my face as I fall into line with the uniforms hurrying between the blocky factory buildings towering over the cracked cement walkways and the worn brick cafeteria. The thought of Tai-ge's face when he realizes his pencils are near useless is worth missing dinner any day. Especially today. The whole Third Quarter smells like cabbage.

The crush of bland clothing streaked with factory dirt closes in around me as I push through the school gate, students with similar tardiness problems rushing back from evening meals that went a tad too long. The hallway outside Remedial Reform is especially crowded, those with work shifts during the day here at night class to get their required dose of history and ideology in short sentences and small words so they can understand. I manage to slide onto the bench at the back of our little classroom before Captain Chen comes in.

My roommate, Peishan, waves from the front row, giving me

a questioning smile when I wave back. She knew I was up in the Second Quarter with Tai-ge and will want to hear about the visit down to the pitch of Comrade Hong's annoyed sniffs. She starts to mouth something at me, but stops as Captain Chen hobbles into the room. The old Captain frowns at her as he limps toward his chair on his ancient pair of crutches, then heaves a deep sigh as he leans them up against the wall. He sits, pulling at the two metal stars on his collar, which had folded inward so that the metal scratched at his throat. The two hash marks carved into his hand look faded and stretched. Remedial Reform isn't important enough to merit a First teacher like the other quarters get. The finer points don't matter much when your days are filled with twisting wire or picking bits of gunk out of the industrial looms. "Did we stop with the Great War invasion, or were we all the way to Jiang?" he grumbles. I try not to flinch.

A boy sitting two seats away raises a work-worn hand, angry red scars lining his palms and forearms like a grid. "You left off with Yuan Zhiwei, sir."

"Yuan. Right." Scratching at his sparse gray hair, Captain Chen turns toward the front of the room, pointing at the portrait of Yuan Zhiwei hung at the head of our classroom. "Salute."

We all stand, each raising a fist toward the portrait. "We stand united, our City dedicated to equality, honesty, and hard work. We strive to protect our homes and families from infection, shoring up our walls against the anarchy poisoning Outside. We destroy complacency within our own ranks. We pledge to follow the teachings of Yuan Zhiwei, each of us dedicated to our own tasks. Thirds to the glory of labor that forms the backbone of our society. Seconds to protecting our walls and defeating our enemies. Firsts, in their superior wisdom, to lead us toward dignity and enlightenment."

And Fourths, I add silently, my mother's face still pulsing in the back of my mind after what Tai-ge said about Kamar discovering our City. *To betrayal. To infecting our own children and murdering our leaders.* Even saying the number four out loud is unlucky. As if just one syllable could bring death and destruction to anyone who heard.

"Shoulder to shoulder we stand, comrades building a society strong enough to find the cure to SS." With that, we finish chanting and sit down, waiting for Captain Chen to start.

He rubs his left temple with two fingers, eyes closed. "Kamar's invasion of our country started with Sleeping Sickness bombs. That beyond anything was their biggest mistake, as SS was not only the cause of our destruction, but also the cause of their own." He pauses to let that sink in, as if this weren't something we've all known for as long as we can remember. Sleeping Sickness—SS— the weapon that bit back at that hand that wielded it. If not for Kamar, the whole world might still be living freely in peace instead of fighting for scraps.

After the moment of silence, Captain Chen continues. "Bombs infected our armies, our cities. Those who weren't infected ran or were killed. Yuan Zhiwei argued not to use SS as a weapon of revenge. Deciding to destroy them with their own weapon would only leave a blasted continent, a pile of ashes where there was once a great civilization. Our ancestral leaders did not listen to him. Yuan led as many as would follow up to this City. They hid in these mountains as SS destroyed everything during the end of the Influenza War. Why would he trap us up here like that and then call it 'Liberation'?"

Peishan raises her hand, smoothing long hair out of her face before answering his nod. Her voice chirps like a little bird, every word measured and confident. "The walls, sir. Yuan Zhiwei wanted to find a cure, and walls were the only thing that could keep out Sephs. . . ." She falters, crossing her arms tightly when she realizes the ugly slur slipped out, but Captain Chen doesn't stop her. "I mean, walls were the only thing that could keep out those infected with encephalitis lethargica—with Sleeping Sickness."

Captain Chen considers her. "They never figured out how to make the engineered flu that causes SS contagious. Why would keeping SS victims out matter?"

"Not contagious." Peishan bites her lip. "But even one infected inside our walls that goes untreated . . . is . . ." She shivers, not finishing the sentence. "Yuan chose this place in particular because it's so remote that Kamar couldn't find us."

"Thank you, Peishan." The captain's nod is a little surprised. He doesn't expect much from a classroom of Thirds, but then Peishan has always been an overachiever. "Did it work? Are we liberated?"

The question annoys me, and I start to roll my eyes, but wrench them back down to my desk when Captain Chen's gaze falls on me.

Once again, Peishan provides an answer. "Our work is Liberation. Seconds fight and Thirds work to make sure Firsts can find the cure and end the war. We are far more free here than any-one trying to survive Outside." The pledge regurgitated, but it's true. Safety from SS and Kamari soldiers is enough for anyone—even a hated Fourth like me—to fight to keep their place inside the City. Peishan is still trembling as if the thought of SS doomed the rest of her evening to looking over her shoulder and watching shadows, terrified an unmedicated SS victim could be sneaking along after her, wondering what her flesh tastes like.

I sit up straight, suddenly noticing the rigid line of my

friend's back, the way her hands grip the sides of her desk, fingers turning white. Peishan's whole body shakes in palsied bursts, her grasp on the desktop the only thing keeping her from falling to the ground.

"Sir!" I jump from my bench and run for Peishan. "Sir, she's . . ."

Peishan slides from her seat, the shakes suddenly stopping as if she's done fighting the compulsion that's taken her. Hands out-stretched, she strides toward Captain Chen, who only has time to fall off his chair as he frantically gropes for his crutches.

I crash into Peishan, my ribs and sternum crushed against her bony back as I tackle her to the floor. Other students in the class spring up from their desks to pull her arms flat on the ground, grab her feet to keep her from kicking. They leave me to lie on top of her, to keep her twitches and screams smashed against the floor, where they can't hurt anyone. Or at least where they won't hurt Captain Chen.

The captain yells for help, members of the Watch sprinting from their posts in the hallway at his call. One of the Watchmen pulls me off my friend, gathering her in a bear hold until her muscles stop straining and pulsing, and her head hangs down, sobs of fear and revulsion tearing from her chest.

"I took Mantis an hour ago!" Tears spill down her cheeks, her hair a tangled bird's nest atop her head. "I'm supposed to be safe!"

I can't watch as they drag her out. No late-night discussion in our room to look forward to tonight. None of Peishan's silly questions about Seconds and Tai-ge and whether we really are just friends. Our room will just be dark now. Silent. Asleep.

Captain Chen's chest heaves as he pulls himself up on his crutches. "This is, perhaps, an unfortunate but appropriate launch into the rest of our class discussion."

Peishan's sobs echo down the long hallway, fading as the Watch carries her away.

"For a hundred years, the City was completely free from SS. We didn't need Mantis. We certainly hadn't seen strains of Mantis-resistant SS. Chemical bombs and the war were no more than an uncomfortable memory. All of this was true, until eight years ago. Now SS is here, rearing up in the places we least expect—the epidemic we were supposed to be safe from." He pauses, and my stomach cramps. "What changed?" He makes a show of looking back and forth over the students, half of us still standing, frazzled from restraining Peishan.

Then, as I knew would happen, his stare fixes on me.

I shrink from where I stand at the front of the room, wishing I could go back to my bench, that I could duck behind the broad-shouldered Thirds, still smelling of the metal and soot from the factories. I don't know why I'm still trying to take these classes; I should have known that having a military captain for a teacher was enough of a promise of misery to just take double shifts at the cannery and stop trying to play at school. Tai-ge had to argue to even get me here, but my stars will always speak louder than he ever could.

Captain Chen's glare stings, expectantly waiting until I look up. "SS has returned to the City, and Kamari heli-planes fly over us daily. *What changed?*" His voice is pinched and poisonous. "Jiang Sev? Care to enlighten us?"

I straighten and meet his stare, refusing to blink, refusing to let him bully me. Hating the way his mouth pinches over my name—my mother's name, the one they made me take instead of my father's. Another kind of brand, just as loud as my scar. "Jiang Gui-hua happened. My mother betrayed us all."

CHAPTER 2

THE ORPHANAGE LOOKS COMFORTABLE IN THE lamplight, the mishmash of peaked tile roofs turned up at each corner and the sprawling glass windows just like a family compound from a feel-good propaganda film. Warmth glows from inside, seeming almost cozy until you catch sight of the plaque nailed above the entrance reading HALL OF WAR-ORPHANED CHILDREN in peeling black characters.

When I pull open the front door, I'm careful not to dislodge the handle from its precarious one-screw tether. It feels good to do something softly, to stop trying to break a hole in the road with my boots, to calm the angry demon stretching inside of me, howling to come out.

My mother the traitor.

Even the mention ignites an illness deep in my belly looking for the quickest way out. As the door opens, someone comes running through from the other side, slamming the heavy wood against my shoulder and wrist.

"Sorry!" It's one of the younger residents. She runs past me without another word, late for a factory shift, no doubt.

I roll my shoulder and look at my hand where the door scraped me, a drop of blood welling at the point of the star burned into my skin—the mark of a traitor. The mark that will never wash away, no matter how many years I spend being reeducated by General Hong.

I clench my fist, trying to tune out the memories of her beautiful voice telling me bedtime stories, of her duets with Aya, which always dissolved into laughter when one or the other couldn't hold their part. She *left* us. She left us for *them*. Every chemical bomb that falls might as well have Jiang Gui-hua's name chiseled into its brassy nose, because she's the one who told Kamar where we are.

My back hunches as I walk into the orphanage's open-air courtyard, gulping down deep breaths of the frozen air. Focusing on any one thing seems too difficult. My eyes dart between the cracked cement ground to the main desk that blocks access to the rest of the orphanage, my hand creeping up to the fleshy inside of my elbow, where the soft, smooth expanse feels as if it's on fire.

And it might as well be. That seemingly insignificant spot on my arm is Mother's last word to the City, delivered through me. Because she didn't just tell Kamar where to find us and our Mantis stores. She didn't just leave half of the First Circle dead in their beds before she was finally caught.

No, she also brought SS back to us personally. To me, her own daughter, in a syringe.

I was the City's first Seph.

I didn't understand what my mother had done to me until later. Much later, when General Hong found time to explain it all to me. All I could think during those first few months was that somehow the Circle and the Reds were all wrong, but even

I couldn't erase the memory of her voice in my room, her face hovering near mine, and the prick of the needle.

The Sister on duty peers over the counter, her bald head reflecting the golden light filtering down from the lamps hung above the waist-high wall between me and her desk. It takes me a moment to get control of myself and find a calm sort of a smile for her. The nuns are supposed to be even more honored than Firsts, giving up everything to serve those who can't help themselves. The ultimate example of society before self.

I don't see a flicker of charity in this Sister's expression. Not surprising. It's Sister Lei, who seems to think her life's purpose is to bring up good members of the City with a switch in one hand and a book with every word Yuan Zhiwei ever said in the other. She actually slapped me once for pretending to compulse. I was chasing some of the younger kids, telling them I was hungry for ears to make them laugh, when I felt a sharp sting on my cheek. "SS is not something to joke about!" she fluted, pointed finger level with my nose. "Especially not for you, Ms. Jiang. I suppose I should expect nothing better, considering where you came from." Then she ordered me to report my gross disrespect during the next morning's self-criticism.

I did, complete with sound effects.

"You're late," she says, standing up. "And you didn't eat dinner."

"Class went a little late. I'm sorry, Sister." The smile isn't so hard now that I'm talking. "I haven't managed to wrench out any of my own teeth, though, so I think we're okay."

"You can joke about SS even now? After what happened to Peishan?" She pulls at her long brown robe, flashing a tattoo of a City seal on her hand. However many slashes were cut into her skin to mark her place in the City, they've been obscured since the day she took the oath to serve. I could probably see if I looked close enough, but for some reason, I think she'd be offended. "Come flouncing in here long after you're due for Mantis? You are putting us all in danger."

Sliding a small paper cup across the counter, she jerks her head toward a water jug pushed up against the metal grate that bars entrance to my home. Not all of us in the orphanage are infected, but separating the sick from the well has never seemed to be something the nuns or anyone else cared about. Not down here, anyway.

Back during the Great Wars, no one really knew what SS was, just people catching sick and falling asleep for too long. Days, weeks, sometimes even months. In those days, people were so terrified of being buried alive because of SS that they went down with a bell at their side just in case they woke up. And not everyone does. It is still almost impossible to tell the difference between the dead Sleep of encephalitis lethargica and the plain dead.

If only that were all SS did to people. Put them to Sleep.

I take the cup, rattling the two green pills against the sides as I get a cupful of water to wash them down. But Sister Lei doesn't buzz the door open.

"There's been a change of schedule. The Watch had to take Peishan to the Sanatorium for observation, and the cannery needs someone to cover her shift."

The deep pool of anger bubbling inside my chest begins to froth again. Peishan. The newest in a line of unforgivable sins to lay at my mother's feet.

I glance down at the pills now cupped in my hand, suddenly not wanting to swallow them. Yuan Zhiwei invented Mantis himself. It's the only way to combat the second half of what SS does to us—the half that happens after the victim wakes up. One moment, you could be sitting and chatting about the weather; the next, singing the City anthem with full vibrato, or trying to pull out your own hair. Or attacking your Remedial Reform teacher. Compulsions aren't exactly random. They just destroy inhibitions and agitate the victim. A bad toothache might have you in the bathroom, trying to extract it with a wrench. An annoying sibling you wish you could smack might end up with strangling bruises. Mantis cured all of that and allowed those of us Sephs who woke up to go about their lives as normal, needing only two doses a day. Yet, about a year ago, Mantis suddenly stopped working for certain people. People like Peishan. The First Circle hasn't even issued a statement about the problem. The victims are just carted away to the Sanatorium one by one, and they don't come back.

"Are they sure Peishan isn't responding to Mantis? She didn't miss a dose or—"

"Her shift starts in eleven minutes."

I look at the floor. What was Peishan's infected brain telling her to do when I landed on top of her? It distracts me from wondering how anyone could manage to survive in the Sanatorium. Uncontrollable compulsions, floors and floors of untreatable inmates confined. I don't know why the City doesn't just let them go. Send them Outside.

I close my eyes, ashamed of myself for even thinking it. The Sanatorium is a blessing from the Firsts. Nothing could be worse than being forced Outside.

Taking a deep breath, I force myself to think instead of a problem I can actually address, like my empty stomach. Only Firsts can help Peishan now.

"Food? Before I go?" The orphanage cafeteria usually stays open for those of us with odd shifts over in the factories, and I don't think I can face another four hours of a sweaty rubber jump-suit and gloves without something to go on.

Sister Lei doesn't even blink. "Comrade Hong informed me of your trespassing in her home this evening, Sev." Her eyes go back to the paperwork on her desk. "You have leave to enter the Second Quarter only for specified reeducation sessions. All of your lessons were canceled for this week, yet you still crossed the wall. If you can't keep your Fourth tendencies in check, the Hongs aren't going to continue trying to reeducate you back into the City's good graces. If I were making the decisions, you'd be doing hard labor like a Fourth deserves."

I quickly swallow the pills, the feeling of Mantis lodged in my throat remaining long after they go down.

It's a hungry walk to the cannery, and a long night of sweating in the rubber getup that keeps me safe from the chemical-laced fruit they cart in from farms Outside. But I can't complain. Not when I know Peishan—or any of the other kids locked away inside the Sanatorium—would die to trade places with me.

Tai-ge appears at the orphanage doors right as the sky falls dark a few days later, bearing an official invitation to sit across the table from General Hong to have my brain reorganized to better fit the City's aims. Something must be brewing up in the Second Quarter for the General to summon me this late. He would have had to ask for special permission to have a Fourth out after dark.

Everything about Tai-ge is still and controlled as he waits for the Sister on duty to buzz the door open. After a Watchman gave me a bloody nose for being out in the Second Quarter alone, Tai-ge always comes to walk me to and from tutoring sessions with his father.

"Let's go around the long way." He edges me toward a side

street that meanders between Third housing installations.

"It's faster to go straight across the marketplace . . . ," I start.

"There's a new batch of soldiers all the way around the market-place walls. They strung them up this afternoon."

"Oh." I let him pull me down the bricked-in alleyway, away from the wall that separates the First laboratories and Second homesteads up the hill from the Thirds. I'm glad, actually, not to pass the City Center's layered tile roof, just above the market-place. After the episode with Peishan, I can't face walking any-where near the Traitor's Arch—the place where they keep *her*.

Everyone talks about how my mother left, how she infected me then ran straight to the Kamari general, whoever he is, and told him where we were so they could try to steal our Mantis. But no one explains why she came back. Why she murdered half the First Circle, all old men who were barely hanging on to life by the tips of their fingers as it was. They do, however, have videos of her arrest, of my father and sister as they were dragged out of our house while I was still waking up from SS. This video shows Mother lying in her bed of glass and tubes in front of the remain-ing Firsts of the Circle. Standing at their head is the Chairman. Highest of the Firsts, too wise to be in the labs anymore, now called to lead us in Yuan Zhiwei's place. It's the only time I've ever seen him outside of paintings. No one beyond the Circle sees much of the Chairman or his family in person. The fact that he came himself to condemn Mother shows just how horrific her crimes were. Those few seconds of his face on the video seem like a doorway into another world, a place I'm not welcome, where I'm not even a person. He stands there under the towering hulk of Traitor's Arch, one flick of his hand sending Mother to her fate.

We all have to watch her at least once a year on the grainy

community telescreens. The Chairman injects her with something as if she's the princess in that stupid story she used to tell me at bedtime, pricked by the crooked spindle and sent into an endless sleep. Everyone in the City Center cheers as they hoist her glass box up to the top of the Arch, on display for all to see. She's still there, eyes closed, kept in limbo between life and death, her every breath pumped in and out of her in crackling bursts.

I have to blink away the thought, because it brings others. *Real* memories from after I woke up—not the ones manufactured from watching Mother's last moments on a telescreen later—of standing before Traitor's Arch, my face hot, and Aya so cold beside me when they finally let us leave our house. Of Father, white-faced and tired, waiting for the Circle to use Mother's crimes to mark the rest of us.

Tai-ge and I circle back behind the blocky factory housing units, the crumbling bricks pasted up and down with big character posters, probably written during the evening's announcements, since most of them have to do with the current campaign to "destroy revisionists" and to "strike at both tigers and flies." I stop looking when I find my own surname in smudged ink.

They haven't hung enemy soldiers up on the wall for months now. The City always leaves their heads bare so it's easy to see they are from Kamar's invading army, their odd-colored hair jarring. Blond, brown, coppery red. Vicious enemies now hanging limply against the bloodstained wall.

The same Watchman from earlier in the week opens the barrier to let us onto the bridge. The Aihu River looks so beautiful when it is lit up for the night that I can't find it in myself to be annoyed at him when he growls at me as I walk past. The reflections from the paper lanterns frolic across the slow roll of water as it flows under the bridge.

"That guard's all bark and no bite. A pleasant change." Tai-ge smiles as he kicks a loose pebble over the side of the bridge and runs to watch it plop into the water. I join him at the rail, eyeing the tollhouse, where the Watchman is still glaring at us.

UNITED TO STOP SLEEPING SICKNESS. The words painted on the old timbers of the bridge make my eyes dance away, back down to the water, where I don't have to think.

We watch ripples from the fallen stone snake out wider and wider, bending the reflected light from the bridge into swirls. The pinpoint light of a patroller blinks across the rushing surface of the river, but it looks oddly big. As though the light smoldering in the river couldn't possibly belong to an aircraft so high up above us.

"It's almost dark," I finally say, taking my eyes off the light and turning to Tai-ge. "Even you can't charm your mother into letting me off if I'm late for reeducation with your father tonight." But Tai-ge doesn't look at me.

"Tai-ge?"

His eyes are still glued to the patroller's reflection dancing across the surface of the dark water. We both look up, as if squinting at the light will force it to pass the way it's supposed to instead of buzzing over us. The light grows brighter and brighter, larger, until I can hear the scream of its engines bearing down on us.

Kamar.

Tai-ge grabs my hand, dragging me toward solid ground, but the light in the sky falls, falls until all sound is blocked out, everything eclipsed by the bright flare of a bomb. My feet leave the ground and Tai-ge's hand twists out of mine as I crash through the railing of the bridge. Splintered wood lashes across my arms and chest, tearing through the dark wool of my coat. I keep waiting for the cement-hard crash that will mean I've hit the water, but all I can feel is a high-pitched squeal that hums through me.

When the impact finally comes, it seems as though I've been falling for hours. I sink in slow motion, the inferno of cavorting lights above the river's surface diluted and weak in the watery darkness above me. Something clicks in my overloaded brain, and I start to fight the water as it sucks me deeper. Panic blossoms in my chest when my lungs begin burning, all the air crushed out of me and what seems like an impossible distance to the surface. I pull off my boots and unbutton my jacket, slipping out of its heavy embrace. Still, even frantic kicking does not speed up the funeral crawl toward open air. The light becomes brighter until it's almost unbearable, and then I break through the surface, gasping in frozen lungfuls of air.

Choking and sputtering, I flail for a few minutes until a chunk of wood bumps my head. I cling to it, coughing all the water out of my lungs before noticing the wood is painted red with one word: UNITED.

The bridge is gone. Plumes of fire above my head blast me with heat, reflections igniting all around me in the water. Face pressed against the plank, I don't look back at the bridge until I am far enough away to feel the cold again. Small, ant-like figures scurry back and forth, frantically attempting to quell the flames devouring the splintered remains of the bridge. The beams splay out like broken teeth. *Where is Tai-ge?* No matter how hard I squint into the bubbling mass of people, my friend's fate remains a hard knot of terror in my chest.

Large columns of smoke billow up from the flames. I can still see the lights of the attacking heli-plane in the sky getting smaller and smaller. On its way back to Kamar.

I take a painful breath and start kicking my socked feet toward the shore. I need to find Tai-ge, to make sure he is safe. At least, that is my intention until my mind starts wandering with cold. *I wonder if*

Sister Lei will call the Watch when I don't show up for reeducation with the General. The thought sends me off into a fit of giggles. I can just imagine arriving on the orphanage doorstep, sopping wet, trying to explain to the angry Watchman from the bridge why I missed my lesson.

I hazily realize that my fingers and toes are completely numb and that every kick toward the shore is getting weaker, slower. The curls of flame dancing on the bridge remind me of a troupe of fire dancers Tai-ge took me to see when I first started reeducation with his family.

When I start to imagine myself running through the flames in a pink leotard, my dream is interrupted by a soft *thud.* I am halfway off the board, not even kicking any longer, but by some chance of fate the pull of the river has sent my raft to shore. I know if I don't get out of the water now, I might not get out at all. My limbs scream in protest, but my toes find the bottom and I manage to crawl out into some muddy grass.

No one is close enough to call for help. The crowds of people forming around the bridge have become one big animal-like blur, not a face to be seen. A prickle of fear needles through the fuzz coating my brain as I watch the shadows slither closer. *Did that thing get Tai-ge? Will it come for me next?*

The shadow thing will see me if I sit up, so I squirm down farther into the mud, clutching the board, not quite sure if it is still actively working to keep me alive. But hiding doesn't work because my hands and feet are gone, and the huge black animal collapsing and trembling by the bridge sends two of its thousands of legs toward me. One wraps around my waist, lifting me high into the air while the other gags my mouth to stop my screaming. The slimy feelers wrap tighter and tighter around my ribs until I cannot breathe, and my vision goes black.

CHAPTER 3

HER VOICE IS SOFT IN MY DREAM, THE SLOW WORDS
familiar. "She could not wake, trapped by the spell. Asleep." A bedtime story.

I try to look at her, but my eyelids won't open. They never do
when I dream about the time I spent Asleep. Her hand brushes
mine, and I want to grab it, to hold on to her, but my fingers
won't move, my voice won't obey when I tell it to call out to her.
My whole body is so still I might as well be dead, except I can
hear her. I can feel her. I'm paralyzed, begging for my muscles to
respond.

"Sleep settled over the whole kingdom: the cook, the butcher,
the guards. The horses and cows. Even the flies. Waiting for one
brave enough to break the spell."

Frozen. Inside, I start to scream.

The beautiful voice breaks. "I'm so sorry, little rose . . ." And
then again, again. The painful words chime in my head, growing
darker and darker as they twist around me. A monster's growl
that squeezes the breath from my lungs, claws sinking in because

I cannot move, I cannot run. My eyes will not open. I have to escape, have to break away, but I am stuck. No one can hear my voice. No one will ever hear the screams trapped in my mouth.

The world cracks apart, and I gasp, air slashing my lungs to shreds. My head feels as though it's about to cave in, pressure from trying to open my eyes threatening to split skin and bone.

I roll over and pain tears through my abdomen. A hands presses against my shoulder, as if the owner wants me to stay Asleep forever. Suddenly, all I can see are tentacles and a black creature squeezing me, the fallen timbers from the bridge burning all around me.

"Sev? Sevvy?" a panicked voice cries. "Someone help!"

The pressure against my head pushes harder until I realize it's my hands covering my eyes, blocking out the light. Shaking, I draw my hands away from my face, my own whitewashed walls and ceiling too bright after the darkness of my nightmare. A face swims above me, familiar but I can't place it. Terror floods over me as the person pins my shoulders against my pillow, threatening to steal my breath and fill my lungs, to leave me cold and still at the bottom of the river. Awake, to feel myself drowning forever.

"Sevvy, please! I'm right here. You're okay. You're going to be okay. Please just calm down. . . ."

The voice pours like honey into my ears, slowing everything down until I recognize Tai-ge's face only inches from mine, lips drawn tight with fear.

I'm not Asleep. Not trapped forever in my own body, waiting for the day the doctors say I'm lost. For them to burn me.

Not enough room for burials inside the City walls.

A nun bangs through the door. "Is she compulsing? Hold her still!"

"No . . ." The word grates in my throat, catching with every wave of pain cascading up from my ribs. What happened to me? I remember walking with Tai-ge and fire and . . . something dark and alien all around me.

The nun pulls my arm from my side, sending a jolt of pain through my middle. It's Sister Shang, a syringe ready in hand.

"No! I'm not having a compulsion." My voice tears through my throat, barely coming out in a hoarse whisper. I try to relax my arm, knowing if I pull against her, the terror of sleep will return at the tip of her syringe. "But if you touch me with that needle, I think I can come up with a better compulsion than lying in bed. Like maybe cutting all your hair off and selling it to Wood Rats as a fire starter." The joke rolls off my tongue, as if pretending that scavenging Outsiders are reasonable enough to trade with will drown out the sound of Mother's hollow apologies still ringing in my ears.

"I'd have to grow it out first. Or did you mean Tai-ge's?" Sister Shang rubs her bald scalp as she pulls the syringe away from me. She's one of the nuns I actually like, usually ready with a joke or an off-the-books snack for days when the factories don't take normal human eating habits into consideration as they schedule orphan hours. "You should be a little more grateful, seeing as it was Tai-ge who found you half-drowned and dragged you to the medics. But if you aren't set on shattering your windows and shaving poor passersby with the glass pieces, then you can take a more conventional dose of Mantis. You're due." She sticks a hand into her brown robe and holds out a packet, two green pills inside.

I take them, holding them carefully in my palm as my breaths come in painful wheezes. *What is wrong with me?*

Sister Shang watches me for a moment, as if to be sure I'm not about to cut Tai-ge's nose off before leaving. The door squeaks as she walks out.

"What happened?" I ask quietly, only now able to take in Tai-ge's battered appearance. His arm is in a red mesh sling, a splint sticking out from underneath his hand, and shallow cuts line cheeks and jaw, as though he washed his face using a bowl of broken glass. That arm looks broken. How did he drag me anywhere with a broken arm? "Was it an SS bomb? Are you—"

"I'm fine, Sevvy." He sort of smiles, cradling his arm as he settles onto the other bed in my room. Peishan's. It's been stripped of sheets, bare mattress bending under him as he sits. "I haven't fallen Asleep or tried to kill or maim anyone, members of the Watch excluded. You, however, have been unconscious for a day and a half and have at least two broken ribs. You scared me just now."

There's a hint of question in his voice that I don't care to answer. I lie very still in bed, every movement sending a jolt of pain through my abdomen, each one grasping at me like the tentacles and darkness from the waking nightmare at the bridge. The hallucination.

I've never had a compulsion before, and he knows it. I don't think that is what he means, though, and suddenly I'm worried I said something in the last throes of my dream or did something to alert him. I may never have had a compulsion, but SS has definitely done other things to my brain I don't have the courage to explain. Compulsions make you believe things that aren't true, dire things, horrible things. They don't make you see things that aren't there.

The monster grabbing me at the bridge is not the first time I've seen the world warp around me, letting in monsters and ghosts that should not exist. I'm already like a piece of faulty machinery here in the City, gumming everything up. What would they do to me if they knew my mind was broken too?

I can't bring myself to tell Tai-ge. Not him or anyone else. I've never heard of any other SS victim actually hallucinating, confusing the darkness inside with the things going on right in front of them. It isn't even what the First Circle would do if they found out that scares me most. What would Tai-ge think if he knew that I'm not just infected? That it's worse than that.

I change the subject. "I've been asleep for a day and a half? Has the canning shift officer come to drag me out in front of the Watch yet? Or is that what you meant by wanting to maim the Watch?"

Tai-ge reaches for a tray balanced on the chest at the end of my bed and pulls it onto his lap, a bowl of cold rice, cooked cabbage, and what looks like canned peaches next to a glass of water . His fingers wrap around the glass, swirling it once before handing it to me and looking meaningfully at the Mantis pills still sitting on my palm. "I couldn't find you that night. I was worried. . . ."

I wait, something other than pain uncurling from under my ribs, my eyes locked on his face with an irrational hope that he'll finish the sentence. But the door opens, and Tai-ge looks up, one of the other girls who lives on my floor freezing halfway into the room when she sees Tai-ge. "I was looking for Peishan. . . . Sorry." She backs out, fear of interrupting a Red General's son chasing her down the hall.

Sighing, I take a sip of the water and swallow my pills.

Tai-ge takes the glass back and sets it and the tray aside. "It took some arguing to get them to take you to a medic at all. And when the medic got a good look at you, I thought he was going to faint. I had to shove my stars in his face before he even let me put you down. He still might turn himself in for aiding Jiang Gui-hua's daughter."

People stopped staring in the streets years ago, and even the Watch hardly notices me anymore. My long hair helps to hide it, but my face belongs to my mother, right down to the birthmark that spreads out from my ear to my cheek. Every comrade has her face branded in their memories along with a good dose of fear and disgust. I rub my cheek thoughtfully and wince at the sliced skin, realizing that my face must look a bit like Tai-ge's right now. "He should have just finished me off. I bet Chairman Sun would have given him a medal. Or maybe a red uniform."

"He was an army medic, double stars and all. No shabby Third doctors for a celebrity like you, Sevvy."

"A single star, then." Not that they actually let anyone add or subtract stars. You couldn't get rid of the hash marks detailing your place in the world even if you wanted to, not unless you wanted to risk looking as though your marks had been burned off entirely like mine. Even if that weren't the case, rewarding comrades for good work with a new set of stars would make people aspire. Compete. Competition makes for arguments and anger instead of duties well performed, according to General Hong. But I don't let the General's chiding voice in my head stop me from making fun. "One star and a job treating nosebleeds up in the First Quarter. Or whatever it is they're excited about this week. Did I see a new pamphlet about a breakthrough in bone remodeling?"

Tai-ge shakes his head, smiling. "So chipper. At least you're off your shifts at the cannery with your injuries. Should I figure out how to get myself a pair of broken ribs and get out of all the extra duties father is giving to me? It doesn't look so bad."

"It just hurts to move. And breathe. And think. I wouldn't

recommend it. In fact, I want my money back. I'll just go shake my fist a little at the guard on the bridge. Want to come?"

Tai-ge sobers a little, twirling the ring on his finger as he does when he's uncomfortable, the City seal stark against the gold. "He didn't make it. They found him downstream in pieces. I think the bomb hit his office dead-on. He left a wife and two kids, both in the youth corps of the Liberation Army. Between you and him, this bombing made a big enough stir for even the Chairman to notice."

The Chairman? He actually came out of wherever it is he commands from up on the Steppe because of me? Curiosity bristles inside of me, battling the flash of regret that flames in my cheeks for making fun of a dead man.

Tai-ge's face slides into something even more reserved. "Which means you should probably avoid shaking your fist at anyone for the next few days. Maybe not even make eye contact."

"I'm not the one who . . ." I trail off. Tai-ge already knows I'm not the one who killed the Watchman, but there are some who won't look closely at facts, only that I was there. Casting about for something to say, I ask, "Is the Chairman upset? Or is it your mother I have to worry about? You wouldn't have been down on the bridge at all if it weren't for me. Did it take a bomb to convince her that I'm not salvageable as a comrade?"

"No. Well, I hope not." Tai-ge's voice is a little strained. "Just stay here. Do what the nuns tell you to do. I'm not allowed to say anything else. But you didn't do anything wrong. This will pass."

"Didn't do anything wrong?" A thrill of fear marches up my arms, and rubbing them sends jolts of pain through my middle. "What do you mean? What will pass?"

"I can't talk about it." Tai-ge frowns. "Stay here and you'll be fine. I'm glad you're awake. I'll check in later to make sure . . ." He shrugs again as he stands, blinking as if he hasn't slept in days, and starts for the door. "Oh, and Sevvy"—Tai-ge turns back, pointing a finger at me—"don't think for a moment that pity is going to get you out of repercussions for trying to destroy my reports. My great-great-grandfather is probably trying to cross back over and kill you as we speak."

"Don't know what you are talking about." I keep a straight face. "I would never touch your family shrine. Or any of your fancy Watch reports."

"Bringing the City down, one wax-smudged document at a time." Tai-ge's smile is real now, stretching wide. "I'm on to you, Fourth. And the nuns wouldn't notice if I lit your mattress on fire or snuck a baby gore in to sleep in the extra bed, so you'd better watch out. Those broken ribs should be the least of your worries." With that, he's gone.

I let my own smile curl for a moment, then struggle to sit up so I can watch him leave the orphanage through my window. But, when I'm upright enough to see the street outside, all thoughts of Tai-ge and smiles flee. Outside, the street is filled with Watchmen, and not the normal City Watch either. The simple cut and subdued colors of their jerkins mark these men as Outside patrollers. Men who are used to death and killing, to hunting and being hunted. Men who have firsthand experience of what untreated SS looks like when left to rot in an infected brain.

The Reds salute Tai-ge as he leaves. He looks back more than once with a troubled expression on his face as he heads off toward the Second Quarter, where he belongs.

CHAPTER 4

WATCHMEN OUTSIDE? WHAT DID I DO THAT WAS so terrible the Chairman feels the need to guard a teenage orphan with no friends and a side full of broken ribs? Missing shifts at the cannery? Did they open an inquiry as to where the traitor was hiding, only to find me sleeping in bed? Fourths are supposed to be inherently lazy.

Perhaps my sleeping through cannery shifts is enough ammunition to finally destroy the annoying Fourth pebble stuck for too long in Comrade Hong's shoe.

Tai-ge told me to stay here. But If I'm going to be arrested, I at least want to know why.

I close my eyes and reach for the tray of stale food balanced on my trunk, trying to ignore the jagged edges of my cracked ribs as they grind together, leaving me gasping. My hands shake as I bite into the bread, not stopping until I've downed most of the food on my tray. Feeling a bit more capable with food in my stomach, I inch my feet over the side of the bed to rest on the floor, breathing through the firestorm erupting through my core. Half walking, half pulling myself along the side of the bed, I make it to my trunk and open the lid, grabbing a bottle hidden at the very bottom.

Da'ard pills are hard to come by in the orphanage. The nuns seem to think painkillers are a waste on kids who are causing most of the pain in the first place. Enduring pain builds character, as Sister Lei might say. In my experience, pain mostly builds my bad temper and lands me extra chores.

Fortunately, Tai-ge slipped me some last year when I broke my arm. It was his fault anyway. He was the one who wanted a look at the First Circle passing judgment on some chemical bomb tactics the Reds formulated. Just to get a look at them, he said. They were holding the meeting in the People's Garden on the Second side of the City Center, where anyone could look if they were motivated enough. We see their faces plastered all over the evening announcements and their names polka-dotting the medical research triumphs passed out at least once a week, but the men themselves tend to stay up on the Steppe where test tubes and elevated conversation are a bit more easily come by. Instead of a good look at the men, I got a good look at the ground when Tai-ge accidentally broke the branch above me and knocked me out of the tree we were hiding in. To this day, whenever we manage to eat together alone, I steal all his white rice, saying he doesn't need the extra weight.

At least I fell outside the People's Garden wall, out of sight. Can't think about what the Circle would have made of the Fourth traitor caught spying on them.

Actually, I do know.

In any case, with the leftover Da'ard pills the pain will be manageable, if not completely gone.

I swig the last of my water to wash the pills down and wait for them to take effect. After a few minutes, I twist experimentally and am rewarded with a dull ache instead of lancing pain.

Stealing a coat and boots from the girls who sleep next door, I prepare to go outside. A heavy winter cap with a brim, buttons done up to my chin, an extra set of stars secure on my shoulder so no one will think I'm trying to hide if they catch me. The ones I wore the night of the bombing must be at the bottom of the river with my coat and boots. The pins are supposed to be worn proudly, a marker for our irreplaceable responsibilities, each of us equal, though our tasks are different.

Something makes me stop. I go back to my chest, push the old clothes aside, and pull out a box. Tai-ge made it for me for my fifteenth birthday. There's a trick to opening it—all the pieces have to slide into place in the correct order before it will open. An ideal hiding place for something I'm not supposed to have. Inside is another gift from Tai-ge from long ago, his name carved deep into the handle in awkward, childish characters. A knife.

Not that I'm going to be fighting anyone. Or even that I could. It just seems right to take it with me, as if bringing Tai-ge's name along will somehow protect me.

The room across the hall has a window grown over with vines, which should have made it impossible to climb through. Those of us who have been here long enough know how to get it open and outside without disturbing the vines, letting ourselves down into a back alley behind the orphanage with no one to sound the alarm that an infected orphan is letting him or herself out.

Peishan and I used to go to the market when we were supposed to be meditating on the Chairman's words, though neither of us ever had ration papers to spend. It was nice to feel as if the long, ugly, straight lines of my schedule couldn't strangle me for the ten minutes I was outside with no one watching me.

I should be able to climb down, eavesdrop until I find out what's going on, then be back in my room before anyone notices.

The climbing part shoots pain through my rib cage even with the Da'ard, and I'm relieved when my borrowed boots find the dirty paving stones. I cringe as the kitchen door, the only door that opens into the alley, creaks. One of the cooks throws some trash out into the alley, the bag falling open to deposit an apple core and some fish bones at my feet. The cook who threw the bag doesn't bother to look out, or he would have seen me, paralyzed and attempting to hide behind the vines' empty skeleton base. Fear curdles through me as I wait for a moment, wondering if the cook will come out to shove the bag through the gate at the back of the alley for the trash collectors to pick up, but he doesn't.

I keep low as I creep around the corner to the front of the orphanage, hoping no one will notice a little Fourth bobbing about in the bushes. I don't think the headsman would be called for my climbing out of my room, but it might depend on who catches me, and Outside patrollers don't have a reputation of being merciful. I duck behind a particularly large bush, hoping I can get close enough to the soldiers to hear if they're talking. Most of them are hanging around the entrance, waiting for something.

"Do you know when?" one of them asks.

"Awaiting orders. Just like you," another snaps. "We're just supposed to keep her contained until all of the evidence can be gathered."

Evidence? Of what? Are they talking about me? I wait, hoping one of them will randomly decide to run through all the details of the situation, but of course none of the soldiers oblige. They just

stand there, watching the street with bored expressions and blowing smoke at one another from their army-issue cigarettes. After
a moment, one comes to lean against the orphanage wall, uncomfortably close to my hiding place.

What would happen if I just asked them what is going on? I
didn't do anything wrong. Even if the City did give me four stars for
my mother's crimes, the First Circle and Comrade Hong couldn't
have made something up completely out of the wind and sky.

Could they?

Maybe a couple of jokes could make the soldiers forget they're
standing next to an orphanage riddled with SS. Maybe they won't
notice my mother's face or my traitor brand. I haven't been around
Outside patrols much, but I bet they need a laugh more than most.
Maybe they've been fighting Kamari soldiers long enough that one
teenage girl with a birthmark won't be scary anymore.

Of course, all of those "maybes" are quite unlikely. And the
idea of approaching an Outside patroller makes me shiver inside
my thick wool coat. Every one of those men has seen death. Every
one of them has caused it, then walked away to smoke a cigarette.

More soldiers walk up from the opposite direction, putting my
hiding place at risk. I slide back between the buildings, only to
hear their gruff voices following me, as if they're coming to check
the alleyway. Not enough time to climb up the vines, so I squeeze
the rest of the way down the alley to the gate where the cooks
leave the trash.

There's a solid wooden gate blocking the back of the alley, a
flap at the bottom only big enough for trash bags to be shoved
through for pickup. The trash gets carted off to the wall and
thrown over. Outsiders, you're welcome.

My nose wrinkles at the stench of rotting vegetables as I

crouch down and look at the flap. It's small and coated in stickiness. But if I'm caught outside my room, will whatever Tai-ge was so worried about happen?

The footsteps echo off the brick of the alleyway as I jam myself under the flap, my shoulders scraping against the sides. I have to turn cockeyed for my hips to fit, barely sliding through as the footsteps draw near. I huddle in the mounds of trash with my back against the gate, knees drawn up to my nose. Waiting for them to stick a hand through the flap and grab me.

"Thought for sure I heard something back here." The gate jiggles against my back as one of the soldiers gives it a kick, the flap swinging with the motion.

"Just rats probably. Don't think I could fit more than my arm through that flap. Keeps hungry kids from trying to sneak into the kitchens, I guess. Have to be a pretty small kid to fit under there."

Or a young lady very motivated not to die under the Arch.

I breathe out as they walk away, waiting until the footsteps are gone before tipping the flap up an inch to make sure they're *really* gone. There's a set of boots facing away from me at the end of the alley.

Carefully letting the flap close, I look at the gate for a moment. But then I get up, lurching down the alley until I find a path to a main street. I brush at my coat and pants. Soybean hulls, burned rice, eggshells are all ground into the wool of my borrowed coat.

I wonder if the Watchmen would find the situation funny. Guarding the orphanage doors to keep the Fourth in, but keeping me out instead.

I'll just have to watch and wait until I can sneak back up. I scrub at the bits of trash and spoiled food decorating my coat, the smell of rot wafting up from the new stains.

No one pays attention to me on the street, my winter-shrouded form only one in the stream of hunchbacked workers shuffling to and fro from the factories. Not wanting to be found by someone actually looking for me, I walk a few streets down toward the market, watching a throng of students lining up to purchase bright red scarves to show support for the army from the safety of an alley. Before I can edge my way into the crowd, a man crashes into me, sending me back into the alleyway.

Pain sears through me, the impact too much even for Da'ard to cloak. I curl up, back to the wall, my arms clutched around my ribs, the world a red haze around me. The man who crashed into me grabs my wrist, hauling me deeper into the dark of the Third Quarter's maze of back roads.

I scratch at his hand, screams bottled up in my throat as he clamps the other hand down over my mouth. A few people do glance at us through the gaps between buildings, but they just look back down at their feet, too tired from long hours and food rations that don't quite fill their stomachs to wonder about anything at all. The pain blossoming all through my ribs steals any strength I might have had from my arms and legs, leaving me to sag limply to the ground. The man scoops me up, then strides down the alley, looking both directions before he opens a small wooden doorway and carries me into the darkness waiting inside. Kicking the door shut, he deposits me on something soft and velvety. A light clicks on, and I'm sitting in what looks like an old-world throne, the chair's upholstery shiny in the sudden light, the wooden arms chipped with age.

Pain hums insistently through my sides, but I refuse to feel it. I ram my elbow into the man's stomach and run for the door. Locked. I stumble along the walls, frantically pulling aside curtains and looking for a way out, but there is nowhere to go. My stare goes back to the man, bent over and clutching his stomach where he stands between me and the door.

"Stop." He croaks in a painful whisper, "I want to help you."

Not one of the curtains has a window behind it. One room with one door that opens out into the street. It makes no sense. The City doesn't build anything down in the Third Quarter unless it has a practical purpose. To sleep in, to eat in, to work in. But here, there are books—real books, not propaganda pamphlets—lining the walls. An intricately threaded rug covers the center of the floor, the reds and golds woven in and out of each other reminding me of something beautiful, something past.

He coughs, putting a hand over his heart. Catching my eye, he moves his other hand to cover the first, two fingers over his right hand, the rest curled underneath. A sign. Mother's sign.

CHAPTER 5

WE USED TO SPY TOGETHER. ME; MY SISTER, AYA; and Mother. Sometimes Father, too, all of us hiding secret notes to each other under the fancy silk upholstered chair in the family room, listening at doors to hear the maid's gossip, me and Aya attempting to sneak into their self-criticism sessions. Father would try to hide the twinkle in his eye as Aya and I fell all over each other laughing when we came back to report to Mother. Just fun and games, though now it seems I should have taken spy games as some sort of warning long before Mother disappeared in a bloody terror. Who else but a traitor would teach her daughters to pass secret messages, to hide in doorways and listen to the Thirds talk for fun? Maybe she was training us, hoping we'd take after her, be part of her network.

Or maybe they *were* just games. Was this man there, lurking in the background of my childhood, watching us play?

We had lots of hand signals, but Mother made this one up. Two fingers over a closed fist meant danger. To freeze.

"Where did you learn that?" I snap, then immediately wish I had held my tongue. My hat was lost in the scuffle outside, and I find myself with one hand to my cheek, covering my birthmark as if that might somehow negate any connection I have to Jiang Gui-hua.

"Jiang Sev." The man's eyes hold mine fast. "I'm sorry I frightened you. There are rumors in the Third Quarter you are responsible for the bomb that destroyed the Aihu Bridge."

"That I did *what*? The bomb fell from a *plane*, for Yuan's sake. Tai-ge was there. . . ." And Tai-ge told me to stay inside. Not to draw attention to myself and it all would pass. But here I am, sitting with a man who must have anti-City leanings if he's trying to help a Fourth, and especially a Fourth with my parentage.

The man continues, "On top of that, three different families in this neighborhood have had kids stop responding to Mantis, and you know whom people will blame. If you are recognized outside the orphanage, you might not make it back there alive. It was dumb luck that my informant managed to tell me you'd gotten away before anyone saw you."

"Your informant? Who are you?" My panicked heartbeat races faster and faster.

"We need to get you out of here." He folds back the rug to reveal a wooden plank in the stone floor. When he pulls it up, there is just enough room to climb down an iron ladder into darkness.

I have no intention of going down the black hole to Yuan knows where with a man who just dragged me into his own personal counter-Liberation study. There is only one place it could lead for me, and execution does not sound good. "Look. I don't know who you think you are . . ."

He doesn't look up. "My name is Yang He-ping. Dr. Yang."

The name nudges some long-sleeping memory at the back of my mind, but I'm too frightened to pull it out. "I don't care. I don't know how you learned that sign or what you have to do with my family or where this stupid tunnel leads. I am not a traitor, whatever my stars say."

Dr. Yang smooths his salt-and-pepper hair away from his face. Lines crinkle around his brown eyes. I'd guess he's somewhere around fifty. Despite the three metal stars perched high on his shoulder, his hand is marred by a series of crisscrossing white scars where his hand marks should be, as if the wielder of the knife couldn't decide where he belonged and gave him five, six, seven marks and hoped he'd fit in somewhere. I finally notice that the crinkles are not only the beginning of his age showing, but part of the smile stretching across his face. "I didn't ask you to lead a revolution, girl. I just want to help. Though if I hear of any job openings, I'll let you know."

"You'll help me get back into the orphanage? Somehow, without anyone noticing, even though they already know I'm out of my room? How?" I can feel a smile crack through the fear pounding at my head. But it is a giddy, uncontrollable smile. Hysteria. I nod toward the ladder. "Where does this even go?"

"The old City. This City was already hundreds of years old by the time Yuan Zhiwei led our people up here to hide, each generation building over the dead bones of the last. There's a whole world left over from Before. It's not a safe place to take a stroll, and the sewers leak through in places, but the Watch doesn't bother much with patrolling down there, and it'll get us to the library. No one will look for you there."

"The First library?" I feel my eyes widen in shock.

"The library will get you within a few streets of the People's Gate, between the First Quarter and the marketplace. The orphanage isn't too much farther, and I might be able to organize a

distraction that will allow you to climb back into your room when
no one is looking. Through the kitchens, maybe?"

"What should I tell them when they find me snug in my bed?
I had a bathroom emergency and no one noticed the door locked?
And . . . the library? Only Firsts are allowed in there. If the Watch
really does think I'm behind that bomb, and then Chairman Sun
finds me skulking around underground or browsing shelves of
anti-Liberation propaganda, my head would be on display at
Traitor's Arch before sunset. No trial. Just an ax."

"You know they don't use axes anymore, Sev. Capital punishment is much more refined these days." Dr. Yang points to my
hood. "You're lucky it's already cold enough we can get away with
hiding your face. It'll just look like you're trying to stay warm.
Take off your stars, keep your hood up, and walk as if you know
where you are going. I can tell you which streets will get you back.
It's your only chance." And with that, he starts down the ladder,
not even checking to see that I follow him.

Truth be told, I don't need directions. I have been to the library
many times. With Mother, before . . . everything happened. The
books lining the shelves are from Before. Corrupted by selfish ideology and philosophy from outside our land. Only Firsts are allowed
inside, using the information to aid in their scientific research, their
minds too high above it all to be tainted by impure ideals. But I know
where all the fairy tales line the shelves. Row upon row of books
filled with fanciful illustrations. Fairies, gnomes, witches and wizards,
dragons, beautiful maidens in distress, and great heroes charging in
to save them. I lived through knight duels and army raids, whispering
ghosts and talking foxes, evil spells and jealous stepmothers. It's sad
that all those books are restricted to incorruptible Firsts. Kids in the
Third Quarter could use dreams with some color.

I still remember settling into my favorite chair, just below the huge picture window, light seeping through the thin-cut jade and onto the floor in a beautiful display. Every hour or so, the colors rearranged themselves into a new picture. When I was very young, my mother and I pretended to capture the lights and take them home with us. Once, Mother gave me a shard of red-tinted jade, bound into a necklace. "This way you can always take the light with you." The image of her beautifully curled hair softly glowing in the colored lights would be forever engraved in my mind.

From that day forward, I always wore the necklace. Yet it somehow disappeared with everything else I loved the night SS took me.

My stars are heavy in my hand. I don't remember taking them off.

"Sev?" Dr. Yang calls from halfway down the ladder. "We don't have a lot of time."

Rough crosshatching on the rungs bites into my palms as I start down the ladder. Stupid, to follow this man. As stupid as wanting to see the library one more time. To stand in front of the picture window and remember life before I fell Asleep. Dark closes around me, the damp air becoming warmer as we descend. When my feet finally find the dirt floor, the overpowering smell of sewage has me gagging. Echoes of running water climb up from deep ditches that frame our narrow walkway. A faint light blossoms in Dr. Yang's cupped hands, throwing dark shadows across his face. "This is just a quicklight, so it isn't going to last long enough to get us out of here. If you run, you'll get lost. Stay with me, and I'll get you to the ladder that will take you into the library basement." Dr. Yang pulls something out of his coat and sticks it in my pocket, the shadows too dark to catch a glimpse of the gift.

"Those might come in handy. Just keep your chin up and don't let anyone look you in the eyes."

Butterflies in my stomach morph into kicks of fear every time the light flickers or my guide makes any noise. Our footsteps are the only sound I can hear on top of the faint chattering of rushing water. The dark seems to press in on me, clouding my lungs with misty fog. I've always been so afraid of the dark.

We pass several ladders rising up from the path, Dr. Yang breaking a new light each time the one in his hand starts to dim. We don't stop, my companion confident at every turn, until we come to a ladder marked with a large golden circle on the lowest rung. Dr. Yang fumbles in his pocket again, producing another quicklight. He bends it in half to break open the center and watches closely as the chemicals mix, glowing a cheery yellow. Shoving it into my hand, he points up.

The metal rungs disappear into the cloud of dark above me. Stalling, I raise my light high to look around us, the yellow glow hinting at graceful curves of stone just behind the ladder. Some kind of statue. But Dr. Yang doesn't give me a chance to look closer, pushing me toward the ladder.

I push back and look at him. "Why are you helping me?"

Dr. Yang is quiet for a moment. When he does answer, his voice is small. "I knew your mother. She was a good person trying to do good things."

"She was a traitor. She might as well have killed my father and younger sister with her own hands, and this . . . whatever is happening today is her fault. Mother deserved what the Circle did to her." My voice bites at my throat. She is the one who made me what I am. Infected. Fourth.

"Luckily for you, I disagree. Ready to go up?" When I nod, he

lays a hand on my shoulder. It feels awkward, as though he is trying to comfort me. "I'll be in contact. Good luck."

The rungs of this ladder are much smoother, worn with age.
After climbing for a few minutes, I look down to see if Dr. Yang
is still at the bottom. I can see his light, but the flare is surprisingly small, sending shudders up my spine. Switching my eyes
to the darkness in front of me is almost worse as the quicklight
illuminates a gargantuan set of hands, palms together and pressed
against a giant's bare chest, the upper portion of the statue I saw
at the bottom.

If I'm only as high as his hands, then how much farther do I
have to climb? Gripping a smooth metal rung with one hand, I
wave the light above my head, catching glimpses of a square chin
and elongated earlobes, like the religious figures that appear in
so many of the history books that landed in the First library.
Religion. Yet another corruption the Firsts say led to our destruction Before. It never quite made sense to me that a belief in
something *more* would have been our downfall, but Yuan Zhiwei
knew what was best for us when he banned religion from the City.
That's why we still follow his teachings.

Looking up so high at the statue bends me over backward,
making my head feel as if it's falling even though I'm latched to
the ladder as tightly as a tick in a mangy dog's skin.

The Da'ard has begun to wear off, so the dull throb in my
sides has turned into a sharp pulse each time I raise an arm to
pull myself up to the next rung. Darkness seeps into my clothes,
each eruption of pain a bite or a scratch from the inside. My
breaths come in short bursts of pain. When my head finally hits
the ceiling, I almost lose my grip on the top rung of the ladder,
my sweaty palms slipping against the cold metal bar. As I jam my

hand up against the rough stone ceiling, my quicklight catches the gleam of a smooth metal handle poking out of the rock a few feet away.

The statue's head looms beneath me, its eyes closed in quiet meditation as the handle above me turns too slowly. The rusted pieces screech as they grind together. I push up, and the hatch falls open with a *thud*, sending a cloud of dust down into my face. I sneeze and drop the quicklight. Stomach turning, I have to lean into the ladder and close my eyes to stop my head from spinning at the light's long descent. My arms and legs shake as I pull myself up through the hole and collapse on a floor so thick with dust that every breath is like trying to inhale cotton. I crawl away from the hole, heave myself up onto what feels like a chair, and pull my shirt up over my nose. A few deep breaths, and my racing heart-beat begins to slow.

After a few minutes of battling the dark, my eyes adjust and I can discern a faint line of lighter black on the floor, which I follow until I find an actual light, deep in the library's basement. Two dusty staircases up and a few minutes of wandering later, I come to an open room that I recognize, with a wide staircase leading to the main stacks. Black marble, just like the rest of this place. Imposing and coldly beautiful.

The picture window I remember so clearly overlooks the stair-case, stopping me as a mix of longing and revulsion fights its way up my throat. The jewel cast of the light as it filters through the paper-thin cuts of stone folds down around the rows and rows of books, their colors so familiar. A beautiful maiden is pieced together in the jade, her curls tumbling from a bed of sleep.

Stuck forever.

Mother always told the story with a dramatic sigh, as if the princess pricking her finger on the spindle and falling asleep wasn't the tragic end to the story, just an unfortunate pause that passed her fate on to the imagination of the listener. Aya and I would make them up together, hiding under our covers, whispering back and forth until Father came with threats of no sweet *bao* for dessert the next day if we didn't go to sleep. Aya would say the evil fairy would be sorry and wake her up, then become her servant as penance. Or that little birds cheeped in her ears until she woke up, and the princess threw water on her royal parents to bring them back from the spell. My favorite idea, though Aya always stuck her tongue out and wrinkled her nose whenever I told it, was that a prince would kiss her awake in true fairy-tale fashion, and the whole kingdom would open their eyes along with her, the evil fairy's spell broken.

But that isn't how the story ends. The princess pricks her finger, falls down as if dead, and her family and the whole kingdom rot away around her bit by bit until it's a place of the dead, a place for ghosts and monsters. She's the one who sought out the evil fairy, and those are the consequences. She deserves her fate.

I look up at the window. It's a relic from Before, when we mixed books and tales with people from far away. Before the world was us against Kamar, the Outsiders who poisoned our air with SS. The picture changes every few hours, all the tiny pieces somehow rattling to a new spot like a kaleidoscope of trained butterflies. For some reason, the library survived the purges of everything from Before when Yuan Zhiwei claimed the City as a safe haven. Setting foot inside is like stepping back in time. Geometric designs on the walls are richly painted in reds and purples, and the supports holding up the roof are carved with dragons and phoenixes, all legends that have been forgotten.

My hand reaches toward the picture window before I can control myself, brushing the woman's long curls. She doesn't look like Mother, but her eyes are closed just the same. Asleep. Dead to the world, and yet still stuck here because of her crimes.

A low cough echoes through the room. I jerk my hand back, knocking two books down from the low shelves as I spin around in panic.

A young man watches me from the other side of the room. His high collar boasts one red star. I feel as though I've seen him before, but I can't place him.

He doesn't look surprised or upset, just a little embarrassed to have caught someone trying to climb a bookcase. Licking his lips and pressing them together, he seems to be trying to keep his eyes on the floor, but they flick up to my face a few times. I am still frozen to the spot, caught like a mouse in a trap.

The picture transforms behind me, the lights dancing to their new places on the floor. Jade pieces realign into a young girl cowering before a black, fanged beast. The change wrenches me back to life.

"Excuse me," he starts, "were you looking for—"

"Nothing," I interrupt. Heart pounding, I nod to him and walk toward the front of the library with my nose in the air.

"Wait!" He's walking after me, the polite smile pasted across his face starting to slip.

I walk faster, the young man only a bit behind me in the twists and turns through bookshelves, though he doesn't yell for help. By the time I push through the library's outer doors, I'm almost at a run. Outside, I duck behind the statue of Yuan Zhiwei, his broad shoulders dusted with snow. His ax points down Renewal Road, toward the City Center building.

The young man comes out after me, looking up and down the street, his face striking a chord in my memory yet again. Was he one of the librarians from when I was young? But I immediately discount that idea. He's much too young for that. And if the Watch is looking for me, it stands to reason they know about it even this far up in the First Quarter. After the young man passes my hiding place, I walk in the opposite direction, slipping behind the library into the strangled maze of lanes backing most of the government buildings in this quarter. Third entrances for the window cleaners and floor waxers.

Going in the direction the young man went would mean passing through the main gate at the end of Renewal Road and trying to cross the bridge that spans the river over to the City Center, which would be a good way to get caught. And I'm glad I can't go that way. I can't face passing the City Center and Mother in her living coffin over Traitor's Arch. Not today. Maybe not ever.

The back streets are still familiar. Walking with my eyes on the paving stones, I join the steady stream of Thirds moving through the narrow lanes, jobs done for the day. Thirds with the odd Fourth scattered through. The Fourths keep their gaze down, whatever rehabilitation they had to go through that allowed them to remain inside the City leaving their expressions blank. Each step seems measured, as though if their stride stretches an inch too far, some First will notice and reassign them to one of the Outside farms or mine labor. Or worse, banish them to the wilds Outside to scavenge what the City and Kamar leave behind. Never able to sleep soundly or stay in one place, because then the other Wood Rats will find you.

To land an assignment in the First Quarter, these Fourths must be reformed indeed, though I think even Firsts have a hard time selling toilet cleaning as glorious labor for the Liberation down in the Third Quarter. A woman jostles my arm as she hurries past. She looks back apologetically but does not stop, almost running to keep up with the flow of workers headed for the gate.

The People's Gate is a sort of back door, allowing Thirds easier access to the First Quarter. It's beautiful, the black marble favored throughout the First Quarter relieved by gray sculptures of men and women holding the base of the columns that form the only direct portal through the wall that divides the First Quarter from the Third. A bridge fits into the gate's mouth like a tongue, spanning the river to allow free access to the marketplace.

For all their beauty, the statues supporting the gate have always struck me as odd. I suppose when the Liberation Army first built the gate, they still thought of Third workers as the center of society, happy in the labor that enabled the City's survival. It seems almost silly to see carved scenes of bricklayers singing through their efforts and factory workers smiling as they present the fruit of their labors to all who walk by. The Third Quarter wasn't such a happy place earlier today. Maybe trying to sing with a lungful of brick dust really takes it out of you.

I don't much want to sing my way through the long hours I put in at the canning factory. My hands are permanently chapped from the steam, and sometimes it seems as though my back will never unbend from hunching over the jars all day.

It isn't a bad job. Tai-ge's family put me there, and I'm grateful. Better than anyone connected to my mother deserves. But when Comrade Hong was presented with the honor of rehabilitating such a high-profile traitor, she wasn't willing to have me track welding dust into the house or cough linen fibers from the textile mills onto her clean dishes.

There's a line at the gate now, each of the workers undergoing a quick inspection by a set of Watchmen before they are allowed to leave. There have never been Watchmen guarding the People's Gate before.

My hand, thrust deep inside my coat pocket against the cold, closes around something hard. My attention on the gate, I don't look down to see what it is, vaguely remembering that Dr. Yang shoved something into my pocket while we were underground.

The Reds pull the woman at the front of the line aside, the flash of four stars at her shoulder sending pulses of alarm up and down my throat. When I finally glance down at the object in my hand, I gasp and throw it away from me with a hiss. A single red star.

I crouch down to look at them, lying on the street. So harmless-looking. Dr. Yang is deluding himself if he thinks I can run around wearing these when a single glance at my hand, or a glimpse of the birthmark on my cheek, would have me on the ground with my elbows tied together before I could even say hello. My fingers close around them, and I stuff them back in my pocket before the workers in line at the gate have the chance to notice.

The setting sun drags shadows long across the narrow streets, all the way to the orphanage's peaked roof, which I can see just over the wall. Was this really Dr. Yang's plan, depositing me in the First Quarter and hoping I might be able to sneak past the tide of Watchmen searching for me in the lower quarters? How can I get back to where I'm supposed to be? And if I disappear, the Hongs, the Outside patrollers, the bloody Chairman himself will think I really was responsible for that bomb. My days of waiting for the ax to fall will dwindle down to single digits.

Across the street from me, a crumbling dragon guards the entrance to a First home. His forelegs stretch around the lintel, but each of his clawed paws are cut off with a deep cross chiseled into the stone, ending in a gray crumble.

The statue's mangled paws grasp at my mind, a thrill of fear dancing down my spine. If I miss my dose of Mantis tonight, it won't matter what the Chairman thinks I did. I might not make it through the night. The family that lives here might not either. The entire block could be dead in their beds by morning.

The red star comes back out of my pocket. I can't think of another way. This must have been what Dr. Yang meant for me to do.

I pin the star to my coat with shaking hands and take a step toward the gate, but a hand grabs my shoulder and tugs me back. I gasp in pain as my ribs seem to grate against each other. The Da'ard must have completely worn off by now. The person gripping my shoulder wears a dark woolen coat, thick hood casting shadows over his face in the failing light. A red star sits on his shoulder, snarling at me like a snake.

"What do you think you are doing?" I whisper, trying to keep my voice from the guards.

He waves to the Watchmen lounging by the wall. "If you try to go through the gate, they will arrest you."

Fighting the gentle pull of his hand toward the alleyway, I stand straight as Dr. Yang advised, my voice taught with a First's impatience. "I have an important errand to run in the City Center, and if I don't . . ."

The boy glances back at me, and I catch a glimpse of white teeth in what I think is a smile. "Don't kid yourself, Jiang Sev. I wouldn't be surprised if all the Watchmen in the City are out looking for you right now. They don't go by halves when it comes to dangerous fugitives. Dr. Yang sent word for me to meet you. The situation up here has escalated."

My stomach twists when he says my name paired with Dr. Yang's. If this First isn't arresting me for wearing a single star— for even being in the First Quarter—then I'm not sure I want to be walking with him. "Dangerous fugitives? I'm sixteen. I've lived in an orphanage helping encephalitis lethargica patients for the last eight years. I am the prime example of what the reeducation campaign is doing for Fourths. The Hongs are teaching me what it means to be a part of a real family. I work at a canning factory every single day to support the war effort." I jerk my hand out of his to show him my chapped fingers. They look much more impressively worn with all the extra scrapes and slivers left over from the bridge. "That all screams 'loyal comrade' to me. I haven't done anything wrong."

"Tell that to the Watch." He looks up the street, where an elderly couple is ambling toward us, hand in hand. "Come on. Let's get out of here before someone decides that two people running around with their hoods up look suspicious." He leads me into a side street and produces a hat and a scarf. "Put these on. It's cold."

"You think a scarf covering half of my face is less conspicuous than a hood? With a manhunt on?" I twitch my hood back and pull the hat down low on my forehead, then wrap the scarf a few times around my neck, tucking the last loop up around my chin. My hair is tight against my cheek, hiding the birthmark.

"*Woman*hunt. If anyone walks by or tries to talk to us, we're a couple out for a walk, understand? Follow my lead and try not to say anything." He pulls back his hood. Somehow, I'm not surprised to see the young man from the library. He inspects the scarf and the hat, one hand hovering next to my cheek where my hair hides the mark. "Don't worry. I won't kiss you or anything."

"What?"

As an answer, he yanks me back into the street and sets a very slow pace. A stroll, like the older couple just passing us. The man gives my companion a knowing smile as we emerge from the alley and stops. "I thought that was you, Yi-lai. Care to introduce me to your friend? I don't think we've met."

Yi-lai's lips part in a grin and he says, "Of course. Premier Sutan, meet Wenli. Her family just came back in after a round overseeing the farm at Lunzi."

"Oh, the Outside farms. I'm so glad I've outgrown having to take my turn overseeing our operations out there. We need the food, and those Seconds and Thirds need First oversight, but just being Outside . . ." The Premier gives a theatrical shiver and looks at me as if expecting me to say something. When I don't, he smiles again and says, "How do you like being back in civilized company, Wenli? What are your parents' names? If they are working with the propaganda team, I've probably already met them."

"Um, no." I manage to choke the two words out from behind my scarf. "They're scientists. Working on biogenetic weapons. Our name is . . . Chen," I say, picking one of the most common names in the City. I hope he takes the stumble as a sign of nervousness. It isn't every day you meet any member of the First Circle, much less the City Premier.

"With General Hong? If I come across your parents, I'll tell them what a beautiful girl you are. Smart, too. You have good taste." He laughs and winks at Yi-lai. "Tell your father hello for me, son."

"Yes, sir." Yi-lai makes his nod almost a bow.

"Oh, and I heard something from the Watch an hour or so ago." He puts a hand on Yi-lai's shoulder, his voice a shade quieter. "Take your friend home. The Jiang girl is making some kind of trouble down in the Third Quarter. I doubt she would try to come all the way up here, but there's no sense in taking the risk. Not with the family's history." He pats Yi-lai's shoulder, his eyes already wandering away. "I'll have to go talk to the General. He must be so disappointed. After all the years they invested in that girl . . . a spy and a murderer, just like her mother. But don't you two worry. The Watch will have her up on the Arch with her eyes closed next to Jiang Gui-hua before you can say 'Sleeping Sickness.'"

Every word drills holes into my chest, and my breaths begin to come out as sharp bursts of fog in the frozen air. Yi-lai's grip on my arm tightens, as if he's worried I might lash out and hit the Premier. But the Premier takes his wife's arm and nods to both of us before leading her down the street.

Yi-lai lets out all his breath at once, as though he's been holding it the whole time. He pulls my arm through his and we walk linked together, moving up the Steppe, the highest section of the First Quarter in the City. "You okay?" he whispers.

"He . . . he doesn't even . . ." I can't make myself say more, waiting for the slow burn of anger to smolder down before trusting my voice.

"Yeah, he's sort of a miserable old bag, isn't he?" Yi-lai gives me a cautious, concerned sort of look when I don't answer, but doesn't attempt any more discussion as we climb higher into the First Quarter, where all the scientists and the First Circle live. Lights bloom all around us in the dusk, street lamps lighting our way up the hill toward the massive homes. Massive like the library, tiered hip-and-gable roofs peek up over the walls surrounding each First family compound.

When my voice doesn't feel as though using it will break glass, I finally end the silence between us. "You're quite chummy with the Premier, aren't you? Members of the First Circle don't stop for just anyone." I grip the stolen red star on my collar, the points like a knife on my palm. "Yi-lai, right? Now that we're involved, would you like to tell me a little more about yourself? And maybe why you're helping me, especially now that I'm suddenly a murderer and a spy instead of an annoying little Fourth?"

The stressed look is back on Yi-lai's face, and he doesn't seem to be listening very closely, concentrating instead on the paving stones under our feet. The quick pace he's set is becoming more and more difficult as my ribs grind against each other. "Would you mind slowing down, at least? I'm kind of broken. It'll be harder to keep up the act if I start crying or something."

He immediately slows a little, but not enough. "Not scared, are you?" he asks.

"Scared out of my mind, and no, that is not meant to be a joke."

"Why would that be a joke?"

"It's sundown."

He looks blank. "Are you scared of the dark?"

"Um . . ." I'm starting to feel eyes on me, peering over the walls of each home we pass. "I have to take Mantis at daybreak and nightfall or . . ."

Yi-lai stops our speed walk up the hill and looks me dead in the eyes. "I didn't even think about that. What are we going to do?"

"Well, if I start to go funny, you could probably take me. I have two broken ribs. And I think you've got me on reach." I stretch one arm out as if to compare, but a wave of nausea and pain washes up from my ribs at the movement, forcing me to carefully arrange it back by my side.

"Are you listening to yourself?" He laughs in disbelief. "Your head is on the line and . . ."

"Yours too. In more ways than one at the moment," I say.

Yi-lai shakes his head. "I'm just surprised. If the Watch ever comes after me, you won't find me cracking jokes." Pursing his lips, he says, "We probably have Mantis in the house, but I don't know where. We'll find it."

"You aren't infected, I'm guessing?" He shakes his head and we continue to walk, passing homes that seem to be getting more and more ornate, the lights glowing out from the windows with warmth. Something about his outline seems familiar, every house we pass washing his features with lamplight. His eyes and mouth especially send a sting of recognition across the back of my mind.

Wait.

I stop, my mouth clenching shut. He doesn't break stride, giving me a questioning tug when I don't follow.

I know where I've seen him. Yi-lai sits in the huge painting set opposite Traitor's Arch in the City Center. Yi-lai and his father, the Chairman. The words come out in a strangled whisper. "You're the Chairman's son."

He doesn't quite meet my eye, pulling my arm a bit harder in an effort to start me walking again.

"You are. Sun Yi-lai. I knew I'd heard that name." The Chairman's family is almost the stuff of legend, like gods from Before living up above us in a flare of glory, hardly ever finding it necessary to show their faces. I put a hand to my forehead, nausea blooming in my stomach like an acid bouquet. "Why did you keep me back from those Seconds at the gate? Is the Chairman going to put me back to Sleep? Like *her*?" I pull away from him, glaring. "I didn't do it! I didn't have anything to do with bombs or with SS or anything that happened—"

"I want to help you." He squares off, looking down at me. "But I won't be able to do it if the Reds hear you yelling."

I blink at his use of the Seconds' nickname. I didn't know Firsts called them that too. "*Why*, then? Why in Yuan's name would you help me?"

He looks at the ground. "You look just like her. Your face, anyway."

Goose bumps prickle down my arms.

"I didn't ask how you recognized me," I hiss. "I asked why you're dragging me from the library, one of two places guaranteed to land just about any non-First comrade in a prison cell, to the other: the top of the Steppe."

"Look, Sev." He grabs my hand again, and we start walking. "I know you didn't blow up the Aihu Bridge."

"That isn't an answer, or even logical. Where are you taking me? How am I supposed to just blindly follow you?" *And what does she* have *to do with it?*

He shrugs. "Where else can you go?"

CHAPTER 6

THE CHAIRMAN'S BASEMENT WINE CELLAR IS CRAMPED.
It seems as if it should all glow with mystery and a special sort of
grandeur, but mostly it's just dusty. A wine rack takes up two walls,
the corked mouths forming patterns in the dark wood. The air is
cool and slightly damp, making me feel as though I need to change
my clothes. No windows. One tiny door that leads into the deepest, darkest corner of the basement. One sputtering bare bulb that
illuminates the last bits of dust clinging to my coat and hands. It
all looks a bit boring to belong to someone who is supposed to be
so wise, his ancestors ask *him* for advice.

The racks leave barely enough room for Yi-lai and me to sit
across from each other, legs uncomfortably crossed. Now that I
have time to look at him, Yi-lai is younger than I thought. Maybe
two or three years older than I am. Too old for us to have been
friends before Mother showed her true colors, though I probably
wouldn't have remembered anyway. The warm light of the bulb
flickers across his face, hollowing out his high cheekbones and
making him look underfed and gaunt. An odd contrast to broad

shoulders and a muscular chest. When he notices me sizing him up, he smiles and opens his eyes extra wide. His eyelashes are so long they practically shadow the rest of his face. He's handsome. And I'm pretty sure he knows it.

"So what do you think?"

"Of what?"

"Do I pass muster? Or are you trying to decide if you can get away if this turns bad?"

"From you? Easily." I mimic his careless tone. "All I have to do is yell that someone is kidnapping the Chairman's son, and I'll be right back where I started. What are you going to do when the Reds storm in? Think we can take them?"

He narrows his eyes, evaluating me from cracked leather boots to messy hair. "Hard to tell. You look pretty skinny under all those layers. But you did grow up in an orphanage with a bunch of infected, so you have to be at least a bit tougher than you seem."

I laugh, tension lifting a bit from my shoulders. I am a little skinny. But he's right: I've had my share of fights. Unfortunately, experience with compulsing ten-year-olds doesn't exactly match up to facing down a Second with his gun jammed against your forehead.

"So, what exactly *is* your plan? We can't hide down here forever. I mean, it is a very nice basement." I make a show of looking around. "But I don't drink."

Yi-lai smiles. "Dr. Yang will get us out."

"Oh, is he best friends with the Premier like you?" Dr. Yang was wearing three stars, and last I checked, the First Circle didn't take advice from that quarter. "What's he going to do, empty the Chairman's wine cellar down their throats until they don't remember anything about a bomb?"

"I meant he'll get us out of the City. No wine necessary. Much less expensive."

"Are you serious?" I jump up, hitting a few bottles on the way. "Out of the City? That is not . . . ! You see *this*?" I thrust my branded hand in his face. "This isn't mine. It is my mother's. I am *not* a traitor, and I am *not* going to Kamar! How could the Chairman's own *son* get mixed up in—"

"No one said anything about Kamar," he answers, not seeming very concerned that my fist is only inches from his nose.

"Who is Dr. Yang? How did he corrupt you into working for Kamar?"

"There *is* no Kamar, Sev." Yi-lai smiles that infuriating smile again. Like I should just shut up and believe that the war we've all been fighting for the last eight years was a bad dream. "It's a ghost. The country that invaded back during the Influenza War fell to pieces when SS spread, just like everyone else Outside. The First Circle just keeps up the lie."

"What do you mean, a lie? The bomb everyone is blaming me for came from a Kamari heli-plane. I saw it. And I work night and day to feed the Liberation Army. It might not pinch up here, but down in the factories we have to sacrifice a lot to support the war."

"Calm down. Dr. Yang will explain everything. Just wait."

I look at the tiny door that leads up to the main house, then back to Yi-lai. If I run now, will I be rabid by the time I get out there? Will they just shoot me down? I hunch against the wall, crossing my arms.

"Your father isn't going to wonder where you've disappeared to? Or get thirsty?" I look up at the wine bottles.

Yi-lai's smile is more a grimace. "He's out with the Reds.

Waiting for them to find you so he can pronounce the City safe again."

I look back down, not sure how to respond to that. The silence begins to itch. Maybe a deep, dark cell under the City and an execution sentence would be better than sitting here waiting for a Kamari spy—or whatever Dr. Yang is—to show up. At least then I would know what to expect.

Not that I have been down in the prison levels of the City. We call it the Hole: floor after floor of slimy pits and a population of rats waiting for anti-Liberation prisoners to be thrown in. Even thinking about it makes me feel constricted, as though my mind is trapped hundreds of feet underground in the dark—the kind that swallows you whole and never gives your soul back. I take a deep breath and close my eyes, trying to blink the image away as the shadows in the corners of our little room start to writhe. When I open them, little ant-size men march out of the black in serpentine lines toward me, each with a miniature weapon flickering in hand. I blink, and they are gone.

I swallow. It's just a hallucination. It's not real.

But then I blink again and the little men are back, converging in on one another, melting together to form something larger: fangs dripping down from a gaping black hole of a mouth.

"What are you looking at?" Yi-lai scoots over next to me, our shoulders are touching. "Sev, are you okay?"

I blink again and it is gone, but sinking dread blacks everything out. I'm ashamed of the tremor in my voice. "Remember when you asked earlier if I'm afraid of the dark?"

As if Tai-ge's angry ancestors heard me, the lights suddenly go out.

I gasp and grab at Yi-lai, but his voice is calm. "It's a blackout.

Sometimes they enforce power conservation, even up here on the Steppe."

The words stick in my brain, but I'm not sure what they mean, lost in the inky black of the little room. The walls close in until I can feel them against my arms and back, crushing my head down toward my knees. My breaths come faster and faster, gulping down black tendrils until they squirm in my stomach, burning and wriggling. Cramps turn to sharp pain as darkness tries to burrow its way back out through my skin.

I feel an arm close around my shoulders, and a quicklight ignites in front of me. "Sev?" Yi-lai's voice is too loud. "What's wrong?"

Squinting into the light, I try to answer, but the darkness constricts around my throat and I can't breathe. His arm tightens down around my waist, and my broken ribs scream in protest. Suddenly, all I can think of are the bottles lining the walls above us. My fingers start twitching.

I jump to my feet, leaving Yi-lai sprawled on the floor. He grunts in pain when I step on his hand to get to the bottles, the dusty glass singing my name in the dark. I need one of the shiny bright blue ones from the top. The blue bottles will save me from those black tendrils inside me. Something in the back of my mind screams at me to stop, but my hands start searching for a way up. I *can't* stop.

The blue bottles are just beyond my reach, so I climb, sending the other bottles sloshing and shattering to the floor. The case shakes under my weight and glass bottles above me fall from their places, breaking against the shelves, bits of glass and droplets of wine raining down on my face and arms. The sharp smell of alcohol fills my nose, curling up into my brain. Glass falls across my coat, catching in the collar and pockets. Holding tight to the case with one arm, I gather the glass splinters together in my other hand and move to shove them in my mouth, but arms wrap around me and a heavy weight bears me to the ground.

"Let me go! I have to swallow them. I have to get them out!" I thrash on the floor against Yi-lai's weight pinning my body to the cement. Darkness worms to my insides, tearing holes through my stomach all the way out to my skin.

"Sev. Stop. It's going to be okay." His breath brushes my ear. His head is an unbearable weight pressed against my neck, holding my head down.

"Let me kill them! Please!" I can feel tears run down my face, stinging where my scratches from before mix with cuts from the glass. If I don't swallow the glass, I am going to die. I know I am going to die. I am going to die. I know I am. Blue glass. Die.

Another light cuts into the darkness around us, and a man swears. "Hold her arms!"

A hand reaches into my coat, and I feel a sharp pain in my hip, fire pulsating out from the bite of a needle. My limbs fall away from me. I am only a bubble of consciousness in the dark room.

"What in the name of the Liberation were you thinking? This girl could be the end . . ." The words fade out slowly as the room swirls to nothingness.

CHAPTER 7

A LIGHT SWIMS OVER MY HEAD. I CAN HEAR VOICES
floating around me, but they don't make sense. A grating voice
whispers, "We have to get her out as soon as possible. They are
starting to realize that she must still be in the City."

"How did this happen? This wasn't supposed to be able to happen!" The younger man sounds angry. "Stop trying to manipulate
me and just tell me what is going on."

"Let me do this."

"No. I made my decision. She's the only one like me."
A picture of the young man, Yi-lai, pops into my head. *The
Chairman's son.*

"If I hadn't come in when I did, she would be dead." The gravelly voice lowers. "We can't risk . . ."

When I force my eyes open, the voices stop. I am lying on my
back underneath a bare bulb and shelves of bottles. Shards of glass
prickle up through my sweater, a slow drip of sweat stinging my
face and neck. My nose is clogged full with the spicy florals of
wine, mixed with rusty iron. Blood. The borrowed gray coat lies

on top of me, covering me from neck to knees, the coarse wool scratchy against my skin. It's cold on the stone floor.

Salt-and-pepper hair and muddy brown eyes slowly come into focus only a few inches away from my face. Dr. Yang.

"I liked you better this afternoon," I say as I try to sit up, but my body doesn't want to move. Every word twinges, shards of glass embedded in my lips and cheek making themselves known. "You are the one who started this ridiculous chicken hunt. Did you set the bomb, too?"

Dr. Yang glares in a way that says I'm supposed to be quiet. "Yi-lai, thank you for your help getting her away from the Watch, but I can take things from here."

Yi-lai, sitting next to me on the glass-littered floor, shakes his head. "I'm not staying here."

"Should I be able to move my arms?" I ask. "I can't move my arms."

Yi-lai looks from me to Dr. Yang, brow furrowed as his voice rises. "You've been watching her all along. You told me to stay away, and I did. *Did* you set the bomb? To convince . . . to get her out?"

My same question, now on Yi-lai's lips, sends flickers of dread flaming down to my core. Did this doctor somehow frame me for blowing up the bridge? He seemed to know everything about me, even the things Tai-ge couldn't tell me, things that wouldn't have gone beyond General Hong's office or the First Circle until they set the Watch on me. But what would the point of framing me be?

Silence in the room draws out like a string waiting to be cut. Dr. Yang sucks in his cheeks and says, "That bomb came from a City plane just like they all do. They're using the situation as an excuse to get Sev out of their hair, and maybe as a warning to . . . others. We can still get her out, but I need you to stay here."

"I'm *not* staying—"

"A City plane?" I cut in. "So now the City is blowing up its own bridges just to get rid of one teenager who no one likes anyway? Almost killing Hong Tai-ge while they're at it? That makes all sorts of sense."

"That's true." Yi-lai's jaw is drawn tight around the words, each shooting with a violent thrust toward the doctor. "How do you explain that? Not even the First Circle would risk General Hong's son. Not unless they had some way to prove he finally gave into Fourth corruption." Yi-lai glances at me. "Sorry."

"You don't think they'd use him as a martyr? General Hong has too much power over the Seconds, so I can very easily see them getting rid of his son as a warning, then using his death to prove that Sev deserved the Arch. This is how they deal with their problems. If SS doesn't take you down, the next step gets more violent." He looks at me and sighs. "It's the same thing that has been happening to you your whole life."

My arms still won't move. What has been happening my whole life? I've never had bombs dropped on me before. And they wouldn't kill Tai-ge. He doesn't have anything to do with this.

Dr. Yang rubs a hand through his hair, making it stand on end. "Yi-lai, you go out and join the hunt with the Chairman, and I'll send word once we're safe outside the walls—"

"It's time, Dr. Yang." Yi-lai's voice comes out in a low growl.

Dr. Yang shakes his head, mouth twisted into a frown. "We had such high hopes for both of you."

"Together, you mean?" I can't help but slip it in. "We've only just met. And he thinks he's too good for me." I am rewarded by a startled look from both of them, the joke cutting through the tense conversation they don't feel the need to include me in.

"And what in the name of Holy Liberation are you talking about? I don't know how many times I have to say this, but I am a loyal citizen. A comrade. I'm not going anywhere."

"A dead comrade." Dr. Yang shrugs. "They aren't even looking to arrest you anymore. The order out there is shoot to kill. You want to die because the First Circle decided it was time? One more traitor to show the Thirds? One more reason for them to keep working down there in the smoke while the Firsts play up here in their laboratories?"

The feeling is starting to come back to my right hand, my fingers twitching through the pins and needles as I consider what Dr. Yang just said. What is this City worth to me? I've spent the last eight years trying to prove my traitor brand wrong. Looking up at my mother and spitting with the rest of them. And did it ever help? They'll never see me as anything more than a traitor's daughter, a Fourth. A living relic of Mother's treason, SS walking. I feel around under the coat, looking for my knife, wondering if it will be enough of a threat for Yi-lai and Dr. Yang to let me go. But it's gone.

Dr. Yang continues over my thoughts. "Who will benefit if you stay and die? What do you think they'll do to the orphanage? To Tai-ge?"

I've always known my being a Fourth is reason enough for anyone to suspect me of any crime, but for some reason the reality is much harder to reconcile in my mind. The City is just; the City is perfectly ideal. The City didn't kill me eight years ago, when Mother disappeared. They let Father take care of me up in our big house on the Steppe while I was Asleep. Might have even let him live if she hadn't come back and marked him as too close to her to be trustworthy. They didn't kill my sister . . . well, not because of her four stars, at least. If there was no hope for someone like me, then why would they have spent so many years feeding me, teaching me, trying to set me on the right path, if my death was always the end goal? I believe there is justice in this place, and I want to find it. "I haven't done anything wrong. And I won't betray Tai-ge or the City like *she* did. *I am not like her!*"

The words cut across a silent room. I hadn't realized I was yelling. Dr. Yang and Yi-lai both look down, embarrassed.

Dr. Yang's grating voice is quiet, almost too low for me to hear. "Do you really want to find out whether anyone else feels that way? You aren't the first person to be used as a warning to families who aren't compliant. Incentive for the Thirds to slave away for sandy bread and dirty water until they die, so long as they believe they need to be protected from what's going on Outside. But Kamar doesn't exist anymore, Sev. The City is killing itself. Your own sister . . ."

I shake my head, cutting him off. What could the City possibly gain by lying about the war? I need someone to tell me what is really going on. I need . . .

Yi-lai finally looks up, catching my eye. "What the doctor is saying is true. If you go to Tai-ge, they'll just kill him, too."

PART II

CHAPTER 8

PULLING MY NEW ARMY-ISSUE COAT A LITTLE closer, I brace myself against the wooden side of the trailer to keep myself from bouncing into a pile of jagged-toothed saws. Fur lining the hood tickles at my nose, a sneeze building uncomfortably in my throat. Yi-lai sits with his legs spread out in front of him, leaning against an army pack, the frame sticking out above his head. He almost looks bored, just staring at the ceiling.

Yi-lai's right about Tai-ge. If the City really was trying to get me under the Arch, and Tai-ge tried to help me, he'd probably end up kneeling under the ax along with me. It happens all the time.

The truck pulling us wrenches to a stop, and this time I can't save my shoulder from banging against the side. My head swims with exhaustion, but my brain won't shut off to let me sleep. Two days alone in the wine cellar gave Dr. Yang time to arrange a way out. Two sleepless days to pace the length of the tiny room, wondering when the door would break down and Reds would pour in like bees swarming an intruder.

Yi-lai only came in once, right after Dr. Yang left, holding a pair of tweezers. I lay there staring up at him for an hour or more while he picked glass shards from my lips and face, the blue and green pieces from the bottles making a bloody pile next to me. I stopped him when he reached for one of my hands to do the same. It hurt, but I needed something to do myself. He mostly left me alone after that, only opening the door to pass food along, to leave a bucket for when my bladder began to press. But every now and then I heard him move on the other side of the door, as if he was just outside, sleeping across the doorway.

We haven't talked about what happened. The bottles and the glass.

I've never had an SS compulsion before. Never. They keep us so medicated that compulsions aren't a problem at the orphanage. But sometimes with the new Mantis resistance, there are near accidents, like with Peishan. Sometimes it's worse, and no one notices it until it's too late. My own sister was shot down by the Watch like a rabid dog. She had been running through the streets with an ax. Now I know what she must have been thinking. My brain knew that my body was going to kill itself, and there was nothing I could do about it.

I've never been frightened of what I am until now. The bitter aftertaste still bites more than two days later.

Life with no Mantis? It is worse than my fear of the dark. Worse than living in a City of people that hate me. Worse than a traitorous mother opening my veins, then abandoning me to a life of hard labor and infection she inflicted on me. Worse even than watching my sister die. Now I know what the monster inside of me looks like. How can I survive knowing any moment it could come back?

Unless I go with them to Kamar, I doubt I'll see another

Mantis pill beyond the ones in the pack Dr. Yang shoved into my hands before slamming the back door of the trailer shut. If Kamar even has Mantis. Isn't that why they keep attacking the City? They're after our Mantis stores. When I run out of pills, I'll have no way to stop compulsions. I'll be a danger to anyone within reach. I know compulsions aren't always violent, but it will only be a matter of time. How can Yi-lai take me Outside, knowing that in a week, a month, I might wake up with my brain wiped of everything that made me Jiang Sev, replaced by a killer?

I almost ask him. But looking past the breath misting out in front of my face, I notice Yi-lai's head lolling against the wall.

He's asleep.

You'd think someone who grew up sleeping on a feather bed would be a little pickier. Or that in the face of escaping with an infected fugitive, he might be a little more worried. But no. I find some space in my nest of self-loathing to be annoyed.

The trailer gives an impressive jolt as we go over a pothole, sending me crashing into him. We both roll back and rub our heads.

"I thought we were on the same side!" Yi-lai complains.

"I'm still not sure which side that is, Yi-lai," I reply. I still have no idea why the Firsts' most beloved son would willingly choose to leave the City, especially for a traitor like me. Dr. Yang has been so adamant about Kamar not existing, but he has yet to even hint at some other destination. Our Outside patrollers are fighting *someone* out here, even if the doctor and Yi-lai don't like the name the City has given them. The bodies strung up on the City Center prove it.

After a few minutes, he nudges me. "You can call me Howl, if you want. I've never cared for Yi-lai. My dad called me Howl when

I was little, and it stuck. I guess I had a good set of lungs. Yi-lai is just what old people call me."

I shrug. "Okay. Howl. You know my name."

"Kind of an odd one. Sev."

"No worse than Howl." I stare down at the floor. I don't even know where my mother came up with the name Sev. Just another thing that set me apart from all the obedient, compliant workers down in the Third Quarter.

Hours later, my stomach is sloshing back and forth with every turn of the serpentine switchbacks until I'm about ready to offer up the coat and all our food for a breath of fresh air. As if Dr. Yang can read my mind, the truck sputters to a stop, the trailer fishtailing a bit in a series of sickening jerks. Voices from outside set my heart jumping. It is hard to tell, but they sound like Reds.

Through a crack between crates, Dr. Yang's head appears in a blaze of late-afternoon light at the back of the trailer, his face unreadable and dark. He is saying something to a harassed-looking man with two red stars decorating his shoulder. Howl and I are tucked behind a huge box of rusty, broken nails, out of sight.

"If there were anyone back here, they would have jumped off a long time ago. I told you, we're just harvesting wood to rebuild the bridge Kamar blew to pieces a few days ago." Dr. Yang's tired voice skids across my high-strung nerves, my skin prickling as I wait for a gun to level in my direction. "There's a side door too, if you want to check that."

The Red shakes his head, voice surprisingly deep. "We'll have to have you unload everything so we can go through it."

"Fine. I don't have anything to hide. . . ." His voice fades as he and the Red walk around toward the front of the trailer.

He doesn't have anything to hide? I curl up as small as I can, trying to control the fear gnawing at my insides. How could Dr. Yang have walked us right through a checkpoint? If he wanted me to live so badly, then why . . . I look up as Howl waves to get my attention.

He points to the side door, low on the wall next to him. Cracking it open, he squints into the sliver of sunlight pouring in. "Hide under the trailer until you're sure it's clear and then make for the ditch over there. There's some tree cover, and they're all up at the front right now."

"We're leaving? What about Dr. Yang?" I ask.

"It's that or let the Seconds drag us back to the City. We're lucky we've lasted in the back of the trailer this long, actually."

I look through the cracked door to be sure the men are out of sight, then slide out and under the rusted metal frame. The ground is frozen, scrubby tufts of dead grass needle-sharp under my hands.

Howl pushes the packs under the trailer before squeezing after me, sandwiching them between us. When Dr. Yang's worn dress shoes lead the Seconds back toward the truck, I crawl toward the opposite side of the trailer to peek out. The army checkpoint must be over by the door where Dr. Yang is starting to swear. This side is completely clear, a few spindly trees marking a ditch that runs along the road about ten paces off. Beyond that, all I see are misty clouds that shroud our mountain range through most of the winter.

Outside. Where Sephs run wild and fantastical gores eat the dead. Even looking out at the unwalled horizon feels exposed and risky, as if creatures of either the human or animal variety lie waiting to eat me alive.

Is it better than death to be stuck Outside? I blink, almost expecting a hallucination to follow a thought so dark, but nothing comes. I won't betray my City or Tai-ge, no matter what Dr. Yang and Howl want from me.

But I would rather be alive than dead.

Wiping my sweaty palms on my shirt, I grab my pack's frame. I know running for it is a better idea than waiting for the truck to drive away and leave us exposed, but my hands shake at the thought of leaving cover for the open ground between us and that ditch. Nothing to shield me from the Red checkpoint but a trailer and an old doctor pulling nails from a box one by one.

But even worse, leaving this last bit of civilization for . . . Outside. With Kamari soldiers bent on finishing the invasion they started so many years ago and Wood Rats gnawing on the remains they leave behind.

I clench my jaw and roll out from underneath the trailer into a crouch. As I slither through the dead grass toward the ditch, Dr. Yang's curses and banging equipment cover the noisy crackle of grass under my hands and knees.

When I get to the trench, I slide over the edge and fall onto something soft. The bank sinks into the ground much deeper than I expected, about seven or eight feet down and three or four wide. Howl's pack slips over the edge, narrowly missing my head. He follows, landing in a crouch beside me.

He grabs his pack and starts to walk, picking his way through the rocks and exposed roots. I bend to grab my things, but lurch backward the moment I set eyes on the ground. The "something" I landed on is actually a *someone*.

Bloated lips and cheeks distort the face in a gruesome mockery of a person who once lived and breathed. I stumble off the body, clapping both hands over my mouth to keep the gasping retch boiling in my throat from bursting out.

Howl doubles back when he realizes I'm not following. My pack lies next to the dead man, touching his muddy jacket and shirt, which have been ripped open by my boots. Broken and decaying flesh spill out from the jagged tears. Three ribs jut out of his side, writhing with insects. A dark brownish red stains the ground all around the corpse.

Howl grabs the metal frame of my pack and shoves me in front of him, herding me away from the body. Tripping over each step, I run.

When Howl catches up with me, he puts a finger to his lips, pointing up. I know they might hear us, but I can't make myself move any more slowly away from the body. I point back to make sure he saw it, wondering how he can be so calm. He just shrugs and whispers, "It doesn't matter. We have to get away from here."

The smell will never wash off my boots. Or hands. I can feel it sinking into me, burrowing under my skin and drilling into my bones. I can't let myself think about the man on the ground. How my feet dug into him. His ribs breaking like twigs under my feet.

We walk until darkness begins to fall in waves around us. Every ten yards or more we find another body, sometimes more than one. I can't look at them, giving each as wide a berth as the ditch will allow.

Howl touches my arm, pointing to the stunted, bowed trees lining both sides of our trench. "I'm going to climb up and take a look around," he whispers, fumbling to unfasten the pack's clasps across his chest and hips. "You okay?"

I shrug, not sure how to answer.

"How are your ribs doing? They hurting?"

My ribs have been complaining the whole way, even though more doses of Da'ard have made it possible for me to move without wanting to extract my ribs and leave them behind. There isn't much more we can do about it. "I'll survive."

Howl props the pack up against the dirt wall, running his fingers over the crumbly surface before he starts to climb. Watching him scale the eight-foot wall leaves me a little unsettled. *How is it that a boy slated for laboratories and test tubes can climb like that?* Most of the Firsts I came in contact with were much more inclined to watch than do.

Pausing at the top, Howl peers over the lip before hoisting himself up. I can hear him crawling through the scrub, each dry leaf crumbling under his boots sending alarm signals down the mountain.

His head pops back over the edge. "I don't see anyone, and we're in a good spot to make a break for better cover, but we'll have to be quick. Hand up your pack."

I slide the bulky frame up the wall until he can reach the pack to pull it over the edge. After I hand off the second pack, I climb before he can come back, throbbing ribs screaming each time I reach up. I force myself to keep climbing, pulling myself higher and higher until Howl's hand reaches out to grasp mine and haul me out of the ditch. Out of breath, I curl up on the ground around the pain, breathing in and out slowly.

Howl drags our bags into the scraggly cover and waits, as if he's not quite sure what to do. Finally, he kneels next to me and leans over, whispering, "I know it must hurt, but we've got to get off the road. Can I carry you?"

I roll over and raise myself to a crawl, going a few feet into the weeds next to the ditch before Howl lifts me to a hunching walk across the road. But as soon as we leave the road's clean slice into the mountainside, the hill is steep, and my feet slide with each step. Howl straps his pack on and drags mine behind him, half propping me up with his other arm until we come to a flatter portion of ground.

"So, what's the plan, Howl?" I finally ask, attempting to stand up straight. My whole side seems stuffed to capacity with jagged edges and points, a firestorm of pain that leaks out through my skin in a cold sweat.

"Get farther away from the road. Find a place to camp tonight near the river. Dr. Yang got us past most of the farms below the City, but there's still a ways to go before we're off City patrol circuits." He looks at the glowing horizon, the sun already halfway gone. "I think we've got about an hour until full dark. Let's see how far we can go."

"Go . . . where? We lost our guide. What about Dr. Yang?" I voice the question both of us must have been thinking.

"Dr. Yang can take care of himself." Howl starts to walk again.

"Yes, but can we?"

Howl holds a branch back to let me pass. "He knows where we got off and will be in contact with help as soon as possible. I can't think that our trail will be difficult to follow for Reds or Outsiders. It will just be a matter of who finds us first."

I shiver at his words, pain blocking my capacity to ask for more. What kind of help could Dr. Yang bring?

The mud on the ground is crusted with ice, footprints of men and women long gone still preserved in sharp ridges that crunch under my feet. Scrubby trees give us a little cover until we make it to where the true forest starts. Before we descend into the trees, I look up at the terraced rice paddies beneath the City, hundreds of sinuously curving steps cut into the mountainside. My last look at home.

A white-water rush of river flows down between us and the farms, and we stay low until the trees twist and curve over us like ancient umbrellas, some wide enough that it would take four or five people holding hands to completely encircle. Even the closely cultivated orchards in the People's Garden look like malnourished children compared to these giants.

When the last touches of sunset are smothered by night, Howl drops his pack under a tree that twists around itself like a girl's long braid, the naked branches spreading out over the wide spot in the river. The dead man's touch still itches away at me, sending me over to the water, the current much slower here than up by the farm. I pull off my boots and set them in the rocks at the edge, where the water can run over them but won't wash them away. Stepping in leaves me gasping for breath, the freezing water stealing the last bits of heat still left inside me.

I grit my teeth and kneel on the riverbank, determined not to leave any trace of the dead man from the ditch on me. Submerging my hands and splashing water on my face isn't enough, so I start scrubbing with sand from the bank. Howl's hand appears in front of my face, holding a bar of soap. He crouches next to me in the water, cupping his hands to splash water through his hair and across his face.

I scour my hands, wishing I were brave enough to go after my hair. The dead stench will never come out, will follow me everywhere I go. The cake of soap is thin enough that after one use, it's almost gone. I set it next to me in the rocks.

"Never seen a dead body before?" Howl's voice echoes loudly against the quiet that blankets the forest.

"I have," I reply, rubbing my hands. They are red with the violent cleaning and cold.

"Not like that," Howl says, taking the soap. He hands me a shirt to dry my hands on. One of his.

Drying my face keeps me from answering for a moment. "I've never been up to my ankles in it before, no. Who do you think he was? Who any of them were?"

"They shoot anyone who comes up the road without stars. They could have been infected. Fighters. People trying to escape?"

People trying to escape what?

"It's too hard to carry the bodies up the mountain, so they just burn the ditches every few weeks."

Lighting a fire seems stupid so close to the road, so we pull out our sleeping bags and eat crusty bread and dried meat from inside them. We agree the quicklights should be for emergencies, so we let the inky darkness fall, watching the sky turn black through the swaying branches. I've never slept outside before, and the noises and the wind play against my nerves like an erhu out of tune.

A long chortling wail echoes through the trees, needling through my skin. Howl and I sit up at the same time and look at each other. His smile cuts through the dark as he says, "What do you think? Gores, or imitations to flush us out?"

"Gores?" Gores are just a fairy tale. Supposedly, during the times Before, the people who lived here used dogs genetically engineered with some sort of hyena DNA on their police and army forces, the animals so large they could bite a man in two. According to the Outside patrollers, they stand taller than Howl's lanky six feet and, now that they're feral, the creatures are set on killing any human they come in contact with. I can still remember an Outside patroller marking the wall to show one of my classes how tall the last gore he'd had to fight was, showing us scars all up and down his side from the creature's teeth. Only the next patroller to come to the class scoffed at the story, sure the last gore he saw was at least three feet taller—all soldier stories spun to give Third children nightmares. "I'm sure there are lots of animals out here, but aren't gores a little . . . exaggerated?"

Howl doesn't say anything for a second, eyes in the trees around us. "I don't think so."

Another cackling laugh slips through the frigid air as we gather our belongings, images of monsters I didn't think could exist prickling the back of my mind. Another wail, closer this time. My ankles and calves protest as we start downhill again, throbbing in time with the crackling pain radiating out from my ribs. Howl stops abruptly, pointing to a nest of boulders jutting up into the tree canopy like a giant's dead hand clawing to escape the ground.

"There's a ledge big enough for both of us." Howl nods to the farthest boulder. "Up for a climb? Nothing will be able to reach us if we sleep up there."

Another animal scream splits the air, creeping down my spine in a cemetery of goose bumps. I nod.

Howl climbs up first, taking each pack as I hand it to him, then helping me. It's an easier climb than the ditch, but the rock feels too smooth against my hands, as though we'll slide from our perch the moment we close our eyes.

We spread out our sleeping bags, setting up our packs as pillows, but it isn't very comfortable. Not that it could be with Howl's back brushing mine. For a strange moment, I'm almost glad to be worried about falling off and being eaten by whatever is making those terrible baying cries, because it means I don't have to feel awkward about sleeping with a boy right next to me.

Another of the haunting cackles rips through the air as I huddle in my sleeping bag. It becomes a game, like watching lightning strike and counting the seconds until thunder breaks. Every cry is closer, and I find myself counting breaths as I wait for the next call to echo around us. Finally, I pull the hood of the sleeping bag over my head, trying to block them out.

Howl rolls over. "Can't sleep?"

"Really? Sleep?" I ask, my teeth chattering.

He doesn't say anything for a minute, and I watch my breath mist out in front of me, two, three, four, five . . .

His hand finds my shoulder through the sleeping bag, pulling me over onto my back. He points up toward the sky, through the waving tree branches. "Do you see that star?" Howl asks. "The bright one?"

Following his finger, dark spreads out over us like eternity. The few stars we could see through smog and light in the City are nothing compared to the thousands of pinpricks letting light in through the shell of the night sky. "That one?" I ask, my hand pointing up with his. Another moaning call screams through the air, and I curl back into the sleeping bag, clenching my eyes shut.

Howl's arm slips under me, pulling me closer. Normally, it would be too close, but the gore's wail pierces every inch of my skin, as if the creature has already found us and taken a bite of me. Howl's presence feels like a shield, a distraction.

"That bright star," he says, "that's Zhinu. She's the daughter of the sun." I open my eyes again, trying to concentrate on what he is saying. "All the other stars paled in comparison, doomed to serve the most beautiful of their number. At the crook of one brilliant finger, they would bring her flowers from Feiyu"—he points to another bright point in the sky—"or travel even farther to bring her a wisp of breeze from He Wu."

His breath mists out over both of us, freezing on the scrubby moss growing out from the rock above us. "But she wasn't content with all of her suitors and servants. She was bored of everything, from the moon's idle gossip to her father's angry blustering against peasants who had stopped worshipping him. *Now, disobedient peasants sound interesting*, Zhinu thought. So she jumped from the heavens down to earth and landed in the middle of a flock of qilin."

"What are qilin?" I interject, looking over at him.

Howl purses his lips, thinking. "I don't know. My mother used to tell me this story, and her grandmother used to tell it to her, and her grandmother before that, so some of the details are a little hazy. Qilin are supposed to be good, I think, but dangerous. Something from a story that couldn't really exist, with beautiful black-and-white hair that trails down to the ground and long fangs for ripping meat."

My thoughts immediately go back to the baying that creeps closer every minute, but Howl's rhythmic cadence draws my attention back to him.

"Zhinu was terrified. She tried to jump back to her place in the stars, but one of the qilin caught the train of her dress between his teeth, determined to eat the beautiful creature. Just as he was about to nibble on her little toe, a beautiful voice sang out over the forest and brought the beast up short. The whole flock ran toward the voice.

"The daughter of the sun followed, curious to know what kind of animal could calm such terrible beasts. But it wasn't an animal, it was a peasant man, handsome, and with a voice sweet enough to rival the cosmic symphony. The moment they set eyes on each other, they fell in love, and were married that day. His name was Niulang."

"Niulang and Zhinu lived happily together for three years before her father, the sun, found her. As punishment for running away and marrying a peasant, he set her in the sky so far from earth that she could only weep tears of sorrow and memory. Niulang killed one of his precious qilin and followed her, hidden under its skin." Howl points up to the sky again, another star twinkling above us as if in response. "But the disguise didn't fool the sun. He built a wall between Zhinu and Niulang, so he would never be able to find her. So they could never be together."

A thick belt of stars winds between the two lovers, the glittering divide millions strong. "So they just look at each other, across the wall?" I ask, my eyes feeling heavy.

I can hear the smile in his voice. "She spends her time weaving her tears into clouds, to protect the earth from the sun's anger. And in return, when the sun's face is turned elsewhere, all the birds fly together into the sky to make a bridge across the wall so Zhinu and Niulang can be together."

My eyes close, baying cries forgotten within the quiet safety of Howl's voice. He settles in next to me, reassuring calm folding over me like a warm blanket.

CHAPTER 9

DAWN FILTERING THROUGH THE TREES SURPRISES me. I feel as though my eyelids just closed, and they resist as the sun's cold rays of light nudge them back open. Howl sits up next to me, dark circles under his eyes marking the sleepless night. When I slide to the ground, I freeze, staring at the ground. Heavily clawed paw prints are dug into the frozen dirt from here to the trees.

Howl crouches down, fingertips tracing the edges of the paw print closest to him. It's larger than his hand. "So what do you think? Believe in gores now?"

I look over toward him, intending to say something flippant, but my eyes catch on the rock face behind him and words won't come. Scratches gouge deep into the stone just under the ledge where we slept, at least ten feet off the ground. They were not there last night when we climbed up.

Howl turns to see what I'm staring at, and half laughs, though there's no humor in the sound as his eyes jerk over the scarred rock.

"Will it follow us? Are we prey now?" I'm proud of how steady my voice is. Almost as if this should be normal. We're outside the walls. Of course creatures would be hunting us in the night.

"I don't think so. Guess we'll see. If anything large and toothy bites my head off, just run, okay?" Howl passes me some hard crackers and water, pulls on his pack, and starts downhill.

"Wait a second!" I call, more to myself than to him, trying not to think of what happened when I was late with Mantis down in the wine cellar.

He stops and watches me pull the pills from the bottom of my pack, tapping his foot as I push two into my mouth and follow them with water, the soft casings sticking in my throat as they go down. Before zipping the pocket shut, I pull out the entire bag of Mantis packets and silently count them.

"What's the matter?" Howl asks, glancing back at the claw-scored rock behind me and shuffling a few steps farther down the hill. "We've got enough Mantis."

"For how long?" I ask. "A few weeks at the most."

Howl sort of shrugs, turning away from me in a sharp huff of breath that steams up around his face as he starts down the hill.

"I'd like an answer to that particular question." I skip a few steps forward, the terror of those glass bottle shards in my mouth still raw.

Howl turns back, head cocked to the side as if he is trying to tease threads of truth from whatever fabric Dr. Yang has woven for him to pull over my eyes. "The City isn't the only place we can get Mantis. You'll be fine until we get to the mountain."

"Get *where*?"

"I'll show you where we're headed the next time I climb up to get my bearings. We should be able to . . . well, Dr. Yang says walking should only take a few weeks if we're accounting for . . ." He gestures vaguely to my midsection, and my ribs give an answering twinge as if they know he's pointing out their bloody, broken faults.

"A month if we run into trouble. We've got more than enough Mantis to last that long."

"A *month*?" I curl around my broken center, attempting to make a joke out of my chagrin, when he raises an eyebrow at me. "We've only been out less than a day and there are already gores trying to eat us. So unless you have something more exciting for them to eat hidden in that pack of yours, I'd have to say I'm less than confident in our chances at survival."

"Gores only hang out where there are lots of people to pick off."

I point at myself. "I wouldn't say I'm ripe, but I'd put myself in the low-hanging, easy-to-pick category."

Howl stops, surprised into smiling again. "We'll be fine. I think."

"Very reassuring." I bite my lip, not wanting to think about the howls from last night. "Even if we do manage to avoid gores and Reds and whoever else might be creeping around out here, what happens when we get to this mountain place, which is somehow not the same as Kamar? Will we be safe there?"

"We'll be *fine*," Howl says again, turning back down the hill without meeting my eyes.

"Will all your limbs still be attached by the time we arrive, or will I have eaten you by then?"

"I'm not going to let you hurt me, even if you do go all Seph-headed. Scars are about as sexy as the Chairman's dirty bathwater."

I think for a second, following his slow meander through the trees, avoiding patches of icy mud. "Is that what you call him too? Even the Chairman's son has to use his title?"

Howl glances at me over his shoulder as he walks, his voice quiet. "Can you imagine calling him anything else?"

I lick my lips, trying to think what to say, images of my own father hazy and shadowed at the back of my mind. He may have been distant, even more so now because I can't think of him without his last moments crowding in to replace everything else. I shut my eyes, trying to replace the terrible images with memories of his arms around me, of the games we played and the special smile he had for Aya and me. However shadowy those memories have become, at least I know he loved me. An odd sort of hollowness replaces the quick rearrangement of thoughts in my head to keep the curtain draped over my past.

Odd, because I never thought a traitor Fourth would have reason to feel sorry for the Chairman's son.

The rest of the week is all steep slopes and fancy footwork to avoid falling into the sea of twisty trees and boulders below us. Howl does take me up a tree to show me where we're going, though the wildly waving branches are almost enough to keep me on the ground. The answer to where we're headed isn't as complete as I'd like, because he just points to a mountain in the distance, blue in the mist. It seems like a part of another world, too far for anyone to make it on foot, too exposed and open, as if the whole world should be divided into sections and walled in as mine has been up until now.

After a few days of walking, Howl points out a funny-looking tree dwarfed by the bent back and gnarled limbs of the elderly canopy above us. "Oh, good. I was worried we were too late in the year to get the last of these."

I look back the way we came, glad for the chance to rest my aching ribs. I hope for a glimpse of the City's gray walls, but the trees are too tall; nothing to see but pine needles and a corroded metal tube big enough to walk through. It almost looks like the carcass of a heli-plane, but different. Older. Shot out of the sky, and now half-buried in the exposed dirt like a gravestone for Before.

Howl shakes the little tree's branches behind me, looking for something. I walk over toward the tube, scuffing my feet in the dirt. My toes uncover two scorched pieces of plastic and a small ring inside, rusted red from exposure. Maybe the only possession left of whoever flew the craft. The band fits over my pinkie finger, like the ring Tai-ge wears, the City seal circling his finger like a shackle.

What if the only thing they find of me is my four stars, corroded to dust?

They sit in my pocket, heavy and sharp.

"Here." Howl interrupts my thoughts, holding something out to me as he walks over. "There's a whole orchard down this hill." He stops, brows furrowed as I lace my hands behind my back, eyes glued to the fruit he is trying to hand to me.

"Do you . . . not like apples?" he asks.

I take a step back, not wanting to touch the fruit accidentally. Raw fruit is poison, one of the reasons the cannery that I spent so many hours sweating in is so important to the City. Ingesting something before the canning process . . . I gasp as Howl casually sinks his teeth into the fruit.

"Howl!" I reach toward him, not sure what to do.

He dodges me, dark eyebrows puckering together. "What?" The word comes out muddy, obstructed by the chunk of apple in his mouth. "I'm sure there are other trees. We'll find something you like."

"Spit it out! Quick, before the juice gets too far into your system!"

"What are you talking about?" Howl swallows, holding the apple protectively against his chest. "It's an apple!"

Years of heavy gloves and eyewear, now here I am trying to figure out how to wrest a raw apple away from Howl with my bare hands, as if I don't know how dangerous it is. "It's poison! Why do you think we have so many canneries in the City?"

Howl's abashed expression would have had me in fits of laughter if the situation weren't so dire, but instead he's the one who starts laughing. "Poison? Fruit isn't poisonous." He shakes his head. "You actually believe all that junk the propaganda department puts out? I guess people don't try to escape if they think that all the food out here is going to kill them."

"Why would anyone want to escape?" I look down self-consciously. "I mean, besides the obvious."

He pulls a branch down, picking another of the hard green fruits to hold out to me. "Here. Try one."

Everything I know screams against me even touching the thing. I had to take a chemical shower once from contamination back at the cannery. My glove cracked and I ended up in the hospital, an acidic tang wafting up from the pulp threatening to eat away my palm. Death by uncooked peaches.

I shake my head. "You've been living on a hill with someone to prepare all your meals since the day you were born. You couldn't know the first thing about what is safe to eat out here."

Howl smiles through another mouthful of apple and shrugs, tucking the second apple into his pocket. "When I don't die, and you are convinced, I'll have this waiting for you."

But only a few steps later, Howl's hands begin to shake. He gropes at his pack, barely getting one of the pockets open before falling to his knees and then onto his face.

"Howl?" My head spins as I try to pull him onto his back, the bulky pack too heavy to move off him. Unclipping it and pushing it off Howl's back, I finally mange to roll him over.

His eyes are white, rolled back into his head, and his skin is chalky and pale.

Why did you eat that stupid apple? I yell inside my head. What now? A finger sweep? Rescue breaths? Heart pounding, I try to remember what to do in an emergency from back at the factory, but the only thing coming to mind is a stupid song the nuns used to sing to us about Yuan Zhiwei's unbreakable ax.

With shaking hands, I turn him onto his side, bending close to put an ear next to his mouth. He's breathing. I lean forward again to check his pulse, but stop short when I notice white powder all over my hands. I run a hand across Howl's cheek, and the powder smears under my fingers.

"Sev!" The whisper has me on my feet and ready to run, heart hammering against my ribs. Howl's eyes open, a wicked smile cracking across his face.

"Sev, the apple! It's killing me! Save me."

"You . . ." I back away as he sits up and brushes the dirt from his shirt. "You dirty Seph! What is wrong with you? You scared me to death!"

Howl wipes the powder from his face, wrinkling his nose as it sticks to his hands. "You'd better watch your language around me, young lady."

"I just about had a heart attack! I thought you were dead! I thought . . ."

"That you'd never be able to speak to me again? The tragic fate of a handsome First you just couldn't save . . ."

The impish smile spreads even wider, and I have to concentrate very hard to keep from slapping the expression from his face. "Come on," he says. "I'm funny. You can admit it."

He's so pleased with himself, it's hard to stay angry. And I can't stop myself from laughing as he tries to wipe the powder out of his hair. Unsuccessfully. "It's stuck in your eyelashes. What is that stuff?"

"Water purifier." He unzips the top pocket of his pack to get at his water skin. Pouring a little water over his hands, he scrubs at his face and hair, the water turning it purple. "Lychee flavored. Disgusting."

"Wasting water purifier just to scare me?"

He rubs the water from his cheeks, shrugging. "I was going for a laugh rather than terror. You haven't spent much time laughing since I met you. I'm trying to help."

I laugh again, but underneath a scary sort of opening suddenly brings itself to light. I thought the exact same thing about Tai-ge back in the City, and did everything I could to fix it. It's what friends do. Is Howl my friend?

I watch as he packs away his water skin and gathers the rest of his things together, a single hash mark on his hand flashing at me like a warning light. Am I friends with the Chairman's son? A week ago I would have laughed at the thought, but Howl isn't what I expected. Not snobby or self-important. He hasn't looked at my brand even once.

Howl finally notices my absent stare in his direction. He smiles. I smile back.

It feels safe, as if Howl is the boy from his story about the stars, ready to sing away the monsters lurking in this forest, in my past. Or tease and joke them away, anyway. He doesn't seem like the singing type.

But, as I follow him out of our campsite, an uncomfortable thought wiggles to the surface of my brain. Howl is most certainly not dead, if a little sticky. If the City lied about raw fruit, what else isn't true about the reality I thought was mine?

CHAPTER 10

HOWL CONTINUES TO STAY VERY MUCH ALIVE, but I don't give in to the fruit. Even if hard crackers have begun to feel like cement piling up in my stomach, biting into an apple feels like some sort of disloyalty to the City. To Tai-ge.

Walking is a slow affair, with rests for me to concentrate on something other than my ribs attempting to poke holes out my abdomen. Howl can't keep still when we're stopped, sometimes pulling up plants with barky-looking roots to eat boiled with dinner, something I do allow, though it makes me look twice at that single line scarred into his hand, wondering how the Chairman's son knows tubers from onions from bloodsucking leeches. He must have been preparing to leave for a long time, figuring out how to survive Outside so he'd be ready.

My cuts and bruises start to disappear, the days slipping by like sand through my spread fingers, mesmerizing and uniform. The cold doesn't bite the way it did up high on the mountain, but it lurks in the open sky and the shorter days, waiting to bare its teeth. Before many days have passed, every tree we walk by starts to look the same, every burr caught in my hair just another task for our chats around the fire at night as Howl tells me stories about other constellations, other worlds, everything except his own life back in the City.

It must be hard for him, too—leaving. I can see traces of something trapped beneath the easy smile that splits his face in two as we walk away from his home and mine. But questions don't go over well. Whatever it is that made him run—that made him help me—stays cloaked, hidden by his mask of smiles, jokes, and stories.

And it isn't so hard to understand. I have my own pain to hide, each step away from the City feeling like a betrayal of something sacred, of the things I knew and loved. I keep track of the days religiously, marking off one week, then two, trying to measure Howl's estimate of walking to this mountain place in a month against our progress toward the blue peak in the distance. It distracts me from wondering what Tai-ge is thinking, doing. The ring I found makes an ugly rust stain on my pinkie, but I leave it there, scratching an ugly circle on the corroded surface, like the City seal.

It feels like a link to him, as if I can toy with it the way he did with his, turning it around and around and imagining he is doing the same. Every day the metal looks rustier, grainer, scraping against my skin. Is that what Tai-ge thinks of me, now that I'm gone? Has his mother managed to convince him I'm as awful and ugly as this old, rusted ring? A sad substitution for the real thing. Never a friend, much less a . . . whatever it was that my traitor brand made impossible.

Going back, even to explain, could be death for both of us. I have to look forward.

Unfortunately, forward is an unchanging view of the back of Howl's head.

The land levels out around us, the river swelling to a huge glassy sheet. We stay close to the water, following the curve of the mountain range south. When the clouds thin, the rounded tops appear, hulking beasts painted over with a child's watercolor set in grays and greens. Once, Howl points out the ghostly silhouette of a building clinging to a bald mountainside, sharply peaked roof gold against gray. A forgotten temple of some god who died along with the rest of this land.

The bag of Mantis feels too light every time I take it out, as if the pills are slipping out behind me in a trail leading back to the City. In another week or more, we'll be . . . somewhere, though I don't let myself think more than that. Is it the same "somewhere" my mother went after she tried to kill me?

But I'll be alive. Not attempting to swallow clods of dirt whole, or carving my initials in Howl's skin. Is that enough? That I've finally earned my four stars, but I'll be alive to wear them?

The trees, the nighttime fires made from Junis (a wood that hardly smokes), the river, Howl's long-legged pace, waking up with frost in my hair—it all hardens into a shield against the knot of homesickness and regret twisted up inside my chest. I feel as though I'm part of a machine: walk, sleep, eat, forget.

Until early one morning, Howl stops.

I peer around him into the trees, and my breath catches in my throat. We've found people. A pile of them.

Howl nudges the closest man over with a muddy boot, separating him from the pile. The body resists, frozen and fighting to remain a haphazard part of the heap. The man's eyes are glazed over with frost, City seal etched out in his brown leather jerkin beneath all the dried blood.

Memories of boots crunching through bones and rotted flesh

dance through my mind, so I decide to sit and watch Howl search the dead men's packs for useful items. At least until my stomach calms down.

As he rummages, the body separate from the rest watches me. The index fingers on both his hands end in blackened stumps, his mouth a frozen crevasse, gaping open in a grimace of ice and blood. *Would you have killed me too?* he asks. *Just like your mother. Killing everyone else to make sure you live. You don't even know why it's a choice between you and me.*

My eyes lock with the dead man's, horror-struck as they film over with black foam. *Are you here to kill me too?* The inky black trails trickle toward his mouth, death grimace twisting into a sneer. *Quit acting like a poor, abandoned child. It's in your blood. Kill me.*

A hand on my shoulder sends a jolt of electricity through my body. "Sev?" the voice snakes through the haze, but cold seeps up through my coat, frosting my ears shut, the dead soldier's icy fingers trying to find my throat.

"Sev?" The voice is louder. Yelling. The blackened face resolves into a pair of brown eyes. "Sev! What's wrong?"

My shoulders lift from the ground and crash back down. *How did I end up lying on the ground?* I can't fight the soldier's iron grip bruising my arms. Water splashes across my face and the dark eyes become a face. Howl. Holding me down.

"Get off me!" I yell, jerking away from him.

Howl lets go, surprised. "You started shaking and fell over." He raises my chin with one finger, appraising. "Are you sick?"

"No! I saw . . ."

"You saw what?" When I don't answer, Howl sits back on his heels, eyebrows creasing in toward each other. "This is the third time this has happened since we've been out here. Not including that first night in the wine cellar." He pushes a flustered hand through his hair. "How could you . . ." But then he takes a deep breath and starts over. "Are you taking Mantis like you are supposed to?"

I feel my face flush. "You hand it to me every morning and night. And watch me swallow."

"Then what is going on?"

I take a deep breath. "I . . . see things. It happened back in the City a lot. Never this bad before. Except . . . except for the bottles." I feel so ashamed. Dirty. Something is wrong with me, and I can't talk about it. Not when a dead man was just speaking to me. "It hasn't hurt you yet, so—"

"I'm not worried about you hurting *me*; I'm worried about you hurting yourself. What do you mean, you 'see things'?" Howl unzips my pack, digging until he finds the plastic package of Mantis Dr. Yang gave me. He doesn't seem to mind that I just told him I've been hallucinating. He just eyes the bottle thoughtfully. "Does it hurt?"

My mind struggles to find a way to deny what Howl has uncovered, to pull the secret back inside of me, where it will be safe, but nothing comes.

I don't remember hallucinations happening at all before my sister, Aya, died, about two years ago. The week after I saw her shot down, I started having frighteningly real dreams. Dreams that woke me up screaming, dreams that didn't go away even after I opened my eyes. It started happening more and more, until I was almost too frightened to go to sleep. Then came the daydreams, dark, twisted versions of reality, like the monster at the Aihu Bridge.

I shake my head, not sure if it is a response to Howl's question or just an attempt to stop the world from spinning around me.

"Just trying to keep you on your toes. Unpredictability: Boys love it. At least that's what the nuns always said in our late-night girly talks. What did you find?"

His lips harden to a tight line, and for a moment I think he won't drop it. But when he finally speaks, his voice is soft. "Nothing. They've all been picked clean."

"Who would be out here killing Reds? I mean, if there's no such thing as Kamar, like you say."

Howl shrugs. "It's no-man's-land from here to the mountain." He says it as if it's a name, not just one of the many mountains we've walked over. "Most Outsiders stay clear. There were only Reds in the pile, though, so it must have been an ambush. Are you okay? You look terrible."

I smooth a hand over my braided hair, picking out a few dead leaves and brushing the dirt from my back. "Better than they do."

Howl glances toward the lifeless soldiers. "Not by much." He puts the package of Mantis into his own pack and pulls out a bottle marked with Mantis's characters. "I'm going to have you switch to these, okay?"

"You've had more Mantis this whole time?" A thread of annoyance cuts at my throat. "I've been so worried we'd run out. . . ." And why would it matter which Mantis I take? They're all the same little green pills.

He pulls out three more bottles, stuffing them all into my pack. "And now you don't have to worry anymore. You can carry it, if you want. Less weight in my pack." He zips my pack closed and uncurls from his crouch next to me.

"The mountain . . ." I say it as if that's the name of the place, the way he did, taking the hand he offers to help me up. "Did they do this?"

"Probably."

"So they are the people we're fighting. I mean, the people the City is fighting."

"Yes." Howl's face shuts tight, wariness cloaking his open smile as it always does when I ask too many questions.

"So, even if they don't call themselves Kamar, how is going to them not betraying the City?"

"Because . . ." Howl can't seem to let go of the word, drawing it out long as if while he's still saying it, he won't have to actually explain anything. "You haven't been out here long enough to understand yet. Come on, we need to get moving. Less than a week to the Mountain, and I don't want to run into trouble."

"Could these Mountain people—the ones who killed these Seconds—be close?" I want to probe more, but dwelling on the dead men replants the Watchmen's black, empty eyes and severed trigger fingers back into my thoughts.

"I don't think so. These bodies have been here for at least a week. . . ." Howl freezes midstep, his head cocked to the side as if he's listening. Each of the tendons in his neck stands out underneath his skin like a starving set of ribs, his jaw set so hard I can almost feel his teeth cracking under the pressure.

It looks almost like . . . fear.

"Howl, what . . ."

He puts his finger to his lips, listening.

Dread oozes through my chest and paralyzes me, the quiet noises of the forest suddenly sinister and dangerous. I can't see anything that should be frightening on the ground or off in the trees. "What is it?" I whisper.

Instead of answering, Howl stalks off into the trees, feet silent on the uneven ground. When he comes back, the tense look isn't quite gone, though it's masked now by a smile. "Come on, we need to check something out."

"What? You look like you're about to dig yourself a cave to hide in."

He squats down, fingers pressing at the exposed dirt, digging around a clump of pink flowers just brave enough to push through into the cold air. Squishing the dirt against his palm into a ball, he then tosses it up into the air and catches it again with the other hand. "Sounds messy."

The knot of fear in my chest is slowly loosening, and pride takes over. I try to sound nonchalant. "What, then?"

Howl points to the ground, which seems unremarkable in any way. "People have been through here. More recently than the group that killed the soldiers. It took me a minute to figure out whether or not they could be within earshot."

"So, not our mysterious and complicated mountain people you won't tell me about?"

His mouth twitches as if he wants to laugh but is too polite to do so. "I don't know if I'd call them 'ours.' Right now I think we have more in common with that detatchment of Reds we found than anyone else out here. Twice as dirty and just about as frozen. I'm not sure anyone else will take us in."

Bending down, Howl wraps his fingers around one of the flowers and pulls, handing the bloom to me.

"At least with the dead guys, I'd know who I was dealing with," I say, raising an eyebrow. But I take the flower, twirling the stem between my fingers.

Howl grins, but his eyes are strained. Worried about whoever is out here and trying to hide it. "Now I can't tell you, because this is more fun. Maybe if I keep my mouth completely shut, you'll explode or something." And he starts to walk.

"Howl!" I call after him. "Aren't Firsts supposed to tell the truth? It's part of your science-Mantis-finding oath thing."

His pack stares back at me, shifting on his back he disappears into the trees.

Running to catch up, I take my place a few feet behind him, though his pace is much slower than usual. "What if you die? I'll be stuck out here with . . ." Myself. The pocket that holds my new bottle of Mantis feels extra light.

The frustration rock solid in my stomach starts to grow until my whole midsection might as well be granite and dragging along behind me. What is it that made him run away? And why doesn't he believe I'll be able to understand it? Even worse than that, if he can't tell me, does that mean he doesn't trust me? That we aren't friends?

I skip a few steps to catch up with Howl. "I heard a story once that the Chairman only employs mutes because he can't stand the chatter from Thirds who can talk. Does that apply to sons as well?"

Howl grunts, fringes of hair bobbing up and down, just visible over his pack from behind him. He doesn't react to the mention of his father.

"My roommate, Peishan, said it wasn't *all* the Thirds serving up in your house. Just the Chairman's hairdresser. She knows all the City secrets, all the Chairman's stupid jokes, and how often he brushes his teeth. He trusts her because she can't tell anyone else, not even her own family."

Silence.

I pull my long braid over my shoulder, more snarl than actual braid at this point. "You already know all of *my* secrets. And you seem to have the no-talking thing down. So if you were planning to start a new career as a hairdresser, I'd be willing to let you try mine."

"I think the only way to fix that braid involves a knife." Howl pauses to brush his fingers across a tree trunk where a few strips of bark have been rubbed away. "Now, how do I turn you off again? Mute would be good right now."

The curt reply stings a little, but I don't let it stop me. "You have to know the magic word. It isn't the name of my firstborn child, or 'open sesame,' or anything about my hair, so don't bother."

Howl doesn't look back this time. "What about 'please'?"

The cold sinks in deep this morning and my healing ribs ache from shivering. Howl stops every ten feet to look at each displaced pebble in our path, making me think of a child wearing his dad's uniform hat and coat, striding around and issuing orders as he plays at being much bigger than he actually is.

"You seem kind of anxious, Howl. Would it cheer you up if I ate an apple this morning?"

He finally looks at me, half a smile pulling at his mouth. "I didn't pick any for you today, so you'd have to fight me for it."

"I'd win, too."

I skip a step back when Howl unbuckles his pack and drops it to the ground, wondering if he means to take me up on that challenge, but he just answers in a conspiratorial whisper, "I fight dirty when I'm protecting my food. Now, if you don't mind, I want to spot the people who passed through here before they hear your voice and die from an overdose of secondhand perkiness. Like I said, I don't think they are soldiers, but I don't think they are . . . our people either. And I don't want to stumble across a nest of Wood Rats by accident. Especially not in the land between the City and . . ." He purses his lips, then amends, "Anyone living this close to the City."

Dropping his pack behind a rock, Howl gestures for me to set my pack down as well. By the time my things are hidden, he's already ten yards away, dark hair barely visible through the underbrush.

We dodge through the woods until I feel ridiculous trying to follow his lead. Elbowing my way through frozen dirt on my stomach and ducking behind bushes seems more conspicuous than walking like a normal person. I'm about to suggest this when he puts one finger to his lips.

Howl huddles under the bare ribs of a bush, the branches sticking weakly out from a dusting of dead leaves. Through the bush, I can see a scrap of mud-green canvas.

The sight of something man-made has me on the ground with my heart pounding, mind full of all the stories they tell about the people who live Outside. After all these days of wandering alone, the idea of other people seemed vague. Unreal. But ahead of us is a very real tent, and real live Wood Rats live in it. The scavengers that survive Outside are definitely something to fear.

Howl gestures for silence again, pointing to his mouth and breathing deeply, a sharp contrast to the short, scared bursts coming from me.

Putting a finger to his lips, Howl touches my shoulder and shakes his head. When he places his other hand on my stomach, it sends a panicked jolt through my abdomen, and I jerk away. Howl rolls his eyes and points to my shoulder. He puts a finger on his own shoulder and breathes in with an exaggerated shoulder movement, shaking his finger. With a hand on his stomach, he takes slow breaths that come from much deeper.

I try it. Much more quiet and controlled. I even feel calmer.

But it's too late.

A *click* sounds behind me, ripping through the cold silence like a clap of thunder. Howl's eyes fasten on something behind me.

I turn to find a weather-beaten old man standing over us, gun trained on Howl. He doesn't blink when Howl's hand slips up into his jacket. He just shoots the tree behind us, sending a flurry of birds into panicked flight. "Don't move. No use for whatever you've got hidden under there."

I agree. I happen to know it's the knife that disappeared from my pocket down in the Chairman's basement. Howl uses it to cut our army-ration dried meat into strips so we can eat while we walk. It isn't very sharp.

"Hands up, both of you." The man's eyes stare at Howl until he does as he's told. "Now stand up."

I roll over to my knees and inch to my feet. Howl creeps up in front of me as he stands, one hand over his head, the other extended out in front of me as though his arm is going to make a difference if this Outsider decides to shoot me.

The man's eyes widen as he takes in the First mark scored into Howl's hand, the scar white against his skin. The angry set of the man's mouth hardens.

"What are you and your little girlfriend doing breathing so loud near our camp?" His voice is a rasp. Harsher than before. "You part of the extermination forces that run through here?"

"The what?"

Howl's elbow presses against my shoulder, an unmistakable *Be quiet.* "We're on the run. Away from the City."

"I guess that explains the First mark and . . ." He gestures to the shiny patch of melted skin that makes a star on my hand. "She infected?" The gun is suddenly pointed at my head instead of Howl's.

Howl's protective arm pushes against me again, tensing as if he's about to jump the guy. Instead, Howl just says, "No. We're not infected. She used to be a First."

The man nods thoughtfully. His voice is still rock hard when he finally speaks. "Care to join us?"

Howl swallows, staring at the gun still pointed at my head. His sleeve grazes my collarbone as he lets his arms fall down, and he grabs my hand.

The weapon clicks again and the man lowers it, waving us toward the strip of green I saw through the bushes. I can just see a small clearing, a canvas tent streaked with mud occupying one edge. A fire-blackened pot suspended over a smokeless Junis fire spouts steam up into the morning chill. It smells like dirt and unwashed humans. And boiled cabbage.

As we get closer, a woman steps out from behind a tree, hair silvered with age. Where the man's years of exposure and hardship crack through, her face wrinkles and bends. Softer. "You okay, Cas?" she asks.

The man nods and pokes a thumb in our direction. "Couple of City strays. Nothing we can't work with, Tian."

Tian looks us over, taking in our dirty clothes and cheeks red with cold. "Pretty far away from the walls to look so well fed. Where are your supplies?"

Howl squeezes my hand before I can speak, "We dumped them a few days back. Thought the Reds were after us and we couldn't move fast enough to stay ahead." Hanging his head, his voice takes on a dejected whine I've never heard before. "We figured with a few days' worth of food and water, we would be able to find help."

"You aren't worried about running around in the woods with nothing? City kids who grew up with Mantis?" She doesn't look angry, just unconvinced. Cas sits down in front of the fire, looking away from us, but his hand stays close to the gun. "What kind of trouble is worse than risking a brush with a clan of infected out here? Not much I wouldn't do to get behind those City walls."

"We had to leave." Howl's voice cracks. "We were as good as dead in the City."

Tian raises an eyebrow, blinking at the traitor brand unmistakable on my bare hand. Or maybe she's looking at both our hands, so awkwardly intertwined. "Sweethearts?" Her voice is tinged with pity.

Howl grasps my hand even tighter, and I know it is my turn to speak. When I do, my voice grates, inches from pretend tears. "It was because of me. My mother, really. There was no point in staying after what she did." It feels odd to twist the truth into this lie.

The old lady purses her lips. "Things are tough even in the City these days, I guess." A trilling whistle sounds from her lips and two men step out from the fringes of the wood, guns lowering as they walk toward us. A young girl pokes her head out of the tent, her hair bound up in a dirty scarf. She gives us a quick glare before clapping the flap shut again.

The dark-haired men sit by Cas at the fire, almost identical in appearance. One is lazily unconcerned with us, the other openly watching and interested.

Tian jerks her head toward the men. "These are my sons, Parhat and Liming. The little one in the tent is June."

One of the men, Liming, catches my eye when she says his name, giving me a start. His eyes are bright green against his sun-dark skin. Green, like the invaders, like Kamar . . . or maybe this Mountain place we're going. I squeeze Howl's hand, trying to get his attention, but he ignores me.

Parhat doesn't look up from the boiling water over the fire. He rhythmically taps a scarred wooden bowl against the three-legged stand that suspends the pot over the crackling wood.

Something inside of me relaxes. It's hard to be frightened of a family cooking dinner. Maybe Outsiders aren't as bad as I thought. Maybe there are people with green and blue eyes who aren't part of the army trying to destroy my home.

They taught us about Outsiders in school. Wood Rats. Scavengers who have defected from the City or Kamar, preying on small groups of soldiers or on one another. But why should Cas and Tian be any more dangerous than people in the City? Maybe the campaign against Outsiders is just another way to keep people inside the walls. Like Howl's ridiculous theory that the First Circle won't let citizens have fresh fruit or they'll escape. Another nightmare to scare the little ones in their sleep.

"My name is Yong-Gui." Howl jerks his head toward me. "And this is Wenli." His tight grip on my hand is starting to pinch my fingers. "Thank you for letting us sit by your fire. It's been so cold."

"Are you coming from one of the farms?" I instantly regret asking as Howl tries to squeeze the bones right out of my fingers. Parhat finally glances up at us. His eyes are glazed and unfocused, darting between me and Howl before twisting back toward his bowl.

Cas turns back to the fire. "South."

I nod. Howl pulls me around to face him. "You've got a bit of dirt on your neck, Wenli." One finger runs lightly along my jaw, stopping just below my ear, sending tingles down my throat. Howl catches my eye and presses firmly just behind my jaw, under my ear, eyes flicking toward Parhat. "Is there any water nearby?"

He knows there's water nearby. We've been following the river. Perhaps this is a bid to sneak away?

Looking back at Parhat, I see that just under his ear he has a scar. It looks almost carved. A cross, cut shallowly over and over again. Looking a little more closely, I see more of them. Crosses decorating the back of his neck, and one peeking out from the cuff of his jacket. Scars. Suddenly I understand why Howl is crushing the life out of my hand. He has never been around SS. I've known hundreds of infected kids over the years. With Mantis . . .

Parhat's eyes move up again to look into the trees. They never seem to rest on anything in particular, just dart back and forth as though he can't keep still. The tapping on the wooden bowl stops, and he looks at us again. Chills run up and down my spine, and I find myself returning Howl's grip. Those eyes are feral. They've never even seen Mantis.

Maybe, in this case, the City wasn't lying.

Tian sloshes a bit of water into another wooden bowl for my neck, saying, "Might as well use warm. The river's close by, but this won't leave you shivering."

I take the bowl with a hesitant smile and sit with my back to the fire. Howl crouches next to me, watching as I scrub away at my face and neck with the water.

Howl brushes a wisp of hair behind my ear and leans toward me with a painted-on smile.

Lips warm against my ear, he murmurs, "They aren't going to let us leave. I have two Mantis pills in my pocket for an emergency. If I give them to you, can you take them without anyone noticing?"

I nod slightly and slip a hand inside his jacket. The pills are in a little paper packet, like the ones Sister Shang brought to me the day I broke into the library. When they are safely hidden under my shirt, I whisper back without moving my lips, "Sure you don't want to just spike the food?"

Howl chuckles like I told him a joke, twirling my stray lock of dark hair around his finger. "There's no way it would be enough. It should keep you with me until we have a chance to get away, though. If they find our packs, they might just take them. Or they might kill us."

"I would never have guessed that." I keep my expression blank. "The gun didn't tip me off or anything. Why didn't you just tell them we are brother and sister so we don't have to act like this?"

"Not plausible. You're a Fourth. Besides, this way I can watch you jump every time I come anywhere near you." The edges of a real smile flit across his face, but it disappears as Liming walks over to break up our chat.

Setting two bowls of food on a rock beside us, he sinks down next to us with a sigh. His eyes are sharp and expectant, pinning each of us in turn. I'm not sure what to say or what he wants, but I can't help but break the loaded silence with a desperately empty "Hi."

He doesn't answer, looking over at the bowls and back to us. When we don't move, he points to them, back at us, then to his mouth. I nod and reach for a bowl, which steams in the cold air. The brownish-yellow liquid smells sharply of rotten cabbage and dirty laundry, the aroma of tubers hiding somewhere underneath. Liming's eyes follow as I bring the bowl to my lips, sipping to allow the arctic chill lodged in my throat to melt. Definitely spoiled cabbage.

The open smile branded across Liming's face feels genuine, but lopsided. Missing something.

Howl takes his bowl and drinks, swallowing with a choke disguised as a cough. "Thank you so much for sharing." The words rush out of his mouth like he's afraid if something isn't steadily coming out, more stew will have to go in. "What is in this? It's delicious."

Liming nods briskly and returns to his place by the fire without answering.

I sidle up close to Howl and try to whisper out of the side of my mouth, "What was that?"

"He can't speak." Howl sloshes his soup around, watching closely as if something alive might crawl out of it. "He doesn't have a tongue."

Not even a mention of green eyes. "What do you mean?"

"I mean he doesn't have a tongue. Cut out, probably. You can tell by the way he moves his mouth." The soup swirls around and around, and he lifts it again to take an exploratory sip. "I don't think they put anything toxic in the soup, so you can go ahead and eat it."

I glance over at Parhat, who is now absorbed in stabbing the ring of ashes around the fire with a stick, a terrible thought burrowing deeper every second. If we don't find the mountain people Howl seems to think are out here, those scars could be *my* future. That blank stare with nothing but infection looking out . . . I can't quite keep the shudder back as it ripples up my spine and down my shoulders and arms. "I'll pass on lunch. How do we get out of this?"

"We'll leave tonight after they all go to sleep. Circle back, get our packs, and run for it."

"The only reason we are still alive is because they think we have Mantis or food or something valuable, right? They need us to take them back to our packs."

"Right. Better hope Parhat doesn't have any violent compulsions."

I think of the wine cellar, the inescapable grip of compulsion, and shiver. Tian walks over, smile plastered across her face.

She pulls us both out of the cold, toward the fire. Where we cannot talk.

CHAPTER 11

SHADOWS JUMP AND TWIST ON THE TENT WALL, the flickers of a dying fire dancing across the fabric. They insisted we take the tent tonight. Even the little girl—June—is sleeping outside. We caught a glimpse of the scarf tied tight around her head before Tian dragged her out of the clearing to gather more wood for the fire. Cas has been planted nearby ever since.

The dirty sweat smell is stifling trapped inside the tent walls, fogging all the way up to where the ceiling is tagged UNIT 314 in bold characters. It makes my mind sink down deep, wondering what happened to the Outside patrollers who must have been the original owners of this tent.

There's barely enough space for Howl and me, canvas wall inches from my nose as I try to make enough room for the two of us to lie down without touching.

Howl spreads out in front of the doorway, palming my knife against his leg, Tai-ge's name peeking out through his fingers. When I asked why they didn't confiscate it, or at least search us for other weapons, Howl shrugged. "I don't think they're worried about us taking them by surprise."

The shadow moves outside, circling around to the other side of the fire.

"What if he just stays there?" I whisper.

Howl glances back at me, shifting a little to allow us to talk, "He's going to. And I think Liming and Parhat are probably watching the other side so we can't cut out the back."

We have to get out tonight. That or face the morning with no Mantis for me. "Are you going to try to sleep?"

"No." His voice is flat.

"Staying up won't help if . . ."

"I won't let anyone come in here, Sev. You're safe with me, I promise." His eyes are black pools in the dark, but I know he is looking at me. "Sleep. One of us should."

Sleep? With Cas's shadow outlined against the tent wall? But some part of me—the part that is tired and hurting from running—says that there is no point in trying to stay awake. If we are going to die, there isn't anything Howl can do. Promises of safety don't mean anything when SS waits outside in the dark, only feet away. And my eyes are so tired, drooping as fatigue twists tighter and tighter around my brain. . . .

That is, until a knife slits through the tent wall a foot above my head.

I roll away from the weapon slashing down toward me, crashing into Howl's back and knocking him onto his stomach. A hand slips in through the gash and folds the flap back, Liming's head appearing through the gap.

He puts a finger to his lips and gestures for us to follow.

Howl and I look at each other. He slithers over me to the rip in the tent, his eyes locked on my face and then skittering away as he touches the rent canvas. "Stay close to me," he whispers, lightly touching my arm. "And be ready to run."

Liming stops us just outside the tent and breaks a quick-light, bathing us in the dim yellow light. He hands me a leaf, folded in two.

Unfolding the leaf, I accidentally tear the green waxy surface, a syrupy substance bleeding out all over my hands. In the center, dark charcoal spells out one word. REBELS?

Howl looks from the leaf to Liming, thinking hard. Then nods once.

What does that mean? Rebels?

Liming pulls us farther along so we are away from the fire, away from Cas's ears. He gestures for us to stay, then walks around a tree, leaving us in darkness.

"What is he doing?" I don't realize that I've spoken out loud until Howl puts a hand on my shoulder. Reassuring, I think. Or maybe just trying to make me be quiet.

The light returns after a few minutes, this time two shadows bobbing in its wake. The quicklight's sickly glow gives the dirty yellow scarf tied over her head a greenish halo. June.

It's hard to tell in the dark, but she looks about twelve, shadows under her eyes carving her face into something more than the child she should be. Her eyes stay fixed on the ground, and I can see her hands clenching and unclenching around the straps of the rucksack on her back.

Liming puts a hand on her shoulder, and then points to me. Grasping his hands together, he points again at me, then at June. Another leaf comes, the word ESCAPE scratched out in shaky strokes.

The unwavering glow of the quicklight lines Howl's face with hard, unforgiving hollows. I can feel refusal blossoming in his throat even before his lips have time to move. The air almost boils with anticipation and violence.

I speak before Howl can shush me. "You'll help us escape if we take her? Yes. We'll do it."

Howl's arm around me tightens. His face is bland, but the whisper in my ear is clear. "We don't know anything about her. The rest of the family will have twice the reason to come after us, even if she doesn't kill us herself."

Liming bows his head, his face crumpled with emotion. Anger and grief twisted in an all-too-human mask. The leaf crumbles in his hand, pieces fluttering to the ground.

June watches them fall, hardly even breathing.

"Is she infected?" I ask in a whisper.

A quick jerk of his head says no.

"Are you?"

His bright green eyes lift from the ground, yellowed and wolf-like in the quicklight. A nod. After a pause, he points back to the tent and the clearing, circling his finger in the air with another quick nod.

"You all are. Except for June."

He bows his head.

"But Parhat, he's so much worse. . . ." Even Tian and Cas seem sane compared to Parhat, if not exactly cuddly. Wouldn't SS have changed them, too?

"SS doesn't progress the same way in everyone." Howl's voice is quiet, even for a whisper as he turns back to Liming. "Why didn't you just follow us back to our supplies?"

Liming puts an arm around June and lifts her face with a soft touch. She looks at us for the first time, and her green eyes pierce right through me. It only lasts a second before her stare is back in the dirt.

"She's your daughter?" The sentence cracks and splinters as it presses its way out of my mouth into the heavy air.

Liming's arm encircling June slips down to her hand to give it a reassuring squeeze. A nod. Almost a smile. A proud smile.

Something opens up inside of me, tears burning behind my eyes as I take in that smile. Longing. Wishing for something that can never be mine. "We'll take her with us. We'll make sure she's safe." A promise I can only hope to keep. But the words are out.

Liming wraps his arms around June, pulling her tight against him. She doesn't move, woodenly enduring the hug. When he lets her go, I can see tears on her downturned cheeks.

He nods to Howl and walks back into the trees.

It's a tightrope walk back to the packs. I feel eyes everywhere, each attached to a gun sight trained on my back as if I'm stuck in a Liberation movie, an audience waiting for any of us to trip, for a gun's metal voice. All we need is some dramatic background music.

About the time we lose sight of the fire, a gunshot sounds through the woods. We drop to the ground, a small hand finding mine in the dirt. A larger one wraps around my other wrist, thumb running across my palm. My lungs refuse to expand, my whole body waiting for Cas's leathery scowl to appear over us in the dark.

The hand around my wrist lifts me up. "He's leading them away. They're running in the other direction," Howl whispers.

Pulling June behind us, I follow Howl to the packs. Howl holds mine up while my cold fingers fumble to clasp the straps around my hips and chest. As he grapples with his pack, I watch June. The moon is dark, but even the night can't hide her huddled outline on the ground, shoulders shaking.

No time to talk now.

Howl grabs my hand, I grab June's, and we run.

CHAPTER 12

MY EYES WON'T OPEN WHEN HOWL SHAKES ME awake in the morning. Taking turns watching through the night coupled with bright sunlight has pain settling across my brain in a poisonous fog. It takes a moment, even after Howl trickles freezing water across my face.

"Stop it! I'm awake!" my voice rasps out in a hoarse whisper.

Peeling my eyes open, I accept the water skin Howl is holding out toward me. He taps his cheek as I sip, studiously ignoring the new member of our group. June is perched up in a tree about ten feet above us, her sleeping bag already stuffed back down into her tiny rucksack.

June's cheeks are pale under her tan, hands clutching her arms as if she's cold. She lifts one hand up to the scarf around her head and pulls it off, throwing it to the ground like a piece of garbage, blond snarls falling to her shoulders.

I blink. The golden halo has been teased into a bird's nest of tangles and dirty leaves. Still, she looks just like pictures of our enemies from the Great Wars. Like the sleeping princess trapped

in her picture window. Blond like the Kamari prisoners they bring
to the City for execution.

My mouth hangs open, not even sure what to say. Howl
catches my eye and shakes his head. He must have seen this
before. Kamari escapees. But if there is no Kamar, does that
make them the Mountain people? Or just . . . people? My mind
twists uncomfortably, trying to fit things together I hadn't
known could come apart.

Howl looks up at June again. "Shall we go?" he asks, lips barely
moving.

I look around, trying to figure out who he thinks is watching
him. "Yes. If you let me eat something on the way."

"Fine." He holds out a green apple. I hesitate, but I take it.

"Has she eaten?" I ask, nodding toward June.

Howl gives a curt nod. "I tried. She took one bite of everything
I offered her, then stuffed the rest down her shirt. I wouldn't be
surprised if she's holding what she did eat in her cheeks."

A wave of pity pricks at my eyes. "She hasn't been eating very
well."

"You don't need to see her play chipmunk to know that."

He's right. June doesn't look as if she's seen a good meal in
years. Cheekbones sharp as knives stick out underneath those
downturned eyes, and her clothing is loose, hanging on her as
though she stole it from an older brother.

When I climb up to sit down next to her, she doesn't even
look. I try touching her shoulder, but she just moves away.

"June?" I catch myself ducking my head, as if I can catch her
eye if I try hard enough. It would probably take lying on the
ground. "You okay?"

A stupid question. Which she answers in kind. Nothing.

"We aren't going to hurt you. We promised your dad that we would take care of you."

Her eyes flicker at this, but she doesn't move. That stillness cuts straight to bone. Tai-ge told me the same thing, breaking my first few weeks of silence after waking up. That he'd take care of me. He'd never hurt me.

I didn't believe him. It felt wrong, as though if what he said was true, then all the things they said about my parents were true too. That I'd never see them again.

"Are you going to run back to your family?" Howl's voice is devoid of any accusation, his eyes up with us in the trees. "Would you be better off with them?"

Her shoulder twitches in what might be a shrug.

I climb back down to the ground. June hesitates a second, but follows. When Howl leads out, June casually stuffs a hand down her shirt, comes up with a broken cracker, and takes a bite.

I look at the apple in my hand and raise it up to my lips. It is sour in my mouth. But I like the way it tastes.

When we stop to eat lunch, June strolls away, glancing back at us once before disappearing into the trees.

Howl starts after her, but I stop him. "She probably has to relieve herself."

He sits back down, craning his neck to watch her until she disappears from sight. "It was too easy. Getting away last night."

"Because Liming helped us."

He looks at his hands. "What if she isn't the abused little girl you think she is? She isn't . . . like you, if that's what this is about. She wasn't abandoned by her parents. She doesn't seem to want to come with us. What if she's out there marking a trail for her family to follow?"

"If the point was just to get hold of the Mantis or food, then why are we still alive?"

Howl shakes his head. "We don't know what they want."

"We can't abandon her." She might not be like me, but I can't believe June is a cold-blooded killer. "Reds will find her, or if she ends up back with that zoo of a family . . . We are her best chance of survival."

"True. But right now, she might be the biggest block between *us* and survival." Howl closes his eyes. "Look. I know I haven't been completely open with you and that it's been hard, but I know something isn't right here."

"I'm *not* leaving her. We aren't Outsiders, and I'm not going to act like one." Tendrils of anger lace through the words, and by the way Howl flinches, I know he feels it.

We stare at each other. Finally, he bows his head. "We'll take turns watching every night. She can't prepare our food or ever be alone with the packs. She can never see you take Mantis. And you're still Wenli, violently in love with a man way out of your league."

The halfhearted joke doesn't quite take away the anger stinging in my veins, though I try to reply in kind. "You wish. I don't even know how to act in love. Back when that was an option . . . oh, wait. It never was." My star brand almost looks like a normal scar under all the dirt. "I have a target painted on my forehead, remember?"

"Let's start by pretending that we're friends. You can tell yourself that I'm Tai-ge and I'll pretend you are my little sister."

I grit my teeth, Tai-ge's name rushing through me like a

sickness. That knot is still waiting to be untied, pain loosed. Something I'm not ever planning to do. "Little sister?" I cough, trying to shake the gravel out of my voice. "I'm the one who suggested that in the first place."

Howl shrugs. "Wouldn't have worked with the Wood Rats. June won't know the difference, though. She's only twelve."

"Fourteen, actually."

The words have both of us on our feet, dull knife in Howl's hands, poised two inches from June's freckled nose. Her voice is lower than I expected.

She doesn't flinch as the knife twitches between Howl's fingers. He puts it away.

"I found these on the ground over there. I think they're still good," she says, holding out two apples.

"Talking now?" Howl takes the apples, looking them over.

Her green eyes go back down, lips pressed together.

I reach out to touch her shoulder and ask, "Are there more up in the tree?"

But June's human moment is over. All I get is a shrug.

CHAPTER 13

THAT NIGHT WE STRING OUR PACKS UP IN A TREE
out of animal reach, spreading our sleeping bags out atop a rock.
For some reason, sleep won't come, Howl's worried expression
lodged firmly in my brain.

When June looks safely asleep, I slide down to where he's sitting, watching the darkness all around us.

"I'm sorry for getting angry," I say, worried the words won't
come out, stuck like sugary candy in the back of my throat.

Howl looks at me for the first time since the argument, surprise flitting across his face. "Is she asleep up there?"

"As far as I can tell. She couldn't get into the packs without
making any noise, could she?" All of the sudden I know I did the
wrong thing, that she is already rifling through our few posses-
sions. That we'll be dead before morning.

Howl's mouth opens in a huge circle of a yawn, hands occupied
with rubbing his eyes instead of covering it. "I hope not."

"I'm sorry that things are so . . . wrong. I want to help June,
but I'm willing to take precautions."

Leaning his head back against a tree, Howl doesn't speak for a moment, fingers tracing patterns in the bark. "Can we be on the same side again?" he finally whispers, shifting toward me, accidentally planting his hand on top of mine. He pulls his hand back, not speaking for a moment as his fingers flex at his side. "Sorry. Not us against June. Just us."

"Yes." I ignore the flutter in my stomach as he looks at me, the hand that touched mine balled into a fist. "But with conditions."

Howl leans in, whispering low enough that June won't be able to hear us, but so close his breath tickles against my cheek. "You want me to trust her? I want her to be what she says she is too. Or . . . what Liming said she is." He glances up at her sleeping bag, peeking over the edge of the rock. "And one point in her favor: I think we can both agree that she isn't infected."

"Unless she has a stash of Mantis somewhere." He sets his hand down again, so close our fingers are touching.

I don't mind. It's funny, because we've been much closer than our hands touching, but this feels different. As if it's on purpose, and without the cover of trying to help me or pretend for Cas and Tian, Howl doesn't seem quite so sure of himself.

I like it. Howl a little unsure. His hand creeping up onto mine. But it seems a bit sudden, almost purposeful. As if he's trying to distract me.

I pull my hand into my lap. "My conditions have nothing to do with her," I inform him. "I need you to come clean."

"Have I led you wrong yet? Trust me a little longer."

I shake my head. "I have no idea what we are doing or why. You call Seconds 'Reds' like old women in the Third Quarter who have had enough of washing uniforms. You aren't acting like a First, or like you're even from the City. You shouldn't even know how to turn on a stove, much less how to track down Wood Rats and dig up tubers. Or see a head of blond hair and not flinch. Up until a few weeks ago, light hair meant the enemy. Dead men with hair like June's, strung up on our walls as a warning against spies."

Howl leans away from me, rubbing his eyes again. "Fair enough."

I wait for him to go on, but he just sits, staring for a few minutes. Thinking.

"Is that the end of this conversation?" I ask. "Trust goes two ways, and if you can't give it, then I'll leave." Even saying it out loud sends prickles down my arms. "I'll find your mountain all by myself."

He shakes his head. "Don't be ridiculous. There's a reason Liming didn't just send June out on her own to find the Mountain. You have to have a guide to even find an entrance. And someone to vouch for you."

I wait.

Howl closes his eyes, his hands tying knots in his hair. "I've lived Outside before."

That night down in the wine cellar, I wouldn't have believed it. But now that I've seen him climb trees and find food, there isn't really another explanation that would make sense.

"I came out with some Reds on patrol a few years ago and we were attacked." Howl's eyes are on the ground, words so slow and careful it's as if he's machine. "We didn't expect a full-blown raiding party right outside the City walls. One of the rebels recognized me and decided to take me back to the Mountain instead of shooting me. For ransom."

Rebels? I want to laugh, but I don't want to wake June. What is there to rebel against? Sometimes down in the Third Quarter there was rebellious talk. Asking for shorter hours, better food. But it never amounted to much more than a day or two of missed shifts and avoiding the Watch. No one wants to get thrown Outside. No Seconds to protect you from Kamar or Firsts to make Mantis for your infected kids. Outside is worse than being worked to death.

Only, if there is no Kamar . . . Howl said I wouldn't understand. That I hadn't seen enough yet.

He's quiet for a long time, thinking the words through. "If you had known the army was fighting rebels instead of far-off, foreign Kamar, how would you have felt about your place in society? The star they burned into your hand?"

I shrug, uncomfortable.

"The Mountain isn't foreign, or even set on killing anyone. It's made up of people who have left the City and people who were surviving Outside. They'll take anyone who wants to be there, and give them something more to live for than fear. And they are organized and successful enough that the City is taking them seriously. If people inside the City knew that, they would *leave*."

I look down at my hands, twirling the rusty red ring on my pinkie.

"You see why the war with Kamar is so important to the First Circle? And the lies about conditions Outside? Stringing prisoners up where everyone can see the enemy's light hair and worry about how close a fictional army is to invading their homes, infecting their children? It's all a propaganda campaign to convince Thirds to work for almost nothing with no way to complain. The forces that the Seconds fight are from the Mountain. They want to *help* Thirds."

"Where . . ." I fumble with the question, not sure how it will sound. "Where do they come from, then? People . . . like June?"

Howl shrugs. "When Yuan Zhiwei locked the City gates, only

certain people were welcome inside. I don't know if that has to do with alliances during the Influenza War, or the invasion they teach us about in school. There are people of all kinds out past where City patrols range, lots of people like June in work camps and farms that belong to the City, but they're kept out of sight. You must know the City hasn't always been fighting Outsiders. How else could a First like you end up with a name like . . ."

I flinch and shake my head, not willing to talk about it. Yes, my mother gave me a funny, foreign-sounding name, but that doesn't mean my family is somehow from Outside. "How did you go from hostage to sympathizer? It's not as if you had anything to complain about up in the First Quarter."

"A former First started visiting me every day in confinement." Howl recites the story as if he's reading it from a book, still look-ing at the ground. "She did SS research before she turned rebel. The First Circle had ordered her to start testing on humans, to purposely infect citizens and set them loose in the City. When she refused, they threw her in the Hole. The rebels caught wind of it and broke her out."

"First-inflicted SS cases?"

Howl's teeth flash in a half smile. "To keep the threat in Thirds' minds. Seconds', too. And you can turn off that respectful voice. I . . . I didn't believe either, at first. The woman who talked to me introduced me to victims. People from the Sanatorium. They don't just do SS experiments in there."

"I know people in there." My voice comes out too low as I think of Peishan, how frightened she was that day in Captain Chen's classroom. How empty my room was after they took her away.

"What could be worse than infected all locked up together?" he asks. "Completely out of control, hurting themselves and anyone else they can get their hands on with no hope of recovery. . . ."

The dark expression in his face stops me cold. The thought of thousands of Parhats, confused and without conscience, left to cut crosses in their arms and hands . . . The City wouldn't do that to people on purpose, would it? I sit back against the tree, tracing lines in the dirt. "So you turned. You started working for them."

He sits forward, the intensity of his voice catching me by surprise. "All Firsts care about is keeping the cheap labor from realizing the Third Quarter isn't much better than a slave camp. 'Shoulder to shoulder we stand, comrades building a society strong enough to find the cure to SS.' City principles are a load of garbage."

I recognize the quote from our pledge, the one I used to recite for every Remedial Reform class, every shift at the cannery. The City was meant to be a place where everyone was equal, each pulling our weight, each taking our fair share. Thinking back to the gargantuan houses up on the Steppe, it's easy to wonder how equal Firsts are compared to the rest of us. Especially when the First right in front of me is calling the City a prison.

I catch myself looking at Howl's First mark, wanting to believe him just because it's there. Even on a traitor's hand, I want that single white line to mean safety. He looks at it too, one finger brushing the scar as if it's graffiti that can be wiped away.

"I call Seconds 'Reds' because that's what they call them out here. Not just because of the pins and the uniforms, but because of the people they've killed. They're all covered with blood."

Howl sits back against the tree. "I've been helping smuggle Mantis out for about two years now." He gestures to my pack. "Dr. Yang gave us more than enough to get you to the Mountain, and the rest will go to the Mountain's Mantis stockpile."

A glow of hope washes over me as he says it. A whole *stockpile* of Mantis outside the City. A safe place to hide from whatever monster SS grew inside of me. But something here doesn't quite fit. "So the bomb at Aihu Bridge . . . That was the rebels?"

"That bomb was air-launched, right?"

I nod.

"Then no. The City has the only aircraft in the area. Rebels don't have access to that kind of power." Howl yawns again, eyes crinkling shut. "That must have been a busy night for the propaganda department, trying to explain how you managed to blast yourself off that bridge. I think it ended up being something about you marking a target point for a 'Kamari' heli-plane."

So, if I'm going to believe Howl, even the SS bombs in the City are self-inflicted, keeping the threat of an army waiting just on the other side of the wall fresh in everyone's mind. It must have just been an added bonus that I was there that night with Tai-ge. Through this new lens, it's easy to see why the First Circle would have used the situation to send me to the Arch. A story about a Kamari spy caught in the act of bringing SS down to where it would hurt the most people would pull Thirds closer to the City than a distant chemical bomb and a burning bridge ever could. Almost like the propaganda department wrote my part. But that still doesn't explain what Howl said while he thought I was unconscious the night the Watch came after me. *She's the only one like me.*

"What does any of this have to do with me?" I ask, cautiously fishing for an answer, wanting to trust him. "Why did Dr. Yang bend so far to get me out of the City? Why did you leave with me if you were doing so much good, ferrying Mantis over the wall?"

"I left because . . . it's just too hard. Being there. Watching people bend until they break. I want to do more. I *can* do more out here." Howl's breath blurs the air between us, his eyes suddenly directed anywhere but at me. "And as for why Dr. Yang wanted you out, you'll have to ask him yourself." He glances toward June. "You should probably get back up there. I'm sorry I didn't tell you where we were going before. Dr. Yang was worried that if you knew, you wouldn't come. That you'd try to run away from us and end up dead along with whoever else they are pinning to that bomb."

My heart starts to pound, Tai-ge's dimpled smile clear in my head. And another, but much blurrier: my father, caught in the tangle of my mother's deception. I can't believe it didn't occur to me before that blame for that bomb might have attached to someone else after I was smuggled out of the City. "Whose life did I trade for mine?" My voice is low, a slow vibration that almost doesn't make it out. "Who is dead because you helped me escape?"

Howl grabs my shoulder, giving it a shake. "Your staying wouldn't have changed anything." When I don't respond, he whispers, "I think it would take quite of bit of hard evidence to get at the Hongs, if that's what you're worried about."

Relief floods through me, but guilt and fear immediately crawl up after it. My escape could be blamed on anyone. The nuns, my teachers, my roommate. Except Peishan was already in the Sanatorium. And if Tai-ge believes I meant to kill him that night . . . at least he's above suspicion. It's not as if I can ever see him again. But is he safe? Dr. Yang said something back in the City about hurting Tai-ge as some kind of warning to General Hong. . . .

"Should we have brought him, too?" I ask.

"Would he have come?"

"No." I wouldn't have either if I'd had a choice.

"Then just be glad you're alive. There's nothing you could have done differently except let them kill you." Howl sighs, and the hand on my arm slips down to encircle my wrist. His fingers feel warm through my coat, comforting. Genuine. "You care a lot more about them than they seem to care about you. No one has thought twice about abusing you for the last eight years."

He turns my hand over, the two of us staring at the brand's star shape melted into my skin. I can hardly find my voice, the words coming out in a whisper. "Some people decided to look past these to find out if I was human or not."

"Tai-ge." Howl looks up at the sky again.

I take a deep breath and let it out, not ready to speak for a moment. The corroded ring around my finger has left a permanent stain on my skin, a rusty fungus-looking smear. That's probably exactly what he thinks of me now: a stain on his past that will be hard to scrub away. But Tai-ge couldn't believe I would have hurt him, could he?

Another deep breath.

It doesn't matter now what Tai-ge thinks. As long as he's safe. His father would never let anything happen to him. "What about June? Are there many more . . . like her in the Mountain?"

Howl blinks. "Everyone gets a fair chance in the Mountain. Wood Rats, City runaways, people from out past this forest . . . No stars, no brands, and no one cares who you are or what you look like."

"Even for me?" It seems impossible that my stars could not mean anything. That people wouldn't look at my birthmark or my star burn and see my mother.

Howl looks at the ground again, choosing his words care-fully. "Whatever happened during the Great Wars, everyone left over just wants to survive. I don't think having light-colored eyes should take away your right to a good life any more than having the wrong number of lines on your hand should."

My head is swimming with information, all of it glassy and distorted, as if I'm peering through murky water. "Why were we so worried about June's family, then? Why don't all of them just go to the Mountain?

"You can't just walk in. They'll let anyone in who's willing to help with a war. Plenty of Wood Rats are content to scavenge on the edges where they don't have to fight. I don't understand what was going on in that family. Liming could have found a Mountain patrol and asked for a guide in."

Why didn't Liming come with us, then? I glance back up toward June, though I can't see her sleeping form from where I sit. "How long did you live out here?"

"Two years. A little more."

"How is it . . ." I shrug. "I never heard anything about you being gone."

Howl looks down at his hands, and suddenly I'm uncomfortable, seeing things on his face that no one ever should feel. He can't even call his father anything but "the Chairman." Was it more important for the Chairman to save face, to keep it quiet that Howl was gone, than to mobilize Seconds to get his son back?

"What did you ever hear about me?" he finally asks, still staring at the ground.

I cock my head to the side, bending so he has to look at me. "I heard at least one pretty little girl from the orphanage wish Third boys were as nice-looking as your portrait. Maybe she meant she wished they were cleaner?" Looking him up and down, I give a mock frown. "Not really sure I agree."

He rolls his eyes. "Well, there you have it. I lived out here. That's how I know where we're going."

"And what tubers are?"

The lighthearted question almost makes him smile. "Right. Tubers."

His hand finds mine again, and the tightness in my chest eases. No more fighting, no more anger. No lying or withholding information. We're friends again. More than that. We could be partners, part of this cause, if it's real. I could help people like June.

People who have no chance, like my sister, Aya, before she was shot down in the street.

People like me.

The City, no matter how I feel about it, isn't an option anymore. Neither is Tai-ge. He never was. And, just like the rest of the City, Tai-ge never could completely forget my brand. No matter what he felt or thought about me, my past was a wall that we both knew he wouldn't try to climb. He never tried to hold my hand. No one ever even noticed that I had hands at all in the City, except to crush them while checking my traitor star. And Howl is right here in front of me, asking me to listen, just to think it through. That maybe I'm worth more than a messy burn. That there's more to life than Yuan Zhiwei and rows and rows of canning jars, and the pieces on the weiqi board numbered from one to four.

Hand-holding has nothing to do with it. I want to believe him. I do believe him.

That night, I dream of Zhinu and Niulang. Except when Niulang first sees Zhinu, his teeth stretch out over his lips, jagged and sharp. Morphed into one of the monster qilin, he chases her back to his den, where the other snarling creatures wait. Her cries surround me, choke me, as her eyes open—deep brown. My eyes.

I wake to find myself precariously balanced against a tree branch on the edge of our rock, slick with sweat. Zhinu's sobs ring in my ears, echoing against the night sky, moon covered by a sea of clouds. My heart drums against my chest as if it's trying to escape its bloody prison.

Howl climbs up from the ground, perching next to me. "What's wrong, Sev?" His eyes wash over June before flicking back to me.

I take a deep breath, trying to erase the image of Niulang's long, sharp teeth tearing through. . . . "Nothing. I just had a bad dream."

He sits for a second, peering at me through the darkness. I can't look at him, as if my dream could somehow reach out and destroy Howl, too, giving the one person I've decided to trust sharp teeth and an appetite for flesh. His hand brushes my cheek, and the awful image goes away, leaving only my friend. Howl is safe.

"Want to talk about it?" he asks.

I shake my head, taking a deep, shuddering breath that sends darts of pain through ribs I thought were starting to mend. "No. I don't even want to think about it."

"Okay." He doesn't climb back down, tracing the pattern quilted into my sleeping bag with one finger. "Do you need anything?"

I shake my head.

"I'll come up." He climbs over me and slips in between me and June. "Maybe we'll get lucky and June will fall off." He smiles to belie the joke.

I smile back, glad that he doesn't mean it. It's odd, but having Howl right beside me does make things seem less frightening. I sleep, and this time the dreams stay far away.

CHAPTER 14

THE MORNING FEELS MUCH LIGHTER. HOWL SHOOTS me a smile before climbing a tree to gauge how close we are to our mountain destination. He doesn't mind when I follow him up, noting that the craggy, sheer side of the mountain we've been crawling toward is no more than a two-day walk away if we go fast. When I smile back, it's genuine.

Unzipping a side pocket on my pack, I extract three packets of powdered purifier for our water. Two lychee, one strawberry. Groping around, I count only five more, all lychee-flavored. I have been purposely giving Howl the lychee ones in retribution for the poison scare. Looks like I'll have to grimace along with him after today.

We're so far down now that the trees are different, the land immediately next to the river thick with long, skinny plants that I hesitate to even call trees. They are thin and dull green in the cold, growing together in clumps to make a bushy taillike burst of leaves far over our heads. The river flows only a few feet deep by the river's shore, water-smoothed rocks sticking up from the calm surface every few feet. I perch on a white boulder that kisses land, half in, half out of the water, a crooked old tree perched next to it on the shore twining snakelike roots around its base.

The water skin comes up cloudy and brown. Odd. I must have kicked up some dirt when I put it under. My second try is also unsuccessful. Confused, I look more closely at the river. Instead of being clear to the bottom, the water is murky.

"Howl!" I yell. "Something is off down here."

June strolls down, kicking at rocks and taking her time. But when she sees the muddy water, she's off like a shot, back toward our camp. Howl is on his way toward me, looking back over his shoulder after June. She throws dirt over the ashes from our fire from last night and begins frantically stuffing our food and utensils into the packs.

"What's her problem?" I ask.

He shrugs, still watching her. "What do you need?"

I hold up the bag of water, the dirt slowly settling to the bottom. "The water is . . . weird here."

Howl jumps back like I've come at him with a knife. His head jerks back and forth between the cloudy water skin and the muddy river. "We have to go. Now."

He snatches the other water skin off the ground and grabs my arm, the two of us running back toward the camp. June already has my pack put together and holds it up for me.

Howl kicks dirt and dry leaves across the campsite, trying to obscure our footprints. June grabs his arm, pulling him away. "We don't have time. Run."

He nods, barely taking the time to buckle his pack across his shoulders before taking off under the umbrella trees, June and me following.

The trees are smaller here, with huge, open, grassy meadows in between thickets. Howl ducks down as he runs to keep under as much cover as possible. June scampers right behind him, pushing to go even faster. Low branches snap across my face and chest, but keeping up is so difficult that I hardly notice. After fifteen minutes of dodging branches and barely keeping sight of the black and golden heads bobbing ahead of me, I'm determined not to be the one who slows us. Unfortunately, a tree root decides differently.

I go down with a clatter. June is on me in seconds, pulling me up and towing me along like a puppy tugging on its leash. Howl slows and lets us pass him, choking down heavy breaths. I'm sullenly glad that he is out of breath too.

"Tell me what we're running away from, please!" I gasp.

Howl coughs, his voice coming out in a growl. "There are Reds here. Using growth regulators."

"Growth regulators?" I ask, looking at June.

She shrugs.

"They accelerate plant growth so much that they die. Makes it easy to clear land for crops." Howl swears as his toe catches on a rock. "When the compounds mix with water, it creates a gas cloud. You have about fifteen minutes to get out."

My eyes find the water skins hanging from the back of Howl's pack, still dripping. "It just hurts plants? Why are we running?"

"It has the added benefit of killing any Outsiders crowding up the land the City wants to use. If you aren't wearing a gas mask, the chemicals will have you vomiting within an hour. By ten, swallowing is a stretch. After a day, your muscles all start to seize up. Then it moves to your lungs. You suffocate. And it probably means there are Reds crawling all over the place through here."

A gunshot sounds over our heads. I flop to the ground. June

is beside me, crawling fast toward a cluster of thick bushes. Howl pauses to let me follow her into the underbrush. June is still moving, hand over her mouth to block the sound of her breathing. Howl puts a hand on her ankle and she stops, all of us going still.

Two sets of boots run past the bush we are hiding under, crashing through the trees. Howl grabs my hand and mouths, *Don't move.*

The boots come walking back, pausing in front of our bush. One set starts back up the path, but the other remains, scuffed toes pointed toward me.

June worms her way deeper into the bush, away from the boots. Howl tries to stop her, but the soldier kicks at the bush, making Howl go still.

We are close enough that I can see the sweat dripping down Howl's face, streaking weeks' worth of dirt into random stripes, indecision twisting his expression until the soldier calls for help. Howl grabs my hand and drags me after June, the soldier's shouts hardly penetrating the sound of blood pounding against my eardrums as he tries to shove through the bushes after us. Worming our way along the ground is quicker than trying to cut through the undergrowth; the soldier punctuates every swipe with another yell of frustration.

When we come out from under our bushes, June is nowhere in sight. Howl unbuckles his pack, throwing it to the ground, and before I realize what he is doing, he starts grappling with the clasps on mine, barely giving me time to wrench the straps from my shoulders. He swings it onto his back, grabs the waterskins with one hand, my hand with the other, and we sprint into the forest.

My feet keep catching on fallen branches, but Howl's grip on my hand keeps me upright and moving. My screaming lungs hardly even register as we duck behind a cluster of tightly knit trees. Our feet aren't quiet, but the man following us doesn't appear. The only sound I hear is my own gasping breaths. Howl lets go of me to stick his hand inside his coat, grasping something. Probably that stupid knife.

We stop behind a cluster of boulders and wait for what seems like hours. Days. My ears strain toward the trail of destruction we just left for the Red to follow. Silence.

When nothing happens, Howl uncurls from his crouch, stuffs the waterskins into the pack, and offers me a hand up. "We have to find June and get out of here."

"Why did you take my pack?"

"Because I'm better at—"

"No, why *my* pack?"

"You have all the Mantis."

"Not all of it. You had that first package that was meant for me."

"But most of it is in your pack. The Mountain needs it." He fiddles with the straps on the pack for a few minutes, adjusting them so they fit his wider frame, and I try not to think of what would have happened to me if we had somehow abandoned all of our Mantis on the forest floor.

We backtrack a bit, keeping our heads down as we listen for soldiers, evidence from our sprint obvious even to me. The trees down here bare their roots from the ground, the ropy twists looping around one another across the top of the dirt. I carefully step over these, hoping a Red won't jump out of the bushes and catch me with my foot trapped in the snakelike mess sprawled across the forest floor. Every time Howl stops to examine the ground for signs of June, my mind screams that standing still will kill us. That we need to move.

"She wants us to find her," he informs me. "She's leaving marks for me."

"The rebels must have been pretty sure of your loyalty if they taught you how to find people in the forest." I look at the tree he is examining and see a leaf pinned with sap to the branch that doesn't match. A Junis leaf. Like June. Cute. "Won't the soldiers see this? That man was calling for help," I whisper.

"Those Reds weren't exactly being careful." He grabs my arm to pull my head down as a branch in front of us starts to shake. But it's just some kind of animal, scurrying away from us up through the trees. Howl takes a quiet breath. "And they weren't wearing masks either, so I hope that means we're out of the danger zone for the gas cloud. I think they were probably just scouting, scaring away anyone left. Not clear-cutting."

I nod, flinching as two birds take off from the tree next to us. We inch along through the forest until we come to a sunlit clearing, sudden brightness blinding me, the panic of suddenly not being able to see like a hand around my throat. But when the spots clear from my vision, it's worse.

"Howl . . . what does this mean?"

Deep scars sit fresh in the bright green of new grass, scuffed footprints everywhere. Howl kneels on the ground, brow furrowed. He picks up two fist-size rocks and hands them to me. "It means June put up a fight."

The rocks are covered in blood.

CHAPTER 15

HOWL DOESN'T BOTHER WITH CAUTION ANYMORE, easily following the drag marks carved into the dirt. It only takes a few minutes before Howl slows to a walk and drops to the ground, peering through the scrub. I'm glad it isn't a question of whether or not we help June, but how. Even if I hadn't promised Liming to take care of his daughter, I wouldn't leave her to the Reds, though it could mean more bullets coming our way, more blood on the rocks.

It's nice to know Howl feels the same.

I drop next to him, catching my breath. He leans in close to me, whispering, "Do you know how to fire a gun?"

"We don't have a gun."

He pulls a handgun from his jacket and hands it to me, the magazine coming next. "Here's another unspoken truth uncovered for you. Can you shoot it?"

I narrow my eyes but save my questions for later as I fit the magazine into place. My parents both liked to shoot with the Reds for fun, but I haven't touched a gun since they were alive. No threat, bribe, or pleading would convince any Red to let me within ten feet of any firearms unless they were pointed at me. I was a fair shot when I was younger, but I've never pointed a gun at another person. Guns are for people who aren't concerned with killing, and I believe my family quota for destroying human life has been used up.

Howl pulls a round, green ball from his coat. Black buttons protrude from each end and a finely etched silver design runs from top to bottom. Two pairs of waxy-looking cones come out next. "Here, put these in your ears. They'll block out most of the sound."

"Is that a grenade? It could hurt June too."

"It's a glorified firecracker. It could knock over the tent, but mostly it'll just make enough noise to distract them. You get June. If things get hairy, use the gun."

We creep up to the campsite; just a camouflaged tent with two packs lying on the ground outside. June's cracked leather boots peek out from the open tent flap.

Howl inches into the clearing, grenade in hand. Pressing one of the black buttons, the ball breaks in half along the silver lines and he pitches the two pieces toward the tent, diving back behind the tree where I sit, wrapping his arms around me and pressing me into the rough bark.

The ground pitches and rocks around us, sprawling both of us to the ground. A blast of hot air screams past us, ruffling the trees and bushes, a few branches crashing down around us. The roaring sound in my ears dampens the shouts coming from the tent.

Howl rockets into the clearing, crashing into one of the Reds who is trying to extract himself from a tangle of fallen tent poles. I don't pause to watch, pulling the earplugs out as I pick my way through the trees to the back side of the fallen tent. A man's hand sticks through the ripped canvas, blood trickling down and dripping from his fingers. My heart stops. Howl said the grenade wouldn't hurt June, but if this man was bleeding . . . I dart in and pull back the covering. The man stares up at me blankly, as if he can't tell if he's alive or not. A metal-framed pack lies on top of him, probably what knocked him over when the tent fell. There's no sign of June.

I point the gun at the Red, feeling a little awkward about it. "She's not here, Howl."

The Red that Howl attacked is on the ground, Howl's foot planted between his shoulder blades. He looks up from tearing strips of canvas from the tent to tie his hands. "Wasn't she in the tent with that guy?"

The man stuck inside the canvas grimaces and pushes the pack off him, starting to sit up.

"Don't move, please. I don't want to shoot you," I say. Not even in the arm, which is the best I can do as far as aiming the weapon at him. "Are you all right?"

Howl steps in to tie his hands, looking at me oddly. "My, aren't you polite. This guy would have shot you without blinking five minutes ago. And he has probably beaten June to a bloody pulp."

"Just because he's forgotten that he's human doesn't mean I have." The gun is steadier now, though still pointing at his arm. I don't think I could miss with only feet between us. "Where is our friend? Tell me."

The soldier shrugs, wiping blood from his cheek. He must not realize that the blood is coming from his hand and all efforts to wipe it from his face are just making it worse. "Wouldn't be surprised if the whole southern garrison is here in five minutes. You two are as good as dead."

Howl shrugs one shoulder. "So I guess it won't matter if we just kill you now. One dead Red closer to breaking the City down." He looks at me, waiting.

There is no way I am just going to shoot this man, but he doesn't have to know that. I cock the gun, the loud *click* ominous in the quiet around us.

"Fine by me." The soldier closes his eyes and starts to hum the City anthem. Thank you, Yuan Zhiwei. Inspiring this man to die for nothing.

I turn to look at Howl, unsure, but he is running toward me. And then there's nothing.

CHAPTER 16

WHEN I OPEN MY EYES, ALL I CAN SEE IS DIRT. IT'S
brownish purple, peppered with little rocks that dig into my cheek.
I slowly move my head, trying to figure out what happened. The gun
is across the clearing instead of in my hand, and Howl is crouching
a few yards off, arms up over his head. *Why is he doing that?* I wonder,
my vision blurring around the edges. *Oh. Because there's another Red.*

The soldier pushes June in front of him, arm wrapped around her
throat, gun thrust into her messy hair. He must have heard us and
dragged June away from the tent while Howl was assessing my marks-
manship skills. Far enough away, the blast didn't knock him over.

The leather of his jerkin is coated with mud, a grayish, dirt-
streaked undershirt peeking through a few tears in the leather. His
back is to me. Perfect.

The world swirling all around me, I drunkenly roll into a
crouch, creeping toward the edge of the clearing, trying to force
my eyes to focus on the heap of branches that fell when Howl
threw the grenade. When I turn back toward the Red, Howl is on
the ground, inching toward the two tied behind him.

"Untie them both. Now." The growling voice sounds too loud, as though the man can't quite hear after the explosion.

Howl makes a sudden move toward the soldiers, but the Red's gravelly bark cuts him off short. "You do that again and she dies!"

I stagger onto my feet, ignoring a sudden need to vomit. The Red, fist full of June's snarled hair, raises her up to her feet. "I'm going to count to three. If those ties aren't cut . . ."

His deep voice grates against my ears, sending chills down to my toes. But he doesn't look around to see me swing the heavy branch into the side of his head, knocking him out.

I drop the branch and try to catch June as she crumples to the ground beneath the Red. Blood streams down her face from a broken nose and a few shallow cuts on one cheek. Her green eyes are open and scared, one bruised black.

Howl grabs one arm and I take the other, and together we drag June toward the edge of the clearing. She lets her feet trail behind us, either too shocked or too injured to help.

Suddenly I wonder why we are running away from these men. They have supplies. Bandages and food. The ground pitches under my feet and I sink down, grateful to have a moment to think this through. But when I turn to ask Howl, I'm alone.

What was I doing again? I can't remember.

My eyes burn, my eyelids suddenly very heavy. Lying down here seems like a good idea. Maybe Tai-ge will come tell me a story to chase away the bad dreams. Like the one of someone shaking me and yelling in my ears.

A light flares and my eyes spring open to find Howl's face too close to mine. He is kneeling over me, holding something that smells terrible under my nose. "Stop!" I feebly bat his hand away. "I don't need help. Where's June?"

"Safe. I carried her first. Normally I would love to sit down and chat, but there is an entire garrison of Reds within a mile and I'm pretty sure you have a concussion." He hoists me up so I'm draped across his shoulders, head and arms down on one side of his head, my legs banging against his chest on the other.

"I can walk. Put me down." It comes out in a slur, and the world starts to spin around me again.

"This is faster than you walking, believe it or not."

My head is right by his ear. From this angle he looks younger, the curve of his cheek soft and smooth. I'm breathing his hair, short and dark and smelling vaguely of sweat and campfire. It suits him. The thought seems to circle around in my head, jerking to a stop with each jarring step. He belongs Outside, all the starch and City pride stripped away. I like it.

"You know"—my voice jars with each long stride—"you aren't bad-looking." The clouds are pressing harder against my eyes and mouth, but from the inside.

"Thank you. I'm strong, too. And very, very funny." He's whispering now and things have gone darker and a few degrees cooler, as if we've walked into the shade.

My head keeps fuzzing in and out, like the scream of heli propellers as they pass overhead, the cadence twisting uncomfortably. Howl's head presses into my stomach as if it is supposed to fit there, and suddenly I am very aware of his arm around my leg, holding me balanced across his shoulders.

Heat floods my cheeks in the moment of clarity. I grasp for something to say that will distract him. "Tai-ge used to take care of me too. "

Howl doesn't answer for a minute. Then he squeezes my arm and says, "I'm glad someone did."

The black around us deepens until he stops, a bright lantern pushed up against the wall ahead of us searing into my eyes.

"Can we put that light out?" I ask, squinting. "I think it's burning my brain."

The muscles in his back and shoulders bend and flex underneath me, and suddenly I'm sitting on the ground next to another person huddled against the wall. Her eyes follow me cautiously as I scoot up closer to her, but she doesn't move away. "June?" My voice sounds tinny in my ears, and my head starts to hurt. "How did you get here?"

She glances over at Howl, hands rubbing back and forth over her arms. He bends down, handing me a leaf that leaks a syrupy sap onto my fingers. The sudden, sharp smell wafting up from the leaf burns up through my nose, sharpening my vision for a moment.

"Keep breathing. It'll clear your head." Howl's back is to us, blocking the worst part of the lamplight, though even the dim ring around him is sending slivers of pain through my head. "Talk to me." His voice is too quiet, as though the earplugs didn't quite do their job earlier. "Tell me about Tai-ge. If you can string whole sentences together, then hopefully it'll mean you aren't broken."

The pain pounding in my head starts to clear all the cottony fuzz from my brain, and I can feel my cheeks heat. "You keep bringing him up. Did you know Tai-ge?"

"Of course I did." Howl brushes his fingers along the wall, following a depression in the stone that looks too regular to be natural.

An uncomfortable feeling joins the ache in my head, trying to imagine Tai-ge and Howl together. Talking. I can't think of anything else to say, avoiding Howl's glance when he raises an eyebrow at me.

He pulls out Tai-ge's dull knife and traces along the depression in the rock wall, shavings of plaster showering down. When the line is big enough, he squeezes his fingers between the stones, and a section of the wall crumbles away. Inside is a black metal box sitting under a thick layer of dirt and broken plaster. He pulls out the box and pries it open, a water skin with about two inches of gelatinous liquid falling out.

The water skin goes to June, who just looks at it in her hands like it's something disgusting.

"It's Choke," Howl tells her. "A nutritional supplement."

"What is this place?" I ask. "How did you know . . . ?"

"We are right on the Menghu patrol circuit," Howl says as he rifles through the box, fanning the cloud of dirt that follows. "This is one of their emergency caches. I stumbled over one of their signs as I was carting June out of there."

"Menghu?" I don't think I've ever heard the word before. It sounds like an old language. One of the dead ones from before the Liberation standardized things.

"The army from the Mountain. Rebels. They have safe havens set up all through here just in case Reds catch them out in the open." Howl dumps the contents of the box onto the dirt floor. "Reds haven't found this one yet, or they would have taken the supplies."

Looking around me, I realize that we must be underground. Light from the entrance doesn't penetrate to where we are sitting, rocks fitted together like a puzzle forming the walls and ceiling. The cave continues past us, but the light doesn't reveal much. The air is cool and dry, smelling of dirt and stale sweat.

"You just . . . stumbled across something marking the cave?" I ask.

"I learned some of the signs when I was with them. I was lucky to have found it when we needed it so badly, though."

Very, *very* lucky.

Howl piles the few water skins and some dried fruit and crackers from the supplies back into the box and comes over to sit by me. Leaning in close, he whispers, "She hasn't spoken yet. I'm not sure what happened, but she's been awake since we dragged her away from the tent, so she should be okay. Even the eye."

June's eye does look pretty fantastic. What was only bluish purple before has now darkened to almost black, her entire eye encircled. She looks back calmly and whispers, "I'm not dead. I can hear you."

Howl smiles. "Good."

June tilts her head and touches her bloody nose, grimacing. "You don't know how to fix this, do you?"

"I can." Both June and Howl look at me, surprised.

"I grew up with orphans as likely to eat their spoons as their morning rice if Mantis wasn't working. The nuns didn't get too excited about anything unless bones were sticking out, so we learned to take care of one another."

June's eyes well up as I remold her nose back to how it is supposed to be, but she holds still. When I'm finished, she resumes staring at the wall. I was expecting a gasp at least. Most kids would have screamed their way through the whole thing.

"Don't touch it for a while, okay? Noses heal fast, but it won't be the same."

She just nods. Like it's happened before. Or maybe she's never looked in a mirror to know what "the same" would be. Her hands rub her arms for warmth, the Choke lying forgotten in her lap.

Howl holds another water skin full of the white jelly out toward me. I wrinkle my nose as I take it, but have no intention of gagging the slimy concoction down. My experiences with Choke have been less than appetizing.

Poking at it through the plastic, I look up at Howl. "So." I wait until he looks at me. "Grenades?"

"Not a real one." He shrugs at my black expression. "I know. We could have saved ourselves some trouble running from the Wood Rats if I'd brought it out earlier."

June looks up, scowling.

"Sorry. I mean . . . I didn't want to attract attention."

I roll my eyes, though he isn't looking at me anymore. "So you do it with hundreds of Seconds watching from upriver?"

"If they've gotten as far as our camp, they already know we're here. When they find my pack, they'll know who we are. We didn't really have time to think of a better way to get June out of there alive."

"How about the gun? Did we leave it out in the clearing?" The Red must have kicked it away from me after he knocked me down.

Howl pulls the weapon from his jacket and slides it across the dirt floor to rest near my open hand. I have no desire to touch the cool metal.

Howl's voice is wry, laughing at himself. "I can't shoot the stupid thing anyway,"

June's eyes rest lightly on the gun, but when she notices me watching her, she returns to staring a hole in the wall.

"Look, I'm sorry I didn't tell you I had it," Howl says. "I didn't know what to expect from you. Whether you had a knife up your sleeve like everyone else. Which you did, actually." He reaches into his coat pocket, touching what I can only assume is Tai-ge's knife. "Telling you was on the to-do list for today, after our chat last night." Howl's hand goes back into his jacket, fishing around in the inside pockets before coming up with another grenade. He sets it between us, the silvery pattern glinting in the lantern's dim cast. "This is all that's left. No more surprises."

"Right." June doesn't look up when I answer, her eyes suspiciously far from the gun. "No more surprises."

We huddle against the stone walls, waiting like cornered rats. Howl and I take turns keeping watch, but visions of soldiers stumbling into our cave keep the circles under our eyes even when we're off duty.

June draws a square on the floor, dividing it into smaller and smaller pieces until she has a grid in front of her. Digging into her bag of belongings, she pulls out two handfuls of pebbles and deposits them on the ground, one pile dark, one light. She inches the lantern a little closer and looks up at me.

"Weiqi?" I ask.

A nod.

"Sure, I'll play." I scoot closer to the board, relieved to have something to distract me from jumping at every noise that filters back into our hideaway. Weiqi is one of my favorite games, the one thing Mother left me that I'm not ashamed of. I love the weight of the stones in my hands, the way their smooth surfaces feel against my skin. My mother, Aya, and I would study at the board, and she'd show us where the holes were, how to attack, when to give up. Aya and I played often. But even though she was much better than I was, able to see patterns where I could not, I still relished the thoughtfulness of the game.

Mother could trounce both of us, even with only one eye on the board. I only ever beat her once. I crowed about it, refusing to play her again for weeks because I knew I wouldn't win a second time. We never did play again, because she disappeared.

June pushes the lighter pebbles toward me, carefully arranging her darker ones in a pile and setting one on the makeshift board.

Smoothing her hair behind her ears, she doesn't look up from the piece, waiting for me to make my move.

I place a pebble on the board, watching her more than the game.

June keeps her attention on the stones, rolling a pebble in her fingers across her lips as she thinks, each piece placed in quick, confident movements. Like Aya as she surveyed her kingdom of stones. About five minutes in, June's mouth curls into a tiny, tight-lipped smile. She looks up and whispers, "Trapped."

"What?" I look down to the long lines I've been making with my pieces to capture territory and realize she's right. I'm trapped. She pulls all the trapped pieces off the dirt squares, arranging them in a tidy row.

Now I am focused. This little girl can't beat me.

But within three moves, I'm trapped again. Two more and the game is over. Howl looks over from his post near the door, whistling in appreciation. "Wow. I didn't know you could lose weiqi that quickly. Remind me not to have you plan any military operations for me."

"No one believes weiqi has anything to do with battle theory anymore. Besides, I was distracted by your loud mouth-breathing."

It isn't true, though. The reason I spent many an hour staring Tai-ge down across a weiqi board was because he was studying ancient war theory. General Hong was convinced the game teaches you how to think correctly. Different battles going on all over the board, drawing in your enemy and trapping them. Blatant attacks. Feints and tricks. Defending territory. It's all there.

I stand up to stretch, my head brushing the ceiling. "You try, Howl. She's brutal."

His pieces pile up in front of June even faster than mine did. "I concede, General June." Howl gives her an elaborate bow from his seat on the floor.

"My turn again." I shove him aside and watch carefully as she sets the first piece on the lines. Eyes narrowed, I watch the light pebbles grow from lines to circles, but I can see where she is going this time. Howl cheers when I capture three of her pieces, but June just grows more and more relaxed, shooting me an impish little smile as she corners five of mine.

We are so absorbed in the game that the footsteps from outside don't register at first. Howl gives a melodramatic groan as more of my pieces slide toward June. "Were you a Hong in a past life? How did you . . ."

"It's coming from over here." A female voice. Close.

We all drop to the floor, pebbles scattering.

Howl creeps closer to the bend in the rock that shields us from the door, gun in his hand. June stays frozen on the ground next to me, the overwhelming feeling that our pieces are about to be taken flooding the cave.

The footsteps crunch closer, careful and slow. The snaps of branches under boots sound like bones cracking. "I don't see anything. Just a bunch of scrub and rocks."

The voice slinks around me, teasing goose bumps out of the skin on my arms. I'm lying so still that my muscles clench until I feel as though my body is trying to morph into something else. Breathing feels too noisy, but I'm running out of air. It seems as if the edges of my brain are crinkling and expanding.

I startle as a rock hits the inside wall, kicked by those worn boots from outside. Howl creeps closer to the door, crouched and ready.

Silence.

The soldier doesn't come in. Doesn't call for reinforcements. Doesn't leave us a bloody mess in the dust. Her heavy tread fades back into the cold whispers of the forest. Howl inches back toward us. "Gone," he murmurs.

June's eyes are wide as she pulls herself up from the ground, leaning against the cold stone in a heap. "You're loud," she informs Howl.

"Sorry. I get a little excited about weiqi. I used to play with my father. The whole family would get involved, rooting for one of us." Howl slides in next to us, our energy spent. "Didn't realize the sound would carry so far."

"Somehow I can't imagine the Chairman playing." Shock still splinters my voice into a barbed mess. "Wouldn't everyone lose to him on purpose?" Maybe weiqi is the one bright spot in their family.

Howl blinks, staring at the dirt on his hands instead of answering.

"I played with my father too." June's husky voice surprises me. She looks up skittishly, like a spooked deer waiting for the shot to sound. I catch her eye and hold it, waiting.

"He didn't turn hard, like the others." Her voice is so quiet I have to strain to hear it, even with the small space between us. "Compulsions . . . He was always sorry."

She seems so much like my sister.

The thought floats out, unbidden. June is so small and wary, too young to worry so much about dying, but with her history etched in lines across her forehead. I always tried to take care of Aya, even when they separated us at the orphanage. I still wonder, if I'd been there when SS took her over, would I have been able to save her?

"I hardly remember my parents." I can't tear my gaze away from her, bowed over the pieces. "But you remind me of my younger sister."

She shrugs and gathers up her scattered pebbles, but I swear I see her face soften. "Want to play again?"

CHAPTER 17

THE NEXT MORNING, THE SOUND OF WHISPERED voices carries into our cave. I sit up, my hand searching for Howl, who fell asleep behind me.

He isn't here.

June is a heap in her sleeping bag a few feet away, her eyes open. One hand snakes out to point toward the entrance. I nod, reaching into the pack for the gun. I've made sure I was between it and June since it emerged from Howl's coat. Just in case.

Sliding along the wall toward the cave's mouth, I let my eyes adjust to the light. It is morning, moments from sunrise. The doorway is masked by a pile of rocks and dead scrub, and Howl stumbling into it was a miracle. But some miracles do happen twice.

There are two forms crouched just outside the opening, hushed voices going back and forth.

With shaking hands, I level the gun at the one closer to me, growling in my best tough soldier voice, "On the ground. Now."

Their heads snap around toward me, the closer one casually raising his hands over his head, looking me up and down as if a gun weren't practically shoved down his throat. His hair slicks back from a face that seems to be all cheekbones and chin. Skin pale in the morning light, his black eyes are unafraid as they meet mine.

My eyes flick to the other shape and my stomach drops. Howl doesn't bother to raise his hands. He just sits there looking vaguely surprised. "Good morning, Sev. Still not sleeping well?"

I keep the gun trained on Cheekbones, trying to mask my trembling hands with the weight of the weapon. "Who's this guy?"

The stranger smiles, revealing white teeth that look a little too pointy. Like an animal's. "I'm Helix. I was out on patrol when you attacked the Reds, but I couldn't get to you until they all cleared out." Shrugging his shoulders uncomfortably, he glances up at his still-raised hands. "Are you going to shoot me or what?"

Helix. His name sounds foreign, like it came from some ancient language that died long before the Great Wars. Kind of like mine. I wait for Howl's nod before lowering the gun, but I don't loosen my grip. Helix's sharp smile gives me the creeps. "Rebel?" I ask.

"I'm a Menghu." Helix rubs the back of his neck as his hands come down. "Not a rebel."

"He's a soldier from the Mountain." Howl eyes the gun gripped tightly in my hands, and I slowly relax my hold on it. "I didn't want to wake you. Seems like the first time you've gone to sleep since we got stuck in there. Sorry we scared you."

Helix's jacket is grayish green, falling past narrow hips and buttoned up to his throat. His canvas pants are tucked into calf-high brown boots, all with a healthy coating of dirt. The front of his high collar is embroidered with a black tiger sitting on a number four.

"Sleeping with a death squad knocking at the door has me a little jittery, I guess. Speaking of which . . ." I look around. "Why are we outside?"

Helix answers, shooting a shifty look at Howl. "There are still some stragglers, but nothing I can't handle."

Something in his voice gives me the impression Helix is a little uncomfortable with Howl. Afraid? But that doesn't make sense. "Why are they out here?"

"Reds are bringing in a set of reeducation slaves to start digging a new mine." Helix's eyes brush my star brand, but he continues without comment. "Gassed the area to take care of any Wood Rats and then combed the outskirts to make sure no one was waiting for them."

"Why would they do that? Gas everyone in the area?" I ask.

Helix squints at me. "Wood Rats are a bit of a nuisance, even for us up at the Mountain. Stealing supplies, spreading diseases. Compulsions out of control. It isn't safe to let them run free through the middle of a City operation, I'd think, so they just get rid of them. I wish we could be so tidy."

The cold shrug that accompanies this account prickles at the back of my neck. Howl, June, and I had to sprint away from that gas cloud, just three more inconvenient presences that needed to be extinguished. But tidying the woods a bit doesn't seem to bother Helix at all.

Helix's voice takes on a certain brand of offhanded pride as he continues, "My patrol was close by when you set off the grenade. Dr. Yang asked us to look out for you, so I broke off to bring you in. It wasn't that difficult to find you after you made all that noise and then suddenly disappeared. There aren't any other caches this way."

Howl looks up from tracing his finger through the dirt, catches my eye, and nods to the cave behind me. I look back toward the opening and find June's wide eyes staring out at us, reflective and catlike in the dark. She edges out, holding my bag of Mantis.

I take it, thoughts in a cyclone around the half-empty bag. None of the Mantis seems to be missing. Did she know I'm infected this whole time? That I had Mantis in my pack, the medicine her family needs? But she didn't take it and run back to them.

"You're late on your dose." She glances at Howl before sinking back into the inky depths of the cave.

Helix's voice grates like sandpaper. "Wood Rat?" He stops cleaning his nails and looks up at Howl. "We going to keep her?"

"What do you mean?" Howl asks.

Helix shakes his head. "Do you even know which diseases she's carrying?"

June reemerges, this time carrying the one remaining pack from the City. She drops it at my feet and then stalks toward the trees, tripping over the rock Helix is sitting back against so it topples over, sending him into a heap on the rocky ground.

He jumps up, growling a word I don't recognize, and reaches for the knife sheathed at his hip. But Howl moves so quickly that my eyes don't believe it when Helix hits the ground.

"You want to bring me and Sev in, then I suggest you skip murdering our friend." Howl's voice is perfectly friendly, but sharp edges underneath are showing through.

"Bring you in?" Helix picks himself up, eyes blazing. His hand grips the knife so tightly his knuckles are white. "What, you get out into the forest and decide you'd be better off with the Wood Rats?"

Howl's jaw clenches and he looks at me for some reason. But

then he returns to glaring at the knife clenched in Helix's hand, waiting until the Menghu lets the weapon go. Howl's face relaxes into a cold smile, the tension melting away as he shoulders his pack. "Good choice. Come on, let's go."

Only a day and a half's walk away from the Mountain. The forest seems too quiet, with swells of twigs cracking and birds flying off for no reason as if the whole southern garrison of Seconds really is only steps behind us. All day long, my arms itch with the sense that someone's watching us, and I begin to wonder if the four of us will live to get to this magical Mountain place at all. Between the feeling that we are being followed and the scowls June is directing at Helix, the chances of survival seem slim.

When we stop to set up camp for the night, Helix's condescending lesson on correct fire-starting technique stammers to an explosive silence when he pulls two fist-size rocks out from under the top flap of his pack. "Did you do this?" His voice is sharp and quiet, eyes on June.

Silence.

Helix rubs a hand across his stubbly chin, taking a deep breath before catching Howl's eye. His mouth hangs open for a second, but he eventually just mumbles something about going to find some good tinder. June smirks at his back until he disappears behind a tree. She grabs the four water skins and heads toward the river.

Howl pulls some rope out of my pack, eyeing the tree branches above us. "Nice to see June acting like a real fourteen-year-old."

"I think we both put rocks in his pack." A smile catches at my mouth. "Helix just hasn't found the ones I put in yet."

Howl laughs as he climbs a tree, looping the rope around one of the branches. "I wish I'd thought of that."

"If I'd known you'd like the idea so much, I would have put some in your pack too. What are you doing?"

"There are gores in the area. They tend to hang out where there are more people to hunt, and I've seen scat and trails all over the place. I thought we could sleep up here on the packs." He smiles down at me from the tree, "Unless you want to see if Helix really is as tough as he says."

I shiver, remembering the huge paw prints and gouge marks in the rock just under the ledge where we slept on our first night out here. How different are things now? Howl and me talking like friends from birth, my ribs almost healed. I hand up my pack, then Helix's, watching as Howl wedges them between two branches and ties them down to form a platform.

June stomps up from the river, dumping the four water skins at my feet, one of them still empty.

"June." Her eyebrows come down at my soft tone. "I don't like him either."

Howl jumps from the tree to join our little chat, whispering, "And I'll put gravel in his sleeping bag tonight, if you two will help me distract him."

She looks from me to Howl, something close to a smile curling at the corners of her mouth. She picks up the empty water skin and heads back toward the river.

"You know, she's only two years younger than I am. My sister's age." Or at least the age she would have been, if she were still alive. It seems odd to say what I am thinking. I haven't ever talked to anyone about my family. Not even Tai-ge. He didn't seem to want to know.

"She reminds you of her. Your sister." Howl watches as June skips a rock across the placid surface of the river, waterskin on the ground next to her. "What happened to her?"

"Don't you know?" I try to laugh, as if the horrific story is some kind of joke. But the laugh wells up in my mouth like bile. "Everyone else does."

Howl doesn't smile. "But you're one of the few who *really* knows. There's a difference between truth and propaganda." He takes a step closer, touching my shoulder. "You don't have to tell me. But I'd like to know."

It's hard to look back, hard to do anything but try to stop the deluge of memories and pictures swamping my mind. I'm not allowed to talk about my sister. Not about my father. None of it. But there they are, staring at me from the back of my head, where they live, buried. I see us all together, me and Father and Mother, Aya holding my hand as we walked together, Mother playing tag with us in the First Quarter park, prodding my reserved father until he laughed and joined us. Of Aya, circles under her eyes, watching silently as they burned Father's body under the Arch. I held her hand, our palms sweaty and slipping against one another as we watched, Mother looming over him in her glass box as if she were the one who lit the fire. I didn't look. I couldn't look. I think my mind made up something even worse than what actually happened.

"She . . . Aya . . ." Saying her name out loud feels so wrong and so right at the same time. "She was quiet. Shy and reserved like my father. She didn't want people looking at her because the attention made her . . . I don't know." I look at the ground. "Curl up inside. She would only play with me." And Mother. The thought of the three of us together plays like a dissonant chord, rattling me. I hastily think of trees, of the sun, of the wind as it paints stories across my skin. Howl listens with his head cocked, silently offering to take a burden that I can't hand over, however much I wish I could. "She loved playing weiqi, just like June. I always felt like as long as we were all together, she'd be able to smile. She'd be happy and safe. I could stand between her and whatever it was that made her so afraid."

I tried to protect her. Tried to make sure the other children at the orphanage left her alone, though the nuns kept us apart. She was assigned to a different family for reeducation, but she had no one like Tai-ge to slip her candies and smile at her when it was hard. Everyone always misjudged her quiet for anger, her reserve for pride. Even at six years old.

Howl doesn't say anything, letting me think and feel without interrupting. I wish he would interrupt.

"Mother didn't give her SS. She caught it in a Kamari air strike . . . a City air strike, I guess." Why would the City want a little ten-year-old with hardly any words, hardly the gall to look anyone in the eye except for me, to fall Asleep? "Two years later, Mantis . . . stopped working. She was in a self-sufficiency class, chopping firewood, and I was right outside the orphanage, hoping to see her when she walked to the cafeteria for lunch. But instead of lunch, she came out with an ax. She was chasing one of the nuns."

I falter. It was Sister Lei Aya chased into the cold, cobbled street, brandishing her ax. And there was a bruise on Aya's cheek when they finally let me see her body later. The suspicion blurts out, something I've never been brave enough to say out loud. "One of the nuns hurt her, and SS made her brave enough to fight back."

Howl knows the rest of the story, that the Watch shot my little sister in the street right in front of me. Like I said, everyone knows. Jiang Gui-hua's daughter proving her true designation: Fourth.

Swinging an ax at the very order of women who had taken her in, clothed, and fed her when no one else would have. Traitors, the whole family.

I knew after that just what it meant to be a Fourth. It meant no one cared. No one wanted us. That they'd rather we were dead than alive. Aya was a hole burned out of my soul with only one Red bullet. I knew if I were to live, if I were to matter, I would have to wipe the brand from my skin. Become a new person. The kind General Hong would recommend for reintegration into normal society. The kind that fit. Aya was a memory I had to blur, to forget in order to keep my smile in place.

But she's there now, sharp and clear in my mind, a crack in my heart.

I look at June, still throwing rocks in the water one at a time. Howl's hand on my shoulder seems solid, as if it's bracing me. June doesn't look at all like my sister, but her silence—her fierce, angry silence—is just like Aya's, who never even for a moment believed anything they said about Mother or Father no matter how many times she had to swallow Mantis pills.

My father didn't deserve to die. He was quiet, but he loved us. He would have saved us, would have fought for us if he'd had the chance. If Mother hadn't made it so they killed him before he could. Reeducation is only for those the Firsts think they can save.

"It wasn't fair." Howl's voice is tight. "She didn't need to die. Didn't deserve it."

"It was so pointless. She was there one minute, asleep in a room down the hall, and the next day . . ." I look up at the sky, framed by the trees. It hurts too much to continue. "It doesn't matter."

"It does matter. That's why we're out here. It matters more than anything else. The people they kill for no reason. Because they're hungry or sick or can't control compulsions . . ." Howl's voice crumbles at the edges, and he clears his throat, avoiding my eyes. "Sorry. Old argument. I don't need to say it to you. I wish . . ."

But he doesn't finish, clearing his throat again instead. Pity and sorrow turn the edges of his mouth down, as if Howl knows what it means to lose people, though I don't know how he could. I stare at him, wishing I knew the right question to ask, how to open the doors to his past so he can let out whatever demons chased him from the City into the Mountain's arms. I want to know.

Howl looks toward the river, watching June. He smiles. "June's cute when she's acting human, don't you think?"

Not ready to talk about family yet. Just as much as I'm not, I suppose. So I give him an exaggerated wink, running from thoughts of my sister, of all the bad in the world just to watch June skipping rocks. That's one right thing. "Cute how? Should I sleep between you two tonight?"

At my joke, Howl falls into line with an exaggerated eye roll. He seems to understand, running right alongside me from whatever it is he's not saying out loud. "No, thank you. You can keep all the little girls to yourself."

"Are you sure? I think a few days back I remember her looking at you from across the fire with something less than outright hatred." This is more comfortable territory, my jagged edges blurring as if joking will make him forget what I said. Will make *me* forget. "Or, if she's not your type, I know a whole bunch of little girls back in the City who would wait on you hand and foot." I grab his wrist and twist his hand down, tapping the single white line there with my finger. "Even if they didn't see this."

He grabs a handful of dead leaves from the ground and rubs

them into my hair. "Because I'm devastatingly good-looking. Yes, I know."

I drop his wrist, scrubbing at the leaves to cover my embarrassment. I never said anything about devastating good looks. What I said after the explosion . . . I had a concussion. It doesn't count.

Helix's voice muscles in between us from behind the tree line. "Come over here, Sev. You can try starting the fire tonight."

It doesn't matter that I can't remember a time when I *didn't* know how to start a fire. I have to get away from the mischievous smile that is sending pulses of electricity through my chest. I sit with my back to Howl, cheeks burning.

CHAPTER 18

WHEN NIGHT FALLS, SLEEP WANDERS AWAY FROM me. The prickly feeling of eyes watching us still leaves me feeling restless and exposed. Helix and Howl volunteer to take turns watching, setting up on the ground to give us more room up in the tree.

My breath freezes in an icy mist above me, but I'm hot inside the sleeping bag, squashed against June. Howl's sleeping bag is probably in some Second's tent right now, so we only have three. Helix volunteered to share, but no one took him up on it. It seems impossible that the outside of the fabric could be so cold when inside it's like sitting in a campfire.

June's face next to me is calm and childlike in sleep. Innocent. Like Aya. Like my mother looks in her box above Traitor's Arch.

Sometimes Mother is just a silent form on the other side of her glass display case in my memories. A doll. Left up on the shelf to remind me of games, of pretending, of silly stories whispered in the dark. She's a pain under my ribs, older and deeper than Tai-ge. The skin has healed over the festering wound, but it spews out in painful spurts when I remember.

Mother's crimes are the reason I spent the last eight years branded a Fourth. The reason I'm out here, peeling the blotchy shadows for movement, waiting for a shot to be fired. She's handed me a life of sleepless nights worrying my roommate's Mantis would stop working. Of being friends with Tai-ge, but not allowed to ever think of more than that. Why I have to worry about broken bottles and glass in my mouth, about the monster buried inside of me.

But Kamar is just a fairy tale. Turned around, does that mean that I escaped because of her? I'm out here with Howl because of the things she did.

If she was a rebel, she couldn't have sold the City's coordinates to the Mountain. They would have known where the City was already from anyone who had escaped the City or the farms. And why would she have left a bloody trail from house to house on the Steppe, First Circle members dead in their beds? What was the point? Why would she have gone back to the City at all after infecting me?

No matter what she did or why, I can't turn Mother's story into some kind of fairy tale. Things aren't going to line up no matter what angle I choose to look at them, because in real life, people aren't separated into black and white like pieces on a weiqi board, good and evil.

There is one thing that is black and white, though. Her hands pushed the needle into my arm, her fingers put the SS monster inside of me. Even if everything from those weeks is a fog of paralyzed nightmares, I do remember the stab of pain, and the feel of my mother hovering over me. She's been rotting away in the deepest recesses of my mind since the hazy days after I woke up, with Seconds guarding my bedroom door and Father being dragged away, head down and hopeless. It's too late to bring Mother out now and hope the decay will have magically disappeared.

I slide down the trunk of the tree, frozen leaves crackling under my weight as I land. Helix rolls over, his eyes softly touching me in the moonlight. But he just pulls his sleeping bag back over his head.

Howl sits up a few feet away, wrapped in his coat. "Something wrong?" There's a line of dirt along his neck that looks smudged into a cross shape, kind of like Parhat's scars. He tries to look down to see what I'm staring at, rubbing at his neck until the dirt is gone.

"Nothing I can put my finger on. Something has just seemed off all day."

One side of his mouth quirks in a half smile. "Sick of walking behind that?" He jerks his head toward Helix.

I shake my head. "More like we are being followed."

He nods, eyeing the trees around us. "I'm with you on that. Will you keep watch up there with June? Just in case?"

The casual agreement takes me by surprise. "You mean just in case it's her family?"

Howl shrugs, meeting my eyes squarely. "Yes. But even if we get attacked by a bunch of hungry gores, it will be nice to have you up there out of reach."

I smile a little. "Don't think I can take care of myself?"

"I mean, if your aim is half as good as you claim . . ."

What he's saying sinks in slowly, dread flowing through to my toes. "You don't have the gun down here?"

Howl's eyes open wide. "I thought you had it. Is it up . . . ?"

I race back to the tree before he can finish his sentence. The twigs and branches scratch my face and arms as I scale the trunk to get back to our packs, back to June. But the platform is bare. She's gone.

"Howl!" My hands are sweaty, slipping against the plastic fabric of the pack as I search for the gun, but come up empty. All but four of the Mantis pills are gone as well. "We have a problem!"

He doesn't answer. "Howl?"

I stick my head over the edge to look and my heart stops. Howl is kneeling in a pool of yellow light, a gun inches from his forehead.

Cas and Parhat stand below me, each with a gun trained on my friend. Parhat looks even more terrifying than before, eyes boring into Howl like he's breakfast. A shudder buzzes through me as I realize that might be the plan.

Tian's voice sings out from the trees, playing down my spine like the out-of-tune strings of a guzheng. "You can come down from there, Wenli. Sev. Whatever you're calling yourself. And bring your new Menghu friend down with you."

Helix? My eyes find his sleeping bag, covered with leaves. Empty.

Howl's eyes catch mine from below and his head gives a miniscule shake. He returns to watching the gun leveled at his nose, almost cross-eyed. "What do you want? We don't have anything of value."

Cas ignores him, his raspy, barbed-wire croon reaching up to wrap around my throat. "We don't need you or your friend here all in one piece, girly. He's going to be missing a leg if you don't get down here right now."

"Okay!" I yell. "I'm coming down."

I take my time, crawling to the other edge of the pack, looking for something that might do as a weapon. A handful of quicklights?

Cas and Parhat would have to lean down and let me stick it in their eyes for the broken glass to do any good. The pack has a metal frame, but after a moment of my fiddling, Tian loses patience.

"I've seen a one-legged rabbit move faster than you up there. You get that rebel down here or you'll see what I mean."

"Cas!" June's husky voice floats into the light. "Leave them alone. I told you already, they aren't worth a brush with the Menghu."

Cas's head swings around, trying to pinpoint her voice. "And I told you, you dirty little mouse, that these folks will fetch quite a ransom with the rebels. We could be set for months. Years, even, now that the new kid is here to get us to the Mountain . . ."

June steps into the dim circle of light cast by the quicklights, mouth screwed into a grimace. "You won't get anywhere near the Mountain." She points to me and Howl. "These two are being hunted by both sides. Between the Menghu and the Reds, you'll be dead before you see a single pill. I took all they've got. It's the best you're going to get if you want to stay alive."

Tian strides forward, reaching a hand out to grab her. June jumps away, pulling Howl's gun from the waistband of her pants, cold metal shaking in the dim light. "Don't. Touch. Me."

Hate twists June's face into something foreign, my insides clenching at the bared emotion on her face. What did Tian do to her?

The old woman's leathery face creases with dislike. "You gonna shoot the only mother you've ever known? Put that down."

The little girl skips backward, away from the advancing Wood Rat. "You are *not* my mother. If you even *touch* Howl or Sev—"

Parhat lunges for her, but his cackling laugh cuts off with the sound of a gunshot.

June looks around wildly for the shooter. Cas's screech pierces my eardrums. More shots ring out, and suddenly the ground is a mass of people running, tripping, swearing. I lose my grip on the packs and fall into the mess, landing on something soft and bony, smelling of rancid sweat. Rolling away, I open my eyes.

It's Parhat, mouth open in a surprised yell that never hit the air. Blood steams up through the cold as it seeps through his hair, dripping down into his ear. Cas's body lies facedown next to him, their quicklights on the ground between us.

I pick one up and immediately find Tian, lying prone a few feet away. Her eyes stare up slightly cross-eyed into the night, almost as though she's trying to see the bullet hole between her eyes. Howl is gone.

"What . . . *happened?*" My voice sounds crackly and unreal in my ears, my panic rising in the growing silence. "Howl! Where are you?"

Helix jumps out from behind a tree, sprinting toward me. A manic smile tears his face in two as he yells, "You're next, sweetheart!"

My body moves before I can even think, crashing low into his legs and twisting so I land on top of them. He covers his face with one arm as he falls, and I take the half-second opening, scrambling up to dig one knee into his back. It takes three slams of his hand into the rocky ground before he lets go of the gun, fingers crunched and bloody.

He pulls me over, rolling on top of me and pinning me to the ground with a knee in my ribs. Lifting my head and shoulders off the ground, he smashes me back down. "What is wrong with you, Sev? Your little Wood Rat is going to get away!"

The sentence ends abruptly as the butt of a gun connects with his skull. He seems to fall on top of me in slow motion, head floating down to crack against my shoulder.

Then Howl is on the ground next to us, pushing Helix off me. "Sev! Are you all right?"

A breath rasps in my lungs as my throat refuses to open. He isn't gone. Alive. His voice is in my ear, urgent and too loud, but I don't pull away.

I sit up, coughing. Inspecting Howl, I try to see if he is hurt, and I can see he's doing the same to me. I can't look away from him, knowing the moment I do, all I will see is death sprawled all around us. Helix did not spare anyone.

"Where is June?" I'd thought Helix was going to shoot *me*, but I suddenly realize he must have been after her or I'd be dead. Fear pours over me in a white-hot sheet. Those shots seemed too accurate for him to have missed one little girl.

Her voice splinters out from the trees, watery and broken. "Here. I'm here."

I breathe out the air frozen in my lungs in relief. We feel our way to her voice. She is hovering over one of the bodies, twisted where he fell, a bullet through the side of his head. Liming.

I close my eyes, and it's *cold. Sickly yellow light swirls all around me, the smooth cement bruising my knees and feet from kneeling too long. He's flopped on the polished floor, buried by the cheers and jeering insults from the crowds behind us. His eyes are open, watching me.* The memories I've long blocked hammer at my brain.

June's stifled sob tears my eyes back open and I kneel next to her, knowing there is nothing I can do to help. My hand on her shoulder can't fill the hole ripped through Liming.

"He was trying to help us." Her voice is numb.

Burying her face in my shoulder, June holds on to me as if I'm

the only thing keeping her alive, anchoring her to this world. I'm
not even surprised when Howl's arms wrap around both of us, and
I can feel his tears hot on my cheeks.

The morning breaks red and bloody.

June leaves before sunrise, appearing back in camp with a tarp
wrapped around some long branches and a fire starter from Cas
and Tian's campsite. We clear a space in the leaves and grass,
holding the blue fabric down with a circle of rocks. Dragging her
father onto the tarp, she covers him with the pine needles and
wood. She stands for a moment at his feet, head bowed. When her
eyes spark open, she lights the fire.

I watch for a moment, his soul ascending with the smoke,
finally free from SS.

Back in the camp, she gathers her sleeping bag into her knap-
sack. Extracting the last bag of dried meat from my pack, she
looks at me with a question in her eyes.

"You can have it." I nod. "But don't leave us. Please. Come to
the Mountain."

Her eyes find Helix, asleep by the tree. His hands are tied
behind his back, but it won't last. We can't kill him as easily as he
killed her family. Some of Tian's hardness rolls over June's face
like a mask, and she just shakes her head.

"What do you want us to do with the rest of them?"

"Leave them for the gores."

Before she leaves, she presses a Junis leaf into my hand and
says, "When you get out of there, find me." And with that, she
turns and heads off into the forest.

She doesn't look back.

PART III

PART III

CHAPTER 19

HELIX RUNS HIS FINGERS ALONG THE ROUGH EDGES
of a cave opening, the mouth jagged like broken teeth. He peers at
the stones until his fingers find a blemish, a patch that is lighter than
the speckled rock around it. He melts forward into the darkness and
goose bumps prickle down my arms. Helix belongs in the dark.

Howl's hand is a comforting weight on my shoulder. "He was
after June, you know."

I look at him, eyebrows raised.

"You were in the middle. June is an Outsider. A Wood Rat.
Helix doesn't . . ." He shakes his head. "No. I'm not going to
defend him."

I nod. I already know this, and it doesn't make what Helix did
any better. Steeling myself, I force my feet to move toward the
cave, my toes dragging against the hard-packed dirt in protest.
The image of Helix's animal smile as he points his gun at my little
sister twists in the shadows. *June. Not Aya. My sister is dead.*

Together, we step into the mouth. The light spot is too dis-
tinct to be natural. It looks like the outline of a cat.

"Menghu." Howl's hand lines up next to mine on the stone. "It's their sign. The cache we hid in was marked like this too."

I fill my lungs until it hurts, until I'm about to burst. *Mantis. This is the only way I get Mantis.* "Let's do this. Before I run."

Howl stares up at the opening as if he isn't sure he wants to go in either, but then nods and leads the way.

Musty air breaks over us like ice water, sinking into my skin and leaving me shivering. The cave ceiling slopes lower and lower the farther we go, until Howl's head and shoulders hunch. Helix breaks a quicklight in front of us, his crouched outline glowing red instead of the cheery yellow I remember from City quicklights. The tunnel drills deep into the rock, twisting so the light is just a suggestion, almost a memory, ahead of us. For once, my imagination stays cold.

I haven't had a hallucination since we came across the frozen pile of soldiers. The bleeding eyes of the dead patroller paint themselves into the black all around me, and I shake my head with a wince at the memory. But it goes away. The dark is just . . . dark.

After what seems like hours of stumbling after Helix's red glow, I startle back when a bright blue light flashes in front of me and a luminous rectangle patch appears in the rock wall. Helix presses his hand to the telescreen, saying, "Lan Helix."

A telescreen? They have those up on the Steppe, maybe in the Sanatorium here and there, but there's not many of them. How can the Mountain just casually leave one Outside to monitor the door?

A cool female voice whispers through me, "Lan Helix, Menghu. Within assignment."

Howl steps up to the bright screen. "Sun Howl."

The female voice doesn't answer for a moment, but the confirmation comes. "Sun Howl, Menghu. Within assignment."

Howl pulls me up to the light, gently pressing my hand against the telescreen next to his. "Say your name," he whispers.

"Jiang Sev." I flinch when the screen pulses blue under my hand. It's a degree or two warmer than the stone around us.

The voice whispers again, "Jiang Sev. Under supervision. Sun Howl responsible. Please immediately process."

The telescreen goes black. Warm air rushes out into the cave, and the darkness ahead of us changes to twilight. Twenty feet in, a light clicks on overhead. The pebbled dirt under our feet changes to metal grates and the smooth rocky walls are swallowed by blue-painted cement.

Howl hangs back, as if he knows I wouldn't be able to stomach walking with Helix where I can't keep an eye on him. We stop when we get to a branch in the hallway. Helix catches my eye and winks, taking off down the hallway on the left without looking back. I repress a shudder.

He didn't say anything when he woke up this morning. Nothing about June being gone, not a word on the four dead Wood Rats. He just grinned an awful, sharp-toothed smile at Howl and led out.

The farther we walk, the less comfortable I feel. After weeks of being Outside, the low ceilings feel too close. The tons of dirt and rock above me feel heavy and unstable, as though the whole place could come tumbling down on our heads at any moment.

The hallway ends with a door marked in bright orange block characters: QUARANTINE.

Howl pushes the door open for me, both of us blinking in the eye-wrenching bright lights of the small room. Windows threaded with metal wire cover the upper half of one wall, looking over five uniformed men sitting at desks. The blue paint on the walls is scratched and dented, as though a gang of angry kids took to the place with shovels.

A young man about my age walks up to the nearest window and presses a button on the desk in front of him. His voice buzzes through the glass, lips not quite syncing with the words. "Nice to see you, Howl. Jiang Sev, I'm Raj. Dr. Yang gave us most of what we need for you to stay."

I lean over to Howl and whisper, "Didn't you say anyone could come in here? As long as they have someone to vouch for them?"

He shrugs. "I don't think everyone who walks in here is as good-looking as we are." He points to a deep dent in the wall, as if someone punched it repeatedly. "Or as well mannered. Must keep them separate at first."

Raj continues, "I'll give you your bunk information and a schedule to go with your assigned collective in just a minute, and if you'll stand still, the computer's snapping your pictures for ID cards. Also, we'd like to do all the testing before we get you settled in."

Howl scratches at his face, several days of beard lining his chin. I think it looks nice, but from all the scratching, I'm pretty sure he's missing the First-grade electric razor he abandoned with his pack. "Not just SS levels? What other tests do you need?"

"Encephalitis lethargica levels first, of course, but we also need to do immunizations, blood typing, a basic physical . . . nothing too exciting." Raj consults a clipboard, checking something off. "Howl, your last tests were updated three years ago. We'll just need levels from you."

Howl quirks his head to the side, eyes narrowed. "Are all the other tests new? I don't remember having my blood drawn before."

"No. This is standard procedure. There might be special

requests from Dr. Yang, but I didn't see anything out of the ordinary."

Raising my hand to get Raj's attention, I cut in. "Whether it's standard or not, you try to draw my blood right now, all you're going to get is dirt. Can we clean up first? I smell like I haven't taken a bath in more than a month. Because I haven't."

Raj blinks. "I suppose that can be arranged. I'll take you down to the Outside showers. You've taken Mantis within the last ten hours, Sev?"

Dr. Yang didn't leave anything out. I nod.

The Outside shower turns out to be one booth, one hose tangled on the floor, no soap, and no door. Next to the shower there's a sink and a squat toilet. From the state of the floor, I'd be surprised if soap of any kind has ever touched the place.

Howl pulls the pack from his shoulders and grabs one of the towels Raj gave us from my arms. "I'll keep watch for you if you do it for me." He snags the towel on a rusted hinge that must have held a door once upon a time, pulling it across the entrance and covering his eyes with one hand. "Won't look, I promise."

Even with that convincing promise, I can't properly enjoy the lukewarm water pouring down over my hair and back. Howl might keep his eyes covered, but the room opens to a hallway.

The time Outside has left me with dirt sunken into my skin, lining all of my joints, and embedded under my cracked nails. It might take weeks to get it all off. Years. Bars and bars of soap, if they have it here. I sigh as I turn off the water. The rusty stain on my pinkie under the ring looks diseased, as if the old metal is causing my finger to rot. I take off the ring and scrub at my tarnished finger. Tai-ge's face swims up through my thoughts, but I don't put the band back on. My past is dead. It has no place here.

Raj walks in just as Howl steps into the booth. "Is everything fitting all right?"

My uniform is too big. I'm pretty sure someone owned it before it came to me, maybe several someones. The loose-fitting pants brush the floor even when I'm standing on my toes, the green canvas fabric frayed at the hem and hip pockets. The black T-shirt has a hole in one sleeve, but I can't argue with clean. The ring goes into my pocket. "It's fine."

Raj's eyes dart toward the shower as Howl starts to hum. "This is your schedule and access card." He hands me a small white envelope. "That's so you can eat before we insert your ID chip."

The card sports a picture on the top left side: me with a healthy coating of dirt and leaves, looking slightly cross-eyed. Great. I take solace in the fact that Howl's card makes him look like he might be drunk.

"I'll just . . . wait." Raj glances at the shower again, water flowing out from under the towel. "I'll get you to the correct wing for your collective."

Howl's head appears above the towel, muddy trails of water weeping down his face. "Don't bother, Raj. I'll show her. Where are you headed, Sev?"

I unfold the papers from the envelope, trying not to blush at Howl's nonchalance about being naked two feet away from us. Even with the towel. "Menghu. Like Helix? Aren't they military?"

"Yes." Howl sticks his head back under the water, washing away the last of the mud. The shower key squeaks as he turns the water off. "Good luck with them. They're all very . . . enthusiastic."

Raj doesn't quite smile. "There are five collectives," he supplies in answer to my unspoken question. "I'm part of Nei-ge.

Administration and leadership. And . . ." He glances up as if there should be something to look at in here besides dirty tile. ". . . late for a meeting. I'll just take Sev up to get her testing done so I can set you two loose."

"Can we talk to Dr. Yang about that? Sev is afraid of needles."

I glance back at him sharply. Afraid of needles? Any infected in the City has had enough needles jammed into them not to care anymore. Look at someone funny and suddenly your Mantis dose needs to go up. Immediately. But I don't say anything.

Covering my eyes, I toss the last dry towel into the shower. Raj picks up the clean uniform meant for Howl from the top of my dirt-encrusted pack and hands it over. The pack seemed cleaner than the floor.

"I can ask, if you want." Raj's voice is uncertain. "I know General Root and Dr. Yang were both very interested in her levels, though."

Howl walks out of the shower fully dressed, rubbing the water from his hair. "Last I checked, SS isn't contagious. She isn't going to infect anyone by walking too close."

"No, but . . ." Raj trails off as we walk out the door, leaving him alone in the Outside showers.

CHAPTER 20

I HAND THE ENVELOPE TO HOWL AND HE STEERS me down another blue hallway that ends with a heavy metal door. He pushes a button in the wall and the door slides open to reveal a tiny, mirrored room. Shiny silver buttons line up by the door, numbered one to eight. Howl pushes number five, the heavy metal door closing slowly. As soon as the door shuts, my stomach drops and I have to slap my hand against the wall for balance. The floor is moving.

"It's an elevator, Sev. Don't you remember elevators from the First Quarter?" Howl asks.

I shake my head. Fuzzy pictures of wood-paneled rooms just like this one flick through my mind, but I must have blocked out this gut-wrenching sensation. I do, however, remember walking up nine flights of stairs to get to my station at the cannery every day.

The door slips back open and my breath catches in my throat. The room beyond is big enough to feel like we're going back Outside, large enough that I'd have to yell to talk to someone on the other side, and ceilings so high I can't actually see them from inside the elevator. Shiny stone walls make a perfect circle around the perimeter, a stairway across the room hugging the bald rock, leading up to balconies and hallways. Windows and openings pepper the walls above us, the highest almost too far to see. When I take in more of the room, I realize there are actually four staircases dividing the large, circular space into quarters. Bright circles of light decorate the white and blue tiled floor. Stepping out of the elevator, my eyes follow the shafts of light up to an impossibly high ceiling in the stone.

"This is the Core." Howl smiles, looking around.

It's as though we're standing deep in a dead volcano's belly, its slack mouth above us turned into skylights. The stairways and window and balconies make me feel as though I've stumbled into an ant nest, the rock above me tunneled through to make way for the bustle of people living underground.

Howl points up toward a large panel of glass set into the stone wall, far above the reaches of the stairways, the glass surface too full of reflected sunlight to see through. "That floor is all greenhouses. They're up high, where the windows can go all the way Outside." He smiles again, as though he's missed seeing this place. "If we ever end up stuck down in here at least we'd have enough to eat. As long as you don't mind being a vegetarian. There are chickens in here somewhere, but they only let us eat the eggs."

"Where's the marketplace?" I ask, thinking of the City's bustling center with comrades trading fabric and canned goods. Everything here is so clean and polished, as if no one has their own place to make a mess.

Howl shakes his head. "No official trade. Everything's issued by Nei-ge according to need. Clothing, food, shoes and socks, paper and ink, everything. Everyone really is equal here."

In the very center of the Core, steps sink down into a circular amphitheater. A large skylight creates a beam of light that falls in a hard circle across the entire sunken portion of the floor, more than ten times longer across than I am tall. The bright light bounces off a gold seal set into the red stone: a large star, with four smaller ones lined up next to it.

"It's left over from Before. Secret military base of some kind, I think. At least I'm guessing from all of the telescreens and the tech and how well it's defended and hidden. We didn't have anything so extensive up in the City, except maybe here and there in First laboratories." Howl nods toward the symbol. "Whatever country was stationed here must have crumbled just like everyone else when SS came through. Places like this were safe from the bombs, so the people inside survived while people Outside turned into monsters."

Monsters. "You don't think . . . Helix?" I stumble over the words, wanting it to be true. At least then I could understand. If shooting at June was a compulsion . . .

"Is infected? No." Howl scratches at his scruffy chin, watching my face, but doesn't elaborate.

We walk toward the drop in the floor, weaving through streams of people flowing into the room from large glass doors. Smells of steamed bread and cooking vegetables waft through the air, reminding me that the only things in my stomach for the past month have been dried, stale, or dirty from being dug out of the ground. People accumulate under a large opening in the stone, wooden beams forming a triangle around a counter, workers passing out plates of food. Groups of men and women sit down on the amphitheater steps, eating and talking.

Something strikes an odd chord. Color. In the City, this would have been a sea of black or gray hair, and varying degrees of olive skin, but here in the Mountain I see olive and pink and brown, and hair that burns gold, white, gray, red, and black. And . . . I like it. I thought it would be hard after a lifetime of fighting invisible Kamar, of propaganda and classes on how to detect genetic deficiency. But these people look like . . . people. As though they belong together. Like I could belong too.

A few of the sitters are staring back. One is even pointing. A ripple goes through the crowd around us until twenty people or more are all unabashedly staring in our direction. The stirrings of hope inside me dim a few watts. *Maybe there's more to belonging here than just walking in.*

"Friendly bunch, aren't they?" I remark.

Howl steps between me and the crowd of uncomfortable stares. "Let's go find your room."

I nod, skin crawling as hundreds of eyes follow us as we walk out.

The halls leading up to Menghu dormitories sport the same calming blue as below, but a telescreen runs the length of every hall. Back in the City, telescreens were for Firsts. And only the lucky ones.

There are three beds in my room, two of them stacked in a bunk and made up with blue sheets, a white blanket neatly folded at the end. The last bed is just a bare mattress, jacked up on stilts above a chest of drawers.

When I walk in, a girl jumps up from one of the beds. She's tall. Almost as tall as Howl, with dirty-blond hair tied back into a ratty ponytail. Her face is heart-shaped and would be pretty if not for the murderous glare that immediately focuses on Howl. "You aren't allowed in here. Men sleep on the other side of the dormitories."

Howl holds up my room assignment. "Argue with Root. It says right here that I'm supposed to be your new roommate."

"Get out!" Rosebud mouth pinched into a frown, the girl jabs a finger into his chest, making the bones laced into a bracelet around her wrist clack against one another. They aren't carved into beads or anything, just bones. I rub my wrist as if the bones are touching me instead of the girl, the last bits of some dead thing up against my skin.

I think she means to push Howl right out of the room, but he doesn't move, trying very hard not to laugh instead.

Before I can intercede, a soft giggle has me spinning around to see another girl sitting on the other bed. She looks about my age, brown hair cut in a close outline around her face. Her light brown eyes are cutely pretty over a flat nose.

Both girls are caked with dirt.

I clear my throat. "I think he means *I'm* your new roommate."

Howl's lips purse in confusion, "No, I don't mean that at all. I'd be a terrible babysitter if I let you stay here by yourself, Sev. Don't you remember? I'm responsible for you until they decide you aren't dangerous." He turns to the blonde, a snarl still wrinkling her nose. "Which she is, actually. So I'm planning to stay."

"Sev?" The blonde flicks a muddy strand of hair out of her face, eyes now focused on me. They're blue. "You're Jiang Sev."

Unease splashes over me like a bucket of ice water. Before I can answer, she spins back to Howl. "That would make you . . ."

"Howl," he says, nodding. "I'm not surprised you've heard of me. Most people have."

She shrugs. "No. I was going to say—"

"—that your name is?"

She blinks at him, not even remotely charmed. "Cale. And my roommate is Mei. Menghu, Fourth Company."

She smoothes her long coat down over her hips, a twin to the one Helix was wearing, dirt and all. Same tiger and number four, except the embroidery on hers is red. Mei jumps up to stand at her shoulder, which is as far as she comes. "She wants you to tell us how amazing we are. She spent years training to be a scout. And now she's training me."

"Are you important enough to get a ration of soap? I think Sev is going to start purposely spreading skin diseases if we don't find some soon." Howl raises his eyebrows at me.

"You're a fighter?" Cale's fingers brush the tiger on her collar as she looks me up and down. "I thought 'Jiang' was a dirty word in the City. If I were a Red, I wouldn't have let you anywhere near the army."

"How do you know who I am?" I press my lips together before the less-polite questions brewing in my throat can come out. If she can slaughter four people in under a minute like Helix, I can stick to polite for now.

Mei answers, full lips framing a very wide mouth. "Your mother, of course. Jiang Gui-hua is a legend. She stood up to the City. Tried to open the walls so Outsiders could have Mantis."

"That isn't exactly the story they tell in the City." I walk out without waiting for a reply.

Footsteps behind me mean Howl is following. After a minute, I turn and wait for him. "Where are we supposed to be going?" The telescreen on the wall flashes a crude pink smiling face, as if it can sense how annoyed I am and is trying to calm me down.

"Right now? How about in here." He grabs my hand and drags me through a doorway. A dusty bunk bed covered by a pile of threadbare quilts is the room's main occupant. Howl pulls a chair down from a stack in the corner, sliding it over to me. "You're upset."

"I'm fine. Let's go get lunch; I'm starving," I say.

"Look, Sev." Howl unfolds another chair and sinks down into it with a sigh. "I didn't tell you about your mother's connection to the Mountain."

I pull my eyes up from the floor. For some reason I thought walking in here would be new. That fitting in would be easy. Just another refugee. But she was here first. "I didn't ask. I was afraid of what you would say."

Howl glances down at the chair I have yet to occupy. "Do you really hate her that much?" Something in his voice makes me sit down and look at him. There's a razor edge hidden under there somewhere, something rattled. "She wasn't the monster they paint her to be in the City. And . . . she's your mother. Doesn't that mean anything?"

I can't meet his eyes. It does matter. But some things matter more. "She *was* my mother. But she chose something else."

"Well, she isn't going to go away. She's a hero to these people. She even gave you a . . . a Mountain name. Her ties must run back before you were even born."

Then all the accusations against her must be true. Asleep for betraying the City. She chose the Mountain over me. Named me for these people, then left me behind, sick from a disease she gave me.

Howl's hand settles on my knee. "Look at me, Sev. We're still on the same team. On our own side. Walking in here didn't change anything. But give this place a chance. I'll walk right back out with you if you decide that you can't stay."

"You want to go live Outside? Smelly tent, rocks in our

sleeping bags, and a Seph to keep you company? And best of all, no soap." I shake his hand with mock severity. Like I can pick up and leave when I've got SS waiting just on the other side of my skin. "I'm in. Wood Rats until we die."

"I'll cook if you clean. We'll build a tree house."

The banter twists the anger out of me. "I wasn't lying about being hungry," I say. "Can we get something to eat before I turn into a crabby old lady?"

Mock horror splashes across his face. "Let's run."

CHAPTER 21

"NEI-GE, JIAOYANG, ZHUANJIA, YIZHI. AND Menghu you already know about," Cale informs me in a bored voice, watching as I take a bite of apple. The names of the collectives all sound as if they're words I should know but have forgotten, each with an ancient sort of twang. "This is the kitchen, if you haven't figured that out." She shoots a look at Howl that clearly implies how unexcited she is to be babysitting me. That, if more babysitting is required, the consequences will be bloody.

"Right, I could just show her . . ." Howl trails off at Cale's glare.

"That isn't what Zhuanjia asked for. They said I was supposed to give her a tour. I'm giving her a tour."

The kitchen ceiling is high, one end a counter that opens into the Core, where plates are being handed off to people waiting in line. I take another bite of apple and set my empty plate down next to a sink, dodging a group of brown-clothed workers cutting vegetables into bite-size pieces.

"You'll end up in here at least once a week for service." Cale points over to the soapy mounds of dishes. "Zhuanjia oversees the actual cooking, of course. They do all the technical work around here. Cooking, gardening, maintaining the transports and telescreens. Some things everyone can help with, so they just supervise. Like in the kitchen. But don't expect service duty in the Heart or anything."

"The Heart?" I smile at her, but she just rolls her eyes.

"The control rooms." Cale points up toward the high ceiling, where all the windows and walkways poke out through the shiny rock walls of the Core. "All the defense systems, transports, telescreens, and patrol communications sync back there. Even the lights have a grid up there, so they can see where problems are and fix them. Nei-ge offices are also up in the Heart."

As we walk out into the Core, I catch a girl in yellow frantically gesturing toward her ear, pointing out my birthmark to her friends. Mother's birthmark. I sigh. Different people, same reaction.

Cale leads us across the Core, rose-colored evening light filtering in through the skylights. "Nei-ge is partly administrative, but all the leaders are elected from each of the collectives."

"And the other two? Jir-something?" I ask.

Cale swats another green-coated girl on the behind as we walk by, the Menghu jumping away. When she sees it's Cale, her face relaxes, smiling when Cale rolls her eyes toward us. "Do you mean Yizhi? They're medics. Jiaoyang does primary education and research."

"How did I end up in Menghu?" I ask, trying to ignore the girls in yellow trailing behind us. "I can point a gun, but that isn't exactly difficult."

"Everyone in this zoo can shoot a gun." The new voice turns me around. "We thought Menghu would appeal to you because of your history with the City."

The newcomer's grandfatherly face creases in a friendly smile. His gray-green military jacket matches the ones I've seen all over the Menghu dorms, but the canvas doesn't quite fit, loosely falling from his shoulders and hanging in baggy folds down past his stomach and hips. Instead of an outline of a tiger at the collar, the rounded edges are embroidered with a simple square on each side, like the space between pieces on a weiqi board. He has dimples. Like Tai-ge.

"General Root!" Another of those foreign-tasting names. Eye rolls gone, Cale gives a deferential bow. "I was just about to bring them up to meet you, sir."

General Root's iron-gray head gives Howl a brief nod. The woman a step behind him gives Howl a nod too. Her skin is ebony dark. "Jiang Sev, welcome to the Mountain. I'm Jen Child, in charge of Menghu operations."

I blink, trying to keep my eyes respectfully on the floor when facing someone so important instead of peeking at the woman as she smiles at Howl. She's beautiful, her wide-open eyes confident when they switch from Howl to me, as though she knows I have never seen someone with coloring like hers before and doesn't care.

Trying to cover my awkwardness, I mimic the General's nod, but his slight pause tells me this was not the correct response. "Thank you," I say, trying to fill the silence. "It's nice to be out of the cross fire."

"Helix tells me you stumbled into more than your fair share of it," the General says. "Get used to it, because the southern garrison is tearing the area apart looking for you."

"They sent the entire garrison out to find us? And failed?" Howl rubs his fingers through his hair with a cocky smile. "Makes you feel good about yourself, doesn't it, Sev?"

I ignore him. "And the . . . Outsiders? June's family?"

"June? Oh. The Wood Rat you dragged out here." He turns to Howl. "I'm glad Helix was able to take care of that situation."

I feel my eyes narrowing, but General Root doesn't give me a chance to respond, focusing his attention on Cale instead. "Take Jiang Sev to get those tests done. Dr. Yang is practically compulsing with impatience. You"—he points at Howl—"I need upstairs. Come on."

Howl hangs back. "I'll finish walking through with Sev, just to be sure she's comfortable." He doesn't shrink under General Root's stern gaze. "Raj mentioned that Yizhi wanted my SS levels anyway. Might as well do it now."

The General gives him a small nod, then walks with Jen Child toward the mirrored elevator doors. Cale immediately steers us down a white hallway that smells of disinfectant, then through a set of double doors marked LAB. The girl sitting behind the front desk smooths long bangs out of her eyes and stands, tucking her open white coat around her. "Jiang Sev? And Howl, of course. I'm Siyu."

I lean over to Howl and whisper, "This is ridiculous. Do they do telepathy injections around here or something?"

"The telescreen let me know you were coming." Siyu smiles. "The system knows which tests you need, and I already have your ID chips ready." She nods to Cale. "I'll take them from here. Follow me, please."

Cale shrugs and shoulders her way back through the double doors, every step a little too hard, as though she's trying to stomp a hole in the floor.

"I already have an ID chip, thanks," Howl says when she's gone. "And Sev already talked to Dr. Yang about sticking with the card for now. She had a nasty infection out in the forest, and Yang thought she needed some extra time to heal before implanting the chip so her immune system doesn't overload."

I glance at Howl, confused. Why doesn't he want me to get a chip? But Howl is the only one I know here, the only person I have a reason to trust, so I play along. "I . . . don't want to spend my first month here in bed." Glancing at the double doors, still swinging from where Cale went through, I add, "My roommates don't seem like the types that would give me a sponge bath."

Siyu smiles over her shoulder at us. "I doubt implanting the chip would have that dramatic of an effect, but I can postpone the order, if you'd like. And Howl, your chip was deactivated when you went undercover. We have to extract it and give you a new one."

Howl shrugs. "I'll get it done when Sev comes back in. They won't starve me or anything." He pulls out the temporary ID card to show her, grimacing over the picture. "Though they might tell me I need to stop stealing Da'ard."

Siyu smiles tolerantly. "The thing we are most interested in is your encephalitis lethargica levels, in any case. Not invasive in the least."

We walk into a high-ceilinged room, the white floor shiny and reflective. Dim lights surround a long white tube on a raised platform in the center of the space. Siyu presses her thumb to a pad by the door and a square of light with two flashing circles labeled RESEARCH and PROCEDURE pop up on the blank wall. She taps RESEARCH and thumbs through different circles that appear.

I'm too distracted by the tube to pay much attention to her. One end is closed off, wires trailing down from the circular wall inside the machine. A pink pad sits under the blinding white lights inside, crisscrossed by what look like nylon ropes. Restraints.

A picture of a brain pulls up on the bright square. Siyu points and a light appears, following her finger. "Levels test gauge swelling. When you are infected with encephalitis lethargica, your frontal lobe swells." The circle of light following her finger tightens, and the picture magnifies, focusing on something that looks like a snake circling the center of the brain. "Which interferes with the way it interacts with the basal ganglia. The frontal lobe is the part of the brain that determines personality, controls inhibitions and self-control. Emotions. Here," she says, highlighting a piece of the snake, "is the part of your brain that regulates sleep. SS causes lesions in this area, hence the sleeping stage of SS. Those lesions also cause the other . . . problems that come after you wake up."

Problems. That's a nice way of putting it. The emotions that aren't being correctly regulated flare out into something terrible, a psychotic break from reality. Fear causes men to turn on their own wives and children; anger drives the incendiary to mass murder in the street. Pain can whisper deep inside an infected's brain, forcing them to cut off whatever hurts. I once saw a little orphan, no more than four or five years old, begin chasing her friends around the orphanage cafeteria with a steak knife, and it was no game.

That little girl meant to kill.

That's what Mantis is for. Regulating those reactions. Tricking infected brains into skipping their moments of psychosis. Except for . . . "Do you have cases in the Mountain that don't respond to Mantis?"

Siyu blinks, and I think it's her version of being surprised. "What do you mean?"

I look to Howl for confirmation. "It is becoming more and more common. Mantis doesn't stop compulsions for everyone anymore." I spent enough time worrying about it back in the City. No more Mantis meant a cell in the Sanatorium, isolation.

A death sentence would be better than SS with no medicine. Not to mention the fact that anyone in the orphanage—in the whole City—could go off at any minute, explosives waiting to blow up without warning.

"I don't think resistance to Mantis is possible." Siyu turns back toward the display on the wall as if that were the end of it, as if I had hallucinated Peishan's sudden compulsion just like I'd hallucinated the monster at the bridge that night. That cold, condescending smile is still pasted on her face as she launches back into her lecture. "Back during the Great Wars, they didn't know what it was. SS is related to the immune system, so it follows other sicknesses. One of the first outbreaks recorded was just after a serious flu pandemic that claimed the lives of thousands. The victims and survivors were well documented, but scientists didn't connect all the SS infections that followed. It wasn't until the Influenza War—the last Great War—that experts began to catch on. Deep sleep, psychosis . . . It trailed after the flu like a shadow. We don't know who first harnessed a flu virus specifically engineered to cause and exacerbate SS, but we do know that the first bombs were used in Asia, part of an invasion that went terribly wrong. Whole cities fell to SS, armies immobile, every other citizen pulling out their own eyeballs or doing it for their neighbors. . . . We're just lucky they never figured out how to make it communicable."

I shiver. If SS were contagious, we'd all be dead, torn to pieces by the end of the first day.

Siyu shakes her head. "Unfortunately, almost all the research from that time has been destroyed, and we've been playing catch-up ever since. Things have stabilized enough over the last few years for us to start looking for better answers than Mantis. We know they manufactured a flu virus that targeted these areas of the brain to cause psychosis and compulsions, and that it has something to do with dopamine levels in the brain, but not how it works or why."

I whistle. "So basically you are telling us you have no idea what you are doing."

She shrugs one shoulder. "Not altogether. But we don't have the resources to manufacture Mantis, and smuggling it out of the City or stealing the ingredients from the convoys coming up from City farms is becoming more and more problematic. A cure is our best option."

A cure? I have to keep myself from scoffing. For all that Firsts claim to be looking for a cure back in the City, it's been more than a hundred years since the invasion that brought SS here. "If there were a cure, wouldn't Firsts have found it by now? They still say they're doing research, but I always sort of assumed they'd given up. Maybe they've started looking again, now that Mantis isn't controlling everyone so well up there. But even if a cure were possible, why are you testing both of us? Howl isn't infected."

Siyu glances at Howl. "We keep everybody on file, especially after time Outside, so we can catch infection early if possible. It progresses a little differently in every person, so by bringing in more test subjects, we have a better chance of isolating the actual cause and effect." She turns her flat gaze on me. "Can you imagine success? A fresh start." She gestures to the tube. "Shall we?"

A true liberation, not just from SS, but from Mantis too. Firsts wouldn't have all the winning cards anymore. If Thirds knew about this, a place capable of curing the real threat—SS—who would stay in the City?

"Fine," I say. "Take pictures of my brain. Save the world."

CHAPTER 22

AS WE WALK OUT OF THE LAB, I START TO ASK
Howl whether it's a requirement to have a personality that resembles
cardboard in order to become a member of Yizhi when he stops
dead in the hall. A Menghu is standing in our way, arms out like
he's going to challenge Howl to a gun duel. "Howl? When did you
get back?"

"Kasim!" Howl barrels into him, and they both end up on the
floor, wrestling like a pair of kids, shouts of laughter echoing up
the hall.

At first glance, I'm pretty sure Howl doesn't have a chance.
Two of Howl could fit inside this Menghu, his barrel-shaped
chest framed by arms larger around than my legs, but Howl holds
his own, latching an arm around his tree trunk of a neck and
squeezing. They act like brothers, wrestling around and teasing
each other as if they grew up making faces at each other across the
dinner table.

I like the look of Kasim, unreserved smile splitting the
Menghu's face as he yells for mercy. And Howl seems his age

for the first time since I've met him, the stress of the City, of Outside, peeling away like an onion. He laughs like he means it.

I like it. Howl happy.

Kasim feels the scrutiny and spins around, ready to pull me into the wrestling match. I skip back out of reach, cheeks flushing.

"Who is this?" he asks with a wide smile. "Bring a trophy home to show off?"

"She followed me in, and I haven't been able to get rid of her." Howl grins at me, standing a good six inches shorter than Kasim. "But she's nice enough when you get used to her. Kasim, meet Sev."

Kasim's eyes widen. "Wow. You always did shoot high, Howl. She's way prettier than you are, even with your sexy beard. And she's famous, to boot." He leans in close and whispers, "He's giving you the royal treatment, I take it? Tours of the Heart? Strawberry shortcake?"

"I've yet to see a single strawberry, Kasim. You want to show me where they are?" He gives me an appraising look, making my cheeks grow hot again. That is not what I meant.

We start again toward the Core, and I listen to them catching up, Howl asking questions about everything from old friends to the food, groaning when Kasim tells him that meat is still something you have to go and kill for yourself.

"And good luck finding it," Kasim adds. "The gores have started cornering patrols, because there isn't much out there anymore. Those things are out of control."

"We didn't have any problems." Howl looks just a little too pleased with himself. He catches me rolling my eyes and grins. "They probably couldn't smell us under all that dirt. See, Sev? There are benefits to being filthy."

"Benefits every Menghu seems to be exploiting to the fullest extent possible," I say under my breath. There was a smear of dirt on the white floor where Kasim hit the ground.

Just as we get to the outer ring of the hospital, a girl wearing Yizhi's long white coat pushes through a doorway in front of us with her head down. She charges straight into me, losing her grip on the black canvas bag slung over one shoulder, sending it to the floor with a clatter.

Rubbing her arm, she brushes long dark brown hair out of her face to go after the things that exploded from her bag when it fell, each grab a staccato burst of cold energy. Scissors, bandages, syringes. I crouch down to help, picking up a roll of gauze before it can escape down a heating vent. Blue eyes meet mine as I hold the gauze out to her, and suddenly I'm frozen, bitten by the blank intensity of her stare. She blinks and reaches for the gauze, shoving it into her bag with the rest of the things that fell when she walked into me.

Spell broken, I avert my eyes in embarrassment, both for tripping her and for the weird moment. "Sorry I bumped you." My voice cracks in the effort not to laugh at myself. "I must have been listening a little too closely."

A teeth-baring excuse for a smile plasters itself across her face, skeletal and unwilling. "I'm Sole. And it's okay. We all hang on Howl's every word, don't we?" The bared teeth turn on him for a moment. "You must be our new celebrity. Jiang Sev?"

She brushes by me, edging past Howl and Kasim as if accidentally touching either of them would infect her with some terrible disease. Howl's eyes follow her as she walks down the hallway, gaining speed until she's running and out of sight, the *pinging* sound of her shoes against the metal floor echoing back to us. He scrubs a hand through his hair, looking lost.

Kasim rolls his eyes and reaches out to squeeze my shoulder. "Sole is kind of a freak. She doesn't mean anything by it."

"You know her, Howl?" I ask. Her empty stare is tattooed on the backs of my eyelids. "Should she be carrying around syringes and scalpels? I'm not going to be able to sleep tonight."

Howl nods with a wry smile. "I knew her before, though. . . ."

Kasim doesn't give Howl a chance to finish, laughing over the top of whatever he started to say. His hand stays on my shoulder and I have to keep myself from shrugging it off. Howl catches my uncomfortable look and raises his eyebrows suggestively.

Not noticing the exchange, Kasim keeps explaining, "Sole is practically a legend around here. She used to be a crack shot. One of the best Menghu. Her parents both got it Outside. Chemical bomb, you know? Just like that, her whole family is gone." He snaps his fingers, looking down the hallway after her. "She used to live in the shooting range when she wasn't out in the forest, blasting the life out of Yuan Zhiwei. Then one day she *cracked*." He pauses dramatically, tapping one of his temples with his index finger.

"Sole came home from patrol, stayed in bed for about a week, and hasn't touched a gun since. She still goes out. Patches people up." Kasim hikes up his brown canvas pant leg, stroking the long white scar that runs up his calf as if it's a treasure. "She fixed me up just a few months ago. Probably would have bled out if she hadn't been with us. But I don't know how she goes to sleep at night. Chicken or something, am I right?"

I take it back. I don't like him.

"A chicken did that to you?" I try to joke, but it comes out a little sour. "Why didn't you bring it home for dinner?"

He lets the canvas fall back down to hide the scar, unfazed by the stupid tease. "Razor-wire trip line. It set off a mine and brought in a bunch of Reds. Sole dragged me back into the trees while the rest of our unit pounded it out. A lot of them didn't make it through."

"Doesn't sound chicken to me." Howl matches his light tone, the whole story seeming even harsher when told so offhandedly. "More like she saved your life."

Kasim shrugs again, a twinge of disgust crossing his face. "Menghu is the only way to go. Protect the Mountain, kill Reds. Sole is such a waste. If she'd stayed behind a gun sight where she belongs, more of us would have come back from that forest that night."

"You wouldn't have."

"Maybe. You two going to practice tonight?"

The abrupt change of subject throws me, but not so much as Howl answering, "I don't think I will. Too many pretty girls laughed at me before. I have to meet with Root tonight, anyway. I doubt we'll be done before it's over."

"What pretty girls?" I ask. "Everyone here is coated in muck."

Howl smiles at me, cocking his head. "Something about grass stains and mud just does it for me, Sev. Forget to brush your hair once in a while and we can talk."

Kasim's laughing too, and I feel my face go red. But Howl tweaks a few stray strands of hair behind my ear that have escaped my braid. "I'm glad you didn't end up using the knife method on yours. Even clean, you look pretty good."

Pulling me aside, he continues, "I need to check in with Dr. Yang. Are you okay on your own for a bit?"

I smile and nod, face growing even warmer at his arm around my shoulders. He squeezes my arm, nods to Kasim, then starts back the way we came.

Kasim walks with me toward the dormitory, leaving the silence between us intact until we get to the steps leading up to Menghu quarters. "So you and Howl really *are* . . . something. That's new, for him."

I ignore the skip my heart gives at what he is implying. "You like him?" I ask. "He's nice-looking, I suppose, in a rough sort of way. You have to remember that he isn't used to washing his own hair, though." *Change subject.* "So, practice tonight? What is it? Self-criticism?"

He tilts his head and shoots me a shrewd look, but he doesn't press any further. "Not a chance. Out here we criticize each other, and do it as loudly as possible. Tonight is dance practice."

"Dancing?" The fire dancers I saw back in the City come to mind, but somehow I can't see Kasim on board with the pink leotards. I suppose I've seen pictures of men stomping around the fire from First library history books. Maybe that's what he means. "How did that get started?"

Kasim's mouth opens into a wide smile as he stops on the landing outside the dormitory, his teeth white against his sun-dark skin. "A performing company got stuck here with all the other refugees when the Influenza War started. They organized dancing to keep people moving, keep them from feeling helpless and depressed and all the stuff that creeps up on you when you're locked up underground. Runaways from the City found their way in here, and it became . . . this. The Mountain." He gestures to the room, the ceiling. The telescreens and the solar-powered lights. "People who knew how to run the electric systems came, we figured out how to grow food inside, and now we're strong enough to fight back against the City. And we've kept it up, holding dances and competitions. Helps the Menghu blow off steam, with missions and training all the time. General Root says it keeps us human." His smile is so large and warm, it makes me want to grin in sympathy. To take some of the burden. "You up for it?"

Give this place a chance, Howl said. Despite the fact that everyone already knows my name, I can still have a new start here. Even if it is stomping around a fire. "I'll come. Will Cale and Mei be there?"

"Are you bunking with Cale and Mei? You'll like them. Most Menghu go, even if it's just to watch. I'll teach you the basics, if you want."

When I nod, he opens the door for me, then runs down the stairs, waving when he gets to the bottom. It is hard not to like the boyish spring in his walk and the fact that he manages to wink at two different girls before disappearing from sight. I like that Howl likes him, but his disgust for Sole leaves me with an odd taste in my mouth.

Cale allows me to follow her to where the Menghu dance together, but skips a step ahead of me the whole way so I have to trail an arm's length or more behind her as if I have some sort of mange. Which, if she's one of those literal types who doesn't understand jokes, Howl did mention skin diseases. She disappears the moment we enter the room, leaving me to stare in shock as men and women dance by me. Each pair is locked in a tight embrace as if no one is watching. The women snap their heads back and forth, turning with their partners in perfect synchronization.

I see Kasim from across the room and wave. He immediately comes over and pulls me to the side of the floor, attempting to show me how to dance. It's hard to concentrate since just standing near all the intertwined couples has my eyes glued to the wooden floor, but that doesn't stop him from twining around me like a cat begging for its back to be scratched.

The only consolation, after an hour of trying to escape, comes when Howl turns up to save me from Kasim's constant reassurances that, yes, we really were supposed to be standing this close.

"Can I walk you back to the dorms?" Howl's nondescript T-shirt is now hidden behind a Menghu jacket, but instead of tigers, the collar boasts two black squares, just like General Root's.

"You're working with Nei-ge?" I ask, pointing to the squares at his collar. "I didn't know you'd be important here, too."

"If your mother weren't so famous, I probably wouldn't even talk to you." He pulls me toward a set of unfamiliar stairs, taking us higher and higher until the walls become panes of foggy glass, the rooms unlit behind them. Opening the first door we come to sends a rush of hot, humid air swirling out around us, and sweat prickles across my face and neck.

"What's this?" I ask as he leads me into the dark room.

"This"—he flips on a light and poses dramatically in front of a line of low green plants, red peeking out from beneath the jagged oval leaves—"is where they keep the strawberries."

CHAPTER 23

THE NEXT MORNING, I WAKE TO ARTIFICIAL LIGHT drilling into my eyes, my internal clock trying to kill itself since there's no sun to tell me what time it is. Cale's and Mei's bunks are empty. Messy, too, the sheets gray in the middle, as if the Menghu couldn't be troubled to change them very often.

Paper rustles loudly in my ears as I put a hand up to my aching forehead. There's a note taped to my hand.

Don't let them take you to Yizhi. All the tests they want are voluntary, so they won't force you. And then, like it was an afterthought, scrawled almost so I can't read it: *Leave your ID card in your room. Enjoy the soap. It took some arguing.*

There's a package of brown waxy squares under my bed. And a box full of little white envelopes. Mantis.

I hug my arms close around my torso, feeling chilly. It's like Tai-ge's warning from the day everything went bad in the City. But opposite. *Don't do what they say.*

As I pull my black T-shirt over my head, the door opens and a young woman wearing a white coat steps in. "I'm here to take you down to Yizhi. Dr. Yang's orders." She turns back out into the hallway. "Follow me, please."

I crumple the note in my fist, feet fused to the floor. She looks over her shoulder, eyes twitching down toward the birthmark on my cheek. Waiting.

"I . . . can't." I look around the room for inspiration. "Dr. Yang . . . mentioned that he needed to talk to me about something this morning before the tests."

She flashes her arm in front of the telescreen just outside my room. "They have you scheduled for the hospital."

"Well, I'll check in with him first. If he changed his mind, I'll come right down."

The Yizhi looks from me to the screen, then shrugs. "See you in a bit, then."

I let out the breath trapped in my lungs as I watch her walk away. When I stick my head out the door, the hallway is empty. After going back to grab my ID card, I flash it in front of the telescreen and a square filled with blue and green bars pops up, the colors marking mealtimes, an afternoon orientation meeting with my section captain, and an hour of service down in the Core. Everything is scheduled down to increments of five minutes to allow for the time it takes to walk between destinations.

The morning hours are marked red, a little message popping up to inform me that I am currently delinquent for a very important appointment in Yizhi.

A shout of laughter rings up the hall, backed by a monotone drone of many voices chattering all at once. Cale and Mei stroll around the corner, fronting a mess of noisy and very dirty Menghu. Mei smiles when she sees me, but Cale just brushes by me into our room.

"They have you training yet?" Mei glances at the telescreen, but I pull my card away from the black expanse and am silently grateful when it goes dark before she can get a proper look.

"Yep. Training. With you guys." I follow Mei into the room and throw my ID card on the bed. Cale eyes me as she finger-combs her hair back into a ponytail, though it's still a mess after she is done. She doesn't do anything about her black T-shirt and canvas pants, still creased with yesterday's dirt. Maybe even last *week*'s dirt.

"I bet Captain Lan will be happy to see you," Mei says. "We had a couple of guys go missing last week. Still don't know what happened to them. You can follow us down. It's easy to get lost at first."

Captain Lan? That sounds familiar for some reason. I bite my lip, not sure how to respond to Mei so unemotionally informing that some of her unit is probably dead out in the forest. "Um. Thanks? I'm still a little turned around on where things are."

Cale rolls her eyes. "I still can't figure out how you got here without Red tire tracks on your forehead." And with that, she walks out. What is her *problem*?

Maybe a good prank would warm things up between us. She could be like Tai-ge, needing a good reason to smile. I wonder how she'd take a good short-sheeting? I haven't seen any spiders down here to put under her pillow. . . .

Mei stifles a laugh at what must be a perplexed expression on my face. "Cale's a little tough on the outside, but she's great once you get to know her. Couldn't ask for a better trainer or friend."

"Does she have a personality under that thick skin?" I tap my lips thoughtfully. "When, exactly, was the last time you heard her laugh?"

Mei rolls her eyes. "Give her time. She doesn't adjust to change easily. New people means old friends aren't around anymore. It's part of life here, but it isn't easy."

She smiles sympathetically at my less-than-enthusiastic expression. "Stick close to me and I'll help you if I can. Just keep your head down. We're gearing up for Establishment next week, so you're in for a rough time."

"Establishment?"

"Nine years since your mother started running Mantis to the Mountain," Mei supplies, stuttering awkwardly when she catches my warning look. "We were just an infected-free safe haven before she came here. So we celebrate."

Mei leads me down four flights of stairs to a high-ceilinged indoor track circled with stadium-style seating. The air feels heavy and used, as though thousands of people have breathed it in before me, leaving it wet and diseased. But I find a vent, clean air streaming down into my face. The dirt-encrusted Menghu I just saw flooding the hallway upstairs are running laps, catcalling one another and racing up and down the lanes. I start around the track after Mei, my tight muscles gasping with relief at just being able to run with no heavy pack and no one chasing me. My ribs, which used to twinge every other moment, aren't even complaining anymore, the bones finally fused together again. The sharp squeeze of stress that wrapped around my brain after Howl's note eases a bit.

A young man strolls down from the upper level of chairs, arranging himself in one of the seats just above us. I can't see his face from across the track, but his outline is familiar, even at a distance.

Helix.

A worm of fear and revulsion crawls up from my stomach into my throat. He's the captain of my unit? Jogging to the edge of the arena, I break away from the Menghu who are slowing their warm-up to form ranks and kneel down against the barrier between the track and the seats. Maybe down here he won't be able to see me.

His skin is a few shades lighter than the dirt-dusted brown I remember from Outside, hair still wet from the morning's shower. His Menghu coat is unwrinkled and immaculate, buttoned up to his chin. Straight as a board, he stands and folds his hands behind his back.

"You're slow this morning," he says to the assembled group. "The boys upstairs are considering us for a special assignment, but you'll have to do better than this to land it. I'll meet you down to the training rooms in ten minutes." Helix nods for the Menghu to start, but instead of walking back up the steps, he glances over the edge to where I am hunched against the wall.

I duck down a little farther.

Helix doesn't come down, but waves to catch Cale's attention. She skips up to him, climbing up into the stands with a cute little smile, all the poison from back in our room clamped behind her teeth.

"Stuck on him like ticks on a cat." Mei appears next to me, mimicking the lilting speech I remember from the Third Quarter.

I keep my eyes on Cale, who is now giggling like a little girl. "Doesn't look like he minds."

"He's just full of himself. Captain Lan doesn't mess around with regulars. You have to earn a rank before he'll even look at you twice."

"Rank?" I catch myself covering my brand and drop my hands to my sides.

Mei grabs my hand, eyeing the star-shaped scar. "Just ranks. It's not a life designation. Fourth, huh?"

I snatch my hand back, instinctively checking her hand for marks. "What do you know about Fourths? Are you from the City too?"

She shakes her head, turning her hand so I can see it clearly. Blank. "Not really. I was born in the Hole. Got shipped out to the farms when I was two. Didn't need a brand to know who was a traitor out there, I guess."

Cale and Helix are now watching us as they whisper back and forth. I pull my attention back down to Mei, trying to ignore the crawl of their eyes against my skin. "How did you end up here?"

"My shift leader killed our guards. We escaped and ran across a Menghu patrol, and they brought us back here. Couple of the girls tested positive for SS, though, so they didn't make it in."

"They don't let infected in at all? Ever?"

"Of course not. Anyway, I've got to go. See you in training."

Helix jumps down from the platform, eyes on me. I look back to Mei, hoping for an excuse to run away, but she's already taking the stairs two at a time, pushing through the flow of green and black uniforms. I start to follow, but Helix cuts me off before I can escape.

Hand on my shoulder, he guides me over to one of the seats, his sharp smile squirming through me. "Aren't you supposed to be over in Yizhi, Sev? Everything okay?"

Cale sits a few rows back, staring down at me.

I pretend to drop something so I can tug away from Helix's sweaty grip on my shoulder. "Fine. Everything is fine."

"They transferred your supervision from Howl to me. I'd like to get you on a training schedule with all the other Menghu, but I can't until you get all of your testing and immunizations done. It isn't safe to have you running around with my soldiers until we're sure you aren't sick."

"Howl says all that stuff is voluntary."

Helix clasps his fingers in front of him. "Letting you live here is voluntary, Sev."

I look down at the floor. Is Helix threatening me? He knows I'm infected, that I can't survive Outside without Mantis. Why would Howl tell me to duck out of these tests and risk being booted out if there wasn't a reason?

Will Helix drag me to the needles himself if I don't jump to follow his command?

I feel Cale's stare locked on to the back of my head, as if she's attempting a telekinetic lobotomy. What if there's something more to the appointment in Yizhi? Something dangerous Howl hasn't told me yet because he doesn't want to frighten me?

Helix's hand is on my leg. "You're making a rough transition, Sev. They would have hurt you back in the City. *Killed* you." He shakes his head. "I can see that you're afraid, and you don't have to be." His finger touches my chin to make me look at him, and I jerk away. His face is still hard beneath the smile, as if it's a mask, covering his fangs.

The hand on my knee moves a little before he stands. Like it's meant to be a caress.

I scoot away again, looking up to meet Cale's cold stare. Maybe if I puke on Helix's shoes, he'll go bother her. She doesn't blink as she returns my gaze, and if looks could kill, I'd be on the dinner menu.

"I've asked Cale to keep an eye on you. She'll make sure things go as smoothly as possible." Helix extends a hand to help me up, blinking back annoyance when I ignore it. "There's no reason to be afraid of anything here in the Mountain."

No reason? The image of Helix on top of me, slamming my

head into the ground, shivers through me. "Thanks. I'll, um . . . I'll go right now. I don't need Cale to take me."

I walk back up toward the dorms, a discordant arpeggio strumming down my spine when I catch a glimpse of someone in a white coat following me. I run around the corner and sidestep through an open door. Two men wearing Yizhi white walk past.

I don't know how long I'll be able to avoid the Yizhi before they send someone who won't take no for an answer.

CHAPTER 24

LATER, MEI FINDS ME IN THE CORE, LOST IN THE crowds of people waiting to eat lunch. A fresh coating of mud streaks across her face and arms.

"What happened to you?" I ask, tapping my ID card against my leg, ready to flash it for a plate and run.

She looks around as if she doesn't understand the question, then comprehension dawns on her face. "The mud? Just training. Where did you disappear to?" She brushes her bangs out of her face, leaving a long streak of brown across her forehead. "What? Too scared of dirt to play with us?"

Mei jumps at me, sliming muddy hands all over my face and arms, laughing as I try to get away. "Now you'll fit in." She giggles. "Too clean and people will wonder if you're pulling your own weight around here."

She laughs as I try to wipe the mud from my neck, the coating of brown sludge smearing deeper into my skin. I have to laugh too, wondering how dirt became such a badge of honor. When we get to the front of the food line, the boy behind the counter looks jumpy. "Jiang Sev?"

I nod, and he gives me a nervous smile. "Telescreen says the Heart sent something down for you. Wait just a minute."

He ducks back behind the partition that separates the serving area from the rest of the kitchen, and I wonder if he'll return with someone from the hospital. Instead, he walks back with an envelope, my name in bold letters across the front.

I pocket the envelope and grab a plate, Mei pulling me toward the stairs leading down into the amphitheater before I can try to escape to ditch my ID card again. Someone catches my arm, pulling me off balance so I drop my plate, splattering pieces of egg and brown sauce across the floor. Before I can pick it up, Howl sweeps the plate out from under my hands. "I am so sorry!" His voice doesn't sound very sorry, though, too busy laughing at the accident. "Let's get this cleaned up, and I'll get you another plate."

"You're alive!" I say with mock surprise, excitement at seeing my friend warring with the thousands of questions buzzing behind my lips like a swarm of bees. And buried in those questions is a twinge of annoyance that he left me alone all day with only vague, slightly creepy instructions to keep me company. But I refuse to show any of this in front of Mei. "I thought they fed you to the gores or something."

He shrugs. "I think the General is just happy to see me. Lots of very long, very pointless meetings."

Mei raises an eyebrow as Howl runs back toward the kitchen to borrow a broom. He tosses me a rag and we clean up the mess together. Howl waits until we're done to give Mei his full attention. "Hi again. Sorry, I don't remember your name."

"Mei." She looks him up and down, her eyes freezing at the single hash mark carved into his hand. "How did you end up out here? Someone stir your tea wrong?" Her voice is suddenly very cold.

Howl takes a step back, scratching his head. "It wasn't the tea. I left because of the window situation." He nods calmly at her questioning look. "There were too many of them. Living inside a mountain seemed so much more exciting."

She presses her lips together. "At least you know how to clean up after yourself. Come on, Sev. I'll save you a seat while you get a new plate."

"Actually, before I threw Sev's food on the ground, I was going to ask her to come up to the Heart." He looks back at me, shrugging off her frigid tone. "Dr. Yang wants to talk to you."

Mei nods to me and walks off without saying anything else. Howl's eyes follow her as she goes, eyebrows creased together. "Did someone spit in her hair?"

"She's from the reeducation farms. Must not have seen your mark when you first met."

"She must be new, or she would . . . well. I guess it doesn't matter." Howl shakes his head and pulls my arm through his, careless of the mud smearing across his coat as he leads me toward the elevator.

Once we're both inside, the doors close, isolating us in the tiny room. Alone again. After so long together Outside, it's nice to not be fighting a crowd. Just me and Howl. Quiet. At least, until his eyes latch on to the envelope sticking out of my pocket. "What is this?" He draws it out without asking permission.

My name blinks back at me, the envelope bulging with something small and round. I shrug. "It came with my dinner."

He raises his eyebrows, silently asking my consent before

ripping the end open, sliding two green pills out on to his palm. Brows furrowed, he looks back up at me. "You still have the Mantis I left you?"

"How did you sneak it into my room without waking Cale?" I take the envelope back when he extends it out to me, but he doesn't answer. Clearing my throat, I voice the worry that has been brewing inside me all day. "Is there something I should be worried about? These Mantis pills aren't right? And the tests in Yizhi . . . ?"

Howl shakes his head, but he looks put out. "No, of course not. Go ahead and take these pills. I just need to talk to Dr. Yang about it again, I guess. They're messing with your dosage for some reason." He shrugs and turns back to stare at the closed elevator doors. "I think I've squared things up with Yizhi anyway, so you shouldn't have any more trouble from them. I checked into it and they were never supposed to do more than those SS scans."

"Are you sure?" I try to sound light, as if hiding today were some kind of joke. "No one ever chased me around back in the City. . . ."

"The City wanted to kill you. I'm just trying to make sure the Mountain doesn't poke any more holes in you than they need to."

"You said this place would be safe."

Howl is quiet for a moment. "It will be. It is. You don't have to worry."

The elevator doors open to a large room, the ceiling domed high over my head. The walkway splits in the center of the room, branching out in ten different directions, each leading to a door set back into the wood paneling. But I can't look at the heavy wooden doors or the mural dancing across the high arch of the ceiling. I'm lost in peering at the shelves and shelves of books. Old leather covers tooled with gilt, brightly colored paper screaming out their titles, tall, short, thick and fat, everywhere all around me.

"We're here a little early," Howl says when we reach the center, a crossroads that could lead anywhere, "because I wanted to show you these."

I can't speak, a wave of something I don't quite understand rushing up through my chest and pricking at my eyes, all questions about needles and Yizhi forgotten. If I didn't know better, I would think it was homesickness. Homesick for a time long before I left the City. Long before I met the nuns, before a star graffitied my hand.

"This is . . . like home. Like the library." The smell of dust and old, creased paper sinks down into me as if it's the only thing that really knows who I am. I catch sight of a title I remember reading over and over, the outline of a sleeping maiden draped across the binding. All I need is the picture window. The picture window and . . .

"Your mother brought the first few. Every time we send someone into the City, they smuggle some out." I can hear the smile in his voice, warm memories leaking out. "There's hope in fairy tales and stories like these. Sleeping Beauty always woke up."

"She always woke up?" I look at the book. "I thought they let her lie there until she rotted. She was the one who brought in the evil fairy. Being cursed to sleep is a fitting end to someone who tries to work with evil and hide it. Isn't that the moral?" It was mother's story, one of the few fanciful tales the Firsts didn't seem to mind leaking all over the Third Quarter.

"Sev . . ." Howl's laugh echoes over us as he pulls the book from the shelf and holds it out to me. "That sounds like classic City manipulation. Read the real story. It has a happy ending."

The painting on the cover at once calls to me and makes me

want to go wash my hands. I know too well what it means to be Asleep, and it doesn't help that this sleeping princess's story resembles my own history so closely. How could the sleeping princess in this story have a happy ending when I know very well that Mother won't ever wake up? That she deserves to be up on display. Asleep.

I wave the book away. There are so many other stories here, tales I've never read that have nothing to do with me. "They're so beautiful." But beauty hardly comes close. This place is a shrine. Sacred. I walk toward the closest shelf, reaching up to pull a book down, Howl's exultant smile at seeing me happy a warm glow in my chest.

Howl steps up to the shelf next to me, one arm brushing mine. He touches my wrist, then slips his hand into mine. "You'll stay, won't you? Mantis aside, it isn't so bad. Safe. Better than the City."

Right now, surrounded by books with Howl beside me, it does feel safe. Like I could fit in here, next to him. He puts the book down and steps a little closer, his eyes trapping mine as he looks at me, all thoughts of the books dulling to fuzzy background haze.

The sound of footsteps breaks the electric silence between us, and heat burns my cheeks. I pull back from Howl to look at the books, not wanting to share this moment with whoever it is walking up the hall toward us. "Didn't my mother work from inside the City? When was she here?"

"After you fell Asleep." A new voice answers my question, slicing between Howl and me as it echoes through the huge room. A voice I recognize. "The First Circle refused to allow our research to go forward. So we left. This is what she wanted to bring with us."

Dr. Yang's bowed worker frame from the City has straightened underneath his Yizhi coat, Nei-ge's squares at his throat. He walks with dignity, authority. The master of this space. He makes me feel small, as if I'm the one who is intruding. "'There is more strength in true beauty and power in imagination than you could ever find in the barrel of a gun.' She used to say that all the time. Gui-hua didn't stay here long, though. She missed you. She couldn't leave you to the City. The Circle."

"She couldn't have missed me." My hand finds the crook of my elbow, the spot where she injected me with SS. The momentary charm of remembering the woman who read me stories before bed instead of the monster who infected me fades. This room *is* a shrine. Worship for an idol for whom I will not light incense. "Or if spreading infection is how you show affection around here, I think you'd better show me to the door."

Patience and tolerance seem almost painted on the doctor's face. "Sometimes memories tell us a story that fits what we think we know rather than the truth. You weren't the first SS victim in the City after one hundred years of safety, Jiang Sev. SS has been used to hurt families not following First Circle orders for years."

I keep myself from rolling my eyes. "I didn't realize you were from the City."

"I was a First at the beginning. Just like you, Jiang Sev."

I look down at my hand, the shiny blotch of scarring all that's left of my First mark. I'm not a First. That life died with Father, with Mother leaving us. And out here . . . out here it doesn't even matter what my scars look like.

I take a deep breath. It feels unrestrained. Free.

Dr. Yang gestures for us to follow him straight across the book room into a tall, arched doorway. I don't follow, looking at the book I almost took, Howl waiting beside me. "Can I borrow one?" I ask. I haven't read a book, a *real* book with no First scientific discovery announcement, no war propaganda, in far too long. I ache to sit down and let myself get lost in a story.

Dr. Yang stops, a funny smile on his face. "No. We don't allow them downstairs. They're too fragile."

I glance at Howl. "But people can come up here to read them?"

Dr. Yang shakes his head. "These stories have to be understood. Appreciated. And explained to those who would not understand. We don't have time for that."

Mother brought them books, imagination, and beauty, and they have it all locked away so no one can touch it. Just like the First library. Only noncorruptibles allowed. My next breath doesn't feel quite so unrestrained.

We walk in single file, the pictures and paintings decorating the hall a stark contrast to the bare walls that make up the rest of the Mountain. It feels odd to have things adorning the walls like medals of honor all around me. The City is bare except for slogans and statues to remember Liberation. A few portraits of Yuan Zhiwei and Chairman Sun, like the one of Howl with his father in the City Center. Anything else would be selfish. Except for the picture window in the First library. I always assumed it was there to catalog the excesses of Before, and I was a little embarrassed at how much I liked it. Maybe the other Firsts liked it too; they just didn't want to share with anyone else.

We finally come to an office, a small window in the sloped ceiling letting in natural light. A heavy desk sits facing the door, and a plaque hangs on the wall, a single syringe displayed like a trophy in the middle of the wood.

Howl starts to follow me in, but Dr. Yang shakes his head.

"Operations has an assignment for you, Howl. Would you go over there now? I would like to talk to Sev alone."

My friend stays in the doorway for a moment, pressing his lips together as he looks at the doctor.

Dr. Yang laughs. "We're fine. She's fine. I promise. No more miscommunications."

A twinge of discomfort thrums through me when Howl doesn't leave. But then he nods and turns back down into the hallway, closing the door after him. Dr. Yang opens his desk drawer, fiddling for a few minutes before placing a leather cord in front of me, a shard of red jade twinkling in the natural light. My stomach drops, and a wave of anger turns my cheeks hot. It's the jade piece Mother gave me. The necklace that disappeared.

Before I can say anything, Dr. Yang reaches across the desk to touch my arm. "She took it when we left, so she could feel close to you."

My voice is as cool as I can make it, though I'm sure the fury at what he's saying bites through. Mother, wanting to feel close to me? How dare he? "Why am I here, Dr. Yang? Even Howl couldn't make up an answer to that one." He doesn't stop me when I reach out and brush the cold jade with one finger, not sure if I can bring myself to pick it up. "You don't usually let Sephs in here, do you?"

Dr. Yang smiles sadly, ignoring the offensive word. "Your mother was a good friend. I've been watching out for you as best I can. I've never regretted anything more than being too late to help your sister. Getting you out was the only way to save you this time."

The necklace draws me toward it, my fingers tracing the smoothed edges, dead faces flicking through my brain. Aya, blood dripping into her open eyes as she lay in the City street. Father, burning under the Arch. "What did you want to talk about, then? My missed appointments in Yizhi? That Howl is convinced I should continue to miss them?"

"Howl has been living in a very stressful situation for a very long time. Can you imagine passing information about your own father? He's paranoid. Worried he's one wrong step, one wrong look away from a shot between the eyes." Dr. Yang sits back in his chair. He takes a breath and lets it out slowly. "Be patient with him. Careful. I have high hopes for him."

The anger simmering inside of me bounces from the necklace to this dismissal of Howl to the doctor's calm assurance that everything he's saying is true. Or that I'll believe him, anyway. Could it be that Howl is just paranoid? I think about the way Howl stood in the doorway only a few moments ago, tension creased across his forehead. I know he doesn't trust Dr. Yang, didn't even when we were back in the City. Is that paranoia or a healthy attachment to life?

The thought curdles deep inside of me. Is my life, *Howl's* life, on the line here the way it was back in the City?

Yang steeples his fingers atop his belly. "There is a way you can help, you know."

"Help Howl?"

"Help me. Howl should recover." He purses his lips, thinking. "This might sound like an odd request, but I need to know what your mother said to you when she came back. Right before the Circle took her. She went to see you first."

The wave of anger turns into an ocean, a brutal storm. I may be here in the Mountain, but I don't have to pretend my mother was some kind of god. And Dr. Yang pretending she was just makes me that much less interested in trusting him. "I was Asleep, remember?"

He nods, sitting forward to drum his fingers against the desk. "And you can't recall anything from that time? Nothing at all?"

I remember her being there, relief at hearing my mother's voice. I wanted to die rather than lie there any longer, unable to move or reach out, open my eyes. Listen to people speculate about whether or not I would wake up, unable to even wave the flies away when they crawled across my face. Mother brought a moment of peace in that awful prison, but her words are just a garbled mess. A broken record telling me everything is going to be okay over and over again. I look at Dr. Yang. "Nothing that would matter to you."

The drumming fingers stop. "She and I were working on something very important when they put her to Sleep. I just wondered . . ."

He just wondered whether the last words she'd spoken to the child she'd tried to kill were about some science project? If some hypothesis would be her top priority on the way to poisoning half of the First Circle? Even if this project was more important to her than I was, as it clearly seemed . . .

Dr. Yang shakes his head and smiles at my incredulous look. "You're right. Why would she tell you anything?" He stands and walks over to a water cooler, draining some water into a cup. "Would you like a drink?"

I shake my head.

"They've got you on Mantis, I take it?"

"About that. Did I hear something about infected not being allowed in? I'm happy to be an exception, but—"

"We don't have the resources to take in just anyone, Sev. I wish we did." He removes his spectacles, rubbing his eyes. "How are you fitting in? Do you like the Menghu?" He speaks as though the conversation is already over. Just formalities to be played out, and he can't be bothered to pay attention.

I brush some of the mud from my arms on to his pristine carpet, letting my thoughts run. Disconnected from everyone, everything. Helix trying to force me to go to Yizhi and the white coats that ghosted after me. My mother being dragged from my subconscious to writhe like a dying snake every time someone recognizes me. "Sure. Everything is fine."

Dr. Yang glances toward the door. "I've asked Raj to take you down to Yizhi for those tests. Just immunizations and a blood draw to check to see what you brought in with you. In the interest of keeping everyone here safe, we need to know what we're dealing with." Something in his face is tight, the words too tidy and clean. He's lying.

With those words, he confirms what I already knew but hoped wasn't true. I'm not safe here. But I just don't know *why*.

I grab the necklace and jump up. "I'd better go, then. My roommate Cale seemed like she might dismember me or something if I didn't get it done."

"Raj should be waiting out in the hall." Dr. Yang smiles, gesturing to the door again. "Cale's a delightful girl. You'll do well with the Menghu." He nods to himself and sits back down at the desk. "Your mother would be proud."

CHAPTER 25

OUTSIDE DR. YANG'S OFFICE, I RUN UP THE HALL-
way and around the corner, barely managing to duck behind a
couch as Raj strolls toward Dr. Yang's closed door. When he's out
of sight, I sprint out of Nei-ge, past the book room, down the
elevator, my breaths coming quickly until I've put some distance
between me and Raj.

Once I feel safe, I pull the envelope of Mantis from my pocket
and the rusty red ring falls out onto the floor. I haven't been able
to put it back on my finger. Even if I had, it wouldn't belong
there, reminding me of Tai-ge when he didn't even give it to me.
I string it alongside the jade on the leather cord and stick it back
in my pocket. Time to move forward. Tipping the Mantis into
my mouth, I swallow it dry, the plasticky pills trying their best to
block my throat on the way down.

The moment of safety doesn't last long. I don't see any
white coats following me until I'm jostling my way through the
Core, in the crowds of people still in line to get dinner. Three
of them keeping their distance, but there's no mistaking the

way the men are watching me, waiting to extract me from the throng.

One steps directly in my path, tucking his white coat closed as he waits for the meandering stream of people to bring me to him. One pushes through a clot of yellow-uniformed Jiaoyang to fall in line behind me, only a few people back. The third waits off to the side. Ready to move if I run.

I don't have anywhere to go, to hide. Trying to duck down into the crowd just makes Yizhi number three start in, craning his neck to keep me in sight. And a ratty blond ponytail, right behind him. Cale's eyes are on me, one hand tucked under her arm, as if she's just waiting for a chance to pull whatever weapon she has stashed there.

A hand closes on my wrist, the man creeping up from behind meeting his mark. He doesn't say anything, hand clamped down so tight I can feel the blood flow to my wrist starting to ebb as he herds me toward the edge of the Core's hustle and bustle. Toward a set of white doors. Yizhi.

"Let go of me." I say it loud, pulling against his grasp. The people around us shrink back a step or two, but no one looks at me. Their eyes slide away like skates on ice, oblivious to the girl who only moments ago drew stares.

I plant a foot on the ground, pulling in earnest, fear bubbling up through my veins. Another man slides in next to me, his arm going around my waist and breaking my stance. My boots squeal against the stone floor as I try to fight, but there's no way to combat both as they drag me toward the door. Cale brings up the rear. I can feel her breath hot on my neck.

But a person materializes in front of the doors to block the way, his green Nei-ge coat dark against the sterile white. Howl spreads his arms wide, blocking the way to the hospital. "What do you think you are doing?"

The men don't let go. Their hands clutch at my shirt, pressing against my skin. Cale steps forward. "We've got orders, Howl. She's delinquent on at least four different immunizations, not to mention the SS levels she's obligated to—"

Howl cuts her off. "Since when did the Mountain turn into a prison where they drag inmates in for testing? That's why I *left* the City."

The man gripping my arm pulls me forward a step, ready to push past Howl into Yizhi. "You know better than the rest of us that we need—"

"Let her go. I'm her supervisor until she makes it past probation. If Sev spreads some terrible disease around the Mountain, I will be responsible. Understand?"

None of them try to correct him, not even Cale. Helix is my supervisor now. But all Yizhi are looking at the floor as if whatever command that made them drag me through the crowded Core is warring with the squares decorating Howl's throat, the lifetime of First authority striking with every word.

Howl steps forward to grab my hand, pulling me away from the men.

The smile I am accustomed to seeing on his face feels strained. "Try to force her again and you'll find yourselves Outside." There's something more than what he's saying, the way the men in white shrink back. Even Cale seems afraid.

He leads me away. The people around us part like oil on water, stares following us all the way across the Core. I can't keep it bottled up, not concerned anymore about who is listening. The look on Cale's face is just like Helix's was right after we met and he joked about "not keeping" June because she was a Wood Rat. Howl gave him one look, and suddenly Helix, the killer, was afraid.

Howl's single star doesn't mean anything here. He's part of Nei-ge, but not an especially important part, I don't think. Why are they all so scared?

Should *I* be?

"Stop." I shake his hand off my arm when we get to the edge of the room. "Tell me what is going on, Howl."

"It's hard to . . ." He looks around, and then plunges one hand into my pocket, coming up with my ID card. Tapping it against his palm, he looks vacantly at the floor, the walls, the ceiling. "I just need to figure out . . ."

"At least tell me why. You know, or you wouldn't be fighting against it. Why are they trying to drag me down there? Why is having an ID chip planted in my arm going to hurt anything?"

"Of course it will hurt. Those things are huge. I can't . . ." Howl trails off, looking around at all the people staring at us over forgotten plates of food. "I can't stand being cooped up anymore. Let's get out of here."

I follow him up the stairs that cling to the glass walls like ivy, up past the greenhouses and over the Core, barely able to clamp the questions vying in line behind my lips. We keep going up and up until I feel as though there must not be anywhere else to go. Howl pushes through an old broken door leading into an unlit, closed-off hallway, the rusty hinges creaking as we go through. Shards of glass crunch under my boots, and the stale darkness prickles in my mind, an answering prickle of fear in my stomach. *No hallucinations. Not now, when I need answers.*

The door opens into bright moonlight, and genuine, uncontaminated, unused air. The fresh coldness rushes into my lungs as though I've been drowning, fossilized in this rock. I feel exposed, as if there's nothing but miles of open space all around me, but I like it. Like an ant, dwarfed by a star slit sky, the blue-tinged moon hanging precariously on strings. Zhinu and Niulang gleam sadly above us, the flowing river of stars between them twinkling with unshed tears. Being Outside feels real, as though nothing that happened down inside the rock beneath us should matter.

But it does. "Howl. You told me I was safe. I don't feel safe."

Howl grabs my hand, leading me out past the door to a narrow pathway that winds its way around the edge of the protruding rocks. My fingers tingle in his grip. We are the only two people on the planet, the only threads of consciousness weaving a pattern into this dark world.

But before we can go too far, I stop, the open space dulling my voice down to a whisper. "Please. Just tell me. What is going on?"

He stops, the whisper contagious. "It isn't a secret, Sev. I don't know what is going on."

My clothes suddenly feel too tight, restricting my air, pushing at the scrapes and tears in my skin, so newly healed. "You have to know something. Otherwise I'd already have an ID chip, a few extra puncture marks, and . . . what? What terrible things will happen to me in Yizhi?"

"Come on." He pulls against my hand, leading me farther down the path. "Only Zhuanjias come out here. Part of the maintenance grid around the solar panels. I used to sneak out here when things felt too close. We can talk without worrying about who is listening."

The Mountain is completely shadowed, the rounded peaks to the north bald against the horizon. A mountain in the distance glitters like a swarm of fireflies over water. The City. Only a month ago I was one of those lights, but now I'm almost nothing. Just a breath on the frozen wind.

We sit in the cold, just looking up at the stars. I don't want to remember today. The crawly feeling of Helix's hand on my knee, my heart still skipping back and forth over the feel of the Yizhi's bruising grip on my arm, the sound of my feet squeaking across the marble floor as those white-coated men dragged me toward the hospital doors. I close my mind, taking deep breaths and refusing to think, peering up into the black. Waiting for Howl to speak.

It doesn't take long, but it doesn't feel comfortable, as if he's inspecting and weighing each word before speaking. "Dr. Yang knows there's something . . . different about you. About the way SS affects you."

"My hallucinations, you mean?"

"Maybe the hallucinations." He leans back, his shoulder brushing mine. "He won't tell me anything. When he asked me to go see Operations instead of staying with you in his office today, they didn't have anything for me. He's trying to keep us apart, keeps trying to get you down to the hospital when I'm not there to go with you . . ."

"Why?"

Howl takes a long time in answering. "I don't know."

Goose bumps trill up my arm. Yang was lying to me in his office, but are my hallucinations really worth extra testing? What kind of extra testing? And it seems as if Howl should know, since he didn't wait until after seeing the doctor to start ducking away from Yizhi. Howl was wary the moment we walked in. Is he lying to me too?

Paranoia. The word sticks in my brain, casting an ugly shadow over everything. It made me angry when Dr. Yang dismissed Howl's concerns, as if Howl is too wound up in himself to discern between reality and anxiety any more than I can when the monsters creep out from the crevices in my brain. But is it possible that Yizhi really is worried enough about me spreading some disease through their hole in the ground that it's worth manhandling me down to submit to the needles?

It's possible. But I know Howl. After our time in the forest, I know when he's going to smile, when he's going to look away. The way he bites his lip when he's thinking. He's doing it now, lips drawn tight. He's never done anything that didn't make sense, that hinted his mind wasn't quite on the same plane as mine. I don't understand, but I believe Howl more than I believe the formerly First doctor.

Howl's eyes are wide open as he looks up at the stars, moonlight giving his dark hair a pearly glow. "I've been helping to smuggle Mantis out of the City for two years now, but they're just hoarding it. This place is supposed to be a new start for anyone who wants it, but they aren't letting anyone in who drains the Mantis stockpile. That's why Liming couldn't come in, why June leaving him behind was the only way. We're caught in the middle of a game of weiqi, and I don't even know who is setting the pieces. Or what it would mean to win." He bows his head and rubs his eyes before looking over at me. "If they give you an ID chip, we're stuck. They'll always be able to find you. I wanted to believe we'd be safe here, but it all feels wrong."

He threads his fingers through mine, something sweeter than fear turning my stomach over. This is why it couldn't be paranoia. I feel exactly the same. Everything here has been just a little bit off from the moment we met Helix and his prickly smile. Howl sitting next to me is the only thing that feels right. The two of us Outside, nothing between us and the stars. The cold is starting to mist my breath, and wind ruffles my hair across my face. But I don't want to move. I don't want to spoil this moment of quiet.

"Sometimes it feels like that's the only possible future." Howl draws the words out, as if he knows what he's saying is wrong. "That I'm meant to end up Outside, alone."

I can't answer, the mirror image of what I was just thinking settling in a heavy weight across my chest. The darkness around me is a little too black, still swirling at the back of my mind. Like a hallucination waiting for the right moment to take hold. No one belongs Outside.

Howl pulls my hand close to his chest as he looks down at the trees so far down below us. I can feel his heart beating through the cloth of his shirt and the rise and fall of his chest as he breathes, both coming a little too fast. "My brother is out there somewhere. He left. A long time ago."

"You have a brother?" I stop, pulling my curiosity into check. "I'm so sorry. What happened? Was he part of the purges? After my mother—"

"Something like that." He takes another deep breath. "I can't help but wonder if I looked . . . if I went far enough . . . It's stupid. He's probably dead."

Not knowing is almost worse than my sister dead in the street. At least I know where she is. What kind of father is the Chairman that he'd lose two sons to the forest? What kind of place is the City that the Chairman could banish his own son and that none of us would ever know? That Howl could have disappeared for two whole years, and instead of telling us, the Chairman pretended all was well. Howl wanting to know about my family—about Aya—suddenly makes more sense.

"I'd bet he's still alive. If he's anything like you."

"What am I like?" Howl is looking down at his knees now, tracing the square on his collar with one finger. "Do you know?" His face is strange in the moonlight. "I don't know if I do. We came running here, and I was *sure* . . . but the way Nei-ge is handling infection and . . . other things . . . It really is just us. Us against everyone else."

Just us. That should be a scary thought. But it isn't, because for the first time it isn't just *me*. I'm not alone anymore. Even in the middle of whatever the Mountain is trying to do. It isn't just me, waiting for the firing squad to have a slow weekend.

"You are . . ." The things I am thinking are hard to say. "Strong. Ready to give up everything for what is right. I don't know how you ever went back to the City. Knowing that you could die any minute if they found out what you were doing. I don't know how you left again either. Your family . . ."

He shakes his head, cutting me off. It must still hurt too much to talk about what he left behind. Or what he's looking for. There's barely enough room for the two of us to sit, our feet dangling over the edge of the narrow walkway, so close I can feel every breath as it fills his lungs.

"Do you think we should just run?" he asks. A joke, but there seems to be a subtle underlying question there.

Would surviving Outside be any different from the life I've already lived? Alone with the trees instead of alone in an overpopulated City or under a thousand tons of rock, hiding from danger I don't understand? Running away from what Jiang Gui-hua has made me.

"If we left . . ." Howl and me running would turn into Howl running away from me, or whatever SS would leave of me. A gore's harrowing laugh floats up to where we are sitting, raising goose bumps on my arms. One of the many kinds of monsters that live Outside. I'd be one of them.

Howl turns a little to look at me. "Could you leave everything behind? Live Outside?"

"Leave what behind? There's nothing to leave. Except Mantis. And you." My stomach twinges, embarrassed at the admission. It's hard to say, but undeniable. Something between us fits. The way we talk, the way we sit, the way we think. It doesn't make sense, but that won't make it go away. I don't want it to go away.

Howl's hand tightens around mine. "You already have friends here. Mei. You've even got Helix drooling after you like a wolf stalking a flock of geese."

I give a grimacing smile. "Even if that were true, the analogy follows. He's probably sharpening his butchering knives right now."

"And you're joking." He almost laughs, but doesn't move away, looking me straight in the eyes. "Most of your life has been balanced against an ax, and yet you still had a joke to tell or someone to cheer up." He looks away, discomfort creeping into his voice when my brows begin to furrow with questions about how he would know one way or another from his pedestal up on the Steppe. "Dr. Yang made me promise to stay away from you back in the City, but I knew you. I wanted to, anyway."

She's the only one like me. That's what he said the first night we met. I still don't know what that means, but I don't know how to ask. It feels too close, as if asking what he meant will sound like I'm asking a very different sort of question.

Our noses are almost touching, and I have to look down. Something stirs inside of me and I want to reach out, to let all this electricity out of my body. He's so close, the static air humming in between us.

"Why?" he asks. "When everything is wrong, why are you still smiling?"

I think for a second. "I never thought feeling sorry for myself did much. Knowing that things are hopeless and lying down for the ax are two different things. My life has always been mine, even back in the City when I didn't have any control over when it ended. No one can tell me who I am or what I am capable of. Not my mother, not the Firsts, not even you."

The silence feels heavy, as if what I said should be offensive. Or laughable. But instead, Howl brushes a hand across my cheek.

"That's why I like you." Slowly, very slowly, his arms fold around me, pulling me up against him. I freeze, knowing that this is what I wanted two seconds ago, but now that it is happening, it frightens me. He smells like spicy Mountain soap, cinnamon, and nutmeg. One hand runs up my arm and brushes my jaw, softly turning my face up toward his. His breath is warm on my cheeks and nose, waiting. My mind races, wondering how this could happen to me. *Is this a hallucination? Am I staring off into space under the stars with my lips burning?*

I don't care. I lean forward a breath. And his lips brush mine. Again. A shiver runs through me, and my hands curl in his hair, brushing his stubbly cheeks.

His fingers trail under my ear, down my neck, as he whispers, "I wasn't lying when I said I'd follow you out of this place. I just can't figure out why you want to take me with you."

CHAPTER 26

SHING. *METAL RINGS AGAINST METAL ABOVE MY
face. My head presses hard into my lumpy pillow.*

Again.

*It's a knife, Cale's face shadowy in the dark of our room. I keep very still as
the blade lashes out again, a brush of air rushing down to dust across my eyelashes.
I'm afraid to even try moving, knowing I'll not be able to twitch a single finger in
the midst of this nightmare. Terrified I'll find myself trapped inside my own skin,
Asleep again and living in a constant stream of hallucinations. The knife's keen
edge strikes again, even closer. Cale's bone bracelet scrapes across my cheek.*

*"Stay away from Helix." Slam. The bed shakes with the violence of the
blow. My lungs won't inflate.*

*"And stop running. We're going to take it," Cale whispers, blue eyes almost
amused, as though she knows I cannot move. "Not even Howl can stop us."*

The knife comes slower this time, tracing across my forehead.

A hand on my shoulder jerks me awake. Mei doesn't stop to
make sure my eyes are open, jumping down from the side of my
elevated bed as a gasp rips from my lungs. I put a hand up to my
forehead, searching for evidence of Cale's blade.

"Inspection!" Mei hops on one foot, trying to tie her boot while opening the door with her elbow. "Put your clothes on before Captain Lan comes through, okay? Cale is already out for your blood."

Out for my blood? The comment drills deeper than it should, my heart still racing from the nightmarish hallucination of Cale's cold blue eyes hovering over me in the dark. I jump out of bed, bumping into one of the support beams in my haste to comply, my hand scraping against loose paint as I grab the bedpost to keep from falling over. I am just pulling on my socks when Helix's slicked head pokes through the door.

Helix smiles as he looks me up and down, but he doesn't say anything, just nods once and pulls back out of the room.

Cale's face flashes by the doorway, shadowing Helix's leisurely check in each room down the hall. I meet her eyes as she passes, but I hate the way my heart races. I'm not going to be scared today. I'm done with fear.

I try to let my mind go to happier things. To last night, just the thought of Howl starting a smile on my face. I finish pulling on my shoes, untangling the laces with cold fingers, wondering where all the flakes of paint decorating the leather came from. White paint. It's all over my hands, too.

When I give the room one last check, my eyes fall on my bedpost. A series of lines cut into the metal, paint scraped away in places where I grabbed it in my haste to get out of bed. White paint.

Was it not a hallucination? Was Cale really testing her knife blade on my bedpost? I jerk with surprise as the door slams open again, ready for Yizhi white or Cale or worse. But it's just Mei, ducking her head as she comes back into the room.

I let my lungs empty, willing my heart to slow. "No training today?" What did Cale mean, they were going to "take it"? Take what?

"Our unit is on active patrols tonight. No training." She looks at the wall, one hand up against the side of her face. As if she's hiding something. "How about some breakfast?"

Howl promised to bring me some breakfast up by the maintenance grid. "I don't know, Mei. I was going to . . ."

"To what?" She looks up, smile stretching her wide mouth. But it's broken. Both of her eyes are dark with bruises, and her lip is split. She ignores my look of consternation, speaking over the question I start to voice. "Come on. Eat with me."

"Mei . . . what . . . ?" I touch my own eye, and she flinches.

"I . . . messed up yesterday."

"What do you mean, you messed up?"

She shrugs uncomfortably. "Helix really wants our unit to be chosen for some operation they're working on upstairs."

"Helix might as well give up now." A male voice intrudes, making me jump again. It's Kasim, slipping into the room and closing the door. "Because my unit could bend yours over backward. Can I trick you two ladies into sitting with me for breakfast? I haven't seen our little celebrity since she first got here." He doesn't even look twice at the bruises decorating Mei's face.

Mei doesn't bring it up either, grinning back at him, but flinching when the crack in her swollen lip breaks open. "Kasim, if they catch you on this floor again, General Root is going to bump you down a rank." She gets up to check the hallway. "Come on. I think it's clear."

Kasim offers his elbow, but I put a hand up. "I'm supposed to meet someone."

"Got something special planned?" He gives me a knowing grin. "Because I happen to know that all of Nei-ge is locked up in some meeting."

"Why would meetings in Nei-ge interfere with Sev's plans . . . ?" Mei's shadowed eyes go back to me. "You're . . . involved with that guy? The *First*?"

A blush creeps across my cheeks, the clear memory of Howl's arms around me last night a warm glow in my chest. "I . . ."

"Yeah, look at the way she's going all red." Kasim's smile is too wide, and he lazily drapes an arm around my shoulders. "You've got me all curious. Howl never had much to do with girls before."

Mei goes to the door again, her characteristic smile turned downward. "I don't know why they let him in here. He's never gone a day without a bath and a shave, walked straight into a cushy job up in the Heart . . ."

Kasim starts to interject, but then looks at me and seems to think better of it.

"I can tell you you're wrong about the bath part," I supply, when Kasim doesn't speak. Mei just rolls her eyes in answer, turning away when I continue. "I was a First until I turned eight. They are people too."

Her voice is quiet when she answers. A growl. "Those slavers don't deserve more consideration than the time it takes to aim. You know why I joined the Menghu? So I can tell them I have a name, not a number. Show the City that I am worth more than the rice quota for the day." She picks up my hand, fingers digging into my star brand. "How can you defend any of them? He's the one who did this to you."

I shake my head. "He's here. Doesn't that mean anything?"

Her fingers loosen from around my wrist. "I guess we'll see."

I look at Kasim, expecting him to speak up for his friend, but he's humming to himself, looking at the ceiling. "Well, Mei, you work on teaching him how to tie his own shoes and I'll make sure to shove my brand in his face every few minutes or so. Maybe we can make him cry. Would that help you feel better?"

Mei laughs, and the intense, violent version of her tucks itself behind that broken smile. "Get him to take out a Red or two. Then we can talk."

I grimace, wondering if Mei can hear the carnage in those words. She doesn't seem hard the way Helix is. Maybe this is Menghu talk, a way to avoid looking the soldiers they're shooting at in the eyes. Mei checks outside again, then gestures for us to follow. "Come on. I'm starving."

When I don't move, she gives me a cute little smile. "Fine. But I'll be back for you later."

Back for me? For all that I want to trust her, I can't help the prickle of alarm that dances across the back of my neck as she slides through the open door. "What for?"

"More dancing, of course." Kasim stands up and looks both ways down the hall before slipping out the door after her.

Later, as Mei leads me down to the dance hall, I catch a flutter of white jacket coming around the bend. Even if Howl did very publicly warn the Mountain not to drag me down to hospital, I don't want to test it out. Unfortunately, the Yizhi is around the corner and walking by before I can get out of the way. It's Sole, the medic I bumped into when I first got here, touching things as she walks by. She glances at me as she passes, but doesn't stop.

The room is crowded, the air clouded by too many people breathing too hard. Kasim appears out of the mob, hand extended.

Submitting to a dance sounds about as exciting as volunteering for torture. It even looks like torture for the Menghu already circling the cement pillars, faces frozen in grimacing concentration. I shake my head, "I'll watch, thanks. I'm kind of . . ." I search my mind for an excuse, the most blandly boring one finally coming out. "I have a headache."

But Kasim hangs by me for a minute. "Is it being underground?" he asks. "A lot of people get headaches from the electric lights. We could fix that. My unit is out on patrols tonight along with yours."

"What do you mean?"

"Come with us. I'll take care of you."

Back in the corner of the room, a couple catches my eye, spinning and kicking across the floor, oblivious to the ripples their flawless performance is creating. They move as though they are one person, the girl's auburn hair bright against her partner's shoulder. Eyes closed as she follows him, she draws the steps out like a picture on the floor. It's a life story, one that makes me begin to understand why the Menghu like to dance so much. It's a fight, a struggle. Just as violent or passionate as training and patrols must be. It suits them.

Mei slides down into the chair next to me, waving at Kasim as he goes off to find a partner who will actually dance. Her eyes follow mine to the red-haired girl as she storms across the floor. "That's Rena. She grew up here, dancing. You can tell the Mountain-born from the rest of us just imitating. The dance is part of them."

Caught up in watching Rena's tight turns, I don't notice Helix until his hand is on my arm. "Care to learn a few steps?" he asks.

Mei flinches when she sees him, hand going to her bruised

cheek. Helix's hand feels too heavy, making me fidget with dis-comfort at his touch. Is Cale waiting just outside, ready to drag me down to the hospital? "No, thank you."

He ignores the rejection, pulling me up with a pointy smile. "I don't usually dance with newcomers, but I'll make an exception for you. Come here. You're just the right height."

Not wanting to cause a scene, I follow, skin crawling as he pulls me in close, his arm curving around my spine. Menghu coat gone, he wears a simple T-shirt and black pants. His unremarkable clothes remind me of a propaganda ad they ran in the City a while back. A picture of a shaggy-furred, fanged monster trying to sit with a group of Thirds during self-criticism. REPORT THE FIRST SIGNS YOU SEE! it said. I always thought whoever drew the poster must have been deluded to think that SS would be so easy to spot. Yet here Helix is, trying to slip in with the rest of us, like he isn't a closeted serial killer.

For all the promise of teaching me steps, Helix just wrenches me around the floor. Every jerk makes me a little angrier until my temper is simmering dangerously close to the surface. His hand wrapped around my back is sweaty, seeping through to my skin.

"So is this how you reeled Cale in? Manhandling her around the dance floor?" I cross my foot under his and he trips.

He recovers, pulling me in again. "You're angry."

"Curious."

"I need to talk to you about something."

"Well, I don't really want to breathe the same air as you, much less talk."

Helix's black eyes hold at my shoulder, thoughtful but refus-ing to look at me as he leads. "Is it because of that Wood Rat?" he finally asks.

Anger rises all the way up to my cheeks. "Is *what* because of that Wood Rat?"

"You seemed much less . . . angry when I met you. *Is* it because of that little Wood Rat? I'd think you'd be grateful, since it was Howl's head on the chopping block that night. You two seem so close."

I shake my head, fingers numb in the grip they have on Helix's arm. "June. Her name is June."

"I saved your life. It's what we do, Sev. Kill or be killed." Helix's voice purrs like a rabid lion. "You don't know who is good and who is bad. I made a decision you didn't agree with, so I must be bad, right?" He gives my hand a squeeze. "Yet I'm here opposing the City, so I must be good."

"No, I stopped you from murdering my friend for no better reason than you had an extra bullet itching in your gun. I'm pretty sure that doesn't leave any room to wonder where you fall." Helix's breath is in my face, slithering down my neck.

His voice twists around me and my ears feel oily just from having to listen. He's caught some of my anger. "I want to be safe. To have a home, a place I can have a family. And June . . . all the Wood Rats . . . could bring that crashing down anytime."

"A fourteen-year-old girl? She was going to destroy your life? I thought everyone was welcome here in the Mountain?" Everyone who isn't infected.

"The ones who want to come in, not the ones trying to kill us for Mantis." Helix glances down at me. "I need to tell you about something. It might change your mind about me."

I push against him, as far away as his arms let me go. "You would have killed her, Helix. Dead because she put rocks in your pack, because she didn't bow down to the scary Menghu. Which wouldn't have helped anyway, considering how you treat your own trainees." I look over at Mei, who is watching us, eyes wide. "When's Mei's death date, Helix? The next time she steps wrong in your war games?"

Helix turns sharply, crashing my head and back into the cement wall. "Is that the best you can do?" he whispers. "Call me a cold-blooded killer? You want to talk about indiscriminate killing, go talk to your buddy up in Nei-ge."

"Get away from me, Helix." I push him away, but he grabs my wrist, pulling me back. His fingers are too long for his hand, curling all the way around my arm.

"I'm more of a friend than you think. I asked for you to be put in my unit so I could keep an eye on you. Warn you."

I raise my hand to explore the bruise I can feel blooming on the back of my skull, my head still ringing from impact with the wall. "What? Stay away from Cale, so she doesn't murder me because I'm standing too close to you?"

Helix flashes those pointy teeth in a smile. "No. That's a fight I would actually like to see."

I narrow my eyes. "You want me to win?"

"Depends on what the prize is."

Helix doesn't expect the slap, but the print of my hand stands out, white against his reddening face. He stops the second blow with ease, swatting my hand away like an annoying fly. We just stare at one another, his hand clamped around my wrist as if it might snake out of his grip to bite him.

"I thought you deserved to know. To make your own decision instead of being trussed up like a chicken and slammed down against the chopping block, you stupid little Seph." He steps back, anger riding every line of his body, the veins at his neck bulging. "Maybe even give you a little excitement for your last few days. You are going to die. You don't even know why. And your friend Howl is ready to do whatever it takes to keep you from finding out."

I turn my back on him, pushing the door open so I can get away before I do something I regret. Something violent.

Helix's voice follows me down the hall, and he's laughing again. "Don't be blind, Sev. Why do you think he brought you here?"

walking up one of the stone staircases spiraling up from the Core, people milling back and forth across the twilight-dark chamber below me. I look up into the waning light, the huge mouth of the Mountain peering up into clear sky.

I don't know where Howl sleeps. Somewhere up here. Skipping past the rabbit warren of rooms and passages, I go up, up to where the carpet is thick and the walls are not cement. Where the telescreen disappears, and the funny little icons flashing after me can no longer warn that my approved activities don't take me anywhere near the Heart.

After running past the book room, past Dr. Yang's office, I burst through a closed door and find myself looking up at the stars, blurry through the high glass ceiling. Two Menghu guards stand at attention next to a door at the other end of the room.

One unconsciously touches his cheek, mirroring where my birthmark sits. Nose in the air, I stride past them, and they don't stop me. Down a dim hall to a door, slightly ajar and leaking light onto the floor. Voices float out from inside the room.

" . . . our only hope. They'd kill her before we got close." It's Dr. Yang, sounding depressed.

"Don't you think that is a bit extreme, He-ping?" General Root growls. "Invasion? Are there no other choices?"

"We might have had success another way, if we could all come to an accord. . . ."

Howl's voice surprises me. "We had a deal, Dr. Yang."

"You knew what was going to happen if everything didn't fall into place." Dr. Yang sounds amused, despite the heavy words issuing from his lips. "Are you volunteering now, Howl? After all these years?"

There's a substantial pause before Howl answers. A whisper. "No."

CHAPTER 27

STARING AT THE CEILING FROM MY BUNK, I TRACE
the hairline cracks in the paint with my eyes. The memory of the
kiss up on the roof tingles through me, but I force it down. My
mother's face keeps popping into my head, her beautiful smile
glowing over me right up until the moment she abandoned me.

Why do I trust Howl? Even Tai-ge couldn't put our not-quite
relationship before who he was. Tai-ge's commitment to his parents, his stars, kept an unbreachable wall firmly between us. It
didn't matter what he wanted, the times I felt his hand against
mine, his eyes lingering a little too long on my face. The times I
imagined looking back, pulling him into an alley, and kissing him,
just to see if there were any chinks in that wall.

I never did it because I knew there weren't. I've had the word
"traitor" chasing after my name since I was eight. Now someone is
treating me as though I'm worth something, and I've been ignoring how weird that is.

I push the thoughts away.

My feet start moving before my brain catches up. I find myself

"You know it's going to come down to one of you in the end."

Even quieter. I almost don't catch it. "Yes."

"That being said," another voice chimes in, "if we aren't prepared to force our resources here, we have to go back to the source. Why can't we get to Gui-hua?"

My mother? Waking her up now wouldn't help much, would it?

Dr. Yang answers, "There's no telling if she would help us, even if we did get to her before the First Circle did. Like I said, the Mantis stockpiles—"

Howl cuts in again, "You know what would happen with Menghu in the City. Whatever their orders, the whole thing would turn into a bloodbath. The people you are trying to save, all the Thirds—"

General Root's voice booms out over his, "This isn't about saving anyone; it's about survival. It's between us and them. It always has been."

My jaw clenches, anger bitter on my tongue. Is that the real stance, what lies underneath all the feel-good, new life, equality business? Anything to get Mantis, all of it, not willing to share a single pill.

And how can Howl just sit back and let him talk like that? His family and friends are all still in the City. Isn't that why all these people left? Because Firsts decide who is going to live and how? Is Dr. Yang going back on a bargain not to invade? After all the help Howl has given them?

A woman's voice pipes up, muffled by the whispers of conversation spidering out from the General's ultimatum. "We could be ready to move out within a week."

"General Root," Dr. Yang interjects, "I don't want any lives to be lost unnecessarily. The reports of SS experimentation and new types of chemical weapons coming our way are frightening. We do need to move quickly in order to secure enough Mantis to support the Mountain, but if I can have authorization to use Jiang Sev . . ."

Use me? Everything goes cold, my breath frozen inside my chest, Helix's warning cutting across my brain.

"Sev?" I jump at the man's voice at my back, managing to school my face into a smile before I turn around.

"Raj. Howl asked me to meet him. . . ."

Raj jerks me away from the door. "I'm sure he did. Howl doesn't like following rules."

I pull against him, straining back toward the meeting, but he's too strong for me. "Please, Raj, I need to talk to Howl."

"No." He stops at the top of the stairs leading to the Core, the height almost dizzying through the glass. Poking at the telescreen, he whispers, "Jiang Sev," and my schedule pops up under his hand. "You'll find out along with everyone else. I'm calling your captain now. . . ."

"No. I'll go. I'm going." I take the stairs at a swift jog, putting as much distance between me and Raj as quickly as possible, worried Raj would send the message, that I might bump into Helix on his way up.

When my lungs start to complain, I slow to a walk, my mind bending around the conversation I so desperately wanted to hear the end of. Dr. Yang wants to use me? What could one infected Fourth do to tip the balance between City and Mountain?

And invasion? General Hong would be first on the list to die, Tai-ge right after him. What could be so terrible that trying to break down the City walls sounds like the best defense? How many Menghu would have to die? Running my fingers along the wall, I walk without seeing, trying to piece things together.

"Sev!" The voice only pushes through my thoughts when the owner grabs my shoulders. Kasim's grin is a little too close to my face. "I was supposed to report five minutes ago and you aren't even dressed."

"Dressed?" I look around at the unfamiliar hallway. Hand-painted numbers hang from the ceiling, the walls made up of tiny broken tiles arranged into a mosaic of animals in a forest. A lizard sits next to me on the wall, tongue lashing out to catch my hand. The movement startles me, just as impossible and frightening as the Red in the forest speaking to me from the dead, or the glass bottles singing my name back in the Chairman's basement.

No. Not again.

"Aren't you coming out on patrol with me tonight?"

I pull my hand away from the wall, brushing my sweaty palm against my pants. *It's just a picture. It can't move.* This hallway must be Jiaoyang. Where all the little kids go to school.

"I thought you were kidding," I reply, still trying to rub the twinges of hallucination away. "How did you find me?"

"Telescreen. Tracks your ID card."

I pull the card from my pocket. I don't remember bringing it with me. "It tracks me wherever I go? Why?"

Kasim shrugs. "Let's get out of here."

Howl made sure I didn't get a permanent ID chip. Talked his way around all of the blood tests and whatever else Dr. Yang is asking for. And somehow seems to know a whole lot more about what is going on than he did last night. Helix's words repeat over and over in my head, spinning until I feel dizzy.

CHAPTER 28

THE NIGHT REACHES OUT TO ME LIKE AN OLD
friend, an unwelcome one that buzzes for attention at the back of
my brain. But the fear that has me wondering if images around me
are real or just inside my head dims behind the conversation I over-
heard upstairs. Kasim's solid presence at my side should be reassuring, but when he reaches out to touch my arm, I jump.

"Outside at last, right? You ready for this?" he asks with a grin.

Kasim moves out ahead of me, letting me catch up to him
under a tree with icicles hanging from its branches in long gnarled
spikes. "This is a routine patrol. Checking for Reds, but none of
them ever come this close," he explains, pressing something hard
and metal into my hand. A gun. A quicklight comes next. "Nothing fancy. Just don't get lost."

He fades into the night ahead of me, and following is impossible. I jog a few steps into the trees before stopping to see if I can
hear him. But then something tugs at my hair, and I look back to
find Kasim undoing my braid.

He guffaws when I grab my hair away from him and reaches

out to swat a moth away from my face. "You move too fast. Too loud." Hand still clenched around the moth, he tears one of its wings off, dropping it to the forest floor.

The casual nonchalance in his face as he crushes the remainder of the moth between his fingers leaves the hairs on the back of my neck standing on end.

Suddenly, he goes still, jovial smile turning a little as he cocks an ear to listen. "That's odd. We're so close to the Mountain. . . ." He glances back at me and then up into the trees. "Why don't you play lookout. High enough no one's going to find you easy." His smile goes back to relaxed and teasing. "Shoot any Reds that come through, okay? I'll be back in a minute."

I watch him disappear into the undergrowth before finding a tree, clinging to the trunk to keep myself from kicking my dangling feet. Fifteen minutes. Twenty. He doesn't come back.

When the darkness around me begins to swirl, I decide it's time to move. I don't want to fall out of the tree trying to run away from cloud monsters or evil tree demons that only I can see.

It's unnaturally quiet down on the forest floor. But then I hear something. A whisper. Wind blows up from behind me, carrying the sound away with it. There are scuff marks against a tree and in the dirt a few feet ahead. When I get to them, I notice a few wet spots on the ground. Blood?

There's a line scratched into the dirt and leaves. A drag mark. The trough in the ground trails away through the trees, and I follow with my nose practically in the dirt.

I come upon them so quickly, I almost fall over to keep from walking straight into the campsite. Four Reds, sitting around the smoldering ashes of a fire. Kasim is on the ground.

Dead.

CHAPTER 29

"SHOULD WE JUST KILL HIM AND GET IT OVER with?" A girl, her head covered by a hood. "There are probably a bunch of them out here. The night patrols are out."

I breathe out. Not dead.

"Nah." The speaker's voice is low and grumbles like a thunderstorm. "Hong wants them brought back. We'll have to drag him to base camp."

"You don't think carting two hundred pounds of Kamari soldier is going to slow us down, Kai? We're supposed to set these things and run." The girl nudges a large flat disk with her foot. *Get up high. Running in will just mean both of our heads on the Chairman's desk.* The gun Kasim so casually handed to me weighs heavily at my side as I climb up a nearby tree. The metal feels uncomfortable against my skin as I steady it across my arm, setting my sights on the hooded girl. I rethink and switch to Kai, the one who seems to be in charge. I can't shoot someone, not even Reds who would happily tear me apart. I won't. I'm better than that, better than my mother. I just have to scare them off. *I can do this. This is Kasim's life.*

But something pulls my attention down, movement flickering at the edge of my sight. An eye blinks up at me from the base of the tree, a giant, muddled outline hidden in shadow. The thing yawns, shadowy hole of a mouth lined with yellowing ivory. Black eyes focus on the ring of Reds ahead of us.

A gore.

A fairy-tale monster, come alive. Even murky and indistinct beneath me, the nightmarish creature I had imagined after that first wakeful night Outside doesn't do the real beast justice.

I drown in indecision, choking back the warning that tries to pass my lips. If the gore charges them, in all likelihood, they'll kill it. On the other hand, Kasim would be the first one to go if they don't. Even if he woke up this very second, his hands are tied.

Instant karma. For the moth.

I shake the thought away. I move my gun down to shoot it myself, but before I can convince my finger to go anywhere near the trigger, a baying call from the forest echoes all around us, pulling the Reds' guns out like a magnet. The four in the clearing jump to their feet. The gore under my branch hasn't moved, ears flicking back and forth at the hunting call from out in the darkness. The girl has two guns out now, standing wide over Kasim.

With their heads pointing toward the strange cry, none of them are ready when the gore under me charges. It zips through the trees, too fast for something its size, snapping toward Kai before he realizes the beast is there. A second gore charges in, hackles raised as it joins the first.

I can't wrench my eyes away from them. The gores are grue-somely beautiful, heavy hyena-like shoulders at least five feet off the ground, spiky manes trailing down their muscular necks to a pointy nose. Their faces are dark brown, eyes sunken in over a mouth lined with jagged teeth engineered for ripping and tearing. But when the first bite clenches down, I cover my face with one hand, tree bark pressing painfully into my cheek as Kai begins screaming, the trophy in a ghastly game of tug-of-war. The beasts crouch down on long muscled legs, roughly shaking their heads back and forth as they go to work on him, powerful shoulders out of proportion with their smaller hindquarters.

The remaining Reds stand transfixed as the gores rip their leader to pieces. One jerks himself out of shock and shoots, bringing a gore around snarling, red blossoming on its spotted neck. The other gore latches on to Kai's bloody leg and drags his body into the trees.

The soldiers finally come together, firing point-blank into the injured gore charging them. Snapping its jaws down on a gunman's shoulder, the gore ignores the bullets as they burn smoking trails through its fur, not forceful enough to penetrate its thick hide. Leaving the Red in a crumpled heap, the thing lunges hungrily toward Kasim. Its formidable jaws rip through the unconscious Menghu's coat before one of the bullets finds its way past the tough hide, dark drops of blood matting the coarse hair at its hip. Keening squeals raise the hairs on my arms, the unearthly cries sending creatures all around us streaking away through the forest. The wounded monster darts out of the clearing, uneven gait spattering blood behind it in a slippery red trail.

The Reds left standing don't have time to lower their weapons before they fall, one after the other, in an ungraceful heap around Kasim. I didn't even hear the gunshots.

A Menghu coat steps in, gun out, switching aim between the fallen soldiers. Pulling the men off Kasim, she twitches his coat aside, eyeing the ragged tears in his chest. Another Menghu stalks out of the trees, and I catch sight of a wide mouth. It's Cale listening to see if Kasim is breathing, Mei standing watch with her gun drawn.

I yell out to them, half climbing and half falling as I come down from the tree, stumbling toward the pile of Reds around Kasim. The gashes in his chest aren't deep, but blood is flowing. Cale's gun follows me down the tree trunk.

"What are you doing out here?" she asks. Casually. As though her finger isn't one twitch away from blowing off my head.

Mei pulls her hood back, looking around at all the dead Reds. She kicks the girl as she walks by, the soldier's head jerking lifelessly against the ground. When she kneels by Kasim, her face is calm. "He's alive, but not in good shape. They must have hit him pretty hard for him still to be unconscious. I think the cuts on his chest are superficial, but this"—she points to his leg, twisted underneath him—"is definitely broken. We need to get him out of here."

"I've got some medic experience. . . ." I falter. Even at the orphanage, they would have sent Kasim to the hospital. Backing away from Cale, I jerk my attention from the gun still following my every move.

Easing Kasim's leg so that it is straight, I pull off my jacket to pad it. With Mei's help, I splint the break with a straight branch from nearby. Not perfect, but it might get us back to the Mountain.

"They were setting those." I nod toward the two disks piled next to the bodies as I tie the splint. "I heard one of the Reds say they were supposed to leave them and run."

Mei rolls one up on its side, brows knitted together as she looks it over. "Too small to be mines. What do you think, Cale?"

Cale's gun is still on me, her eyes narrowed. The weapon tucked into my coat pinches at my side, my hands shaking a little as I try to concentrate on Kasim, not the thoughts that must be running through the Menghu's head.

She blinks. Finally lets the pistol fall. Dropping down by one of the Reds, Cale looks over at Mei. "You got one of them, Mei. I'm proud of you." She stuffs something in her pocket, stepping on the dead girl's hand as she stands back up.

"Can you lift him?" Cale asks as she stoops behind Kasim, threading her arms under his wide shoulders to pick him up. "Or are you really as useless as I thought?"

I kneel at his legs, balancing the splint on one shoulder and wrapping an arm around his other knee. He's heavy. Too heavy. But I'm not going to admit that now. Mei grabs one of the disks and follows.

As we walk by the Reds' packs, Cale catches a toe on a loose strap and skips a step, landing on one of the disks still lying on the ground. The light in the center of the disk flashes red, white . . . and then my ears are inside out, boiling with noise, the bright white of an explosion all around me, tearing at my hair and clothes. A loud hissing fills my ears as I try to pick myself up from the ground. I break a quicklight, but the air is so clouded with dirt and gas it's like being underwater, my eyes straining to identify dark shapes in the blur.

When things start to clear, Cale lies crumpled on the ground at my feet, Kasim an inanimate heap next to her. Fragments of the disk lie smoldering all around them, burning holes in Cale's coat. As I take it all in, smoke blooms around her head, her tangled blond hair bursting into flame.

I frantically roll her over in the dirt, batting at the fire's crackled touch until it's dead. Her eyes don't open. Anxiously checking for a pulse, I take a few breaths to calm myself enough to be able to feel it.

It's there. Fluttering like a hummingbird's wings. Bending close to her upturned face, I feel faint brushes of air against my ear.

Mei crashes down next to me, and I have to look twice to make sure I'm not giving in to a hallucination. Black plastic obstructs the bottom half of her face, curling up over her nose and into her mouth, clasping a mesh filter, making her look like a monster from the First library fairy stories. She rips through her bag and pulls out another one like it, shoving it up against my face and helping to untangle the rubber clasp. "Check Kasim!" Her breath rasps through the mask in a tinny hiss as she pulls Cale's mask out. "Get his mask on if he's breathing."

Kasim's eyes are open when I get to him, but he bats my hands away when I start looking for the mask. I have to turn both of the Reds over before I find his bag. When I hand him the mask, he just looks at it. Taking it back, I try to fit it over his mouth, but he jerks away, landing an open-handed slap across the back of my head.

Mei tries to pull him up into a sitting position, but he fights her, too. She lets him slump back to the ground, and pulls me in close. "We have to move. I don't know who else is out here . . . or what. We've made so much noise. . . ."

She picks up fragments of the disk and shoves them into her pack, far enough from Kasim that he can't reach her. "I'll stay with him while you go for help," she says. "Can you get Cale back?"

The filter on Cale's mask is painted with sharp teeth, a grotesque imitation of the monsters that just ran away into the forest. Pushing back a shudder, I boost her up, sliding her over my shoulders. The bone bracelet she's always wearing flops off onto the ground, so I pick it up and tuck it into one of my pockets.

By the time Kasim and Mei are out of sight, my steps are already heavy. Running back toward the Mountain soon becomes walking, then trudging. It feels as though Cale has gained a hundred pounds in the five minutes I've been carrying her.

A rustling in the bushes off to my right turns my head. Eyeing the leaves as they sway in the wind, fear kicks through me, Cale's unbearable weight pinning me to the spot. A low growl whispers toward us and something large moves, leaves swirling around its shadowy outline. A pointy nose and black sunken eyes swish through the curtain of vines. The thing's mouth opens wide in an excited *yip*, yellow teeth jagged and bloody.

The gore charges us, its graceful bounds lopsided by dark trails of blood running down one of its legs. Cale is on the ground and my gun is out before my mind registers that I am about to be torn to pieces, but my shots ring out in quick succession.

The barreling hulk seems to trip and fall midstride, momentum tangling its legs, sending it to the ground in a heap, nose twitching inches from my feet. It snaps at my boot and I trip over Cale in my hurry to put distance between me and its sharp snout.

It thrashes closer to Cale, eyes on her unmoving form. Hungry, even moments from death. I level my gun, find its eye, the cold metal reflected in the endless black pupil. Fire.

CHAPTER 30

OUR DORMITORY IS SO QUIET. IT SEEMS WRONG, as if after all the gunshots and death tonight, my room should be part of the war zone. Mei lies across from me with a pillow over her head. As if nothing happened.

Cale woke up as I carried her in. They have her on a monitor in a sterile white room over in Yizhi. No word on SS levels yet, but they are watching her.

She didn't look at me once. Wouldn't even ask what happened. I left with her toothy mask in my hands, not sure what to do with it. I didn't even remember that I wasn't supposed to be in the hospital until I caught one of the Yizhi workers pointing at me, two more joining with him to watch as I brushed my way out the door.

The team that brought Kasim in took him straight to surgery, but the healthy warmth in his eyes was back by the time they hustled him past me in the hall. He was cracking jokes with the boys carrying the stretcher and winking at Mei.

They have him locked up somewhere too. Just in case.

I didn't know what to do next, so I followed Mei back to our room. To sleep.

At least Mei is succeeding.

I can't close my eyes without seeing the gore's fluid leap toward me, or Kasim's blood pooling in the dirt all around him, or the Reds sinking to the ground in slow motion. My mind keeps replaying it all over and over until I have to get up.

As I wander up and down the Menghu halls, my bare feet ache with the cold. This whole place seems to be submersed in ice water. I walk until I'm high up above the Core, dangling my feet out over the hundred-foot drop through the railing. The height pulls at me, pressing at my lungs and tingling in my head. It makes me forget all the things lurking just behind my eyelids.

I look up when someone slides down next to me, shifting his legs over the side to kick beside mine. Howl's eyes have heavy, dark circles underneath them, making him look years older. But he still has a smile for me.

I turn back to the edge, not sure what to say. Howl knows more than what he told me outside. Knows what it is Dr. Yang wants. But he has deliberately kept it from me. Why? He was arguing for people in the City, arguing not to let the Cales and Helixes in the Menghu ranks near unarmed citizens with a gun. I put a hand to my forehead at the thought of Cale, my stomach writhing with the image of her coat burning, the gore's jagged teeth as it opened its mouth wide . . .

"Are you all right?" Howl finally breaks the silence.

I close my eyes. "I don't think I ever said thank you."

"Thank you for what?" His voice is rough. Tired.

"For getting me out of the City. Away from this." I hold my hand out, scar stark and white against my skin. Helix's comments climb up into my thoughts, pitched against the argument I over-heard in the Heart, demanding to be let out. But the words don't come, stamped down beneath the gore's black eyes.

He takes one of my hands, rubbing his thumb across the brand. "Did it hurt?"

"I don't remember." I want Howl to be the person I got to know in the forest. The person who carried me away from the Reds when I had a concussion and cried with June when Liming died. I have to trust someone.

And I choose Howl.

I chose him when I pushed the last hope of Tai-ge out of my mind. And Howl chose me back, not caring where it led him, who would be angry. I finally understand what he meant that first day when he told Dr. Yang that I was the only one like him. He's the only one like *me*. Banished from the City. Running away from our pasts. We're both outcasts from the place we once thought of as home.

"I can't stand the Menghu," I say. "I think I'm done."

Howl raises an eyebrow. "You want to go back?"

"No. Not to the City." There wasn't much of a life in the City for me even when the Firsts still were willing to tolerate my presence. I can see that now. With an execution order on my head, I'd almost rather let the gores do it than stand under the Arch with my mother watching from above. "I can't fit here. I don't want to. If it weren't for Mantis . . . I just want to go live in our tree house Outside. With huge electric fences to keep everything out." My own safe haven. Where I can break myself into little pieces in peace.

Howl catches my eye and puts a finger to his lips. He slips a hand into my pocket, coming out empty. "I couldn't find you on the telescreen. I saw you from down there." He nods toward the floor stories below us. "You don't have your ID card, right?"

I must have left it in Jiaoyang before going Outside with Kasim. "No. Are they . . . ?" I look around the way he did, but no one is in sight. He's worried about our voices carrying. Whispering as softly as I can, I say, "They're listening, too? Not just tracking me."

He nods. "We can talk in Nei-ge. Or Outside. But they are definitely keeping tabs on both of us."

"Why?" My voice is flat. The idea should bother me, but I can't find any emotion left over to worry.

"That is a very complicated question." Howl pulls me up from the balcony and we walk down the hall, a tingle sparking up my side as he slips an arm around my waist. He whispers too, now, "Maybe we should ask June about it."

June? Does he mean he's reached the end of wanting to stay here too, and this is the safest way to say it?

"Should we ask her?" I glance self-consciously up at the screens around us, wondering if someone is watching right now. Nervousness and an odd fluttering at the word "we" attempt to penetrate the fuzz coating my brain.

"I think it would be the safest option." He looks both ways. "The sooner, the better."

I don't have any fear, the gore attack blocking out what "going to ask June" would mean. No Mantis. Outside. Facing the unknown. "Maybe if I make it through the night, okay? It's pure luck that I'm not half-digested right now. We can talk about it in the morning."

Howl's angry tone surprises me. "I don't know what Kasim was thinking. If I had known . . ." He rubs his eyes. "That's

why I'm up, actually. General Root wanted to show me the disk
Mei brought in. It's an SS mine, but nothing like I've ever seen
before. You found them setting the mines near the base of the
Mountain?"

"I found them dragging Kasim away by his ankles. The disk
was just a bonus." I shake my head, an image of Kasim's leg bent
askew shivering through me. "Is Kasim going to fall Asleep? And
Cale?"

Howl shrugs. "We'll see, I guess. It doesn't make sense. The
City knows we have Mantis. And the effectiveness of these things
would be tiny, only infecting three or four people at the most."
He pulls something out of his pocket and presses it into my hand,
then puts a finger to his lips. "I'll walk you back to your room."

"What is . . ."

He shakes his head, glancing at the telescreen.

It's as long as my pinkie and rubbed smooth, like a river rock.
Thick at one end, it narrows to a point under my fingers. There
is a leather strap tied around it. A necklace. I keep it balled in my
fist, hiding it from anyone who might be watching.

Night-lights follow us as we walk, little points of illumina-
tion dribbling out over our feet. As we pass a closed door, Howl
squeezes my arm and taps the sign at the side of the door marked
SERVICE.

Meeting his eyes, I nod. I'll remember where the door is. Are
we really going to leave? But what about . . . me? SS?

When we get back to the Menghu collective, he bends in close,
lips brushing my ear. "Be careful. Don't talk about it. Three days
from now." And points back down the hallway.

The service stairs must go Outside to the maintenance grid.
I nod and hold up three fingers. Establishment celebrations Mei

told me about are in three days. Maybe the Menghu will be too distracted to notice we're gone. He stands there, grim-faced. I want him to laugh, to smile again. "I had fruit for breakfast this morning. It was amazing. Thank you for convincing me it isn't poison."

His eyes crinkle up at the corners, full mouth curving into that smile I was hoping for. I want him to come nearer, to turn how close we are into something real. I want everything to be right. His fingers sweep the hair out of my face, messy from my unsuccessful sleep.

"You are beautiful, you know that?"

No one has ever said that to me before. No one has even wanted to. I have to look down, closing my eyes for a second before looking up to meet his gaze.

Howl puts one hand to my cheek and kisses my forehead, leaving me unbalanced, but calmer. I couldn't sleep before because of bloody memories. Now I won't be able to sleep because of that kiss warm on my forehead.

Helix can go die. I don't even know what he was talking about. In three days, it won't matter.

CHAPTER 31

AT BREAKFAST THE NEXT MORNING, MEI IS STONE-
cold, food forgotten in her lap. I take a look around the room
before walking over. No one moves toward me, so I slide down
onto the step next to her, but something in my pocket sends me
right back up.

A bone bracelet. Cale's, from last night.

I pull out the hundreds of tiny bones, all threaded together
with fishing line. I can't think the bracelet would be very comfortable to wear, with all the pieces sticking into you and catching on
things. But to each her own, I guess.

Mei's eyes fall on the bracelet. "Where did you get that? You
shouldn't have any."

"Any what?" I hand it over. She holds it in a white-knuckled
grip in her lap, resuming her gloomy silence.

Another girl I recognize from the dorms slides in next to us.
"You two were shadowing Kasim and Cale last night, weren't
you?" she asks, twirling a bracelet on her arm. Bone, kind of like
Cale's. "Are they going to be okay?"

I wait for Mei to answer, but she doesn't look up from her eggs.

"Kasim wasn't out of surgery when I left, but everyone seemed to think he'd pull through all right," I say. "I think they're just going to watch them for the next few days."

Another girl joins us, toying with a necklace, striking ivory against her dark skin. Bone.

They're everywhere. Another bone bracelet on a Menghu a few steps down. Necklaces, anklets sticking out from underneath green canvas. The pattern is the same on every one, the same tidy rows of bone.

Mei is still clutching Cale's bracelet as though it's made of gold. Suddenly, I realize where I've seen that composition of bones. In an anatomy book Mother made me read through before she left.

They're finger bones. Trigger fingers.

Hundreds of pieces wired together at the joints to make each pointing finger. Interlocked, clasped, dead in that bracelet. It couldn't be. My mind flashes back to that first week in the forest with Howl, the soldier with bloody stumps instead of trigger fingers. And last night, Cale stooped over the dead Reds.

I felt so apart from everyone here, as though I would never be quite comfortable. The rigid military schedule, nothing that belongs to me, and the technology bubbling out of the walls wherever there is space. But that wasn't why. Looking around with fresh eyes, I see hundreds of dead men. Each missing a finger or two.

I rake Mei up and down with my eyes, looking for her set, but she's clean. Grabbing her wrist, I pull her up away from the group. When we're out of earshot, I whisper, "Where are yours, Mei? Why don't you have any?"

"Any what? What is wrong with you?"

"The bones. The fingers. Everyone over there is wearing a list of people they've killed."

"Oh." She shrugs, disinterested. "Don't you know? The Menghu keep track. The General doesn't like it, but . . ."

"You keep score." My voice sounds flat in my ears. "Where are yours?"

The question hangs in the air between us, but Mei doesn't even blink. "I'm still in training. I'm not allowed."

She leaves me standing there, everything finally clear. Helix's *shoot first, smile about it later* policy isn't a savage exception.

It's the *rule*.

They really are going to invade the City. Howl's argument last night that invasion would be a bloodbath seemed so dramatic, but he's right. The way Mei looks at Howl's First mark, the way any of the Menghu talk about the City . . . They wouldn't be doing it for the Mantis. Invasion would be revenge. A delight. A chance to add to their jewelry collection. It isn't just Helix and Cale who are the monsters. If the Menghu invade, *no one* will survive. My fingers find the rusty ring on the necklace around my throat.

A pair of hands grabs my shoulders, and I spin around to fight them off, tripping over my boots. At first all I see is a woman in a white coat, her arms coming up defensively when I wrestle my way out of her embrace. But it's Sole, the concern in her eyes at war with the way her mouth twitches into that odd grimacing excuse for a grin. "You're so pale," she says. "What's wrong?"

I don't have anything to say, the burn of realization still coursing through my veins.

"Still in shock from last night? Deep breaths, Jiang Sev."

I want to run as my eyes latch on to each new set of bones

on the people around me. Run and tell Howl that we can't wait another three days. I have to keep Tai-ge from becoming just another trophy, fingers stripped down and bound into a bracelet at some Menghu's wrist.

"I heard you stood down a gore to protect your roommate. Cale, right?" Sole is still talking. Oblivious to the twitch that keeps jerking her shoulder up toward her head. She used to be one of them. Killers. "You two must be close."

"Close?" I shudder the thought away. I don't even remember pulling the trigger last night. That thing just folded up in front of me like a paper doll in a fire.

"And you're already taking keepsakes." Even her voice is cold.

"Keepsakes? Like those bracelets?" I ask.

"I don't think I would have stuck my hand in a gore's mouth." She points to the long white tooth hanging from a leather cord around my neck. Howl's gift from last night. It seemed as though it was meant to be a secret when he pressed it into my hand, but I haven't discovered anything exciting about it. After staring at it for a long time this morning, I threaded my mother's piece of jade and the rusty ring onto the leather next to it. After some thought, I added my star pin and put the necklace on. Past, present, and future.

"Is that what this is?" The thought of the gore's long, pointed teeth spearing toward me makes me want to take the thing off and wash my neck. "Howl gave it to me."

"*Howl* gave that to you?" Sole leans forward, her eyes hungrily taking it in. "City Howl? The Howl you came in with?"

"Yes. Are there other Howls?" I shift uncomfortably, covering the necklace.

She shrugs, eyes latched on to my hand sheltering the tooth.

Someone taps my shoulder, and I'm grateful, wanting to get away from that intense stare. That is, until I look up and see Helix.

"You're needed downstairs. Now." His face is carved into an eternal frown.

Mei is waiting for me by the door. "Cale didn't wake up this morning. She's Asleep." Horror leaks through the cracks in her voice. *The Mountain isn't letting infected in. . . . What if contracting SS means Cale can't stay here anymore either?* The way Dr. Yang was talking about stockpiling Mantis last night makes me think the odds aren't good.

"And Kasim?"

"They won't tell me what's happening with Kasim." Mei swallows. "He's awake, but something's wrong. They won't let anyone see him. Yizhi asked us to come down to Cale's room. They're hoping we can help them figure out what was going on with those disks."

I shake my head, starting to back away, but Helix is right behind me. I can't go to Yizhi. Not after all this time running away. Not even knowing what it is they want from me. Not with all the dead walking around on display. "They won't need me."

But Mei drags me through the door, Helix following close behind. A pair of Menghu are on the other side waiting for us, and I catch one with a hand on her gun, crowding in after Helix as we start toward the doors that lead to the hospital.

The white walls in Yizhi make everything seem cold. Medics sporting gas masks flow in and out in a constant stream, all giving Mei and me a wide berth, squeezed onto a bench in the corner of the room.

Mei's angry reserve from this morning seems to have sucked

her dry, her head lolling sleepily against the wall as she draws crosses down her leg with one finger. Cale looks pathetically small under her blankets in the center of the room, dwarfed by the large hospital bed. Like a child.

I feel like an unwilling spectator at a fight, waiting for the bloody show to start. I can't just sit and watch while Cale's heart monitor beeps slower and slower. But pacing the short length of the room isn't helping. Why are they keeping us down here? It could be weeks before she wakes up.

I catch myself rubbing the gore-tooth necklace between my fingers. The smooth surface is stained ivory and no longer sharp, as though it has been many years since it was taken from the gore's mouth. As my fingers explore the wider base, they stop at a small ridge I didn't notice before.

Restlessly walking back to the door, I hold the tooth tight in my hand, as if squeezing it might somehow get me out of here. A masked Yizhi squeezes by me to shift a tube in Cale's arm, connecting it to a bag of clear fluids hanging up above the bed.

I remember what it felt like to be Asleep. The terror of not being able to move, not even twitch. Voices all around you saying that you might as well be dead. That you could be already. I tried to tell them. I tried to reach for the doctor, to shake some sense into the hand that was constantly feeling for my pulse. But nothing worked, nothing moved. My body was a prison.

I shrug the feeling off, looking back at the tooth. I almost drop it in surprise. It's glowing.

I can barely tell in the brightly lit room, but there is definitely a light inside of the thing. When I pull along the ridge at the top, a line appears and the tooth comes apart in two pieces, something falling out and rattling on the floor.

The medic by Cale's bed looks around for the source of the sound, but I bend down to pick up the fallen object before she sees, pretending to stretch. It's black, about the size of my thumbnail. I hold it in my fist, flinching when the back of my hand begins to glow.

Slipping into the bathroom attached to the room, I turn the light off and sit on the edge of the low sink with my fist balled around the object. The entire back of my hand glows orange, black characters spelled out in the faint light. It says, Where are you? I can't find you.

I unclench my hand and the characters disappear. When I clench it again, a set of character radicals appears along the side of my hand, a purple circle of light pulsing below my pinkie knuckle, as if it is asking me to write my own message. Cale mentioned Zhuanjia was experimenting with some new communication device. I press one radical and it appears in the space below, a small box blinking for me to write out the rest of the strokes for my desired character. I type the words In Yizhi with Mei and Cale slowly, not used to putting characters together this way.

Leave. Now, he responds.

I flip the light back on and return to the room, now empty of medics. Mei jerks awake as I walk by, expression hard as her eyes follow me. The guard sitting outside looks up when I open the door. Her hand is on her gun.

I go back into the bathroom and bring up the set of radicals, writing out, Not an option.

The reply comes almost instantly. I'm coming.

Fitting the thing back into the tooth, I make myself go out of the bathroom, switching places with Mei as she jumps up from the bench, hands restlessly touching everything on the walls, the equipment crammed into the room, then ducking down behind Cale's bed.

"Mei?"

Something rips. Suddenly, she's up, eyes wide with something I can't identify. Fear? Her chest is heaving and her hands are hidden behind her back. "Mei? What are you doing?"

If I didn't know better, I would think . . .

She runs at me, a long piece of wire stretched between her hands, and it's around my neck before I can yell. The force of her running knocks me over the edge of the bench and onto the floor, Mei straddling my stomach. I manage to get a hand under the wire before she pulls it tight, but she's much stronger than I am, and the wire is starting to cut across my palm, my windpipe, air choking out of me as she pulls. Her breaths come in shuddering gasps, face twisted with panic.

Three gas-masked Yizhi burst into the room. Two pull her off me, trying to contain her flailing limbs as she kicks and hits. Mei catches the third medic in the stomach with her foot, knocking a long syringe out of her hand. I roll over onto my side and grab it, flinging the wire away from me. The two holding Mei manage to get her facedown on the floor, one holding her arms, the other her legs. I jab the syringe into her exposed hip. She immediately goes limp.

"What in the name of Yuan's bloody ax is going on?" I yell. The nurses don't answer, impassive behind those masks. "She isn't infected! How could she—"

Something jabs the side of my own leg, and everything goes gray, spinning into black.

CHAPTER 32

I WAKE TO AN ENDLESS WHITE BLUR. MY ARMS and legs won't move at all, heavy, as if I've been buried alive and the earth is pressing down against me. For a moment, my mind panics, racing through all the memories I have of being Asleep, trapped inside my body but awake, listening. Helpless.

As I struggle against my lifeless arms and legs, my lungs start to contract, giving me less and less air. Is this how I'm going die? Gasping for air in my brain while my lungs refuse to listen?

But my eyes are open. I can look around me, even catch a glimpse of my nose. I can't be Asleep. No one falls Asleep twice. A calm settles over me as the thought sinks in. My fingers start to twitch and my toes tingle. My neck seems to have strength and I lift my head up. I'm not lost. My body is here, strapped to a pink mat, my necklace pulling at my throat. The numb heaviness weighing my body down must be the last of some kind of sedation wearing off.

The whiteness around me is familiar, the nylon cords coiled around my arms and legs something I've faced before, but I can't place it. A light over my face comes on and a soothing female voice purrs, "Please hold your position. Two minutes, twenty seconds remaining." I'm in the levels machine again.

A door slams as I twist against the restraints. The tube starts to hum, vibrations throbbing through me. The end of the tube pops open and my mat moves out, inch by inch, until my muscles clench with impatience. When my head finally emerges, it's Sole who is standing over me.

She's rattled, fingers shaking as she fumbles with the restraints. There's a shiny silver table pushed up next to the tube, bright lights focused in hard circles on the reflective surface, pooling at the end around a drain. A tray of sharp-looking instruments is arranged next to it, a clear mask sitting on top, connected to a tall silver canister by a long tube.

Sole's hand shoots forward, an offer to help me sit up. I take it, shivering as the cool, sterile air floods through the paper hospital gown that seems to be all I'm wearing. My feet are unsteady when they hit the floor, and I have to lean against Sole to stay up. She still hasn't said anything.

"What is going on?" I ask, fear thrilling through me as we move toward the metal table, my eyes catching on a particularly lethal-looking scalpel. Was it Sole all along? From that first frozen smile to now, leading me toward an operating table?

She doesn't stop at the table, dragging me toward the door. "No questions right now. Just move."

The door opens to a loud siren echoing around an empty office, the telescreen flashing red and black with the word FIRE racing up and down the room.

"Should we be running?" I ask.

She keeps dragging and pushing me along toward the door that takes us out into the main Yizhi hallway. "Howl set off the fire alarm upstairs so I could get you out. If you try to run right now, you'll just fall over. They pumped enough tranq into you to drop someone twice your weight."

"Why?"

"We don't have much time before they figure out the fire upstairs is just a bunch of smoke and the cameras all go back online."

We hobble down the blue-and-white-checkered halls, the drone of the alarm pounding against my eardrums until they must be bleeding. We finally come to a long, unfamiliar hallway dotted with heavy wooden doors every few feet. Sole pushes through the first door on our right.

A simple room, single bed neatly made with blankets patched in blues and greens. Sole deposits me on the quilts, moving back to the door. "I need to report to my station. If I leave now, I might be able to convince Root that I had to come up from level one. Stay here. Hide in the shower if anyone tries to come in." With that, she runs, dark hair streaming behind her.

I push through the only other door in the room, pulling the communicator out of my gore-tooth necklace. Light tile and glass shower doors shine in the lights, too clean to belong here in the Mountain. Flipping the light off, I squeeze my hand around the communicator. The characters glowing on the back of my hand are unhelpful.

It simply says, Wait for me.

CHAPTER 33

WORSE THAN BEING CHASED. WORSE THAN HIDING.

Waiting.

Sweat pours down my forehead from underneath a chin-length wig, though the cold air mists with my every breath. I adjust my borrowed tool belt, too tight over the brown Zhuanjia uniform Sole procured for me. Howl said it was too risky to go down to Sole's rooms, and he had to show me something out here in order to make our escape work, but if this takes much longer, I might have to start pretending to fix something in order to fool the cameras trained on this solar panel maintenance platform. That would bring unwelcome attention even faster.

A Zhuanjia ducks out of the metal door, face hidden beneath a billed hat. The small tube of inhibitor spray Sole gave me is supposed to stop an attacker for a few minutes, which would give me a chance to run, but where to? He walks toward me, head down, inspecting the walkway, so I can't see his face.

Pressing myself up against the wall, the inhibitor spray feels slippery in my palm. It fits in my hand perfectly, small enough that no one would know it was there until their eyes started burning, but that won't do much if I drop it.

The Zhuanjia draws closer, shielding his face against the sun, only seconds from noticing me. Do I spray him, then push him over the side? No, the fall would kill him. Leave him here for someone to find?

Just as I'm about to do . . . something, the young man looks at me, and I realize he isn't shielding his face from the sun. He's shielding brown eyes I'd know anywhere from the cameras. Howl.

I sigh in relief, the tube going back in my pocket as I follow his lead, trailing behind him along the narrow ledge cut into the side of the mountain that leads around to the base of the earth-colored solar panels. He slides between two of the panels, off the path.

"Are you okay?" he asks when I follow him in. It seems like a stupid question, but I appreciate it nonetheless.

"They didn't saw anything off." Just remembering the table all set up to cut me open gives me the shivers. "What is going on? Why did they suddenly decide to steal my kidneys? And Mei . . ."

"Not your kidneys." Howl takes his hat off, twisting it between his hands. "I thought they'd do more tests, not that they'd just try to . . ." He rubs his forehead.

"There must be other people here with SS, Howl. I'm not that annoying, am I? My hallucinations can't be that special." Trying to stay lighthearted is all that is keeping me from dissolving into tears. I can feel them, white hot behind my eyes.

"Others with SS, it's true. Three more this week. You were a test, in the hospital room across from Cale. Mei was the control subject. The mine you brought back is carrying a new strain of SS, one that transfers from person to person instead of having to contract it from a bomb. Kasim is showing all the signs of post-Sleep behavior and never even went through the sleeping stage. . . ." He points to the pocket of my Zhuanjia uniform, where a bit of red fabric is sticking out. "What is that?"

I can't answer for a moment, my breath catching in my throat. SS, contagious. SS infecting people without even making them fall Asleep first. The entire Mountain could be a slaughterhouse in minutes. The whole world will be trying to slice off their own fingers within months. There's no way they have enough Mantis stockpiled to keep everyone lucid. "What are they going to do? What are *we* going to do?"

He leans over and pulls the red fabric from my pocket. "What is this? Where did you get it? Did Sole give it to you?" His fingers pull at the pieces. "It could be bugged. Don't say anything."

"No, it's just . . ." I'm still reeling, mind blank. "I made it for you." It's a red flower, tied out of an old piece of ribbon I found in Sole's room. The long hours of staring at the wall before Howl could meet me were too much.

He holds it up, the ends of panic replaced by surprise, looking from the folds of rose-colored ribbon to me.

"Sole told me that you make good-luck charms for . . . for people about to go out on patrol or . . . or something dangerous. . . ." I stumble over the words. She'd stumbled over them too, presenting them to me like some sort of offering during the long wait in her room, as if she was trying to show me that the people who had almost cut me to pieces had good sides to them too.

Howl's face softens. "For Boyfriends. Girlfriends. Husbands and wives." His mouth is starting to curve into a grin. "So they're with you when you go. And to make sure everyone knows you've been spoken for."

"Right." My cheeks heat up and my hands twist into my shirt

of their own volition. I made it with butterflies in my stomach, nervous that he would just laugh at me. But it's too late to worry; the flower is in his hand, so I might as well see it through. My hands reach out like they belong to someone else, settling on his shoulders. "But if you are asking me to marry you, then my answer is no. I'm only sixteen."

He laughs and leans forward, closing the gap between us, his hands pressing into my waist and back. "Thank you. I've never wanted something like this. Not until now." Howl's head is heavy on my shoulder, holding on tight.

I hug him back, surprised by his reaction. "I hope that is a good thing."

Howl pulls away, pressing his lips together. "I need to tell you something. Something that I should have told you the moment I dragged you off the street in the City."

"More important than the fact that the Mountain is probably already boiling over with loose infected?" I look down the slope, my mind teetering on the rocky edge below us, wondering how far down it goes. "Should we just make a break for it right now?"

Howl's fingers brush my chin back toward him. "Dr. Yang suspected something odd was going on, so Kasim and Cale have been quarantined since the moment they took their masks off. They can't do anything else until they figure out how long this new contagion lasts. The Mountain isn't going to turn into a slaughterhouse unless someone else steps on a mine and doesn't tell anyone."

The medics all knew and they did nothing. They wore their masks, breathing filtered air while Mei poisoned herself sitting in Cale's room. "How will they know when it stops being contagious? Is Dr. Yang just going to keep sending people into Cale's

room to see if they start having compulsions?" The bite of anger
in my voice isn't meant for Howl, but he shrinks back a little.

"You were the one they were testing in that room. Mei was
there to make sure it was contagious to normal people."

"I'm already infected. Are they trying to see if being exposed
again makes me worse? If I become contagious too? Or if Mantis
will stop working like it has in the City?"

Howl scrunches his eyes closed, hands tightening on my shoulders. I want to brush them away because it's starting to hurt, his
fingers digging into me. "They wanted to see if it would affect
you because you aren't infected. You've been cured."

"Cured?" I pull away from him. That doesn't make sense.
With a cure, there would be no war. No Mountain, no City. We
wouldn't have to fight for Mantis anymore. "You haven't been
messing around with Da'ard, have you? There is no cure. If there
were, they would have found it a long time ago."

Howl is already shaking his head. "No. The Mountain doesn't
have the cure. And to the best of our knowledge, the City doesn't
have it either. The cure is what your mother was working on when
she came here with Dr. Yang. And she succeeded. With you."

He rubs his cheek, uncomfortable for some reason, but the
rest comes out in a rush. "That is why those primary kids have
been staring at you since the day you walked in here. Not just the
primary kids. Anyone who saw that birthmark. You are hope. The
end of SS. The cure."

It's my turn to shake my head. "That's impossible. It doesn't
even make sense. Why would the City have put my mother in
Suspended Sleep for creating a cure?"

He shrugs. "Your guess is as good as mine. But that is why
she left you. Not to save the Mountain, and not to give Mantis

to Outsiders or to win any wars. It was because the City put you to Sleep and wouldn't let her help you. The moment she and Dr. Yang had something she thought would work, she ran straight back to your bedside."

"The *City* . . . Why would they have put me to sleep? SS wasn't even supposed to be there before Mother brought it back." Everything seems to burn red around me, Howl's face blurring. The City gave me SS? But *why*? The City told me my mother hated me enough to inject me herself. . . . I can't even finish the thought, General Hong's deep voice enumerating my mother's many crimes in my head. The City did it. *The City did it?* And she left only to figure out how to fix me?

Dr. Yang told me they used SS as a punishment, as a warning for people venturing across the line of First rule. That I wasn't the first SS case at all, just one in a long string of warnings of what it meant to defy Firsts. If she was like Howl, questioning what the Firsts were doing . . .

No, it isn't possible. I remember her coming back, the press of a needle in my arm and her voice . . . but that was after I was Asleep, wasn't it? I knew she'd come back, I knew she'd given me something. Did I somehow make up memories to go along with the stories General Hong told? Pinching and pulling the nightmares until they fit? "What about my hallucinations? And remember the first night we met, when I tried to kill myself? That wasn't an act to make you feel sorry for me."

"And it scared me halfway back to Liberation days." His smile falls crooked. I want to reach out and smooth it out, to put it back the way it's supposed to be. "Those hallucinations were side effects of the pills you were taking. Firsts have been working nonstop to re-infect you, to see if they can beat the cure. The medicine they were having you take instead of Mantis can cause patients to demonstrate SS symptoms, and they were experimenting with it to see if they could get better results. The orphanage accidentally gave you a little too much that day, so the hallucinations turned into a full-blown compulsion."

I hadn't ever had a compulsion until the night we ran. The story fits so many things together so that they finally make sense. I didn't start hallucinating until the weeks following my sister's death. Perhaps getting rid of Aya gave the Circle the idea to get rid of me, too, using my poor, sad little life as one last experiment to force the disease Mother had purged from my system on me. When they realized Thirds saw Aya as yet another proof of my family's corruption, I became a tool. The last Jiang to go out in a flame of compulsions and insanity, the last of the sleeping princess's family to be punished for her crimes. An ache springs up inside of me, filtering through my chest all the way down to my toes.

I want to believe this nonsense.

I want to believe that I'm free. That the black ugliness waiting under my skin is just my imagination. That we can run.

My breath catches on something even deeper, more painful. If she did cure me, does that make the monster who lives above Traitor's Arch the mother I loved after all? A refugee from the City because they wouldn't let her help me? My hand finds the jade strung around my neck, the sharp edges pressing into my skin. It would mean she loved me and died for it. Worse. Spent the last eight years imprisoned in her own body, unable to die because of it. All for me.

Something clicks in my head, another puzzle piece landing. "I started having hallucinations again when we got here. They aren't nearly as bad, but . . . Dr. Yang is doing the same thing to me that they were in the City, isn't he?"

Howl nods curtly. "Dr. Yang didn't tell me they were going to continue the tests. It has something to do with figuring out what part of your brain changed, what your mother did to cure you."

"But the levels tests, the pills they're giving me . . . It isn't enough." That's why I ended up immobile in the levels machine, a bone saw lying next to me with my name on it. That's what Dr. Yang was asking the council to do that night. "They need to dig deeper. All those tests they were asking for, the people trying to drag me into the hospital . . ." It wasn't until this moment that the horrifying truth occurs to me. "Wait, you *knew*?"

He shakes his head, his tone a plea. "Dr. Yang promised not to hurt you. He told me scans would be enough, that he'd be able to just look at your brain and see what had been changed and how. I wanted to believe him. I knew the pills Dr. Yang gave us when we left the City weren't Mantis, but I didn't realize what they were doing to you at first." He blinks as though trying to banish something in his thoughts. "You were so scared. Convinced that something was wrong with you. That day, with the dead soldiers . . . I started giving you the real Mantis, the stuff meant to go back to the Mountain. Then when we got here . . . I can't tell you how many arguments I had with Dr. Yang. How many times I followed you to make sure you were okay."

"But you knew the whole time I didn't have SS. That I didn't have to worry every single day my mind was slipping, that I wasn't going to wake up one morning and kill you?"

"You wouldn't have believed me, Sev."

I open my mouth, the beginnings of anger curdling across my tongue, but then swallow it down. He's right. I wouldn't have believed him. Not after so many years of believing it was only a little green pill between me and compulsion's tight grip.

"Don't they suspect that you had something to do with me disappearing from the operating table?" I ask, but Howl won't meet my eyes. There's something more that he isn't saying.

"I'm not the likeliest person to be hiding you. For a lot of reasons."

Howl lets go of me as I start to squirm away from him. I need space. To think. "What do you mean? You're my only friend here who isn't currently in quarantine. Of course it would be you hiding me—"

"We have another problem," Howl interrupts, looking up toward the path. "When you disappeared, Nei-ge voted to invade the City. Root says with this new strain of SS, we don't have a choice. No cure, and even the Mantis stockpiled here would never be enough if SS starts spreading from person to person."

I can't take in all this new information. I wish I could slow it down, make it stop.

"They are going to announce the invasion at Establishment and head out within a few days." Howl's voice sounds broken. "They're sending Menghu into the City."

Everything inside me goes still. My panic that SS could spread like lice in an orphanage at any time, discovering the truth about my mother's supposed crimes, hearing that the Mountain wants to cut me open—everything bows to a vision of Helix pressing a gun between Tai-ge's eyes, Peishan lying cold in the Sanatorium, Sister Shang weeping in front of the orphanage while it burns . . . "If the Menghu go into the City, it would be a massacre."

Invading wouldn't be about Mantis for any of the Menghu. It would be about killing every City-born in sight, about trophies, about revenge for everything the Mountain has had to go through in order to survive.

"Howl, what do we do? Tai-ge, your family . . . They'll die."

Howl's laugh is unnerving, with a hopeless edge I didn't expect. "There's nothing we can do to save my family. There never was."

"A cure would stop the invasion. It would stop this whole stupid war." The realization that I might have grown up Fourth for nothing boils inside me, but I close my eyes, trying to think of the cure, of what Mother must have been fighting for.

She was trying to *save* me, not kill me. Mother wasn't fighting for the Mountain or Kamar. She left to finish her SS experiment here so that she could cure me. If what Howl is saying is true, then she was fighting to cure everyone.

Am I brave enough to let Dr. Yang have the cure so that her work doesn't come undone? To walk back into the Mountain and close my eyes forever so that the SS nightmare can finally be over?

If I do, does that make me like her? If what Howl says is true, she gave up everything to save me. Could I give up everything to save the world—to save the Mountain, the City, the people like June running free in between—from SS?

If it would have saved Aya, I would have done it without hesitation. If it would keep June safe now, I'd do it. And Howl . . . I look at him. He lied to me; he's been lying to me since the day we met . . . but I'd still do it to keep Howl from ever feeling SS's monster claws in his brain.

When I open my mouth, Howl stops me. "You don't have to die to stop this. We can't rediscover the cure, just the two of us. But I know someone who can."

"What do you mean?" My head hangs as if it's already severed, already being dissected and labeled. But Howl's words bring me back up, hope flaring through me like alcohol under a match.

"We need your mother. We need to wake Jiang Gui-hua up."

CHAPTER 34

ESTABLISHMENT DAWNS WITH NEW FALLEN SNOW.
I can't see it or taste it, cloistered in Sole's room the way I've been
for days, but the air feels different. Patrols are all coming in for the
festivities tonight, wet with the sky's melted offering.

Sole bars the door as passing field medics stop to say hello.
Excitement buzzes through the halls, conversations humming
constantly outside the door. Even hidden beneath the wig and
a long white Yizhi uniform, I feel exposed, as if whoever was
slated to cut me open will notice the line of my skull or the width
between my eyes and recognize me.

When Sole has to leave for Establishment games, she locks me
in. "My ID chip will open this door, but no one else can just walk
in. Don't answer if anyone knocks."

"You're kidding, right? I'm not dumb enough to let anyone in
here."

Sole's head ticks sideways and she blinks four times in a row
before answering. "Yes. It was meant to be a joke. Here, Howl
told me to give you this."

She holds out a book, and I recognize the sleeping princess on the front. *Sleeping Beauty*, but with a happy ending. I take it, and Sole wipes her hand on her tunic three times, as if trying to destroy some unseen germ colony deposited on her hand from something so old and dirty.

The whole time I've been stuck in Sole's room, she's been kind. Kind but odd. Staring at the wall for long periods of time, never making eye contact. Laughing when we haven't even been talking. But it's less unnerving than it was at first.

The only thing that bothers me anymore is the way she looks at the gore tooth strung between the four stars and my mother's jade around my neck. I had to hide it away in my pocket. Every time her eyes touched my neck, it felt like she wanted to take a bite out of me.

Sole gave me her medic pack, full of food, water purifiers, medicine, a hammock. A padded jacket with rough fur lining the hood. A huge brown blotch stains the left side, but I don't care to ask where it came from. The hours left to wait seem to be stretching out as I pace, hundreds of times longer than they should be. If only I had someone to play weiqi with.

The book could be good company for the last hours I have to wait, but I'm still not sure I can bring myself to open it.

I reorganize my things in the borrowed pack one last time before settling down on the bed to look at the peaceful sleep of the princess on the book's cover. The long hours of silence have been painful. Thinking hurts too much. About being cured, about my mother and why she really left. There are so many pieces still missing, but for the first time, the raw edges of hurt where she lives in my chest aren't nauseating pains of betrayal. It's just a sad story that I don't know the ending to yet. What if, just like Howl said, Sleeping Beauty really does wake up? What if she isn't really the villain after all? And if she isn't, who is?

It hurts. Every thought of her still leaves me feeling broken and alone. But now I can ask her myself. I can have the truth from her lips.

I check for the syringe that Howl pressed into my hand before we parted. It's the same syringe I remember seeing in Dr. Yang's office, mounted on a plaque like some great award. Howl told me that Dr. Yang was a member of the research team my mother headed, studying the effects of SS. But he discovered this instead: Suspended Sleep. Similar to the first stages of SS, induced by a simple injection, but controllable. This syringe is full of the only thing that can wake the subject up.

He gave up everything, his First status, his family, to follow Mother here, thinking that his breakthrough might be a step toward the cure. Instead, the First Circle used his discovery to put mother to Sleep.

Maybe he regrets it now. Making the poison that closed her eyes forever.

Breaking out tonight is still the best plan we can come up with. With most people inside celebrating Establishment, there won't be as many patrols or guards out. Howl will put in an appearance at the festivities tonight so no one will go looking for him until morning.

I put the book down, not sure I can handle the hope that a happy ending would open up inside of me. Stories are just stories, however much we want to believe them.

Sole's room is small, a bed and a desk packed into the tiny room. Piles of paperwork black with spidery handwriting spill over the scarred wooden surface of the desk, a few loose leafs on the floor and under the chair. I turn one over and it's an inky monster, black teeth bared in a snarl. Next to the beast, a little girl cowers, hiding her head under her arms.

Pushing the sketch away from me, I notice a drawer that is cracked open, a set of eyes staring out from the gap. I pull the drawer open and four people look up at me from the blacks and grays of a framed watercolor. A family of four, mischievous grins matching across all of their faces. The mother has Sole's clear blue eyes, the color scratched in long after the original paint dried, her hand intertwined with that of the man standing next to her. The young man seated in front of them looks a little too straight-backed for the grin on his face, probably elbowing the younger girl sitting next to him. She would be just like Sole except for the unmistakable joy in her face.

I don't notice another person in the room until a hand comes down across their faces, grabbing the portrait away from me. Sole holds the picture to her chest, eyebrows drawn low. "What do you think you are doing?"

"I-I-I'm sorry," I stutter. "I shouldn't have . . . I'm sorry."

The anger on Sole's face drains at my downcast eyes, leaving the contrite apology hovering between us. She sighs, running her fingers along the wooden frame. "You can look if you want."

She takes a long look at them, nose close to the glass, before holding it back out toward me, pointing to the young man. "He taught me to shoot a gun. Chan."

"Your brother?"

"Yes. They were all . . . They all died together. About ten years ago. In the forest. The Reds . . ." She shivers as though trying to shake the memory loose. "It's still difficult to talk about. They were trying to steal food from one of the convoys going to the City."

"I'm so sorry." It's uncomfortable to watch her, raw grief quaking through her.

"When it first happened, I was so angry." She glances at me. "I'm sure they've told you. The moment I was old enough, I joined the Menghu. I was the worst of them. Completely out of control. Took out every Red I came across. Signed up for every mission. I hardly ate or slept, I was so busy taking revenge for what the City did to my family."

I hand the picture back to her, Kasim's words coming back to me. *One of the best . . .* She sees the question in my face before I can hide it away, too personal to ask.

"You want to know why I stopped." She pulls a stray hair behind her ear with a trembling hand. "Why I shake and can't look anyone in the eye."

She abruptly turns away from me, walks back toward the bathroom, leaving the picture on the table. When she comes back, there's a box in her arms, rattling with each step. It drops to the floor at my feet with a clatter.

"I started taking things from the people I killed. Little things, so I could keep track. For my parents, for my brother."

Sole, too? "You mean like the bracelets they all wear?"

"I think I was the first to keep score." Sole's voice is dead. "Though I never took fingers."

I back up a step, my legs hitting her bed. Sole has always seemed like she didn't fit in somehow, as if she was rebelling against something here, so when it was Sole who hid me in her tub, I didn't question it. Suddenly, that seems like a gross misjudgment.

She points to the box, sending a chill down my spine. Is she even worse than the rest, with a box of severed ears or bloody feet in her bathroom? When I don't bend down to look inside, Sole pulls the lid away herself, thrusting her hands down inside.

A doll. One that I've seen before.

The City mass-manufactures the same doll for all the kids. I had one when I was little. I remember her braided yarn hair and her red uniform. Did Sole kill children, too? I feel myself shrinking farther and farther down against the bed, wondering if I jumped off the operating table just to land in the butcher shop.

Her eyes eat at the doll, voice evaporating from her lips so I scarcely catch the words. "About six years ago, on patrol, we found a set of Reds outside the City. A man and a woman. We shot them before they could even blink, heads blown open all over their gear. The tent was ripped to shreds, but then a little girl rolled out and started to run. That's when I realized that they weren't Reds, they were just a family trying to escape the City. But my partner shot her before she ran five steps."

"She cried while she died. I held her, but she was scared of me. I made it worse. They could have been my family. Running away from the Reds and their guns, the Firsts and their experiments. All dead." Tears trail down Sole's face, and she holds the doll to her chest as if it's a real child. I lean over to look in the box, full of odds and ends. Books, rocks, rings and necklaces. "I keep them now to remember what I've done. I switched over to Yizhi, but no matter how many lives I save, I can't give any of these back. I can't give back the lives I've taken.

"The Menghu can't remember that people out there, even City-born, are *people*. That they have families, parents, brothers and sisters, kids. That they all deserve a chance to live, to grow old with the ones they love. I can't keep taking away from them what some stupid Red took from me. The Menghu think it is a game, a tally." Her voice starts to shake with emotion. Anger. "It's worse than SS. They *choose* to be monstrous."

"Why do you stay here, then?" I ask.

"I have to make up for what I've done. Even if it means saving the monsters who are making it worse. They are people too, even if they've forgotten."

The sentence sticks in my head, and I remember the Red I refused to kill back in the forest. "We need to do something. To stop this."

Sole looks tired, lifting her gaze to hold mine for the first time since she grabbed the painting from my hands. "I am. Getting you out of here . . ." She gestures to the door. "That is all I can do."

Her eyes jump between me and the door, and for a second I think she might run away—run from her past. But when she speaks, it is for me. Needle sharp. "But before you go out there, before you put your life in Howl's hands, you need to know something about him.

"My partner . . ." Her voice breaks, the jagged fragments slicing through her composure. "My partner, the one who shot the little girl? That was Howl."

CHAPTER 35

SHE KEEPS TALKING, BUT THE WORDS RUSH PAST me as though she's speaking some dead language, meaningless. Noise. Sick panic seeps up into my lungs and throat and the words erupt out of me. "City-born Howl? My Howl?" I can feel frenzied laughter rising in my throat. "That isn't possible. Wouldn't he have still been in the City when it happened?"

She's shaking her head, and for one bright moment, I believe she means a different person. But then her ragged whisper snakes into my ears, the poison slowly killing all hope. "Howl isn't City-born. He's not even a refugee. I grew up with Howl. Our parents were friends, killed by the same attack. He was just as bad as I was. We were partners, destroying the City one comrade at a time."

Not possible. Those are the only words in my head. The only thing I can think. Why would he pretend to be from the City? "What do you mean, killed by the same attack?" I'm pretty sure I would have heard if the Chairman had been murdered.

"Our parents were killed outright by a bomb, but our brothers, Chan and Seth . . ." She stumbles over the names like hot coals, pausing for a moment. "They were infected. The Mountain didn't have Mantis back then, so the minute they woke up . . ." She trails off, eyes wandering as though she's lost her train of thought.

"You mean they were put down? Like sick animals?" The calm tone shrouding the disbelief in my voice is starting to shred.

She laughs, a bitter, unhappy sound. "You don't believe me. No one understands anymore. Any infected inside the Mountain—any at all—would have tried to killed all of us. We didn't have Mantis to keep infected from hurting people or hurting themselves. We didn't even have tranquilizers. When the people who lived here took the rebels in, infected weren't welcome. Almost one hundred years underneath this rock, afraid to do more than turn on the lights and use the greenhouses because it would bring attention down on us. The Menghu weren't even organized until a few years before I was born. We knew what would happen with just one compulsion, just one person out of control in the dark.

"They weren't shot outright. When they woke up, they had to leave. Just as effective as a death sentence." Her fingers find my pocket holding the gore-tooth necklace, drawing it out. "This was his. Seth's. He must have given it to Howl before he left."

Her face crumples. "Seth and I . . . We were close."

My hand closes around the necklace, the shard of jade cutting into my hand as it presses against the long white tooth. Everything seems so still, as if the world has stopped. "If Howl is from here, then how did he end up in the City?" As the Chairman's son, no less. What she's saying simply isn't possible.

"Dr. Yang brought Gui-hua to the Mountain." Sole startles back when I stand up at my mother's name. "They were so close to finding the cure, and there Howl was, ten years old, no parents to protect him. Dr. Yang infected him, then they used him as the trial. They succeeded. Your mother disappeared the next day with all the documentation. She went to the City to save you and never came back. Whatever Gui-hua and Dr. Yang discovered together, Dr. Yang couldn't duplicate it without their notes.

"Howl was all they had. Dr. Yang waited until he was older, to see if it stuck. When he turned sixteen, they decided the tests weren't enough, They needed more. Another person who was cured to compare him to or to dig deeper. They didn't have the first, so Dr. Yang set a date for an operation. A dissection, really, to look at what Gui-hua did during that first procedure. Dr. Yang didn't even pretend Howl was going to live through it, he just assumed Howl would be happy to give himself up for the good of everyone else. Howl went out on patrols the day before it was supposed to happen and didn't come back.

"The Menghu tracked him down Outside, but he wouldn't come back. Howl could hold his own against any of them. Dr. Yang managed to talk to him, convinced him to help run Mantis back to the Mountain until some other solution presented itself."

"And then he met me." My whole body is numb. "Some other solution." I was Howl's ticket back home. If Dr. Yang had me to dissect, then Howl would be free.

"He took the promotion into Nei-ge and went straight back to Kasim and his other Menghu friends."

I can't even hear the rest of what she is trying to say because a deeper, uglier memory crawls up out of my brain, context finally crystal clear. *You know it's going to come down to one of you in the end.* That was what Dr. Yang said. And Howl answered, *Yes.*

Howl knew. I'll bet Dr. Yang started sharpening his knives the moment we got here. It explains how well Howl fit in, how quickly "we" meant the Mountain instead of the City. Why I never heard a word of remorse for leaving. Not about family, friends. Nothing.

The fear I saw in Helix and Cale's faces when Howl stood up to them suddenly takes on a frightening animal quality. If Howl isn't who I think he is . . . then who is he really?

No.

Howl had the whole time we were in the forest to slip and show corruption lurking underneath his chipper exterior. If he were truly as horrible as Sole is saying he is, I would have seen it. I would know.

My thoughts flick back and forth, trying to speed through all of my conversations with Howl and Dr. Yang until something inside me snaps. I can't think anymore. My hands are shaking and my legs are unsteady under me as I back toward the door.

"I can't believe it. I knew Howl in the City." Sole looks up as I cut her off, my voice breaking uncomfortably close to a sob. "He had parents, a family . . . People there knew him. Even I knew who he was."

There's nothing we can do to save my family. There never was. I push Howl's words away and stumble out into the hallway. "It can't be true. Howl would never . . ." The painting of the Chairman's son hanging across from my mother. I've seen it thousands of times. It *is* Howl. It has to be.

She's the only one like me.

I thought he'd meant we were both . . . but if Sole is telling the truth, then he really meant . . .

Sole bows her head, voice shaking like an old woman. "I wish it weren't."

I run.

CHAPTER 36

I HAVE TO FIND HIM.

I have to concentrate to keep from chanting the words out loud. The Core glows with the flush of lanterns and fairy lights. High above the crowded room, long streamers hang down in a pavilion, the top so high that the twinkling lights don't touch the white, filmy fabric.

Tables surround the amphitheater where people are talking and laughing. The fountain centered on the cafeteria entrance is turned on and spouting red. A beautifully made-up woman leans down to dip her glass into it. It looks like blood.

I hardly recognize any of the Menghu because they are all so clean. They are easy to pick out, though, candlelight glinting on the dead fingers clasping at their wrists and necks.

Have to trust him. Howl wouldn't lie to me. Not about who he is, not about being cured, not about . . . I can't make myself finish the thought. Because if he did bring me here to take his place as the cure, then that's exactly what he would have lied about. *Everything.* I never would have followed him out of the City if I hadn't believed the mark on his hand.

Dancing couples crowd the sunken amphitheater floor, obscuring the golden star seal with a haze of swirling skirts. Masks obscure all of their faces, jeweled, feathered, and painted alike. It looks like a dream, a scene from another world. Maybe dancing is what this place was built for. Before the world revolved around SS.

Patting my blond wig down a little farther over my forehead, I stick to the shadows, black sweatshirt borrowed from Sole painfully casual in comparison to the sparkling scene before me. He isn't anywhere. Not in the amphitheater seats, not at the tables. Leaning back against the wall, I bump my fist against the clear glass in frustration. Why should I believe Sole? Staring off into space as if the world the rest of us live in isn't what she sees. The box full of trophies stolen from her victims. The frightening drawing I found on the desk. Can I trust someone so obviously damaged?

No.

The dancers below stop and clap as the song ends, the swell of instruments marking the beginning of a new one over the speakers. Most of the dancers remain on the floor, but stay on the outside, watching. Waiting for something.

A girl with fire-red hair flounces to the center, her black skirt twirling up around her hips as people laugh at her bravado, clapping and cheering her on. Rena.

She twirls again and strikes a pose, pointing into the crowd. Chuckles echo up to me as the crowd pushes a young man forward into the center of the floor. He's laughing behind his black mask, shaking his head as Rena circles him like a shark. Finally, he stands up tall, throws a hand out toward her as the music starts up. A demand.

Rena's bright coppery head glints in the lantern light as she coyly walks up to him. She lashes out suddenly, kicking his hand, but he catches her foot and draws it toward him, pulling her out into a split. The onlookers cheer as they start to circle the floor.

I can't help but move closer, drawn by the dramatic strikes and pauses, kicking in and out between each other's legs, her long ponytail snapping back and forth as he leads her across the floor. Hiding, I feel as though I'm just on the edge of something important, something that I should understand, but can't.

They pause in the corner of the floor near my hiding place, arms wide as they pose together, cheers following them in ripples from around the steps. The young man lunges, backing away, and she follows, running after. And that's when I see it.

Stuck through the top button of his shirt. A red flower. My red flower.

Howl's eyes are dark behind his mask, the intensity between the two of them like a rubber band twisted and ready to snap. They look as though they were born in each other's arms. Born here, born Menghu. I can't tear my eyes away, dread and despair seeping in through my nose and mouth, the very air around me toxic. I keep waiting for clouds to start swirling down from the ceiling or shadows to leap out and rake at me with their sharp claws, but this isn't a hallucination. This is real.

Helix's voice rings in my head: *You are going to die. You don't even know why.*

Howl, who can't dance. Howl, who can't shoot a gun. Howl, who says we are our own team, not a part of this place. Howl, who told me he was from the City, and that we were going to escape this place.

Howl, who brought me here to die.

* * *

I don't know how I get back to Sole's room, whether anyone notices my uneven stagger through the halls of Yizhi. When I open her door, she's waiting for me the way I left her, head bowed, tears glistening against her light skin. Eyes fixed on her hands.

The last threads of hope inside of me flare up, bright and rebellious inside my chest. I want to fight for him, for myself. Trying to find a place for the Howl I know inside of this terrible story.

"Even if he did lie about who he is, he saved me from that operation. Or sent you to do it, anyway. He's done nothing but stand between me and Dr. Yang. We're leaving, right? If I am the sacrifice he's offering to the Mountain, then why am I still alive? Why didn't he just hand me over the first day we walked in?"

Sole bites her lip. "Howl is a survivor. No matter what, no matter the cost. When he first brought you here, it was for you to take his place on Dr. Yang's table so that he could come home. He knew what was going to happen to you. He *knew*. Everyone knew."

"But he changed his mind." Even trying to wrap my brain around that thought leaves my lungs constricted, twisting the air out of me. How could his intentions ever have been so foul? "If we wake Mother up now—"

"He hasn't told you about any of this. Why?" Sole's voice is quiet but unapologetic. "What if waking your mother up doesn't work, Sev?"

"If it doesn't work . . ."

"Whatever Howl has convinced you of, about how important you are to him, about . . . this." She holds up one hand, something cupped in her palm. "It's not the whole picture."

A jade bracelet. It's lying on top of a note, bold characters I can hardly make myself recognize.

It says, *For good luck. I love you, H.*

A present. Like my flower. Made with love. Or with something much, much worse. My fingers twitch toward it, as if holding something he made will tell me that Sole is lying.

"I love you." The words sound twisted and evil coming from Sole's mouth. "Perhaps that's true. But Howl loving someone more than *himself* . . . ? If it comes down to a choice between you and him, Howl will be the one who lives. And, if it's possible, the Mountain will be what comes second. The things he did before . . . even Helix has been trying to keep away from him." She swallows, her throat pulsing. "Why else would Howl have lied to you? When it was *your* life on the line? When you could have escaped and put him back in the surgery waiting room?"

The silence between us is tangible, liquid. My mind is crushed under the weight of what she is saying. I want to believe that what the note says isn't a lie, isn't bait to keep me here, to string me along just a little longer. But even if Howl does love me, how could I expect him to love me more than he loves his own life?

If he'd told me about being cured, that my life may mean thousands more could be saved from SS, I might have come anyway. I might have walked straight to the hospital and handed Dr. Yang the scalpel.

But he didn't tell me. He didn't tell me anything. He actively kept it from me, flirting with me, kissing me when I asked too many questions.

The last bits of fight inside of me smolder to ash, that tiny flame extinguished. I pull the gore tooth from the leather cord around my neck and set it on her desk.

CHAPTER 37

THERE ARE TWO MENGHU WAITING JUST OUTSIDE the service entrance door. For me? Was Howl not even going to go through with our escape? The immobilization spray has both of them down before they know I'm there.

We were supposed to meet at midnight. Was he going to lead me up here and pretend he wasn't a part of us being captured? Or were all the disguises about to be dissolved once and for all? The last time Howl was planning on saying, *Oh, I forgot to tell you . . .*

The ropes Howl was supposed to stash aren't here. I have to go back to Sole, to send her into the Zhuanjia supply closets to steal some. Everyone is in the Core celebrating, so all she has to do is walk in.

When I get Outside, I keep my hands busy, cutting telescreen wires that Howl told me he'd disable. Every step uncovers more evidence that Howl didn't mean to leave tonight at all.

When my way out is clear, I brush the new dusting of snow from the anchors set for Zhuanjia workers, and thread my rope through them. Shouldering the extra webbing, I slide the rope through the clasp on my harness and take a deep breath, scrunching my eyes closed as I lower myself over the edge. I try to concentrate on the rope, the way it pulls at the feed on my harness . . . but I can't keep my eyes away. I have to look down.

There's nothing to see. Straight up and down, rocks jaggedly disappear into the dark below me. My breath sticks in my throat, my chest and arms tingling as though I'm covered in ants. I can't even see the ground, hundreds of feet down to the first treetops, black circles in the night. Turning back around, I try to focus on the rock, my feet slipping against the icy edge.

I don't have any choice. Breaths coming fast, I walk down the side, lowering myself with the rope.

I have to reset the lines twice, pulling them down after me when I hit a ledge. The rope threads through my hand-tied anchors, a sorry-looking setup. My life rides on knots that my fingers are tying for the first time. Just as I'm starting to feel confident, my pack catches on a tree limb, pulling me away from the rock face. I kick to find purchase with my feet, and my fingers catch between the line and the feed. I let go with a yell. The branch cracks under my weight, the sickening lurch of free fall clutching at my senses as it gives way under me. But it's a short fall, only a few feet to the icy ground.

The frozen air swishing through the trees sends goose bumps prickling down my arms inside Sole's bloodstained coat. I lie in the dirt for a moment, pebbles digging into my legs and side. I don't have time to think about being cold. There is nothing left in me except escape.

The hammock folds around my tired body like a cocoon, hiding me from the bright arrows of light lancing down from the full circle moon. Zhinu and Niulang glare down at me, asking why. Reminding me of that first night, of him. I'm waking up from a dream that was always too good to be true, where Niulang was a protector, Zhinu's love. It turns out he was actually one of the frightening beasts, the qilin from the story instead of the man. I exchanged Tai-ge's reserved smiles and steady friendship for Howl's full gore-tooth grin, believing the lies as his teeth snapped closer.

Which leaves me with nothing. All I am is the traitor that Tai-ge could never bring himself to touch. Hunted in this empty forest by the same men and women who are going to break through the City walls to kill everyone I know. The pieces for this game were placed long before I sat down to watch. My stone, who-ever it was who placed me, is dead.

It's only a matter of time before the Menghu come, trained like wolves to sniff out their prey. I can't find the emotion to care.

I breathe in and out, stretching my ribs until my lungs burn, the shadows from the trees fluttering across the sheltering layer of my hammock. There is no room to regret, to think that this is what I should have expected. I am solid, a rock. Incapable of feel-ing anything. I can't let the doubt or the desire to trust Howl even now take over. To look over my shoulder and expect him to come running after me like this was all a mistake. I am too hard to feel. Too hard to remember that, for the first time, I really am alone. Friendless. Banished. Too hard to notice the despair killing me slowly like dry rot.

CHAPTER 38

SUNRISE. I HAVE TO KEEP MOVING. I STAGGER
downhill, knowing I won't last long if I don't find water. The air
clear of winter's low-lying clouds, I can see the rounded tops of
the mountain range disappearing into the northern horizon. The
City clings to the side of one of those mountains. And if I can
find the river, it will take me back. Back to the Reds, to Traitor's
Arch. Back to the people who weren't shy about why they wanted
to kill me.

Back to Tai-ge. Back to Mother. Maybe waking her up will
stop people from killing one another, stop SS. Or maybe it will
just stop them from killing Tai-ge, keep him off the list of people
I loved who are now dead.

When I finally stumble into the river's smooth-rolling current,
I sit, mindlessly running a stone along the sharpened edges of my
metal stars. Unprotected and Outside. Howl still has the knife
that Tai-ge gave to me, my only weapon stolen even before we left
the City walls. My stars will have to do as a defense, the edges
honed until they can cut. A brief image of me attempting to stab

a gore with my tiny pin flashes before my eyes. I shake my head to clear it. What else can I do?

Food finds its way to my lips when I remember that I am supposed to eat, though the first time I look in Sole's borrowed pack for sustenance, my hands find the book Howl gave me instead. The one with the sleeping princess on the front, and the promise of a happy ending. I can't even touch it, staring down at the glint of gilt on the front cover until I can force my fingers to zip the pack closed.

What would a happy ending mean to Howl, anyway? Happy the way Zhinu and Niulang were? Separated by a wall of stars in the sky, seeing each other behind the sun's back with help from a world's worth of confused birds? Or perhaps just a life—any life—would be happy for him as long as his lungs still move air in and out of his body and his heart still beats, regardless of who around him has gone silent.

Every day the sun watches my slow progress along the river, and every night the moonlight is the same, stolen from where it should belong. I find myself looking over my shoulder as I walk, expecting Howl's white smile and Kasim's boisterous laugh to emerge from the trees at any moment, the two of them ready to drag me back to the tubes and knives. Why haven't they caught up with me yet?

Finally, a shadow blocks the sun rising over my lonely hammock. The flap that protects me from rain, insects, and my nightmares is stenciled with a human outline. It wrenches back to let in the full blaze of pink morning sun. A crane startles from branches above us at the quick movement, wings stainless white against the patchwork sky. The person's face is obscured by the black curls of a gas mask, but I recognize the green Menghu jacket buttoned up to her throat.

She doesn't cut me down immediately, head cocked as though she's not quite sure what kind of butterfly she's found in this strange cocoon.

I'm glad it's over. No more running, no more pretending. I don't have to think anymore. I don't have to breathe.

I reach my hands out, wrists together so the Menghu can tie them. "What took you so long?"

She tears the gas mask from her face, letting loose a cascade of blond curls. "What did they do to you, Sev?"

June.

PART IV

CHAPTER 39

WE WALK IN SILENCE. SHE ALWAYS WAS GOOD AT silence. I don't ask her where she got her uniform, and she doesn't ask me where Howl is. Her presence brings me back to the forest, aware of time passing for the first time in days.

"Where are you headed?" June's question sounds like cold iron, inhuman and airless through the gas mask. "Or are you just going . . . away?"

"The City." I have to warn Tai-ge about the invasion. Even if the rest of that place almost deserves the Menghu, I can't let him be killed. And there are others that I can't justify leaving for the Menghu to piece together in bracelets. My roommate, Peishan, locked away in the Sanatorium. Sister Shang. I can't let them be shot down just because of where they are standing, like my father was.

And Mother. It feels like checking rat traps back in the orphanage. Dreading what I'd find, but knowing that leaving the dead creatures would just draw more rodents . . . I have to look. I have to know once and for all why she left me. And the only way to find out is to ask her. The syringe in my pocket feels like another limb, a part of me. The kiss to cure her awake.

She could be the end to SS and this stupid war. The end of people dying and forcing other people to die for them . . .

"You can go back to the City?" June interrupts my thoughts. "The Reds weren't after you, they were after——?"

Howl. I cut her off before she can finish the question. "Things have changed."

"The Menghu aren't following you, though."

I stop, letting the statement sink in. "They must be."

She arches an eyebrow at me, glancing behind us into the woods. I blush at what she isn't saying. If they were after me, I would already be back at the Mountain with my throat slit. Running away from the Menghu shouldn't be as easy as falling down a mountainside. I'm their cure. They wouldn't just let me walk away, would they? Maybe they just moved their focus onto Howl instead. That thought gives me a twinge of guilt, even after everything he's done, but I stamp it down, smothering it under all the lies he told me.

June just shrugs, handing me a handful of dried apricot slices, the flesh feeling gummy under my fingertips. "Eat that. You look like you've missed a few meals."

I hold the apricots in my fist, squeezing them between my fingers. June sighs and pries my hand open, taking one of the orange fruits to hold in front of my nose. "Eat it."

The taste burns, my tongue curling up in protest, but I still swallow. It slides down my throat and settles in my stomach like a rock.

June's mask stays attached to her face, a green hood covering her bright hair. Rumors about contagious SS must have spread like a fire through the Outsiders, though she won't tell me how. June isn't the helpless little girl I thought she was. She's smarter than me, better off than I ever was.

When we settle down for the night, she pulls an envelope out of her pocket, rattling it as she holds it out to me. Two green pills fall out of the paper into my palm. I shake my head, tears stinging behind my eyes.

"I don't need it anymore." If I did, then I would still have a mother and Howl might have actually loved me. I would have a home instead of wandering around out here, an outcast. "I wish I did."

Trekking back to the City blurs into one long day of heavy feet plodding mercilessly forward and one long night of terrible nightmares, each one featuring Niulang transforming into one of the qilin monsters he attended and tearing after Zhinu through the forest with his teeth bared.

When we get close to the City, June and I use the ditches to get past the farms, playing dead whenever patrols wander by. June swaps her green coat for a leather jerkin stamped with the City seal. I find one as well, the ditches populated with many uncomplaining donors. Remembering the dead man stamped with my boot prints from the first day Outside leaves me wiping dead smell from my shoulders and arms, and I keep catching myself holding my breath to keep the death from going inside me.

The inlet leading to the Sanatorium sewers is on the cliff side of the City. It isn't that hard to slip past the guards, because they're all concentrated in front of the City's main gates, the few Seconds who notice us just nodding as we walk toward the thin path that curves around the back side of the mountain.

My stomach churns as I size up the single, icy board running out to the sewer outlet, a simple hole in the side of the cliff. There's a chain bolted to the cliff wall above the board to aid the unfortunate Third who was required to unblock the sewer pipe. From here, the wind pushes up on my arms and face as if I'm a bird getting ready to take off over the terraced rice paddies, each strip of water reflecting the blue sky like a mirror from hundreds of feet down. Beyond that, mountains pop up from the ground, laden with robes of green as far as I can see. The City wall zigzags far above my head, gray stone following the lines of the mountain in a disorganized-looking sprawl, a square-shaped turret almost directly over us.

I swallow the dizzying height down, curling my fingers around the chain. I don't have time to be scared. I don't even have time to look down. Failure to get in means Tai-ge will die.

June grabs my hands before I can take a step, shaking her head. I try to smile to reassure her, but my face has forgotten how. "Don't wait for me. A war is about to start."

Her eyes don't waver, a faint blush staining her cheeks as she pulls again. "Don't leave me." The first words between us in days. "I'll keep you safe."

Taking care of me when, only a few weeks ago, I thought I was taking care of her. I couldn't save Aya, and now my new little sister is trying to save me. I don't have the heart to tell her that there is no such thing as safe. Not Outside or In. But I nod. "Come. But this could be as messy as a gore's dinner party."

Inch by inch, June right behind me, we make our way to the outlet, a coating of brownish slime staining the rock underneath the opening. My heart sinks when we get close enough to see the ice-plastered grate covering the sewer, bars set so closely together

I can't even get my arm through. But, on the far side, two of them are cut.

I bite my lip. Does that mean Menghu are already here? Is Helix already inside, waiting for the right moment to open the City's main gates?

Even with the cut bars, squeezing through leaves my ribs feeling bent. Dirty water pools around me, soaking my pants to the knees, the stench of rotting garbage curling in my nose. But the filth down here doesn't scare me so much as what must be waiting for us up in the Sanatorium.

Parhat's wild eyes; Mei's bared teeth. My sister with her ax. The Sanatorium is full of men and women who are infected. I've had nightmares about ending up in the Sanatorium since the moment they set the first stone, since the first instance of infection trumping Mantis.

I don't have to worry about Mantis not working for me anymore. I just have to get through the Sanatorium without being eaten. I remind myself that the infected aren't monsters, they're victims, and if I want to save my friends from the true monsters of this world—the City and the Menghu alike—I have to push forward.

My quicklight breaks, catching the slow ripples of water around me in an eerie glow. The water trough narrows as we walk along, cement walls closing in around us as the roar of rushing water down the channel finds my ears. There should be a cement wall, about fifty feet high, with sewage rushing over the side up ahead—the City's insurance that Outsiders won't sneak in this way, and City dwellers won't use it to sneak out.

By the time we get to the wall, the sound of rushing water fills me up, echoing off the cold cement until it feels like the dirty water is inside of me, all around me, that there's no reason I should still be able to breathe. Water careens over the side from above, leaving only a foot-wide section of cement clear of falling water. I slip on my gloves and pull out the rope and the two sets of metal disks that Sole stole for me when I ran from Howl. Part of the plan that wouldn't have worked if she hadn't raided Zhuanjia storerooms for me, getting the materials Howl was supposed to bring when we escaped. Two attach to my boots, one strapped to each hand. The disks are magnetic, bonding with the iron reinforcement through the cement, sticking like glue with every move upward. I skate up the wall, concentrating on the dark above me to avoid thinking about what will happen if I fall, if I move too far to the side and the roaring water grabs me from my delicate perch to go crashing into the sewage channel.

Howl's voice whispers in my mind, *The sewers will take us straight up into the Sanatorium. There are no connections to the old City underground, but they will get us past the walls.* My shoulders hunch up around my ears, and I stop for a moment to shake his warm touch from my head. I need to concentrate. It only takes a few more lung-wrenching minutes to pull myself up over the top, and I give myself a second to choke down breaths of sewage-infused air before turning the magnets off in the disks and carefully dropping them back down for June. The red of my quicklight flickers over her spider-like crawl up toward me, much faster and more sure of herself than I was.

After June scales the wall, we continue down the narrow walkway next to the channel until the next screaming fall of water. This one, however, has a ladder ascending into the darkness above us, the rungs slippery with muck. As I climb, my quicklight begins to wane, so I break another at the top to reveal a cavernous cement room, the water coming from a break in the wall across from us but confined to its channel running the length of the space. Ladders crawl up the blank faces of the room, and drains dot the floor every few yards, the cement shiny and damp.

We climb the ladder on the far wall, coming to a high-ceilinged hallway. The area is still unlit and unrelieved cement, but there are doors cut into the deep gray walls every ten feet. The first door I come to has three hand-size windows across the top. My footsteps draw a scuffling sound from inside, and reflective retinas peer out at me from the cell. "I'm not gone yet," a voice scratches out, wobbling like an unbalanced top. "Not yet."

The voice repeats itself over and over, rising into a scream that follows me all the way down the hall, past door after door of other frightened eyes blinking after my quicklight.

Flickering light ahead means people. Firsts?

June drags me into the inky blur of an alcove, grabbing my quicklight and stuffing it under her heavy leather jerkin. The deep murmur of voices penetrates my hood.

". . . entire floor locked down. At least until the Watch comes back from Outside. They've spent the last two weeks pasted to the City gates like graffiti. Our security here cannot be set back in priority. One exposure . . ."

A voice interrupts, rasping through the mesh of a gas mask. "We understand the importance of what you are doing, but the Watch is spread thin at the moment. We've lost three farms already. My soldiers . . ."

The first man cuts back in, "This ridiculous experiment is ravaging the Wood Rats as we speak. We have no way to stop it! We can't set foot Outside without risking exposure! We can't even tell who is infected because the Sleep stage can't be regulated anymore. A single night's rest could be the first stages, or even less, and we have no way of knowing who is infected and who isn't. Dr. Yang couldn't have known. . . ."

Dr. Yang? The name echoes out behind them, the last word I catch from the exchange before their voices disappear into the dripping gray prison. I pull my boots off and pad after them in my wet socks, but I can't pick apart the hollow echoes bouncing off the cement walls. Frustration bubbles through me as I lean against the wall, stuffing my boots into the pack. Is Dr. Yang involved on this end too? Is that how he knew about the contagious strain of SS?

And did Firsts release it into the wild as an *experiment*? As though they could just document the effects and file it away, never expecting it to affect them? That's the same kind of hubris that got the world into this mess in the first place. Some of the resolve I felt back at the Mountain resurges in my chest, warmth burning holes through the lead cocoon protecting me from my feelings.

Tai-ge will know. The Hongs will be able to do something, whatever is going on. The thought is a bright point in the darkness. Taking a deep breath, I turn to go back to June.

But my head jerks back, crashing into one of the metal doors.

A cackling laugh stabs through me as I fumble to detach the hand tangled in my braid. I can't see anything, the assault snaking out from the small window leading into the cell behind me. Sputtering hoots of laughter die down, smothered as the prisoner pulls again, shoving the end of my long braid into his mouth.

I wrench away from the cell door, the hair at the nape of my neck tearing at my skin, but the prisoner is stronger. He lets me pull just far enough away to smash me back into the door with a *crack*. The contact resounds through my head like a bell tolling, sick dread flooding through me as another hand reaches out from the holes in the door, fingers digging into my chin from behind.

My fingers find my star pin, leather cord cutting against my throat as I tear them from the necklace. Using the stars' sharpened metal edges, I saw through my braid, the star pin's points glancing across the hand clutching at my face. The arms recoil back into the cell with a howl, my severed braid snaking after them.

The irregular ends of hair scratch at my eyes and mouth as I run, my hands too busy keeping hold of the stars, feeling for my mother's jade and the rusted ring on the leather cord to brush them away. My whole body convulses with fear and revulsion, slimy fingers crawling across my skin in ghostly memory of the Seph's touch.

I grab June's hand and we sprint down the hallway, wetness clinging to us like a diseased haze. She doesn't question it, but pulls me to a stop when we get to the first stairwell, the severed remains of my hair a harsh revelation under the bare bulb.

I lean back against the wall, pulling my hair away from her, trying to let my gasping breaths calm. The white-knuckle grip I have on my stars refuses to unfold, as though my fingers are permanently bonded to them. My palm throbs as the metal stabs into my palm, a dribble of blood squeezing out of my fist to drip on the floor.

Cocking her head, June twines a finger around a lock of hair, ending jaggedly at my cheekbone. The shadow of distress in her face is enough to get me talking again. "I'm fine. Let's go." I tie the broken leather cord back around my neck, stars and jade bloody red next to the ring. "The Menghu could be waiting right outside the City. We have to go."

The gray cement wall boasts a large red number four centered above the flight of stairs. At the top of the staircase, we come to clean, rose-colored tile, utilitarian and boring. Each hall seems like an endless string of doors, with red handles marked ALARM set into the walls every hundred feet or so.

Offices. Each inhabited by a ruthless monster, every case of SS blood on their hands. How do Firsts work in here, so close to their victims? Do they worry that someday their charges will get out? My hand trails across the glass door protecting an alarm handle in the wall. I suppose the moment anything unusual happens, everyone runs.

The first person we see has his face buried in a pile of papers, a single red star glinting in the harsh lights as he walks up the hall toward us. I duck through a doorway, June slipping in under my arm, before he looks up.

The room is a small office, gagged by loose papers overflowing from the small metal desk and gray filing cabinets that line the walls. June stays by the cracked-open door, eyes on the man as he passes. I slide into the chair at the desk, interest caught as the miniature telescreen set into the wall blinks white and blue. A file pulls up in response to my sitting down, the words MEDICAL TRAINING black against the screen. A group of pictures pops up underneath.

My eyes catch on one familiar face near the bottom. Peishan, my old roommate from the orphanage.

I select her picture and it fills the whole screen, bringing up an ant's march of text denoting time spent in the Sanatorium, notes on how often and how much she eats, how often she has bowel movements, and a long list of other statistics and notes. Next to her face reads BULLET RECOVERY TEST SUBJECT: STOMACH. And a date.

"What is today's date?" I snap at the screen, at once feeling proud and awkward that I know how to work a telescreen after my time at the Mountain. Black characters crawl across her face like a spider, and I blink. Today's date is two days *before* the date next to her picture.

She's been here in the Sanatorium since before I left the City, since her outstretched fingers reached for Captain Chen in our Remedial Reform class all those weeks ago. Mantis stopped working for her, but she went quietly once her compulsion was under control. How did Peishan end up with a bullet in her stomach? And if Peishan somehow did get shot, why would Firsts let her sit in the hospital for days with a hunk of metal in her stomach before treating her?

I scroll through the details of her file, looking for something, *anything* to explain how someone safe inside the Sanatorium could be nursing a gunshot wound, images of Cale storming through the dimly lit halls blackening the edges of my vision. But there's nothing. Just a blue box marked SIMULANT with that date two days from now tagged underneath and a short blurb about treatment: SIMULATED FIELD TEST. MEDICS HAVE TEN MINUTES TO STABILIZE SUBJECT AND EXTRACT BULLET.

Something here doesn't make sense. I click out of Peishan's file and scan through the other notes, but there are no other circumstances or problems listed for Peishan. . . . It's not until I click into a file labeled SECOND FIELD TESTING that I find my answer.

Red sharpshooters have a test the same day as Peishan's scheduled bullet removal.

Horror chokes me as I let this sink in. They're going to shoot Peishan in two days, and then let the student medics try to sew her up before she dies. Is this always how they train Red medics?

I press through to the other case files up on the telescreen, recognizing two from my shift at the cannery and four more from the younger kids at the orphanage. People I didn't even know were infected. Now each one has an expiration date fixed beneath their grainy pictures. June snaps her fingers, jerking my attention away from the telescreen. She's still hunched against the door, watching the hallway. She points back out, but I hold up a hand, silently asking her to wait.

I put my head down on the desk to clear my thoughts. How did all these people get SS? All orphans or Thirds. A bright red box on the screen flashes, catching my attention. I click into the boy's case file, and instead of a blue box marked SIMULANT, this record has a red one with the word PLACEBO noted in large characters.

I flick back through the other case files, but this is the only one flagged red. The rest are all flashing the blue SIMULANT. Most of the records are labeled FIELD STUDY, but three of the ones I sift through have a black bar cutting the subject's picture, bold white characters blocking out the word RESEARCH above their foreheads instead. Bone reconstruction research. Heart and lung recovery and reconstruction research. Brain trauma research. I think back to the new pamphlet that came out right before Dr. Yang dragged me underground all those weeks ago. Wasn't it something about bone remodeling?

They built this place to house infected that aren't responding to Mantis. But why would Mantis suddenly stop working? Siyu, that nurse back at the Mountain, seemed to think it was impossible.

Firsts gave me medicine to make me think I had SS. Why couldn't they do that to any number of orphans, Thirds, people they don't care about? Are there drugs to make you think you fell

Asleep, too? My throat constricts as I think of my mother in her glass coffin. Of course there are.

Perhaps they started using SS victims for their experiments, giving them placebos instead of Mantis and then claiming they were *resisting* the Mantis so they had a healthy number of subjects to cart off to the Sanatorium for research. But now they don't even have to give real SS to the people they want to experiment on. With their SS "simulants," Firsts can cause an "outbreak" anytime they need to refill the kennels, but with an added benefit: When Thirds watch their families fall to SS, it keeps them scared, just like the bombs the City drops on itself.

And the medical discoveries kept us convinced as to how wise and powerful Firsts are. That maybe, someday, they would find the cure to SS. That their place above us was right. How many dead bodies are attached to each discovery? The Sanatorium is just one big operating table, allowing Firsts to play without anyone being able to complain. Or even realize what is going on.

Contagious SS, this new strain they gave to Cale and Kasim . . . did Firsts invent it in the Sanatorium? Disgust balloons up from my stomach, my throat tightening around the acid boiling up in my esophagus. If they use SS to control the City, are they even trying to find a cure? I doubt it.

I flip through pictures, faster and faster until I can't even see the faces, just looking for the red and blue SIMULANT and PLACEBO boxes. About half are red, most of those who are actually infected with floor designations in the wet, dark halls I just came from below. They were all denied Mantis, so who knows how many have lost control of their minds from compulsions or solitary confinement? And the rest of the people here, blue SIMULANT boxes blinking over their pictures, are all unknowing, unwilling volunteers in a City-wide medical experiment when there's nothing wrong with them.

At least Howl wasn't lying about everything. The Sanatorium really is full of gruesome medical experiments. The thought pops up, a spot of hope in a gaping abyss, but I push it away. Howl doesn't get any points for telling the truth about one or two things when he lied about literally everything else.

Sitting up, I motion June over, pointing to the picture in front of me of a girl with a prim little smile. "They're going to kill her. They told her she has SS to force her into the Sanatorium, and now they are going to kill her."

June scans the rest of the screen with an appraising air, shrugging one shoulder. "Are they running out of Mantis?"

"No. They're reading all the old medical journals and trying to regain some of what doctors were able to do Before. This girl is a lab rat—a lab rat who allows Firsts to stay in control here." I slap the table. "How do we fix this?" The same feeling of helplessness that I've always felt facing down the Sanatorium makes me feel glued to the table. Paralyzed.

June glances back out into the hall. "How about we get out of here before trying to solve any other problems? You can't help anyone if Firsts catch us in here."

The hallway outside is bare once again. Artificial lights glare down on the shirt underneath my jerkin, brown and slippery with sewer sludge, raggedy hair hanging in an uneven mess across my shoulders. June looks equally bedraggled, her gas mask and hood making her look as if she belongs here. Just another terrible science experiment.

Kneeling by the next pull-handle alarm we come across, I stuff my feet back into my boots, pulling the clasps tight against my calves. Next, the gas mask goes on, my face hidden behind its metal screen.

Now the alarm. I rip the glass door open and pull the handle from the wall. The high wail of a siren starts to keen through the building, and the hallway floods with confused Firsts calling to one another to ask what is going on. Three members of the Watch elbow their way up the hall, eyes falling to the broken handle chafing in my hand. I yell to them before they get close, my gas mask distorting my words. "Breakout on four! They're newly infected!"

The lead Watchman swears and pulls a mask over his face. "How did they get down there? Testing is supposed to be restricted to ten. Actively compulsing?"

I pull at my torn Watch jerkin and muddy clothes. "I wouldn't say they were friendly."

"You alert Captain Zhao on two; I'll set up a block."

I nod as though I know what he's talking about and catch June's arm, the two of us riding the flow of confused uniforms up toward the ground floor and the exit. After a confused shuffle up a few flights of stairs, natural light pours into the cement stairwell. Pushing our way out, June and I run down the hallway, large windows that look out into a courtyard flowered in pinks and reds set into the walls every few feet. A knot of threadbare children stand out in the garden under the outstretched hands of a statue of Yuan Zhiwei. The stone's red veins look like streams of blood all over his hands and face.

Their heads follow the tide of the panicked Firsts, eyes wide with alarm. An older girl bends down in front of them, wiping away tears. A girl I know.

I slam through the doors and the kids scatter like cockroaches under a light, leaving Peishan alone under Yuan's hands. She faces me with firm resolution, only a hint of fear in the line of her jaw. Her hair is stubbly and short, different from the sleek locks I remember.

"You need to get out of here." My monster voice makes her cringe away as it leaks through the gas mask. "Now. Come with me."

She holds her ground, brow furrowing. "Sevvy?"

Surprised that she recognized my voice, I pull the mask down around my neck, and her face goes grim, more disturbed by me than by the gaping mouth of the mask. "Get away from me, *Fourth.*" Her eyes run over June, catching on to a blond snarl escaping from June's hood like a fish on a hook.

"Fourth? Suddenly you care?" The children regroup in the corner farthest from me, eyes wide with tears forgotten in the presence of this new enemy. I can't leave them here. Not to target practice and dirty syringes. "Come on!" I grab for her hand. "We need to get you all out of here."

"Why don't you just shoot me now?" she spits. "I'm not joining Kamar. Murderer." She twists away, running to stand between me and the kids.

My heart stops. "What are you talking about?"

"What's the count now, traitor? The people on the bridge. The guards you took out when you escaped. There's even a body-cam video of you braining one of the soldiers Outside with a tree branch. And Sun Yi-lai . . ."

"I did *not* kill Sun Yi-lai." His name rips through me like a rusty scalpel. Sun Yi-lai? Shouldn't the real Sun Yi-lai be living in some laboratory up on the Steppe, unaware that a rebel used his name to seduce me away from this place? "But I do know that if you don't get out of here, you will all die."

Fear and anger war across her face. "We might as well be dead already. We are all infected, thanks to you and your friends in Kamar. Half of the orphanage stopped responding to Mantis after you left."

Peishan's file was marked SIMULANT. All those nights in our room when she whispered how afraid she was of the darkness lurking inside herself, and Peishan was never even really infected. The City just wanted that fear to keep her in line. "Peishan, please—" I start.

"You didn't even stay to tell your pal Sister Shang good-bye."

My breath catches in my throat. Sister Shang was the last one to see me at the orphanage, right after Tai-ge left. Did the First Circle think she helped me escape? All she did was give me my fake Mantis dosage and a comforting pat on the head. "What did they do to her?"

"Same thing that happens to all traitors." Peishan's voice is acid. "Same thing they are going to do to you."

My attention strays down to a little boy peeking out from behind Peishan's legs, tears streaming down his cheeks as his eyes dart between me and the lights flashing in time with the alarm sirens. I recognize his face. Corneal transplant. That's what his file said.

Even if I can get them to come with me, will it help? I look at June, still hanging back by the door, one eye on the streams of people as they rush by. I would never have left her to be hurt by Cas and Parhat. How are these kids—or any of the people here being hurt by the City—any different? They don't deserve to be left here any more than June did.

Any more than I did.

The Menghu are going to attack. Even if they weren't, the City is going to destroy this little boy's eyes. Make him blind. The City took so much from me. Dr. Yang and Howl did too, with their lies and their plans. . . .

Pain throbs deep down in my chest. For the first time, I can do something. I won't let the City hurt this boy. Not any of these children. I don't know who is infected and who is not in this little group, but if there is a cure to SS, then life doesn't have to be *this* unfair. I can't let the City or the Mountain do this to anyone else. Not when I can help. I won't let myself fail as I did with Aya.

It's time to be what Peishan wants. What the City taught me I was.

Time to be a monster.

"Look," I growl, pulling out my sharpened stars. "You are coming with me whether you like it or not."

CHAPTER 40

IN THE GENERAL RUSH TO GET OUT OF THE
Sanatorium, we manage to sneak into the Third Quarter. Dr. Yang's
entrance to the old City takes a few minutes to relocate, but the
tired Third workers, ruffled by the sounds of sirens coming from
the Sanatorium, don't pay us much mind. I leave Peishan tethered
to a pipe at the bottom of Dr. Yang's ladder with Sole's borrowed
pack, the younger children hiding under June's open wings. June
agrees to wait for me down in the dark, this particular mission
better done alone. The Second Quarter is easy to reach from here,
a ladder leading up only a few houses away from my destination.

It feels like years since the night we played that last game of
weiqi, though it's only been a couple of months. I climb through
the window into his room, the same bloody redness overwhelming
the place as if the murderous hand of the City has pawed through
all of my friend's things.

The first hour prickles with anticipation as I wait for the door
to swing open. I smooth down the uneven remains of my hair,
one side curling up by my cheek, the other brushing my shoulder.

He'll give me a hug and tell me how glad he is to see me and then we'll run to tell his father about the invasion. The second hour of waiting is harder, wondering what will happen if it's someone else, his mother or father who finds me. The third hour I spend lying with my face on the carpet, smoothing my hand back and forth to make designs in the short fibers. Wondering if Tai-ge even lives here anymore, if he's even alive. When the door finally clicks open, my stomach flutters with nerves, my head light with exhaustion.

When Tai-ge's tired eyes light on me, he stiffens, his mouth hanging open. But he doesn't rush forward, doesn't hug me or even say my name. His brow drops, anger curling through his handsome face like a plague. He glances out into the hall, softly clicking the door shut. Back against the door, he focuses on the floor. "Give me one reason why I shouldn't just shoot you."

I guess disappearing with an execution order on your head says something about your guilt. But he isn't calling for help, either. "Because I am here to save you," I say. I can't put it any more simply than that.

His hair is longer than I remember, full mouth tightened like a vise against his jaw in a skull-tight stretch. "From what? Another bomb?" He lowers himself down into a chair, eyes finally meeting mine.

"They are going to attack. I don't want you to die. Please come."

"So you *are* one of them," he says. The pain in his face strikes me like a physical slap.

I shake my head. "No, I . . ."

Tai-ge stands back up, cutting me off. "I thought it was a propaganda campaign to stop complaints down in the Third Quarter. Send Fourths Outside where they belong to do hard labor. Traitors can never be rehabilitated. Leave honest work to the Thirds, fighting to the Seconds, and let the Firsts take care of us all." He laughs without a speck of humor. "I tore the Hole apart, accused the First Circle of kidnapping you." His fists hit the wall in frustration, voice dripping with pain. "I attacked the head Watchman over in the Sanatorium when he wouldn't let me in." He turns around, grabbing my arm in a bruising clutch. "And here you are. Alive and well."

I don't move away, grabbing his shirt to pull him in close. His shirt is creased and smells of stale coffee and a tinge of something harder. His muscles tense, and it's as if I'm hugging a statue, an unforgiving boulder. I look up into his face, but the soft, serious Tai-ge I know is lost in granite. "I didn't have anything to do with the bomb on the bridge that night. Howl . . ." I choke on his name. "Chairman Sun's son . . ."

"It's easy to blame the dead."

I take a deep breath, letting it out slowly to soothe the pricks of anger threatening to rip through my blanket of calm. "You don't truly believe I'm guilty or you wouldn't still be talking to me. You were with me when the bomb hit. It fell from a plane."

"A rebel plane." He angrily pushes me away, and I trip over the carpet and fall into his desk chair.

A rebel plane? I clench the chair's armrests, my fingers turning white, breath trapped in my chest. "You know the war is a front. You know Kamar isn't real." When he doesn't answer, the air presses in on me, panic brewing deep in my chest. Tai-ge lied to me. At this point, is there anyone left who *hasn't* lied to me? "You know about the Mountain. And the defectors. And reeducation camps all around the City for traitors like me and Outsiders that the City manages to pick up. All this time, you *knew*, and yet you let me believe my mother sold us to some foreign invading army?"

"It isn't that different, Sev. What happened to her was just. The camps, all of it, are the way we keep this place safe."

It is *different.* I want to yell it at him, but I ask a question instead. "What about me? How is condemning an eight-year-old to half a life for something her mother did *justice*?" The words burn off my tongue in rapid succession. "I met a girl in the Mountain who had been in a labor camp since she was two. How is *that* just? You tried to beat your way into the Sanatorium—do you even know what they *do* there? The City isn't about safety, it's about cheap labor, about thousands of lives at First disposal. That's why there are people out there fighting the City, Tai-ge. They want something better than this."

"Don't try to tell me you know more about the City than I do." His voice is quiet now, dangerous. "You are only alive because I kept them away from you. I thought you were innocent, and you weren't. That bomb was meant to kill me, and you just stood there and waited for it, joking with me in the moments before I was supposed to die. You were going to be a martyr, just like your mother. Taking down the General's son."

I should have expected this. But I can't leave him here, even if he lied to me. I can't lose one more person. I have to make him see. "Tai-ge, I *do* know more about the City than you. The rebels don't have access to helis or planes. There's no way they could have bombed the bridge, and there's no way I would have stood there waiting for them to kill you. This place is bombing itself to—"

"That doesn't make sense. I don't want to hear any more of this."

"You are my only family. You are the only person I trust, in the City or Outside. You know me. And I'm telling you that I don't want you to die. I didn't on the bridge and I don't now. The whole City is about to become a battlefield. I don't want *anyone* to die, and you can help me stop it."

He turns to face me, the movement so slow I wonder if the world has come to a screeching stop around us, focused on this one moment. "I would have done *anything* to protect you." He slumps against the bed, burying his face in his hands. "But I can't believe you now. Don't make me call the Watch. Just leave."

"But, Tai-ge—"

"Get out, Fourth."

CHAPTER 41

MY BRAIN IS NUMB. I CAN'T DO ANYTHING BUT cling to the branches outside his window, pretending that I'm in a world where Tai-ge trusts me. Loves me. That I'll wake up and he'll still be my friend.

The leaves around me are so tranquil. I wonder if they could be Asleep, slated for destruction like everything else in this City. All the times I've sat in this tree to throw slimy leftover noodles into Tai-ge's room as a joke or just to wave and have him smile and wave back. Is this the last time I will ever see Tai-ge? Will he even live through the night? The ring cuts into my palm as I hold it too tight.

Tai-ge's outline against the drapes has stopped throwing things and is now sitting again with his head buried in his arms, like a two-year-old waiting for his mom to come in and tell him it will be okay. It'll be a long wait. I doubt Comrade Hong has ever comforted anyone.

There's only one thing I have left. The haze of smoke obscuring the stars over the City glows orange and red with the beginnings of a new day. By the time I face the City Center's red tile roof, the sun peeks up over the horizon, a spear of fire waiting to burn the night away. If the living won't listen, it's time to go ask the dead.

I creep past the openmouthed snarls of the lions that guard the City Center, eyes unable to avoid the portrait hanging high on the back wall. The Chairman's blank face looks down at every person who enters here, hand on his son's shoulder. I let my eyes fall, unwilling to wonder why it was I thought the boy appeared so much like Howl. How did he fool everyone? Even the Premier we met in the street assumed Howl was the Chairman's son, though his face was covered at the time. The resemblance of the portrait sticks in my brain like a knife. It does seem remarkably like Howl. But it isn't him.

Traitor's Arch is set at the back wall across from the portrait, the white wood curving up about two stories, flanked by long red-and-black banners that run from ceiling to floor. Stairs mimic the bend of the Arch, leading up to the second-floor balcony that runs the length of the room, cutting the tall windows at every wall in half. Displays of City history and triumphs sit in glass cases on the balcony every few feet, seeming small and insignificant under the high ceiling. From every point in the room you can see her, standing in her glass case like a princess waiting to be kissed, her upright coffin the keystone of the Arch.

It's the first time I've seen her face since that terrible day my eyes closed in Sleep, every other memory of her driven out by the horror of not being able to open them. In all the years she's been here, I couldn't even make myself look up at her. They bring all the schoolchildren through at least once a year to scare them, to give a face to the terror of SS, Kamar, and traitors all in one monstrous body. I could never force myself to take it in, stare always trained above or below her glass prison. Mind carefully blank to allow the voice explaining her many crimes to ricochet around in my skull without my noticing the words. Espionage. Intentional propagation of SS. Murder. A little demon gnawing at memories I knew were mine, to make them fit into this much more gruesome shape.

Sunrise yawns through the high windows, bathing Mother's prison in bright pinks and oranges. I shy away from the white-painted wood of Traitor's Arch, carved figures bowing under the weight of Mother's display, arcing over a simple white chair. This must have been where Sister Shang died. Her name is carved at the base alongside hundreds of others who died in this chair. SHANG SUNAI.

My father's name is here too, the edges of the characters still sharp where the tools gouged them into the wood.

Finally, I force my stare up. Of all the things Howl lied about, was my mother one of them? Did she try to kill me herself? Or was she trying to save me?

My feet are lead, the toes of my dirty boots streaking the floor with mud as they drag across the floor, dread and anticipation warring inside of me, knowing the hurt should be gone after all these years. But it isn't.

The light falls in flaxen strands, tumbling over the waves of hair that curl down to her waist. Calm and peaceful. A certain pride emanates from her unlined brow, full lips slightly curved in a smile. White embroidery covers her black dress like mold, arms crossed over her chest to show the First mark on her hand, the single red star pinned over her heart. She's beautiful standing up there. Asleep.

On the second-story balcony, a small platform allows you to walk around to the front of her coffin and look at her up close. To see the monster where she stands braced up inside her prison. But for me, her features burst open all the old pain, a gush of regret bringing me to my knees in the face of my tormentor, the woman I loved so much.

Now I have something with which to fend off the bitter, lost little girl inside of me. Hope. If only a drop.

I pull the syringe from my belt, steeling my heart. Whether Howl's story was just part of the deception or actual truth, I tell myself there's nothing left of me to hurt.

I cut through a tangle of wires that hook to an alarm up above her cage, as if she could somehow wake herself up and escape. Howl described this part to me too, just in case we couldn't both come in. How to cut the wires and open the front panel of her coffin, which tube to clip the syringe into out of the mess of lines feeding into her back. I watch for a moment, holding my breath as the serum spills through the maze toward her veins. What if it's just sugar water? Yet another part of an elaborate joke. Only one way to find out.

She blinks.

And then the world turns over. Her eyes—the same eyes I see in the mirror—shift into focus, warming my skin.

"Sevvy." The croak belongs to a woman on death's doorstep, moments from crumbling into powder. "I've been waiting for you."

She isn't what I remember, lithe beauty lost in her brittle body. Her head lolls against the metal brace holding her upright like a porcelain doll, tied up for display but not for play. Her eyes fight to stay open, long eyelashes dark against her cheeks. Papery, cracked skin folds experimentally as she fights against the dead weight of her limbs, struggling to move. She makes me afraid. Not for myself, but that she might crumble and burn in the direct sunlight.

"Come on," I say, lost in the maze of tubes and pins trapping her in the box. "Let's get you out of there."

Her laugh is dry and hoarse, dead leaves swirling in a gust of wind. "I'm not going anywhere, Sevvy. I doubt I have more than a few minutes to live, now that I'm awake." Her gaze flicks over me and her mouth bows and crooks, white teeth sticking out. It takes a minute for me to realize she is trying to smile. "You are beautiful. So beautiful."

I shake my head, trying to banish from my mind the only other time that has been said to me. "Here"—I offer my shoulder— "lean on me and I'll try to get you free. The Menghu are coming. I need your help to stop them. I need the cure."

She ignores me, the smile creeping up larger as she reaches out to touch my hand and clasp my fingers. Her skin feels wafer-thin and dry, as if all that's left of her is paper and old memories. "You escaped the City. You must have. I used to hear your voice with that Second family when they brought you up here to see me. Waiting to hear you was the only thing that kept me alive. I knew one day you would realize . . ." Her voice starts to buck and rear, as though she's losing control. A tear slides down her cheek, and the hand in mine gains strength, clutching at me.

Gui-hua takes a breath, rattling in her lungs as she lets it out. "You know about the cure?"

I nod, her eyes scorching mine in intensity.

"The Circle already had the cure to SS. I'm a fool." She stops, coughs racking her lungs. "They told me to stop my research.

SS cases started to crop up in the City, and I wanted to solve it, didn't want to try to hide it from the Seconds and Thirds like they told us to. I didn't realize Firsts were the ones infecting children and families. The Circle told me it was a waste of time after all these years to search for a cure at all, that my talents were needed elsewhere. When I kept going. . . . That's when you fell Asleep. It was a warning. To make me stop.

"But with your eyes closed, your heartbeat so faint . . ." She stops again, and this time it's emotion, not her dusty vocal cords, taking control of the words. "How could I stop looking for the cure?"

Warmth blooms inside of me, tears washing her face to a blur. Is Howl's story true, then? She didn't pump my veins full of SS as a last insult to our family before she defected, only to find the Watch waiting to drag her to the Arch. Mother came back, knowing she would probably get caught to save me. She didn't make a cure for Outsiders. Not for the Mountain. It was for *me*. The years of stinging hurt rear up inside of me, rebelling. But I push them back. Was Gui-hua Jiang, the traitor, the *child-killer*, really just trying to protect her daughter? Her fingers closing around my wrist feel like they are meant to be an embrace, but she's cold, her fragile grip breaking as she sags farther down.

Mother's eyes focus on the leather thong around my neck, and her trembling hand jerks toward the shard of jade glowing red in the morning light.

"Dr. Yang." Something like fear flowers in her clear black eyes and she tries to lift her head. "You know him, or you couldn't have that. He took it. . . ." Her hands twitch against the restraints I am trying to unfasten. "Listen to me." Her voice gains strength, sickly vibrato thinning to a murmur. "You need to leave now. Run. North. Port North. To the family."

"I don't understand." I take the hand that is grasping toward me, holding it tight.

"He must be here. He knows he needs me to reproduce the cure. He never could quite put things together."

The intensity in her expression is lethal, her whole face caving, burning to feed her last reserves of energy into me. "He took me to the Mountain. But when we succeeded, he wouldn't let me leave. Dr. Yang didn't want peace; he wanted power, to use the cure to control. I hid the formula from him and ran. Hid until I could get back to you. The family . . ." She trails off, eyes wandering as though she's lost the thread of what she was saying.

"When I got back here, Dr. Yang had gone before the Circle to say that I had formulated a cure and was going to use it to overthrow them. They arrested me. But not because they wanted the cure. The Circle already had a cure." Her voice fades, despair trickling down her face in wet trails. "They wouldn't give it to anyone but their own. If you go to the family—"

"Mother! What family? What are you talking about?" The last restraints open, and she sinks down to the floor, head on my shoulder as I try to support her weight. The trailing tubes pulling at her are starting to show red feedback. *You have to live!* I want to shout at her. *I don't know what I'm supposed to do!* If I can just get her out of here, we can go to . . . My mind stops. Go where? No one is going to help us.

"Your father . . . We escaped. . . . We tried to escape. But Dr. Yang was waiting for us when we came for you and your sister." She looks down at her body, shudders flickering through her like an earthquake. "They threatened Dr. Yang. Told him not speak of a cure to anyone, then put me to Sleep. Left me to rot."

Her words are becoming twisted with tremors, almost

impossible to decipher one from the next. "Go. Port North. Find them. Don't tell him. Don't tell Yang He-ping. . . ."

"I don't understand!"

Her mouth curves into the smile that I remember. "I love you, little rose. Now run."

Her shakes quiet, and her hand's white-knuckled grip on mine goes slack. "Mother?" I ask, my voice tiny and insignificant, dwarfed by the huge room, by the blood pooling underneath us on the floor and all over my hands. Her beautiful black eyes dim and stare out above me, unseeing. Empty, as though I can see the space where her life used to be and is no longer.

Alone. Again. With no answers. Just an ache in my chest, my heart beating faster and faster as if it wants to follow her wherever she went.

Cold metal sears an icy ring at the nape of my neck, and the quiet calm of Dr. Yang's voice scrapes against my nerves like a razor blade.

"Thank you, Jiang Sev. That was just what I needed."

CHAPTER 42

"WHAT ARE YOU DOING HERE?" THE CYLINDER jabs harder into my neck as I try to inch away.

"Getting what I need to finish this whole mess. She was so selfish, your mother. I didn't realize she had hidden our work until I had already destroyed the First Circle—or rather, everyone who knew how to perform the cure procedure."

"You are the one who murdered all those Firsts? And let them blame her?" The tears in my voice are just beginning to wet the conflict raging inside of me. Sorrow for a whole life lived hating my mother, anger that I couldn't do anything to save her, just like she couldn't do anything to save me. Angry to be alone again. Holding her close against my chest, I squeeze my eyes closed, tears dripping down my cheeks. It's hard to concentrate on what Dr. Yang is saying, my brain screaming at me to do something when all I can do is hold her wasted body closer.

She's dead. And the man who did it is about to kill me, too.

"Firsts use Mantis to control their labor force, even bombing their own City to keep up the appearance of being at war. To keep the infections spreading. They could have given the cure to every-one, but they saved it for themselves. Killing them was justice." I can feel him shifting closer. "The whole Third Quarter might as well be a slave camp. And no one can complain. Not while my First compatriots control Mantis."

"What does that have to do with you?"

"It has everything to do with all of us. Firsts control the City with SS, with Mantis. More than the City. Fourths out on the farms, con-victed because they see that something is wrong." His voice is grim, but respectful. Envious. "Thirds shelter behind Firsts and Seconds like a protective shield. Believing they are comrades, each quarter performing their appointed duty. But it's all a lie. Parents down in the Third Quarter bring their compulsing children to doctors who deal out sugar pills so First medical experiments can continue in the Sanatorium. Third workers don't know that the heli-planes dropping SS bombs on their families take off from Second airfields. Even if they do suspect, how can they fight? It has to stop."

"Then why is there a gun to my back? Why did my mother have to die?" I scan the empty building, grasping at wisps of insubstan-tial, ill-conceived plans to escape. "Let's help the Thirds."

"Only a select few of the Firsts know about the cure, the highest in their ranks, who doled the cure out as a reward, a sign of authority. The Circle. When a young, upstart First started to make headway on discovering their secret, they did everything they could to stop her. Gui-hua wanted to save the world, but she couldn't see that she was putting her faith in the wrong people." He turns me around to face him, not batting an eye at my mother's lifeless face. "Who is there to trust here or anywhere? The people who hand SS to their own chil-dren? Or the Menghu, who kill indiscriminately, convinced that every light needs to be snuffed out but their own? No one could be trusted with the cure but us—Gui-hua and me. But when we finally put all the pieces together, she stole the whole experiment, all the data. Handed it straight to the Firsts. I had to do *something*."

"*You* put her to Sleep." The syringe Howl took from Dr. Yang's office takes on new meaning. A triumph. A trophy. The anger building inside me threatens to tear through my skin, biting through the confusion of sorrow and regret. "You let her decay up here for *ten years* because she didn't want to work with you?"

"They didn't know it was me who put her to Sleep. The medics knew it wasn't the same as a normal SS infection the moment they saw her. They went through the whole ceremony of the Chairman pretending to inject her for the cameras." He starts to laugh. "And they didn't know how to wake her up. She was the signature on the devastation I left when I destroyed their access to the cure. All of the scientists who knew, all of the records. Nothing left but a group of old men who remember what used to be. Still, they work with me almost every day with no idea that they could be next ones to die. That they put the wrong person to Sleep." Dr. Yang's smile is so triumphantly ugly, worming its way through his doctor's calm. Finally, he can boast. "The scientists here are untrained. Unimaginative. Able to create terrible pain in the name of science, to control with fear, but not much more. They were completely unprepared to reinvent the medical miracle Yuan Zhiwei's discovered. When the armies came with SS, he saw the opportunity to set up this empire and became the little king of a little kingdom, the promise of a cure keeping the slaves hard at work while the cure itself kept him and his own safe as the rest of the world fell to pieces. Gui-hua was the First Circle's only hope to rediscover the key, the cure, if only they could get her awake. I only wish I'd been there when the Chairman found her."

Dr. Yang lowers the gun a hair, chuckling. It still points to my chest. "I knew she went somewhere else first. I knew she wouldn't be stupid enough not to leave a copy of everything we achieved. She trusted you. Loved you. I knew she either had told you where it was already or would, given the chance."

A light dawns in my mind. "You couldn't reproduce the cure, could you? Not even with Howl right in front of you. Not even with both of us opened up on an operating table."

"There was never much of a chance that examining brain scans would have resulted in any helpful—"

"She was smarter than you are. She figured it out, and you just watched. How long did it take before you realized there was no hope? That Howl's brain would never be enough? How did you convince him to help you?"

"Howl would have done anything to come home. He has been a very effective tool, doing everything I ask without even knowing I asked it because he believes he knows the true state of the world. That he's smarter, faster, more moral than I am. He thinks he knows me and what I want. He thought I wanted you on that hospital table with your head cracked open, so he saved you. Convinced you that coming back here and waking your own demons was the only solution. If Howl hadn't been so taken with you, I still could have convinced you, given time. But fear worked the fastest. It always does." Dr. Yang's grin speaks horrors and violence, prickling down my neck. "Intelligence doesn't come in only one form, Jiang Sev. I got what I wanted after years and years of delicate manipulation. This all would have been so much easier if Gui-hua hadn't chosen to come back here instead of saving the world from SS. But now things will come out right. Now I finally know where it is."

The words sink down to my stomach, a hard rock of cancer threading its way through my body, waiting to kill. "It wasn't between the world and the City. It was a choice between me and you." The door of the glass coffin is cold and unyielding against my back as I try to inch away from him, fingers grasping for something, anything. "She chose curing her daughter over starting a new world order, with you in charge. You want to use the cure just like Firsts use Mantis. To hold it over our heads and start your own slave pens. Why did you wait? Why drag me out to the Mountain? Why didn't you just bring me here years ago?"

"Would you have told me anything if I'd just ripped you away from Tai-ge without reason? Would you have believed back then that she wasn't a monster without Howl to show you why the City was wrong, without Mei and her City-inflicted scars?" He smiles as he says it. "You had to want to leave yourself, to know this place was going to kill you and to make your own decisions, or Jiang Gui-hua would have seen the puppet strings and wouldn't have told you anything." He scowls. "She did such a good job on you. But the world is more important than one miracle."

He jams the gun hard against me just as my fingers find the tangle of wires that protected the City from my Mother's return for so long. I wrench them away from the door, pulling them up from the floor in one swift motion.

An alarm blares, and the gun in Dr. Yang's shaking hand wavers as he looks up in surprise. Red and white lights flash all over the Center, but I don't have time to cover my ears. I'm over the edge of the balcony, sliding from one of the long banners framing Traitor's Arch to the ground. Above me, Dr. Yang's swearing bleeds through the overwhelmingly loud siren coiling and striking at my eardrums. His face disappears behind the empty glass box just as something crashes into me from behind, slamming my head into the shiny marble floor, leaving nothing but darkness.

CHAPTER 43

I NEVER APPRECIATED THE HOLE'S NAME UNTIL this moment. Shadows compose the very air, soaking through my thin shirt and into my skin. Damp stones make up the floor and walls, radiating cold. I can't have been here long, but I already feel as though the jagged remnants of my hair have begun to mold. I am blind, masked by a world that has never seen the light of the sun. Seldom even brightened by a torch or quicklight. I'm actually glad.

If the heavy stench of decay is anything to go by, I'd rather not know what I'm sitting in.

The dark doesn't speak to me anymore, empty of all the nightmares. It's so quiet down here I can hardly think, my own breaths ringing in my ears, every scrape against the stone deafening. My eyes keep trying to adjust, to make some sense out of the static deadness surrounding me. Eventually, I have to close them to stop myself from hoping, from jumping every time my brain tricks me into believing the darkness is thinning. Silence presses against my eardrums as if I'm deep underwater, the air so thick I have to remind myself to breathe.

She's dead. Just like that. A few minutes with the woman who blighted my existence for eight years and she's exonerated. Allowed to be my mother again. Then gone forever. Half a smile tugs sadly at my mouth, her last words a temptation to forget all of my years alone. I wish I could be her little rose. But, instead, I am the one who woke her up. Whether I can piece Mother back into my life or not, I am the true betrayer. I gave Dr. Yang the key my mother died to protect. Port North and the family. Our family? Is my name so painfully foreign because Mother isn't from the City at all? That doesn't make sense.

I can only hope it means as much to Dr. Yang as it does to me. Nothing. He's right, the world is more important than one miracle. But my life isn't standing in the way of curing the world of SS. If he's the one who controls it, somehow I doubt he'll use it to cure anyone but those who will bow to him.

The Watch didn't chase Dr. Yang, didn't even blink when I screamed my head off that he was escaping. Shrieking that she's dead, that they didn't understand. They just saw Jiang's cage open with her fugitive daughter running in the other direction and came to their own conclusions.

Which, strictly speaking, were correct.

My future is blank. All I have to hope for now is that June will realize I'm not coming back. Maybe she can get Peishan and the others out of the old City before the Menghu descend like a killing frost.

Something inside me wants to replay the situation with not just me, but the way I thought it was going to happen back when I was still in the Mountain. If Howl had meant to come here with me to wake her up, would my mother's secrets now be in Dr. Yang's hands? Or would I? Would "Port North" and "the family" have been enough to keep us going, enough to keep the merciless survivor buried down deep inside of him?

I close my eyes, trying to stop the line of thought, to bat down the tiny flame of regret flickering inside of me. I'll never know. I can't. Howl is a road that can never be walked. The fact that he was willing to lead me to my death, joking and teasing the whole way . . . My head rings in the silence, the blackness pressing in on me, every breath wringing my lungs as I try to extinguish the betrayal tearing at my insides. Someone who can do that . . . Sole was right. Howl is not anything close to the caring and warm person I thought I knew. He's just like Helix. Cold inside. A killer. His mask is just more cunningly carved, an art honed over years and years of fooling those around him. Of surviving.

If we had come here together, I would probably be lying right next to Mother, eyes closed forever.

I sit trapped inside my thoughts for hours. Days. Years, for all I know, before I hear sounds. Shouts bleeding through the thick walls, muted by my cell door. Running footsteps. Screams growing louder and louder until it's right outside. Three or four men yell to each other over the top of an inhuman screech, flailing limbs thumping against the heavy wood of my cell door. Each blow shivers against my ear, pressed against the wood, drinking in the sound. Tumblers fall as a key breaks the lock, and the whole fight spills over right on top of me.

A boot connects with my chin, and my head hits the ground, ringing with the impact. A soldier's heel grinds my open palm into the stone floor before I can roll away to the edge of the tiny cell, banging my arm against the rough stone wall. Curling up in the corner, I wrap my head and neck in my arms, half protecting myself, half blocking out the unearthly screams as a man is thrown into the cell, kicking and wrestling as though his life depends on it.

"Give them back!" he screams. "I need them back! My eyes! What about my eyes?" The Watchmen slam the door, vibrations reverberating through my bruised jaw. The prisoner is at the door, fists pummeling the wood until his bones must be broken.

A Watchman's heavy breaths mist through barred window, the yellow flare of a quicklight blindingly sharp after the unrelieved dark. "All yours, Fourth, since you made him what he is," he yells over Seph's screams. "Better hope he stays self-destructive, because neither of you are going anywhere."

His meaning catches at my lungs like pneumonia, my breaths coming quickly but never making it into my system. So it isn't even going to be the execution block. Unless this guy has nice compulsions. Like brushing other people's teeth. Or chewing gum.

The Seph continues pounding on the door as the quicklight fades, then spins to look at me. "Scream." His voice's ragged ends barely come together for the word to make sense. "Scream! Now!"

When I don't respond, he lunges at me, and the demanded scream rips out of me like a barbed hook out of a fish's mouth. He crashes down on to the floor next to me, scuffling against the stones as his hands search for me. I brace myself, the muscles in my arms aching, frozen with tension as if they'll never move again. Waiting.

But nothing happens. I can't see him, but his breath touches my eyelashes, washing over my face and down my neck, everything still. My skin crawls. He must be inches from me, just waiting for infection to order him to strike. Tears tickle my nose and cheeks, but I can't brush them away, can't even force my lungs to inflate, afraid any noise at all will trigger the time bomb lying beside me.

His hand grazes my elbow, fingers trailing up toward my shoulder, following my collarbone to rest in the hollow at the base of my neck. Trapped. And it is in this moment that I realize how badly I want to live. I don't want to die down here in the Hole's inky depths. I want to live so much that it burns, the blank shell slated for destruction forgotten in my silent fight to survive.

"You okay, Sevvy? Did they hurt you?" I jerk away from the whisper, hitting my head against the wall. His voice must be tearing his throat to rags after all that screaming, but it's calm. Sane. The hand on my collarbone slips up under my chin, to my cheek. "I think they're gone."

Tai-ge's voice. Anxiety thick in his deep tones when I don't answer. I can't. I curl forward, gasping for air as I wrap my arms around him, the sobs finally shaking out of me. His arms pull me in tight, my head tucked under his chin, the slow rise and fall of his chest the only thing I understand.

"What are you doing down here? How did you find me? Why did you find me?" The questions trip over themselves to get out of my mouth.

"They told everyone when they caught you. I think they might have had a parade if rebels hadn't started popping out of every nook and cranny in the Third Quarter."

I sit up in alarm. "It's happening. What is the Watch doing? Are Thirds being evacuated?"

Tai-ge's voice goes quiet, anger seeping out from the cracks. "I was there. I watched them pour out of the Sanatorium and start ripping into the factories. The dead are everywhere. People just slumped all over each other, shot down before they could even run. And instead of helping, I came down here. But there were no heli-planes. No chemical bombs."

"I told you they didn't have planes." My nightmares of Menghu loose in the City would have been bleak enough without the exhausted hopelessness in his voice, confirming that even my bleakest of dreams wasn't enough. I can just imagine the Menghu calling to one another, keeping score as whole families crumple at their feet. More bracelets to make.

"All the people I am supposed to protect, dying by the hundreds. And I'm down here making sure you are all right." My heart twinges in my chest, pressure building in my throat at the condemnation clouding over me like a poisonous gas. "I had to come save the traitor. . . ."

I reach out toward him, grabbing his wrist so hard that his bones crack. "Listen to me, Tai-ge." He doesn't pull away, waiting for the defense he refused to hear earlier. "I did not kill anyone. It was all a setup. Dr. Yang convinced me that if I left—"

"Wait, Dr. Yang? Yang He-ping?"

"You know him too?" The confirmation bites at me.

We are quiet for a few minutes, Tai-ge's hands groping for something in his pocket. A quicklight. After so long in the cell, even that small light seems blinding. The yellow glow hollows out his eyes, changing my friend into a tattered ghost. "Yang He-ping is one of the lower Firsts. He has done a lot of spy work with the rebels. It was Dr. Yang who warned my father the rebels were moving. We didn't think they could get in."

"It was Dr. Yang who argued to send Menghu into the City. Of course he told you they wouldn't be able to get in. He's the one who killed half of the First Circle all those years ago. He's the one who should have been molding over Traitor's Arch. The deaths, this invasion, it's all because my mother found the cure to SS."

His head is shaking before the sentence even hits the air, anger yellow and sickly in the quicklight. "Stop lying to me. I don't want to hear it. Why did I come down here?" He stands up and peers out the small window in our cell door. "Why do I still want to protect you when I know you are using me?"

Tai-ge tenses when I touch his shoulder. "Because deep down you know the things the City says about me aren't true. You know I could never have set that bomb, and you know I'm right about the planes. You are the only person who believed in me, who thought my life was worth more than the price of an execution. And it's still true." I let my hand drop. He isn't responding. He doesn't believe it anymore. I can feel the emptiness yawning under me, my resurrected hope sinking back down. "I left because you mattered more to me than my life. And I came back for the same reason. I would never lie to you."

Tai-ge holds up the quicklight, softening the grasp of night around us. "Do you really believe your mother had a cure to SS?"

"I'm living proof."

CHAPTER 44

TAI-GE'S ACCEPTANCE BRINGS THE WHOLE STORY
pouring out, a torrential downpour of pent-up information and
feelings. Except for one thing. I can't bring myself to tell him about
Howl beyond the bare bones of our working together. The humili-
ation and hurt are still too raw to touch.

At the end of the story, Tai-ge pulls another quicklight from
his boot, smoothing the tube back and forth over the hem of his
coat. "And Dr. Yang? Our spy?"

"He's had a foot in both City and Mountain since before my
mother died, playing one off of the other. Just think, Tai-ge. Firsts
set a contagious form of SS loose Outside. Dr. Yang was ready for
it the moment it hit the Mountain. He must have been involved
in formulating it and setting it free. The Mountain decided to
invade the City specifically because of it. Not enough Mantis to go
around. If Dr. Yang has his way, contagious SS is probably spreading through the Menghu, and it will infect everyone in the City not
killed in the fighting. So what do we have left?"

"Lots of extremely impulsive people? With weapons?"

"SS everywhere. People getting hurt. Looting and cruelty. If Dr. Yang comes in with the cure, it'll be like Yuan Zhiwei all over again. Except instead of Mantis, he's offering *real* freedom from SS, not just a stopgap. Who wouldn't go run straight to him? Dr. Yang will be a king, a *god* who fixed our broken world. Just like Yuan Zhiwei."

The truth of the statement stares up at me as if it were sitting there all along but I was too blind to see it. Dr. Yang never needed my brain. Not mine or Howl's. If he really thought he could reproduce the cure, then Howl would never have gotten away the first time. I would never have seen anything of the Mountain but the sterile white of Yizhi. All the threatening from Yizhi and Helix and Cale trying to drag me down . . . *They* might have believed Dr. Yang needed to cut me open, but in reality it was all just to scare me into coming back here and waking up my mother. He was manipulating Howl, manipulating me, manipulating both the City and the Mountain. He didn't need my brain—he needed Mother to tell him where to find the work they had already done.

"There are Firsts in the City who have been cured. Dr. Yang could have used any of them if rediscovering the cure were as simple as analyzing a cured brain. He needed me. Not because mother cured me, but because she would only tell *me* where she hid their work. She wouldn't have trusted anyone else." I rub my eyes, which ache from lack of sleep. "He must have suspected that Howl had second thoughts about throwing me under the knives, so he used him. Must have started feeding him information about my mother, hoping he would pass it on. Practically handed him the serum to wake Mother up. Then, for the final touch, he shoved a scalpel in my face to make me run back here."

Tai-ge shakes his head. "Sevvy, you can't know . . ."

A laugh starts to bubble up inside of me, but there's no humor in the broken sound. "I should have put it together the night after I escaped." I jump up, unable to sit still. But pacing back and forth in the tiny cell just makes it worse. "The Menghu would have picked me up before I even made it down the rope. The whole Mountain should have been on lockdown the moment Dr. Yang noticed his antidote for Suspended Sleep was missing. I was too upset to think much about it at the time, but Dr. Yang must have done something to stop them from coming after me. He let me go so I could get here. To her."

Another thought calcifies along with that revelation, a spot of cancer drilling holes through skin and bone. It never was a contest between Howl's life and mine. We could have . . . But I take a deep breath and let all the anger for Dr. Yang and this whole situation stream out of me. Nothing changes why *Howl* brought me to the Mountain. Whatever Dr. Yang wanted from me, Howl didn't know. He thought it was a choice between us, and he chose himself. Even if he did have feelings for me, if it had come down to that choice, I don't think I would have won.

I shake my head, not willing to speculate. Not willing to try and defend him or try and unwind the events, the conversations in my head. What might have happened. It's too late. Our story was over before it even began.

"And she told you." Tai-ge breaks into my frenzied thoughts. "Your mother told you where the cure is. And Dr. Yang was standing right there."

"She told me, but I still don't understand. Have you ever heard of Port North?"

Tai-ge taps on the door experimentally, frowning at his fingertips when they come away with slivers from the rough wood. "No.

There are Kamari . . . or some kind of settlements northeast of here, but . . . we need to take this to my father. If both sides know a cure is within reach, then there will be no reason to keep shooting at each other. Catch Dr. Yang before he gets out of the City, show both sides the way he has been manipulating us, and stop the fighting. We can all talk this over like civilized people."

"The Menghu *aren't* civilized. Invading for them is like a national holiday. They're all rabid to kill City-born. And why would your father listen? General Hong doesn't exactly trust me."

"Add that to the fact that the whole Second Quarter thinks I've got SS"—Tai-ge breaks our quicklight, sending the room into darkness with the tinkle of glass shards hitting the stone floor—"and it's hopeless." Fiddling with one of the long metal wires from the broken light, I can hear him working on the door. "But we have to try. Otherwise, everyone out there might as well be dead already."

"What are you doing?"

His voice sounds amused. "You think I'd come down here without a way to get out? It was a gamble, but I hoped that if I was unruly enough, they'd wait until the 'compulsion' stopped to search me. With everything else going on up there, I figured they wouldn't take the time to follow safety protocols." The wires scratch against the door's metal lock. "We were lucky. I thought I was going to have to search this whole prison for you. But I got a set of Seconds with a healthy sense of irony."

"Irony?"

"Because the City blames your mother for SS. If my compulsions killed you . . ." He pauses. "Wait a minute. The door isn't even locked."

"What?" I stand, reaching out to test for myself. He already has it open, but only a crack, as if the lock already being undone might make it safer to leave the door closed. "Why would they leave the door unlocked?"

Tai-ge doesn't answer, hand clenched around the edge of the door.

"Well." I put a hand on his shoulder. "Let's hope it's a good omen and get out of here. Maybe your great-grandfather didn't like the candles on your family shrine and was glad I stole them to smear all over your watch reports. Maybe he's helping us."

"Great-grandfather would have hated you."

"That is a terrible thing to say to a person." I think for a second. "Even if it is true. But we have to get out of here, no matter why the door is open."

The hallway outside is black, silence a heavy blanket over the long line of doors. A creaky hinge brings me up short a few feet down. The cell doors are all open. We're the only people here.

"Is this level usually empty?" I ask.

Tai-ge shrugs. "On the way in, I was too wrapped up in fake compulsions to notice."

We don't see anyone in our hallway or on the stairway up, not even a single guard there to make sure prisoners stay where they belong. When we break out into sunlight, it's too bright. The rays burn into my retinas as I stumble away from the cement staircase leading down into the Hole. Tai-ge stops, shading his eyes against the beams magnified by huge windows overlooking the City from the lower edges of the Second Quarter.

The room is deserted, the prison station sign over the front door hanging crooked. The street outside should have been teeming with the midday markets selling meat and canned goods for the evening meal. But it's empty. As if the whole City is Asleep.

My feet slip out from under me as I step in a pool of spilled water, a cup broken in the middle of the floor as though someone dropped it midsip. Papers lie in messy heaps, spilling over onto the floor. Tai-ge runs his finger along the inside of a tall cabinet set into the wall, doors torn open and askew.

"The rifle cabinet is empty. They must have been in a hurry." His eyes follow a trail of debris, cupboards, shelves, and tables all lying on the ground, stomped to matchsticks. Drops of dried blood coat the whole scene, as if someone decided to ransack the place with nothing but his bare hands.

"Someone let all the inmates out." Tai-ge is at my shoulder, pulling me away. "The rebels must have had allies down there."

"Why didn't we hear the locks go? Can they control the doors from up here?"

Tai-ge nods. "It must have been when I was still screaming. Let's get out of here. It wasn't just political prisoners down there, and I don't want to find out if any of them stayed back."

Outside, the normal cloud of smog hovering over the Third Quarter burns black instead of the normal brown-tinged gray. I can see the flames from here, wooden dwellings falling as if they're no more sturdy than dried flowers. Heli-planes circle over the chaos like vultures waiting for their prey to give up their last breath.

"Where are all the people?" I ask.

Tai-ge points down toward the smoke. "Either down there fighting or heading up to the heli-field. Or hiding, I guess." A red polka-dotted curtain twitches closed in the house facing us across the street.

"The heli-field?"

"The army heli-fields are down below the City, but there's an

emergency landing pad and some hangars up in the First Quarter."
He scans the City beneath us. "My father is commanding from
the First library. But how are we going to get him to listen? They
aren't going to just let us in, not when they sent me screaming to
the Hole an hour ago."

"Why didn't they give you Mantis?" I ask.

"It's all gone. The Firsts took it all or are hiding it somewhere
to keep it away from the rebels. The minute the attacks started,
every single pill went missing, airlifted from the heli-field. Father
has probably already killed someone, he was so angry. I saw two
other Seconds in my class get sent down to the Hole before I
decided to come find you."

Did they know? I wonder. How deep are Dr. Yang's claws in the
First Quarter? Is he pulling out everyone loyal or valuable to him,
letting everyone else die? Are all the City heli-planes his now?

The tiered eaves of the library tower over the First Quarter,
easy to see even from the Hole's entrance so far over in Second
Quarter that it's almost to the wall. My boots pound against paving stones worn smooth by thousands of feet as we cross over the
Aihu River using one of the many bridges that connect the Second
and First Quarters with no wall or checks in between, unlike
the walls that pen in the Thirds down the mountain. I lengthen
my stride to keep up with Tai-ge, feeling odd at being together
again. He looks different. The lines I remember from the previous
night in his room are still there, his face molded into a permanent
frown. He was serious before, buttoned up to the throat. But he
could laugh, too. I can't imagine the statue running beside me
laughing ever again.

We're too low down on the Steppe, most of the roads twisting
away from the library and up toward the lab district, but we slide

through alleyways, the blocks of lesser First homes, and follow the wall that bars Thirds from coming into the First Quarter all the way to Renewal Road. I grab the tail of Tai-ge's coat, just about dragging my arm out of the socket to pull him behind a wagon abandoned in the street as a group of Seconds march by, their synchronized steps ringing out across the wide road.

Just over the wall and bridge Howl stopped me from crossing . . . only a month or two ago? . . . the City Center towers over the central market, windows heavy-eyed and blinking in the late-afternoon light from underneath the three tiers of red tile roof. It's hard to believe that it is empty now, the single occupant finally released.

Tai-ge's eyes are on the tall building as well. "Sun Yi-lai." He points, the Chairman and his son peeking from their portrait inside the doors, barely visible from our hiding place. "He disappeared the same day you did. Did Dr. Yang take him, too?"

I shake my head. "Howl looks kind of like that painting of the Chairman's son, so I thought . . . well. It doesn't matter what I thought now. I'm not the only one he managed to fool. He had the Premier talking to me as if I were a real person the day I left the orphanage. They couldn't have taken him, too, or I would have seen him. I don't know where the Chairman's real son is." I still can't let myself focus on that portrait, Howl looking back at me. No, not Howl, however much I wish this coincidence could make his story and not Sole's true.

Hugging the buildings, we move forward, stopping to cower just beyond Yuan Zhiwei's statue as a cluster of Seconds tromp up the road. The statue glares down toward us, as if he'd alert the Reds to our presence if he could.

Just as we run across the street, one of the Seconds does look back, catching sight of me as Tai-ge and I dive toward a lesser

First family's bright red door to hide. He shouts, and all the men immediately turn back in some formation, guns up and ready.

"Come out or we shoot!" the captain yells, fear and adrenaline transforming his voice to a monster's growl. "Yuan knows we need all the men we can get, so if you're friendlies, then come out!"

Tai-ge bites his lip, looking at me. "Stay close to me. They won't shoot you if it means shooting me, too." Then he slides out from our hiding place in the doorway, hands high up over his head.

CHAPTER 45

"FATHER WILL LISTEN TO US." TAI-GE DOESN'T bother to whisper as the men jerk us up the library steps, the building poking out from the spread of structures below as if it were refusing to bow to the war bubbling around its feet.

"You don't think he'll be worried that you showed up with me? Right after being sent to the Hole?" I jerk my arm away from the Second who is pulling me along, standing up straight as I walk through the library's propped-open doors.

Inside, afternoon light streams through the square windows, forming a necklace of sunlight around the pagoda's high ceiling. General Hong's broad figure stands tall, the focal point in a maelstrom of red uniforms. A raven-haired beauty stands over him preserved in the picture window's jade, little men around her skirts forming darker patches that splotch across the City maps covering the marble floor.

The General doesn't look at us until our escort pushes us down at his feet. "My disobedient son." He turns to me, features a mirror of Tai-ge's but made from stone and iron instead of flesh.

"And his traitor playmate. Was it you who let these foul rebel creatures into our City?"

Tai-ge raises his chin to speak, but a shrill screech cuts off whatever he was going to say. The floor pitches under our feet, the force of an explosion hammering down on General Hong, crashing him down on top of us. The air fills with an ear-piercing smash, my eardrums blocking everything but a high-pitched tone. I try to scramble out from the General's heavy frame, the air smoldering all around me. Arms wrench me back from under the picture window. . . .

Only there is no window, just a smoking gash in the wall, all the bits of jade lodged in the floor and walls behind us. It's Tai-ge dragging me away, but he freezes when his panicked gaze lands on his father's slumped form, back peppered with yellow and green shards of jade and bits of rocks and wood. The library's stone and timber groan overhead. Still, Tai-ge doesn't move, as though he's waiting for the tattered human remains to pull themselves up off the floor.

Grabbing Tai-ge's arm, I drag him away from General Hong's still form, over a man slumped in a pool of red, his leather jerkin torn to shreds, dodging the men and women still left standing as they scream and run back and forth in panic.

The stones shake around us from another explosion as we sprint down the stairs, but the unholy noise fades as we follow the twisting hallways to a place I've been once before.

A trapdoor and a ladder.

The rungs slip under my hands as I rush down, an involuntary cry ripping from my lips as I miss a step. Tai-ge moves slower, his boots scraping against the metal above me. When he steps down from the ladder, the ground quivers under our feet, a muted *boom* filtering down from above. Things seem too quiet, too still down here in the old City, nothing but us and the statue sitting silently behind the ladder.

Most of the Red's nerve center must have been in that room. Maybe the Firsts that were coordinating with them too. How many of them are now dead from the Menghu-planted bombs? My heart pounds with the thought of what almost happened . . . what *did* happen to General Hong, who died as a human shield. Whether he meant to or not.

What will the Menghu do now that the man giving Red orders is lifeless in a pile of broken jade and stone? And with Firsts flying away with all the Mantis, what are all of the infected going to do?

The hunt up there is going to turn nasty, especially as night falls.

Tai-ge's arms wrap tight around my back and shoulders, pressing my head into his chest. He feels sticky underneath the T-shirt. Chalky dust covers both of us. I can feel it in my nostrils, mouth, and throat, the grittiness on my tongue making me want to gag.

"I'm sorry." I don't know what else to say, the General's mangled body clouded by some kind of fog in my mind, as if I can't feel anything at all.

Tai-ge hugs me tighter, chest expanding under my cheek in a deep breath. But he doesn't say anything.

"We still might be able to stop the fighting." I hate the cold sound of my voice. "If we find someone from the Mountain high enough to give orders and tell them what Dr. Yang is doing—"

"We have to get out of here, Sevvy." Tai-ge's voice breaks, too small in the darkness enveloping us. "This isn't a fight we can win, just the two of us."

"Get out of here? No one knows about Dr. Yang." I think of Peishan, June, and all the little orphans stranded where I left them in the sewers. Are they safe? And even if I don't have crowds of friends welcoming me back, no one deserves to be cut down just because of Dr. Yang's greed. It's just an extension of what happened to Mother. To me. "If we don't tell the Mountain who it is they really should be fighting, this invasion will kill everyone we know. For no reason." I grimace. "What about your mother?"

"We need to leave. Before the compulsions start."

"Tai-ge, are you okay? Your father just . . . saved us. Accidentally." But what I mean is that he died. Even with the detachment I feel about what happened upstairs, I still can't quite bring myself to say it out loud. Fear stabs through to my chest as I wonder what will come next—how many more will fall like birds at a glass window before the end of today. This whole City is going to crumble if we don't do something. But what? It's like the days at the beginning of the Influenza War. The last Great War. So many infected people jammed together that the idea makes my head spin. And it's happening again, right above us.

Tai-ge pulls his head back, letting me look up at him. "We can't do anything here. We can't stop the fighting. But we can go find the cure. And people to help us make it, distribute it . . . If no one has SS, and no one can use it as a weapon, what will they have to fight about anymore? If we get to the cure before Dr. Yang does, everything could change." He takes another deep breath. "The entire Circle is already gone. Most of the First Quarter, too, and I think Mother might have been roped into going along with them. If we can find their camp, she and the Firsts still alive might be able to help. . . ."

Before I can object to leaning on the First Circle for *any* kind of help, much less his mother, who left him in the City prison during an invasion, running footsteps echo up the tunnel and a faintly glowing quicklight bobs toward us. A red quicklight.

Followed by a trickling trail of yellow ones.

Tai-ge pushes me behind him, easing the gun from the waistband of his pants to point it at the floor. By peeking around his shoulder, I can see the small dots of light looming larger. Their faces are all shrouded in the serpentine coil of gas masks, the leader's red light too far out to cast any light on his hooded features.

The leader, who appears to be wearing a Watch uniform, draws up short about ten yards away, squinting through the quicklight's glow to make us out, pulling the whole procession to a dead halt. *Where did a Red manage to pick up a quicklight from the Mountain?*

The heavy dark pushes in on them, making them look small, harmless. But the leader's hand twitching into his jacket has nothing harmless about it. Tai-ge takes a deep breath, his ribs expanding out against my arm. "Don't move," he says. "We've already got a gun on each one of you."

Head cocked, the person holding the red light moves forward, pulling back a hood to reveal long golden hair. "You must have a lot of hands, then, since there are only two of you." She steps toward me. "Is that you, Sev?" Once again, June appears as my guardian angel.

Tai-ge levels the gun at her head. "Who are you?"

June raises an eyebrow at Tai-ge before looking back at me, giving me time to inch my way between them, pushing Tai-ge's gun down. "She's a friend, Tai-ge. From Outside."

"A friend from Outside?" Tai-ge's serious calm cracks a bit. "A sentence I never thought would pass my lips."

The line of yellow lights gathers around her, the children from the sanatorium holding hands in a long train with their lights tied to their coats, all masked. One sniffles a little and June stoops to wipe her cheeks with a handkerchief and tuck loose strands of hair behind her ears.

"Are we safe?" I ask, wondering if we have more time than I think. "The Menghu haven't found their way down here yet?"

Peishan's voice breaks through from the back of the line. "No, we aren't safe. We only moved because the fight spilled underground yesterday morning. We've been peeking out every now and then to grab food and water. They set the hospital down in the Third Quarter on fire. What is going to happen to us now? The walls have been breached; there are Kamari soldiers everywhere—"

"We're going to get out of here. Somehow," I answer. She glares at me but doesn't argue.

June speaks again. "Peishan managed to steal some Mantis and a stash of quicklights before the fighting started. We got the masks up there too. All from a bunch of carts headed up the hill, stocked up with all this junk."

"Dr. Yang must have started early." Tai-ge looks at me. "I guess that explains why my father couldn't get any medicine out of the hospitals."

Peishan slumps down on the ground, smiling from behind her mask when June pats her on the shoulder. Purpled circles under her eyes coupled with her bald head make her look sick. Vulnerable. Too young to be scavenging for Mantis in a burning hospital. She and June make a good pair.

When Peishan catches me looking at her, the smile disappears. "What happened to you? Weren't you going to take out General Hong's family or something? You never came back."

I ignore her, pulling June and Tai-ge over close so we can talk. However much I want to stop the violence happening over our heads, Tai-ge is right. "So the sewers are blocked down by the Sanatorium?" I ask. "What are the odds of getting out that way?"

June shakes her head, the darkness around us spilling all over, turning her half machine, half little girl. "Menghu aren't asking questions, they're shooting everyone not wearing a Mountain uniform on sight. And there have been bombs down in the Third Quarter, so leadership might be kind of hazy at this point."

Tai-ge scrubs a hand through his hair. "SS bombs? Everyone should calm down then. Fall Asleep."

"This new strain doesn't do the same thing to everyone." I think of Mei, her eyes wide and frightened. She dozed in the hospital, then woke up compulsing. Not like any SS case I've ever heard of. And the doctors I overheard down in the Sanatorium seemed to think this strain was capable of moving much faster in the victims. "We might have people compulsing in hours. Maybe less. Picking our way through a whole City of infected isn't going to happen. And it's contagious, so no one will be spared."

"Then what chance do we have?" Tai-ge's eyes flick between me and June. "Where is there to go? Infected must be outside the walls too."

"What if we go up?" I ask.

"Up . . . where? Even if we get over the wall at the top of the First Quarter, there's no way out. It's just cliffs," Tai-ge says.

"Helis are swarming all over the City like starving mosquitoes. They must be still moving in and out of the City heli-field. If we take one . . ."

June rolls her eyes. "Full marks for thinking big, Sev, but I don't know how to fly those things and neither do you."

Tai-ge smiles, the first inklings of the boy I grew up with showing through his iron mask. "That, my Outsider friend, is where I come in handy."

CHAPTER 46

THE OLD CITY IS A BLACK MAZE, MY LIMITED EXPE-
rience combined with June's hours down here the only thing our
group has to go on. We know how to get back to the fight, but
none of us knows how to get up to the Steppe without leaving
the tunnels. The roar from the Third Quarter screams louder and
louder each time we stick our heads out into open air.

After another unsuccessful check aboveground, June touches
my arm. "Wait until night. Compulsions might have already
started, but after dark the soldiers won't be able to see us. If we
can stay ahead of them, we should be okay."

Tai-ge looks at her, glimmers of respect behind his expression.
"She's right." Running his fingers along the metal of the ladder,
he shrugs. "And if the infected start compulsing, maybe soldiers
will be too distracted to pay attention to us."

The thought of waiting makes my skin crawl, memories of
Cas, Parhat, and Mei too close to forget. "We have to go *now*. You
don't understand, Tai-ge."

June shakes her head. "But I do. We can at least back up against a wall down here and keep watch. We can hide. Infected can't follow compulsions to hurt us if they can't see us."

I meet her eyes, stale memories shady on her face. The pressure of being trapped pushes in on me from all sides. But there is nowhere safe. So I nod.

We stay underground until darkness falls completely, the sky a purpled bruise fed by smoke from the burning factories. Even in the shadows, I feel as though our every move is being watched, as if soldiers are waiting to drag us onto the bloody cobblestones only a few streets away. We make our way up the Steppe until homes loom over our heads like fairy-tale castles, a First family name spelled out over each door.

Silence dampens everything up this far, everyone from this part of the City either fighting or evacuated or dead. Of all the homes we could hide in, there's only one with a clear view of the heli-field: the house of the god. Of all the mansions we could break into, at least we can be sure the Chairman was one of the first to be flown out. Or killed.

The battle going on seems miles away, a whole world apart from the quiet glamour of the Chairman's home. His is the last in a long line of colossal homes that perch on the cliff that ends the Steppe. Tai-ge stares out through the window that overlooks the heli-field, nose almost pressed against the bubbled glass.

It feels odd to be back here, where it all started. I have to stop myself from trudging down into the basement to sit on that wine cellar floor. To remember the bottles, Howl's desperate bear hug to keep the shattered glass from my mouth, the comforting words that everything was going to be all right. He didn't know that it was impossible. That even the elaborate dance he choreographed to get me to the Mountain as a sacrificial lamb wasn't going to be enough payment to resume his old life. Fooled by Dr. Yang, just like the rest of us. It almost makes me feel sorry for him.

Almost.

On the main floor, a set of three windows stand two stories tall, looking down on the thousand-foot drop of bare rock. June is busy ransacking the house, filling bag after bag with food from the cellar. Other things too, like paper and pens, knives, batteries.

"For bartering," she says when I give a questioning look to the matched set of knives she is wrapping in paper. "There must be someone out there who wants them."

She loads everything into my pack, eyeing the book Howl gave me with interest before throwing six cans of peaches on top of it.

The minutes tick by, and we all watch Tai-ge play lookout, waiting for a heli to land. Waiting for the chaos that must be boiling down in the Third Quarter to bubble up and spill into our laps. Helis buzz in and out, the huge balloons of gas fluttering over propellers, pounding the grass circle with torrents of air.

Peishan sits on the other end of the window, looking out over the rest of the City. Her fingers tap against the glass with pent-up energy. The roiling black cloud down by the factories drifts up toward us, the old brick-and-timber buildings bright spots of flame in the early morning air. A black mass bulges out from the smoke, hordes of people running to and fro like rats swarming on a trash heap. Every second, the flames push the crowds closer and closer to the streets that lead up toward the Steppe.

I can't watch anymore. I can't think about the shots being fired, the families dying in their beds because I didn't move quickly enough, because I couldn't stop Dr. Yang, convince General Hong to end the violence . . . and that I am up here, cured, while infection spreads through the riots going on down there. I can't think about what will happen to us when the crowds find us, Menghu and City alike calling for our blood. So instead of envisioning the rioting crowd breaking over us in a wave of violence, I look down. The height tingles through me, my imagination replacing all the real danger with the cliff just on the other side of the window. What it would feel like to fall, air rushing by, catching my lungs in a gasp . . . I can face this fear.

Tai-ge gives a shout, pointing at a newly landed heli, red-clad airmen rushing to connect a fat tube into its belly. "That's our ride," Tai-ge yells. "Everyone get ready to run."

Men scurry back and forth under the huge machine, ducking their heads under the twin propellers and hosing down the glass deck, the great circle window an eye that watches us. I can only hope the pilots are less observant. I step up to join Tai-ge at the window.

"I've only been working with the Watch for a few months, and they don't do training on models with passenger room," he whispers. "But it's the only one big enough for all of us."

Everyone shoulders at least one bag, even the littlest girl, who can't be more than five, walking lopsided under her load. Eight little kids, all with gas masks strapped tight over their faces to keep SS far away. Tai-ge pulls one of the masks over his chin, then hands one to me.

"I don't need this, remember?" I ask.

He wordlessly points to my birthmark. We can't hope to take the heli by force. That leaves the chance that they'll recognize Tai-ge, but not the rest of us. Not me. I pull the straps over my hair, feeling the rubber pull out a few strands as it settles across my nose and mouth like a muzzle.

The street outside is bare, but June pulls up sharp as we step onto the cobblestones. "There, there, and there." She points. I squint over at the buildings where she is pointing, but nothing special jumps out at me. Tai-ge jerks his head in a nod as he unholsters his gun, whispering, "Run. I'll cover you."

She collects her charges around her like a mother hen gathering her chicks, checking each set of small hands to make sure they have something to throw. They jog down the street with Peishan in the lead and June bringing up the rear, then take a sharp turn toward the heli-field. A figure breaks from the early morning shadows, sprinting after them. June shoots him down without a blink.

A chill runs through me, the man's body lying twisted in the street not twenty feet away. Two more figures spring away from the building across the street, headed straight toward us. Tai-ge aims for feet and legs, bringing both down before we take off after June.

A bullet sings by my ear, burying itself in the cobblestones a few feet in front of us, Tai-ge dragging me along as I try to see where the assault is coming from. Two more bullets find the walls behind us before we can duck into a doorway.

"Seconds? Protecting the airfield?" I pant, dumping some of the cans weighing me down. "Or Menghu?"

"Either way, someone doesn't want us out here." He peers around the doorway, jumping back when a shot rings out, exploding in a spray of pebbles.

"I think June and the others are okay. They're already around the corner." It seems like such a small distance. Only another fifty yards. Fifty yards that might as well be fifty miles as far as the snipers covering the airfield are concerned. I peek back out, expecting another shot, but instead there's a man in the street. Walking toward us.

"We've got to go, Tai-ge. Can we make a run for the heli?"

Tai-ge nods, and we burst out of our hiding place, running from doorway to doorway. But no fire comes. Not a single bullet. When we get to the end of the street, I glance back again. The man is following us, only a dozen or so yards behind.

I miss a step. It's Howl.

"Holy Yuan! Move it!" I yell, wrenching Tai-ge around the corner and leading him in a full sprint down the middle of the street. As Howl breaks around the corner, Tai-ge pulls me through a doorway into an open hangar, the large door open on the grassy field where the heli's twin propellers beat at the air.

June waits by the far wall, arms outstretched over the cluster of children. I can hear Howl yelling from outside, still in hot pursuit. Slapping my hands over my ears, I run across the open space. Tai-ge is right beside me, both of us almost crashing into the wall, unable to stop our sprint. June's gun is out, but she's confused as she points it back toward the door. Toward Howl.

Two men come barreling in after him, gas masks secure over their Menghu jackets, so I don't recognize them. Howl's hands are empty, and his run is an off-center lope, like the wounded gore that charged me Outside. He's still yelling, but I can't hear, the reality that June and Tai-ge are about to shoot blocking everything else out.

I reach for Tai-ge's arm, grasping to pull the gun's ugly nose away from its target.

But it's too late.

Five blasts lash out from either side of me, the crack of the bullets ripping through me as if I'm the one in front of the gun instead of Howl. Tears squeeze out from my closed eyes, but I can't look, horror freezing me to the cement floor. Wishing inside that it really was a misunderstanding. That Howl really did love me, that he came for me just like Tai-ge did. But it isn't true, and the young man lying on the ground in the middle of the hangar can't say anything to change that.

Even with all the justification coursing through my brain, I take a step toward him. Howl couldn't be the unmoving mass lying on the floor, just a bundle of clothing, an empty shell. My friend. My . . . something else. Something more. Every fleck of blood I have cleaned up over the years in the orphanage, every bone I set flashes through my mind like some sick catalog of experiences I wish I could erase. None of those fixes look anything like the holes blasted through Howl's coat.

But then his head jerks to one side, shoulder twitching up toward his neck.

Someone grabs my hand before I can go any closer, dragging me out into the open field. Tai-ge's yell to the Reds refueling the heli is lost in the deafening racket of propellers. Two men look up from underneath the great white craft, immediately heading toward us with guns out. But when Tai-ge pulls his mask down, they slow. Lowering the guns, the man closest to us gestures for Tai-ge to follow.

June keeps a hand on her hood, posted at the bottom of the ladder to help the kids find their feet on the way up. Peishan stands at the top, pulling each one up and setting them down on the floor. The two Reds watch us warily, glancing from Tai-ge to the sorry train of shaved children as though they are starting to realize that even Hong Tai-ge shouldn't be allowed to cart along such a ragtag entourage.

As June puts both hands to the ladder to follow the last child up, the wind from the propellers tears her hood back, curls whipping around her face in a golden tempest. The Reds start back, guns trained on her obviously foreign figure. I jump between her and the metal barrels. Tai-ge is at my side, barring their way to her.

One of the soldiers darts forward, and I crash into him, pulling the gun down. Time slows as I wait for the other to shoot. Pins and needles dance across my skin, every nerve prickling as I steel myself for the bullet.

But nothing comes. Instead of a shot, the ground starts to grumble underneath me, the deep throb of hundreds of feet pounding against the dirt reverberating up through my bones. The Red underneath me pushes me off, scrambling for the ladder leading up to the heli as men and women pour out across the field toward us. A blast of fire arcs up over the hangar, greedy fingers tearing into the wood and metal supports, huge columns of smoke making an X across the sky.

Struggling up from the ground, I look up in time to see June kick the Red trying to climb the ladder in the face, her eyes darting across the sea of people sprinting toward the heli, panic pinching at her mouth. "Get up here *now*!"

I rush to comply, Tai-ge at my side, but we're only at the bottom rung of the ladder when the crest of the wave breaks over us, terrified screams mixed with the roar of soldiers setting about their horrific work. Shots zing past as Tai-ge wraps his arms around me and presses me face-first into the ladder, trying to block the deluge. June scampers up to the heli's hatch, shoving children in ahead of her. Once inside, she peeks down at us, her hand twitching toward the door control.

A man howls, his hands grasping around Tai-ge's protective hug to scratch at my neck and shoulders, but before the Seph can do more than gnash his teeth, he falls under a blow to the head. People are pushing up against us, the metal grid of the ladder pressing painfully into my chest and ribs, and between Tai-ge trying to protect me from the violent crowd and the ladder, I can't unpin myself to climb.

Tai-ge shoves back against the press of swinging arms and weapons, giving me an opening to wrench myself back from being pinned against the ladder and climb. The crowd slams back up against him by the time I'm free, so now it's his chest crushed up against the metal rungs, but I hold a hand down to him, helping to pull him up from the mess.

Up. Away from the rioting mass of humanity and violence, but they never seem to get any farther away, men and women crowding up after us, throwing one another off the ladder and snaking up to catch at Tai-ge's boots.

June's hands reach out to grasp mine, her nails digging into my skin and the hatch's metal lip biting into my stomach as she pulls me through. By the time I turn to help Tai-ge, rioters from the ground are trying to climb over him into the heli, and all I can see of him are his white-knuckled fingers barely attached to the ladder.

Together, June and I grab his wrists, dragging him the last few feet, pruning the frothing mass with our feet. When the door swishes shut, several arms and legs catch between the door and the wall, flailing until I can push them out of the heli to let the door whisk closed.

We all sit for a second, unnatural quiet inside the ship filled with every gasping breath coming out of me, every drop of sweat and blood that hits the floor.

A dull *thud* echoes up through the shuddering heli-plane, the walls echoing like a bell. Tai-ge scrambles up from the floor to the captain's chair and the wall of blinking lights surrounding the cockpit window, almost tipping over as his feet try to run faster than his body can unfold from the ground.

Another crash rings through our craft, and the floor seems to bend underneath me, the screech of metal drowning the children's screams. But Tai-ge whoops from the front as we finally move. Up.

I can still hear banging on the metal hull, the people attached to the ladder outside crying to be let in or too far gone to know they need to jump. But soon all the sound dies down, nothing but smoke choking out the blue sky in front of us and the insistent whir of propellers snaking in through the vents.

The force of the aircraft moving upward pins me to the floor, but I don't even want to get up. Screams still echo in my ears, the scratch and pull of frantic compulsions and those just trying to escape. But it isn't enough to block out the memory of those gunshots, of Howl slumped on the floor. I take a deep breath, trying to force the air into my lungs, but it's too quiet, too still in this little room to try and blank out the misery threatening to drag me under.

Howl took me to the Mountain to die. He was going to let me die. I keep saying it, over and over, as if the dull singsong voice in my head will blank out everything else I'm trying not to feel. Was he somehow still alive after those bullets hit him? Is he now, in the middle of that riot?

June puts a hand on my shoulder, her eyebrows drawn down. "We're alive." It sounds like an argument.

We. I'm not alone.

Tai-ge tears his eyes away from the smoke streaming past the cockpit's clear glass just long enough to ask, "North?"

I try to sit up, to smile at Peishan and the cluster of children still softly crying into their masks. June is right. We're alive. Alive to go get the cure. Alive to help all the Sephs who will flood through the forest, infecting those they don't kill. Alive to make sure nothing like the full-out war beneath our feet ever happens again. Alive to stop Dr. Yang from tricking the world just like he tricked me, and forcing us to accept a new world set on his terms.

Alive and ready to fight. I am no longer a piece in someone else's game. I am ready to play this game of weiqi. And this time, I need to win.

I wipe a hand across my face, dirt-smudged palm coming away wet. "Yes. Go north."

AUTHOR'S NOTE

There are three things I should probably make clear about this book.

First, I wrote *Last Star Burning* in English with an English-speaking audience in mind. The language in this book is supposed to be a version of Mandarin, or what Mandarin could look like after it's been isolated and changed over a hundred years. That being said, if we're going to compare the way language is handled in this book to Mandarin as it is spoken today, there are some things that don't make sense. For instance, you can't abbreviate things with a single letter in Mandarin. Mandarin doesn't have letters. Each syllable is a single character, so abbreviating Sleeping Sickness to SS doesn't really make sense. I've treated most issues like that as a translation problem. If I were a translator adapting this book from Mandarin, I'd have to make decisions about which words to use and how, knowing a literal translation wouldn't make sense, or a translation without a little bit of extra explanation wouldn't be accessible. Hyphens are stuck here and there to help separate out syllables when it seems like correct pronunciation would be impossible for English speakers without them.

Second, encephalitis lethargica is a real disease. We don't know what causes it exactly, but it has very real effects on those who suffer from it. The disease as it appears in this book is just my idea of how, if scientists had the tools and the desire, it could be refined and weaponized. Sleepy sickness (as it is called in the real world) is not contagious, can cause a paralyzed sort of sleep, and, in some cases, can cause episodes of both self-harm and violence against others that seems almost compulsive. If you're interested in learning more, the first book I read about encephalitis lethargica is called *Asleep: The Forgotten Epidemic that Remains One of Medicine's Greatest Mysteries* by Molly Caldwell Crosby. It's full of case studies and information about real people and real doctors who dealt with this disease both after the Spanish flu epidemic and during other periods of history.

And third, there are some elements of Chinese history, especially the Cultural Revolution under Mao Zedong, that influenced me as I was building Sev's world. This isn't meant to be a direct representation of anything in particular that happened in the People's Republic of China. If you'd like to read about what actually happened during the Cultural Revolution, *Wild Swans: Three Daughters of China* by Jung Chang and *The Private Life of Chairman Mao* by Dr. Li Zhisui are both a good start. There is a reference to a Mao quote in the first line of the book, which Sev bungles. Mao originally said, "A revolution is not a dinner party, or writing an essay, or painting a picture, or doing embroidery; it cannot be so refined, so leisurely and gentle, so temperate, kind, courteous, restrained, and magnanimous. A revolution is an insurrection, an act of violence by which one class overthrows another."

ACKNOWLEDGMENTS

There are so many people who had a hand in this book that it feels as if we could probably take over the world Menghu-style, but maybe with books instead of guns. Victoria Wells-Arms, my lovely agent, wouldn't need a weapon at all, disarming people with her incurable perkiness and killer instincts. My wonderful editor at Simon Pulse, Sarah McCabe, would probably use the cutest picture ever of a pug as a distraction, then go for the jugular with her red pencil. Both of these ladies pushed me to sharpen Sev's story until it could draw blood.

Thanks are also required for the extended members of the *Last Star Burning* battalion at Simon Pulse: Mara Anastas, Mary Marotta, Liesa Abrams, Jessica Handelman, Michael Rosamilia, Carolyn Swerdloff, Catherine Hayden, Michelle Leo and her team, Christina Pecorale and the rest of the S&S sales team, Katherine Devendorf, Chelsea Morgan, Rebecca Vitkus, Sara Berko, and Aubrey Churchward.

There are so many people who read various awful stages of *Last Star Burning*, and I am grateful to all of you for encouraging me rather than trying to kill my book. A special thank you to Shenwei Chang for the insights they provided on language, culture, and many other things.

I'm so grateful for my mom and dad, who made books part of our family culture. I still hear Tolkien in my dad's voice as I read because he's the one who read it to me first. They taught me from a very young age that I could accomplish anything I wanted to, so long as I was prepared to work for it, and were suitably not surprised when I told them *Last Star Burning* was going to get printed on actual paper with a cover and everything. Thanks to both of them for knowing I could do it, telling me I was doing it, and then saying they were proud of me afterward.

My mother- and father-in-law are also very much a part of this list. Sherri Sangster listened to me talk about writing ad naseum, watched my children while I wrote, jumped up and down for me when things moved, and sent me on dates with my husband when they didn't. She waded through my first drafts, gave me honest feedback, and still was okay with me being married to her son at the end, so that's something. Thanks to Greg Sangster for always having a new book idea for me should I run out, usually involving mud, knives, and communist Southeast Asian countries.

Thanks to my oldest sister, Sarah Dunster, who, though she is blond and quite stubborn, is a much better person to look up to than Cale. She proved to me that writing isn't a dream so much as an accomplishment, and you should probably read her books. Also to my other siblings who are fabulously supportive and encouraging, including Juan, Bailian, and Zhongying, who mostly make fun of my Chinese.

Most of all, thanks and all the props and acknowledgment in the world to my children. They gave me some lovely titles that, though they did not make it to the final cover, still make me happy. (My favorite is Fight the Bad Guys. Maybe when I write my father-in-law's crawling-through-the-jungle book, that's what it will be called.) To my wonderful, patient, perfect husband, who dealt with all the craziness, obsessiveness, ups and downs and unders, thank you, thank you, thank you. He shares all his time, confidence, honest opinions, and love, and there aren't words to express how grateful I am for him. I couldn't have imagined a more perfect partner in life.

And, last of all, though certainly not least, thank you to whoever is holding this book. You are awesome. I wrote this book for you. Please don't use it as a weapon.